Kobo
A Story of the Russo-Japanese War

by

Herbert Strang

Double 9
BOOKS

Kobo
A Story of the Russo-Japanese War
by Herbert Strang

ISBN: 978-93-62761-32-3

Published by

DOUBLE 9 BOOKS
2/13-B, Ansari Road
Daryaganj, New Delhi – 110002
info@double9books.com
www.double9books.com
Tel. 011-40042856

ABOUT THE AUTHOR

George Herbert Ely (1866–1958) and Charles James L'Estrange (1867–1947), two English writers who worked together on several children's adventure books, wrote under the pen name Herbert Strang. In the late 19th and early 20th centuries, the pair contributed to the boys' fiction genre with a variety of books written under the collective pen name Herbert Strang. Charles James L'Estrange was born in Hampstead, London, on November 6, 1867, and George Herbert Ely was born in India on October 24, 1866. They were both students at London's Dulwich College. Young readers were drawn to Herbert Strang's adventure stories because they frequently dealt with themes of bravery, patriotism, and discovery. By using a pseudonym, the writers were able to continue building a steady reputation for themselves in the boys' literature market while producing a large body of work. They have several popular series, such as "The Adventure Series," "The Airship Boys Series," and "The Marooner's Island Series." The books added to the canon of young reader adventure fiction because of their captivating characters and thrilling stories.

CONTENTS

Chapter I
A mere Chinaman

Flotsam — A Commercial Correspondent — A Story of the Sea

The P. and O. liner *Sardinia* was some twenty hours out of Shanghai, making a direct course for Nagasaki. Few passengers were on deck: it was drear and cold this January afternoon, the sky grey and sullen as with coming snow, the sea rolling heavily under a stiff north-easter that blew cuttingly through the Korea Strait. But beneath the bridge, somewhat sheltered from the wind, sat three figures in a group, talking earnestly. The eldest of the three, John Morton by name, a big shaggy Englishman of forty-five, sat enwrapped in a heavy ulster and a travelling rug, his legs propped on a deck-chair before him. Every few seconds a voluminous cloud of smoke issued from his lips, and floated away like a pale miniature copy of the vast black coil from the funnel above. John Morton was correspondent of the *Daily Post*. At his left sat a round little Frenchman, with fine-drawn moustache and neat imperial, a comforter about his neck, a cigarette in his mouth. Armand Desjardins was also a correspondent, representing the *Nouveau Figaro*. The third member of the group was much younger than his companions. He was a tall, slim young fellow, with bright hair and frank blue eyes, his cheeks tanned the healthy brown of outdoor life at home no less than by the winds of four weeks' sea travel. The collar of his long frieze ulster was turned up to his ears; a low cloth cap was perched on the back of his head. Nobody could have mistaken Bob Fawcett for anything but a Briton.

He had just answered, smilingly, a remark of the vivacious little Frenchman, when the attention of the group was attracted by the quarter-master clambering hurriedly up the ladder to the bridge, the ship's biggest telescope under his arm. He handed it to the captain, who, with the chief and third officers, was looking intently towards a spot a few points on the port bow. After gazing for a minute or two through the telescope, the captain handed it without remark to the chief officer, who looked in his turn and passed it also in silence to the third. The three men below rose to their feet and went to the port-rail, scanning the horizon for the object of the officers' curiosity. Nothing was to be seen save a limitless expanse of dark, green billows, heaving with the swell.

There was a short colloquy on the bridge, after which the third officer ran down the ladder on his way aft. He was intercepted by the little group, who raked him with a gatling-fire of questions.

"Only a raft, or wreckage, or sea-serpent, or something," he said in reply. "Perhaps sea-weed."

"But you vill examine?" said Desjardins. "De sea-serpent is a subject of im-mense interest to de savants of all nations."

The officer laughed.

"Well, monsieur," he said, "get a good glass and you'll have a chance of seeing for yourself; we shall pass it within a short mile."

By this time a speck was visible far ahead, which gradually disclosed itself, as the vessel drew nearer, as a half-submerged spar with a tangled mass of rigging. Bob Fawcett and his companions had ceased to take any interest in what appeared to be merely floating wreckage, when they were surprised at hearing the clang of the engine-room bell signalling successive orders. The steamer slowed down, then with helm hard a-starboard crept up to within a hundred yards of the object, and came to a stop. A boat was speedily lowered, and the passengers, drawn from below by the sudden stoppage on the high sea, crowded into the bows, and looked on with breathless curiosity as the third officer steered gingerly up to the spar. It was possible now to make out a human figure rising and falling with the heave of the sea, its outlines half-hidden by the surrounding cordage. The quarter-master was seen to open his huge clasp knife and cut several strands that apparently lashed the castaway to the mast, and the men who had supported the inert body while this was being done lifted it gently into the boat. The passengers heard the third officer's voice shout the order to give way, and in less than three minutes the boat was being swung in upon the davits, and the *Sardinia* was again forging ahead at full speed.

The castaway, an inert, sodden, unconscious figure, was lifted out of the boat and carried below, to be handed over to the ship's doctor.

"Is there any life in him?" asked Bob Fawcett, pressing forward to the third officer.

"As dead as mutton, sir, in my belief. But we'll do what we can for the poor beggar."

He passed on; and, catching a glimpse of the castaway as he was borne down the companion-way, Bob noticed that he had but one ear. In a few minutes the passengers had resumed the occupations and amusements which the incident had interrupted. The curiosity of the most of them finally evaporated when it became known that the figure saved from the sea was nothing more romantic than the body of a Chinaman. Bob Fawcett was not a sufficiently hardened traveller to take the matter so lightly. But learning on enquiry that the doctor had little hope of the man's recovery, and that in any case his resuscitation would take some time, he went back to his companions, and found that they had been joined by another passenger—a stranger to him. The new-comer was a stout, brown-bearded, spectacled man, with cheeks puffy and sallow. He leant heavily on a stick, and every now and then rammed his soft wide-awake down upon his head, evidently in apprehension of its being swept away by the breeze.

"Feel better?" Bob heard Morton say as he approached.

"Ach ja!" was the reply. "I do feel better, zairtainly, but not vell, not vell by no means."

"You'll be all right soon. Fawcett, let me introduce you to Herr Schwab; don't think you've met. He came on at Shanghai, and—well, hasn't been visible since. My friend Mr. Fawcett—Herr Schwab."

"Glad to meet you, sir," said Bob, lifting his cap. The German was a second or two behind in the salutation, not from lack of native courtesy, but because his hand had to skirt the limp brim of his wide-awake and come perpendicularly on to the crown, which he raised between finger and thumb.

"Most delighted," he said with guttural urbanity. "I lose much zrough my so unlucky disbosition to sea-illness; it keep me downstair all ze time since ve leave Shanghai. Ze loss of food, zat is nozink; it is ze gombany. Vy, I regollect, ven first I voyage to Zanzibar it lose me vun big order for bianofortes. At Massowa zere come on board a Somali sheik vat vas fery musical. I vas below—fery ill. Vat could I? Ze sheik, he buy concertina from ze rebresentative of concertina house. Now ze Somali, zey all blay concertina; zey might haf blayed biano!"

"And are you in pianos now, sir?" asked Bob, smiling.

"Vell, yes, but primarily I am in literature. I haf ze honour to rebresent ze *Düsseldörfer Tageblatt*, a journal of fery vide circulation in Werden, Kettwig, Mülheim, Odenkolin, Grevenbroich—zobsgribtion, twenty-zree mark fifty, payableinadvance."

He handed Bob a card with these particulars duly set forth, and paused as if for a reply.

"Unfortunately," said Bob with a smile, "my screw is payable in arrears; I'm afraid I shall have to wait a little."

"You say screw!" responded Herr Schwab instantly. "I haf also ze honour to rebresent ze solid house of Schlagintwert: ve can ship you best assorted screw f.o.b. Hamburg at truly staggering price."

He drew from the pocket of his ulster a sheaf of papers and looked them rapidly through.

"No," he murmured, "zis is botato spirit; zis is batent mangle; zis is edition de luxe *Stones of Venice*; ha! ve haf it: best Birmingham screw. Allow me, vid gombliments."

Bob caught Morton's eye as he pocketed the price list, and strenuously preserving his gravity, said:

"Thank you, sir; I shall know where to come. But I fear that with war in the air your journey may not be profitable."

"Ah! Zere you mistake, my friend. If it is peace, I sell botato-spirit Birmingham screw Ruskin edition de luxe batent mangle; if it is var— zen I rebresent ze *Düsseldörfer Tageblatt*; ve circulate in Werden, Kettwig, Mülheim, Odenkolin—"

"Magnifique!" exclaimed Desjardins. "You save de price of passage in all case. To compete vid you Germans, it is impossible."

Herr Schwab smiled indulgently.

"Business are business," he said. "In peace, ze Chinese, ze Japanese, ze Russian—zey are all vun to me. But in var, I am instructed by my house— ach! I should say, my journal—to agompany ze Japanese field-army."

"By all accounts," said Bob, "it'll be a case of the patent mangle and not the pen this time. A fellow in the smoking-room has just been saying that there's no earthly chance of war. He had it from a native merchant in Hong-Kong, and somehow or other they're always the first to scent out news."

"No var!" exclaimed Desjardins. "Vat den shall I do? Vat shall I write for de *Figaro*! I have no patent-mangle!"

"You'll have to write poetry," said Morton; "geishas, plum blossom, and that kind of thing. You'll be all right. But I'm helpless. Couldn't do it to save my life; if I could, *Daily Post* wouldn't take it. Fawcett will come off best of the lot."

"I'm afraid not. They wouldn't have sent for me to help with their range-finders unless they expected a rumpus, and soon. If there's no war, I shall get a month's notice and my passage home.—Hi, steward, how's the castaway?"

The steward came up in answer to Bob's hail.

"Doin' well, sir; most surprisin'. Doctor himself can't make it out nohow. Says the Chinee must have the constitootion of a elephant. Captain's with him this very minute, interviewin' of him; he can't speak English, but there's another Chinee in the steerage that's doin' the interpretin'. He's a big ruffian of a fellow, the castaway, a regular hooligan to look at—and only one ear and all. I've just sent some vittles for'ard for him, sir."

The steward passed on. A little later, when it became known that the interpreter had returned to his quarters, Bob announced that he was going to see the man, and was at once joined by Monsieur Desjardins and Herr Schwab, the former in eagerness to get material for a paragraph, the latter in obedience to his motto, "Business are business". Morton refused to budge.

"Saw plenty of Chinamen, dead and alive, in the war, ten years ago; all alike," he said.

Accordingly the other three made their way to the steerage, and, finding the Chinese interpreter, were soon assured of his willingness to tell all he knew for a consideration. It was Bob who paid.

The man who had so narrowly escaped drowning was, it appeared, a Manchu Tartar—a big muscular fellow nearly six feet high. When once he regained consciousness he had made a surprisingly rapid recovery from his long immersion, and had told his story with great readiness. He had been making the voyage from Chemulpo to Yokohama in a Korean junk, which had been capsized by a sudden squall, and had gone down, he feared, with all hands. Luckily he himself had managed to cling to a considerable portion of wreckage, and to hold on long enough to lash himself to the mast. He was sorry now that he had not waited for a steamer; it was only his strong family affection that had prompted him to sail in a crazy junk, and he would certainly never do so again. He had a brother in Tokio, the owner of a small curiosity shop. News had reached him in Chemulpo that his beloved brother was at the point of death, and without delay he had embarked on a rice-laden junk that happened to be sailing for Tokio, in the hope of reaching that town in time to see his brother before he died.

"'Plenty muchee velly good piecee man," concluded the interpreter approvingly.

"Extraordinaire!" exclaimed Desjardins in admiration. "Dat is sentiment; it is noble, it touch my 'art."

He laid his hand on that section of his rotundity which might be taken to conceal the organ in question, and sighed with enjoyment.

"Ach! it is not sentiment," said Schwab, "it is business. Ze brozer haf curiosity shop—vell, ze ozer brozer vish to inherit imme'ately, vizout drouble. He must be on ze spot."

"Come now, Herr Schwab, don't spoil our little romance," said Bob. "Poor fellow! he's had a rough time anyhow. I wonder how he lost his ear."

"Bad time indeed," said Desjardins. "Pauvre diable! Ve must make him a collection, and you, Monsieur Schwab, you are business man, you shall collect de moneys."

Herr Schwab, who had evidently foreseen that the Frenchman's sympathy might take this practical form, began to decline the proffered honour, but the chorus of amused assent left him no option. Then, finding that he had himself to pay the tax, with German thoroughness he devoted himself heartily to the task of seeing that no one else escaped, and by the time the vessel opened up the lights of Nagasaki quite a respectable sum had been gathered for the Chinaman's benefit.

Bob, being on official business, had instructions to proceed direct from Nagasaki to Tokio. Most of the passengers, however, among them his recent companions, were remaining on the *Sardinia* as far as Kobe, with the object of seeing the world-famed beauties of the inland sea. The last words Bob heard as he went down the side after the final farewells were a guttural protest from Herr Schwab, with whom his enforced contribution to the Chang-Wo fund was still rankling.

"Business, my dear sir, are business; sentiment is sentiment. Zey should nefer be mix. Damit basta!"

Chapter II
Rokuro Kobo San

An Incident in Ueno Park—Japan at Play—Journalism in Japan—A Japanese Gentleman

Shortly before dusk, one day in the week following the arrival of the *Sardinia* at Nagasaki, a stalwart figure in the coat, pantaloons, and clumsy clogs of a Chinaman slowly ascended the flight of steps leading to the Ueno Park in Tokio. The time of cherry-blossom was not yet; the trees stood bare skeletons against the gray sky; the ground was lightly touched with rime; it was not the beauties of nature that attracted the sauntering visitor. He seemed, indeed, to have no special object in view; but an observer might have noticed that wherever he saw a group of Japanese in conversation, he passed them with a very deliberate step, and always on the right-hand side, even when this necessitated some little squeezing. Only an observer of more than usual intentness would have connected this curious fancy with the fact that the Chinaman had lost his right ear.

He came by and by to a tea-house—not one of the large and well-appointed establishments which a Samurai would willingly have entered, but a structure little more than a shed, with tables ranged outside beneath the trees, and a few musumés sitting with folded hands and crossed feet on a long low bench covered with a crimson cloth. The Chinaman hesitated for a moment; it was cold, and hardly the evening for al-fresco refreshment. But something attracted him towards the shed. He sat down on one of the benches, and was soon contentedly sipping the weak almost colourless decoction supplied to him by the smiling girls as tea.

For half an hour he sat there, sipping, watching the passers with his yellow almond eyes, thinking Chinese thoughts, silent, almost motionless. Then he pulled his padded garments more closely around him as though for the first time feeling the cold, rose, bowed low in response to the still lower salutation of the attendants, and resumed his slow walk. There were fewer people about now; no talking groups; nothing apparently to attract the remaining ear; and Chang-Wo, shuffling along on his clogs, hurrying his step a little, passed beneath the bare oaks and gloomy pines towards the Buddhist temple near the gate.

Dark was beginning to fall; there were few rickshaws to be seen; the visitors to the famed Toshogu shrine had melted away. Only here and there a woman trudged homeward with her baby on her back and a bundle in her hand, or a shaven Buddhist priest sauntered amid the trees.

Turning from the path to shorten his way by crossing a secluded glade, the Manchu came all at once face to face with a small figure hastening in the opposite direction. He moved somewhat aside, to pass on, but with a suddenness that took his bulky form utterly aback, the shorter figure, that reached not much past his elbow, flung himself upon the Manchu with a cry like the snarl of a tiger, springing up at him, clutching at his throat, and hanging on with desperate fury. The shock was so unexpected, the assault so unprovoked, that the bigger man, his hands hampered by his capacious sleeves, was taken at a disadvantage, and gained nothing from his superior build. In a moment he was on the ground, and the Japanese was kneeling on his chest, retaining his grip on the prostrate man's throat, and striving with all his might to strangle him. But his advantage was short-lived: the Manchu regained command of his muscles, and exerting all the force of his arms thrust the assailant from him, wriggled over, and pinned the puny frame to the ground.

Scarcely a sound had been uttered, whether by Japanese or Manchu; but now, as the latter proceeded with vindictive and triumphant malice to retaliate upon his helpless victim, a half-choked cry, as of an animal at the shambles, broke the silence of the glade. Instantly, as though in answer, a tall great-coated form, the form of a European, came out from among the tree-stems. A glance apprised him of the position: a small man, black in the face, was being throttled by a man twice his size; and with a rush the new-comer hurled himself upon the Manchu, wrenched the Japanese from his grip, and saw that he was only just in time, if indeed not too late. For the small man lay inert, huddled in his kimono; and the Englishman placed his hand over his heart, fearing that he was already dead.

But his doubt was soon dispelled. In a few moments the little fellow moved, gasped, and sprang to his feet, his slanted eyes asquint with excess of rage. It seemed that he was about to fling himself on the young foreigner before him, so much was he blinded by passion; but recognizing in a moment his mistake, he looked round for the big Manchu, and found that he had disappeared. With a muttered word of thanks to his preserver, he rushed madly in the direction he supposed his enemy to have taken, and the Englishman was left to himself in the gathering darkness.

Bob Fawcett had a half-smile upon his face as he walked back through the park and the crowded streets to his hotel. It was his fourth day in Tokio, and he had already seen many strange things; nothing, perhaps, stranger than the deadly earnestness with which the little Japanese had sped after an enemy who could have crushed him with ease.

"I wonder what it was all about?" he thought. "Plucky little Hop o' my Thumb! I suppose he's the stuff of which the Japanese army is made."

He would have liked to know what had brought about the unequal fight, but speculation was vain; and besides, it was nearly dinner-time, and the meals at his hotel were punctually served. Punctuality was, in Bob's eyes, the only virtue the hotel possessed. He did not like the heavy carpets, the cumbrous four-poster in his bed-room, the general stuffiness that resembled only too closely the fusty musty atmosphere of certain hotels at home. He wished he could have put up at a Japanese place, lived in the Japanese way, eaten Japanese food, for he was of an enquiring turn of mind. But he had been strongly advised to put up at a house run on European lines, and for the present he could not but recognize that the advice was probably good.

On arriving in Tokio four days before, and reporting himself at the Japanese ministry of marine, he found that his services were not immediately required. He was asked to hold himself in readiness to assume his duties at a few hours' notice; meanwhile his time was his own. It was unlucky that his arrival in Japan was in the very middle of the New-year celebrations, for business being at almost a total stand-still for a fortnight on end, the two English merchants to whom he had brought letters of introduction had gone away with their families for a holiday, and among the two million people in Tokio there was not one that he knew. There was company at the hotel, to be sure, but it consisted chiefly of tourists and globe-trotters eager to "do" everything, and Bob had never had a taste for frantic sight-seeing. He accordingly chose his own course, and wandered about pretty much by himself, taking the keenest interest in the novel scenes that everywhere met his eyes.

A stranger could hardly have arrived in Tokio at a more interesting time. For ten days after the year has opened Japan is more characteristically Japanese, perhaps, than at any other period. It is one universal festival. Among the upper classes visits of ceremony are exchanged; the streets are crowded with rickshaws drawn by coolies in fantastic costume—mushroom hats and waterproofs of reeds. They worm their way through throngs of adults and children bouncing balls, playing at battledore and shuttlecock, flying kites, tumbling over each other in their happy frolicsomeness. Shopkeepers are to be seen carrying specimens of their wares to their customers; brightly-clad geishas add grace and picturesqueness to the scene. Every variety of costume is to be met with, from the correct frock-coats of the government officials to the strange mixture of billycock and kimono which lesser folk sometimes affect. Every house is decorated; here and there a juggler or a showman provides elementary entertainment at the price of three-farthings, and the unwary visitor, enticed into a booth by the promise of great marvels, finds that the magic is nothing more startling than an electric shock, or that the advertised fire-breathing dragon is no more than a moon-faced performing seal. At night paper lanterns dangle from every rickshaw shaft, making the streets a moving panorama of fairyland; and from the low one-storied houses proceeds the quaint barbarous music of the samisen—the native guitar twanged by smiling geishas entertaining their employers' guests with dance and song.

Bob spent many delightful hours in witnessing these things, and in strolling through the streets, looking into the curio shops, sometimes venturing a discreet purchase. But amid all the merriment there seemed to him to be a something in the air—an undercurrent of seriousness, which was the theme of incessant talk in the hotel smoking-room. Was it to be war? That was the question which was discussed from morning to night. Everybody knew that negotiations were proceeding between the foreign offices at Tokio and St. Petersburg: what was the result to be? Opinion veered this way and that. Russia apparently would not keep her pledges: would Japan fight? What were the rights of the case? Was Russia merely concerned with holding an ice-free port and developing her trade, or was she aiming at aggression and conquest? Was Japan strong enough to enforce unaided what the diplomacy of European powers had failed to accomplish? Would China come to the assistance of her conqueror? Would Britain be involved in the struggle? These and similar questions were canvassed to the point of weariness; and Bob all the time felt that it was talk in the air, for nobody knew. There was no excitement, no mouthings, no boastfulness. The little soldiers in their trim uniforms were not much to be seen in the streets; yet it was not long before Bob learnt that preparations were quietly, unostentatiously, being made to throw vast armies across the Korea Strait; and as to the navy, was not his presence there in itself a proof that the government was determined to have everything at the top of condition should the struggle which many deemed inevitable actually begin?

On the second morning after the adventure in the Ueno Park, Bob, having finished breakfast, went to the reading-room to glance at the papers preparatory to his usual stroll. There were illustrated European magazines in plenty with which he was familiar, and a five-weeks' old copy of the *Times*, which he looked through without much interest, the news being so obviously stale. There was the *Japan Mail*, a little more interesting, in which he was glad to find an account of the last match between the Australians and Warner's eleven, as well as news of the British doings in Tibet and Somaliland. But having brought himself up to date with those journals in his own tongue, he turned, as he usually did, to the native papers, and stared at them as earnestly as though only assiduous poring was needed to give him a thorough grasp of Japanese. He wished he could read the strange hieroglyphics—some shaped like gridirons, others like miniature barns, others like the little dancing imps drawn by school-boys with a few straight lines on the margins of their grammars. He wondered what meaning lay behind the strangely picturesque tantalizing characters, and sighed as he replaced one of the papers on the table.

"Not understand, sir?" said a passing Japanese waiter, with the smiling courtesy of all the hotel attendants.

"I don't, I confess," replied Bob, returning the smile. "What do you call this, for instance?"

"That, sir? That *Ninkin Shimbun*—very good paper. My uncle belong that paper one time—prison editor."

"Prison editor?" Bob looked puzzled.

"In Japan, sir, newspaper two editors one time. Number one editor he write War Minister bad man. Policeman he come say: 'Be so kind cease publish hon'ble paper; hon'ble publisher, hon'ble printer, hon'ble editor be so kind enter hon'ble prison'. Number two editor he go prison, number one editor he stay home."

"I suppose they pay number two well for that," remarked Bob laughing.

"No, sir; my uncle very poor man. His wages four yen a month; but no spend much, in prison every time."

"Poor fellow! He earns his four yen."

The little waiter's countenance took on a lugubrious expression.

"He prison editor not now no longer," he said. "Everything change in Nippon. These days number one editor go prison, number two he out of work. My poor uncle sell *Ninkin Shimbun* Shimbashi railway-station."

At this moment the hall-porter entered, and bowed to Bob with a deep Japanese obeisance.

"Japanese gentleman, sir, beg you be so kind give him interview."

"Oh! who is it?" said Bob, thinking that it must be the bearer of the expected summons from the minister.

"Japanese gentleman, sir; say you not know his name. But he very great man, he very noble Samurai." Then, looking with an air of imparting important information, he added: "His name, sir, Rokuro Kobo San."

Surprised that so important a personage should have been chosen to wait upon him, Bob rose and made his way across the corridor to the reception-room. The porter shut the door behind him, and as he advanced a slight figure stepped lightly across the room to meet him. Whatever dim picture of a Samurai Bob had formed in his mind was banished at the sight of a trim, exquisitely-dressed Japanese, wearing a frock-coat that would have done credit to Poole's, and carrying with practised ease a silk hat, which might have been twin-brother of Bob's unused Lincoln & Bennett. He was short, though perhaps rather above the average height of his nation. In feature he resembled the Japanese of better class whom Bob had seen at the government offices, but with an indefinable touch of added refinement, due partly, no doubt, to his Samurai blood, but partly also, as Bob surmised, to his evident familiarity with western civilization. He was sallow, like all his race; his jet-black hair was thick and strong, and a narrow moustache graced his upper lip. It is always difficult to judge the age of an alien in race, and Bob had little or no experience to guide him; but the impression made upon him by his visitor's general bearing was that he was in the prime of life.

"Good-morning, sir," said Bob pleasantly.

"Good-morning, sir," said the Japanese with perfect accent at almost the same moment, bowing with inimitable grace. Bob instinctively bowed in response, but felt that his salutation was awkward and stiff by contrast.

"I trust, sir, that you will pardon my intruding upon you at this hour. I feared lest I should not have the opportunity of thanking you in my own person for the very great service which you have rendered to me and to my house."

His mode of speech was measured, even, and perfectly correct, somewhat stilted perhaps, with an old-world flavour that belonged to a courtlier age than our own.

"You may remember, sir, two days ago, in our Ueno Park, you rescued one of my countrymen from the hands of a Chinaman, who I have every reason to think would have killed him but for your generous intervention. The Chinaman was a man of evil character, a desperate man, a villain; the Japanese, who owes his life to you, is—my servant. I thank you."

"Really, sir," said Bob, somewhat embarrassed, "it was a very small matter; I merely hauled the fellow off, and he bolted."

"To you, sir, it may have been a small matter. It is an instinct with your countrymen to help the man who is down. To you it is a mere nothing; but to me, it represents much, very much. The man you rescued is my servant; his forefathers have served mine these five hundred years."

"I am very glad, sir, that I happened to be passing just at the moment. May I congratulate you on your man? He tackled the big Chinaman with fine courage."

"He is a brave man indeed, but he grows old. Ten years ago he was with me in the China war; he was in his prime; there was not his equal in our army. The Manchu, as you saw, is a man of more than common strength, but in single fight with my servant at Feng-huang-cheng he escaped with difficulty, and the loss of an ear."

"The loss of an ear!" repeated Bob. "Surely he cannot be the man we picked up off Nagasaki?"

Kobo San's expression betrayed just a hint of enquiry, and Bob proceeded to give an account of the Chinaman's rescue. This was the beginning of a long conversation, which, starting with Kobo's previous relations with the Manchu, drifted away into a variety of subjects, giving Bob every now and again a suggestion of his visitor's extraordinary range and versatility. He was clearly a man of wide reading and many interests, had been a great traveller in his younger days, and spoke as though at home equally in all the great capitals of the west. So interested was Bob that he did not notice the increasing number of rickshaws halting at the entrance to the hotel, depositing guests laden with strange bundles, the spoils of long chaffering in the Naka-dori.

This influx was the sure indication of approaching tiffin, and when the Japanese rose to take his leave, Bob awakened to the fact, and with some diffidence begged the pleasure of his visitor's company. Kobo San, however, explained that he had but just time to keep an appointment with his excellency the minister of war, and while courteously expressing his regrets, extended to Bob an invitation to his own house on the following day. Bob accepted with genuine pleasure, and escorted his visitor to the street. The two shook hands almost with the cordiality of old friends.

As Bob turned to re-enter the hotel, he encountered the little waiter gazing after the retreating form with a mixture half of admiration half of awe.

"Rokuro Kobo San, he very great man," he said, confidentially. "He kindly send my poor uncle to hon'ble prison."

Chapter III
A Samurai's Home

A Japanese Interior—An Oriental Menu—Tales of Old Japan—The Quarrel with Russia—Chang-Wo—Raiding the Raiders—Good-bye

"Takaki ya ni

Noborite mireba—"

Bob rubbed his eyes, and became conscious of a crick in the neck. He thought for a moment he must be in a railway-train; the sensation was just the same that he had experienced on a night journey to London, when he had had a compartment to himself, and lay stretched on a seat with his head on the elbow cushion at the end. But no: he had never heard in England such a thin soft voice, singing in utter tunelessness such strange words—

"Kemuri tatsu;

Tami no kamado wa

Nigiwai ni kere".

He lifted his head from the low neck-rest, and remembered. The voice came through the wall of his room; but it was not a wall—only a slight paper partition. It was evidently time to get up. He flung off the wadded quilt, and sat up—not in bed, but on the stretch of straw matting that formed almost the only furniture of his room. The neck-rest fell down, making a slight noise; the voice in the next room ceased singing; he heard the swish of soft garments; a few moments later a sliding paper panel in the partition was pushed back and a form appeared—the form of a little Japanese carrying a bath and a pitcher of water.

"Morning, sir," said the little fellow with a smile and a bow. "Bath in morning, sir?"

"Thank you," said Bob, springing to his feet. "By the way, I don't think I have heard your name yet?"

"My name, sir, Taru. You sleep well, sir?"

"Oh yes, though I found the head-rest a little strange. Was it you singing just now, Taru?"

"No, sir; no sing at all. The little lady, hon'ble mistress, sir; O Toyo San."

"Indeed!"

Bob forbore to ask questions. He had only arrived the night before at Kobo San's country house near Nikko, tired and chilled after the uphill railway journey from Tokio, and quite ready to retire to his sleeping-chamber after a cup of warm saké. It was three days since his first meeting with the Japanese gentleman who had called upon him at the hotel. During those three days Kobo San had proved himself a most delightful companion. He had taken the young Englishman here, there, and everywhere about Tokio: to an entertainment at the Maple Club, where Bob had seen the prettiest geishas in Japan dance to the barbarous music of the samisen and the koto; to a wrestling match between two huge athletes; to a theatrical performance which, though tragic in intention, gave him considerable amusement, so strangely were the actors' faces painted, so ludicrous (to the European eye) were their gestures and grimaces. Bob was intensely interested in all that he saw, and sincerely grateful to his indefatigable guide; but his delight was increased tenfold when he received an invitation to spend a few days at Kobo San's country house; it was a unique opportunity of seeing for himself something of the domestic life of Japan.

Two things had struck him specially during those three days. The one was that Kobo San was a man of great note and influence; wherever he went he was treated with exceeding respect and deference. The second was that, though he himself knew almost nothing about Kobo, Kobo appeared to know a good deal about him. No confidences had been given, none asked; but Bob had the strange consciousness that his new friend was perfectly acquainted with the errand upon which he had come from the island empire of the West to the island empire of the East. When inviting him to Nikko, Kobo had said "My house is within easy reach of the telegraph", as though to reassure him that if the summons he was expecting should come suddenly, while he was there, nothing need hinder his prompt obedience to the call. Bob had never learnt how his host had discovered the whereabouts of the stranger who had rescued his man from the one-eared Manchu. The explanation was simple. The Japanese, finding his vengeful hunt for Chang-Wo fruitless, had next day made enquiries at all the European hotels, and learning that a young Englishman staying at one of them somewhat answered to the description he gave, had sat down on his heels at the gate for hours, and waited there until the man he was in search of passed by.

And now Bob was actually a guest in the house of a Japanese samurai. The house was really a sort of two-storied bungalow, standing on rising ground, and approached by a flight of stone steps. A mountain rose sheer into the sky behind it; a stream dashed over a cascade, filled a fish-pond in the neat garden, and plunged into the river below. There was no furniture to speak of; nothing but straw covered with finely-woven bamboo, spotlessly white, a pot or two of flowers, and a curious-shaped stand for a paper lantern, by which, as he learnt afterwards, Kobo San sometimes read at night. But his surprise was mingled with admiration. The walls were plastered with sand of varied hues, inlaid with fragments of shell and mica; the ceiling was of light polished wood crossed by bars of a darker colour, and supported on light posts. Near the ceiling ran a long strip of exquisitely-painted paper; along the bottom of the wall a narrow border of the same was fixed. On one wall, from floor to ceiling, there was a kakemono,—a painted panel, representing storks standing in water dotted with moss-grown rocks. In a corner was a sort of inlaid cabinet let into the wall, where the futon, the thickly-wadded quilts, were kept; for every room in a Japanese house is a bed-room in case of need. Let into the floor was a charcoal brazier, with which alone the room was heated. Everything was spotless; the harmony of colour was perfect; and Bob could not help contrasting this charming simplicity with the elaborate tasteless furniture of the conventional English home.

While he was still admiring, Kobo came in. But it was a different Kobo from the frock-coated gentleman he had known in Tokio. His host was clad in the costume of his country,—the flowing wide-sleeved kimono, his feet encased in the mitten-like tabi—socks with a separate pocket for the big toe. He bowed very low as he entered the room, and there was a slight smile on his face as he explained:

"When I am at home, as you see, Mr. Fawcett, I preserve the old customs—the old dress, the old manners. I work in the present, I take my recreation in the past. Did you sleep well?"

"Very well; though I woke once with the idea that I was falling out of bed."

"Ah, you will soon become accustomed to the makura. No doubt you are now hungry."

He called, without raising his voice, and from the distance came a long-drawn answering cry: "Hai-i-i, tadaima!" Presently there entered two ladies, followed by four maids bearing food on little lacquer trays. The ladies went down lightly on their knees and bent over till their heads touched the ground, murmuring "O hayo!" Bob was somewhat embarrassed, but Kobo said something in Japanese; the ladies rose, advanced, and said "Good morning!" with the prettiest accent imaginable. Kobo explained that they were his wife and daughter, O Kami San and O Toyo San. Bob would have taken them for sisters, so alike were they in the graceful kimonos of lilac-coloured silk, girt with rich brocaded obi. They knew but a few words of English, but Bob felt almost instantly at home, so simply and charmingly did they welcome him.

Soon all four were seated on cushions on the floor, while the four musumés knelt in front of them, offering the first course of Bob's first Japanese breakfast. It consisted of beautiful white cakes made of bean-flour and sugar, and little cups of weak tea. This was followed by a sort of fish broth in lacquer bowls, with a condiment made of shredded daikon—the Japanese radish—mingled with green herbs. Bob found that he had to pick morsels of fish from the broth with a pair of chop-sticks, dip them into the condiment, and poke them into his mouth; and his first clumsy attempts with these novel utensils did not call the shadow of a smile to the faces of his polite entertainers. Then came prawns in batter, fish cakes, rice in bowls of gold lacquer, preserved plums, crystallized walnuts, and other dishes, in many of which fish figured in some form or other: all in such midget quantities that Bob felt he would still be hungry if he swallowed the portions of all four. He felt as Gulliver might have felt at a state banquet in Lilliput. At his side throughout the meal stood a beautiful porcelain bottle filled with saké, a liquor tasting like weak beer and water. Bob did not like it, but he had accepted Kobo San's invitation, and he was resolved to endure without flinching all that Japanese hospitality might involve.

When the meal was finished the ladies withdrew, and Bob was asked by his host to accompany him in a drive. At the door the former found his boots, and the latter a pair of sandals, which he fastened by passing a thong between his big toe and the rest of his foot. Outside there waited two handsome rickshaws with their coolies, who set off down the hill towards the magnificent avenue of cryptomerias that stretches in one almost unbroken line for twenty miles.

That was the beginning of as pleasant a week as Bob had ever spent. He grew accustomed to the simple ways of the house: took off his boots instinctively on entering; learnt to squat more comfortably on the floor, and to enjoy the novel fare; even to tolerate the plunky-plunketing of the koto when O Toyo San played to him, and sang strange songs which she tried in her pretty broken English to translate. On some days Bob was left much to himself; Kobo received many letters and telegrams which kept him busy for long hours in his own room, and at such times Bob would chat with Taru, the servant, who gave him many precious bits of information about his master's family, always with infinite discretion. Kobo was the descendant of a long line of samurai, who had themselves been the vassals of a daimio or great baronial family illustrious in the history of Japan. Taru himself remembered the time when Kobo's family had fought in the great civil war from which dates the wonderful advance of modern Japan. Previous to that time, foreigners and all things foreign had been regarded with the intensest hatred by the Japanese; Kobo's father had been among those who fired on the foreign settlement at Hiogo in 1868, and had been condemned to hara-kiri by the Mikado. Bob learnt the terrible details of that mode of execution, when the condemned man, without a murmur or a sign of reluctance or fear, deliberately took his own life at the bidding of his lord. Kobo was a boy of nine when his father thus died; he had grown up under the new system; he had played a considerable part in the Japanese Diet, and had won great honour in the war with China; and he now enjoyed the peculiar confidence of the Mikado's government. Taru did not explain what position he held, and Bob, for all his curiosity, did not care to ask; it was evident that the man held the master in boundless veneration.

Interesting as these talks with Taru were, Bob was most of all pleased when his host, in the evenings, after being invisible all day, entertained him with stories of his country's history, and recounted the picturesque tales of old Japan. He learnt of the long tyranny of the Shoguns, who kept the titular sovereign, the Mikado, in strict seclusion and usurped all his powers until the great Revolution of 1868, when the restoration of the Mikado overthrew the Shogunate for ever. He learnt about the old class distinctions: the daimios, great feudal princes owing vassalage to the sovereign, holding their fiefs on condition of doing military service; the samurai, the warlike retainers of the daimios, themselves chieftains of large bands of warriors, and often more powerful than their lords; the priests of the two religions, Shinto and Buddhism, some of whose wonderful temples in Nikko Bob visited in company with his host; below all these the trading and farming classes, who were held of no account, however wealthy they might become. He learnt of Japan's strange awakening that followed the Mikado's final triumph over the Shogun: the abolition of the feudal system, the disarming of the samurai, the eagerness to learn western ways, the readiness to adopt western inventions. Besides all this, he heard some of the legendary stories of old Japan, and one evening saw Kobo dressed in the old armour of the samurai, a combination of chain-mail and armour-plate, with penthouse shoulder-pieces, nose-piece and gorget, helmet and greaves, a long spear, and two swords worn one above the other on the left hip. Bob was carried back to the days of chivalry in Europe, when knights in armour went out adventuring, soldiers of fortune selling their services to any potentate who would employ them; and he understood something of the fierce energy and enthusiasm which, withdrawn from mere warlike enterprises, had found an outlet in Japan's astonishing development in commerce and industry.

Most of all, Bob was struck by the glimpses he obtained of the samurai ideals. Kobo never talked about his honour; it was not a matter either to boast of or to prove; but from the stories he told, and his manner of telling, Bob recognized that his ideal of honour equalled, if it did not even transcend, the ideals of the preux chevaliers of Christendom. In the old days, the samurai's devotion to his feudal chief was the pole-star of his life. He allowed nothing, not the direst tortures, not death itself, to stand in the way of his duty as he conceived it. In the Sengakuji temple in Tokio Bob had seen the tombs of the Forty-seven Ronins, the national heroes of Japan, whose story as he heard it now from Kobos lips was an epic, an Iliad that was literally true. The Ronins, whose very name means "wave-tost", were samurai, and their lord having been compelled to put himself to death, they formed themselves into a league to avenge him against the man whose treachery had brought this woe upon him. Unfalteringly they pursued their aim, though they knew that the end must be to themselves also death. Against all difficulties and machinations they held on their course unswervingly; their lord's enemy was slain; and with serene cheerfulness they accepted the inevitable doom, and forty-seven, slew themselves in the manner prescribed.

Kobo's conversation was not merely about the past. He spoke of the difficulties at that moment facing his country—difficulties due in great measure to the interference of western powers. With an increasing population, a soil of which a large part was unfit for cultivation, and rapidly-growing industries, Japan needed outlets for her energies, and was determined not to be debarred from her legitimate markets in Manchuria and Korea by restrictions imposed upon her by Russia, which had stepped in and robbed her of the fruits of her victory over China. It was now no secret that a critical stage had been reached in the negotiations between the two empires. Russia promised but did not perform; Japan was biding her time. Would she fight? Bob could not refrain from asking the question. Kobo smiled.

"You saw that little quarrel between two rickshaw men in the narrow road yesterday. They could not pass; neither would yield to the other; they bowed and smiled and discoursed pleasantly for a long time. Then all at once, as you saw, the eyes of one shone, his features set themselves with grim purpose, and he secured the right of way by a heavy stroke that rendered his adversary helpless. Our diplomatists will be polite until the last word is said, and then—"

The information was not merely on Kobo's side. Bob felt that, while the purpose with which he had come to Japan was perfectly known to his host, some further account of his antecedents was due to him. One evening, therefore, he spoke of his parents, of his home in the hill-country near Penrith; of his school-days at Glenalmond, and the vigorous bracing system there; of his early taste for mechanics, and his subsequent years with a Glasgow engineering firm and at Glasgow University. He spoke modestly of his experience, enthusiastically of his work, and hopefully of his prospects; and Kobo, listening without any outward sign of sympathy, said a few simple words of encouragement, which Bob appreciated much more than if they had been extravagant and fulsome.

One day a chance reference to the Chinese war of 1894 prompted Bob to ask a question on a matter that had engaged his curiosity ever since his little adventure in the Ueno Park.

"Chang-Wo?" said Kobo with a smile. "Yes, I will tell you about him if you do not mind listening to a somewhat long story. It was in the autumn of '94. I was then a captain in the Eleventh regiment. Our general, Count Yamagata, had driven the Chinese across the Yalu, and we had made a dash on Feng-huang-cheng, only to find the place a heap of ruins. But we captured a vast quantity of stores, and it was while we were making arrangements for the disposal of these and for the advance of our main army from Kiu-lien-cheng that word was brought to General Tatsumi of a disaster that had befallen one of our transport trains. It was one of those tiresome little contretemps that cause loss and annoyance without affecting the general progress of a campaign."

"We had several affairs of that kind in our Boer war," remarked Bob. "But I interrupt you, sir."

"A half company of infantry escorting a large quantity of war material had been ambushed by a force of Manchus from the hills on our right. Nearly all our men had been killed; the remainder, with the wagons, were carried off into the mountains. The leader of these guerrilla warriors, or brigands as they would more properly be described, was a certain Chang-Wo, a notorious freebooter, who had collected a formidable band of outlaws, and was playing for his own hand. The news was brought to us by one of the wagon-drivers, who had cut the traces of his team and made good his escape. He told us that the brigands were very numerous, but owing to the suddenness of their onslaught he could not give us definite particulars. It was clear that the attack had been most skilfully planned, for the captain in charge of our column was an officer of great ability.

"The general could hardly allow such an attack to pass unpunished. He would have sent cavalry in pursuit of the brigands but that the hilly country was entirely unsuited to them. It happened that my infantry company had been the first to scale the defences of Kiu-lien-cheng, and General Tatsumi selected us to track the marauders down. But he gave us only twenty-four hours. If we did not overtake them in that time we were to return; he said he could not afford to waste a company on a wild-goose chase in the hills. Accordingly I set off at once with my men. The brigands had four hours' start of us, and unluckily we had no information as to their route. But the chances were that they would make with their booty for their stronghold, and we discovered that that lay some two or three marches distant among the hills. It was fifteen miles to the spot at which the ambush had been laid; that was four hours' march, so that the enemy were altogether eight hours ahead of us. We had only sixteen hours left of our twenty-four. Could we accomplish our task? The one point in our favour was that Chang-Wo was encumbered with booty. No doubt he had impressed natives to carry it: wagons would be useless in the hills; and laden coolies perforce go slowly.

"Just as we were starting, it occurred to me that we might make use of the river if boats could be procured. After a little searching we found enough flat-bottomed craft to embark all our men, and we punted down the river for some sixteen miles, saving our legs, and making excellent progress, for we were going with the stream. We kept a sharp look-out on its banks, and at last my man Taru, an excellent scout, declared that he saw traces of a recent fording of the river by a large force. We landed, following up the tracks, and prepared to march them down.

"We had not gone very far before we came upon a coolie dying by the wayside. He told us that he had been brutally maltreated by the Manchus because he had been unable to carry his load. From him we learnt that the brigands had passed seven hours ahead of us. It was one o'clock in the afternoon. My men were in grand condition, the boats having saved them a fatiguing march; and the Japanese infantryman—pardon my saying so—is hard to beat at forced marching. By dusk we had covered thirty miles over the hills. Then a few of my best men went ahead to see if they could more definitely track the enemy. The night was still young when they returned. They had found a large camp about six miles ahead; watch-fires were burning, but the bivouac was but loosely guarded. Chang-Wo evidently believed that he had outmarched any pursuing force. We at once pushed on.

"The brigands were engaged in high carousal when we came within ear-shot of their camp, which was pitched in a hollow of the hills. I sent a scout forward; he returned with the news that they appeared to be about to carry out an execution. I could not doubt that some of my unhappy countrymen who had fallen into the Manchus' hands were to be the victims, and I knew that their death would be neither speedy nor painless. Sending a score of my men to the further side of the hollow to cut off the brigands' retreat, I waited only long enough to give them time to take up their position; then in dead silence the rest of us charged down among the gang. The sentries were so much interested in what was proceeding in the camp that we took them quite unawares, and we were in the midst of the camp almost before the alarm was raised.

"It was a good fight, a capital fight, while it lasted; but my men had a score to pay off, and they were bent on teaching the brigands a lesson. My servant, a very tiger in battle, made direct for the big Manchu, Chang-Wo, and aimed a cut at his head. But the blow was warded off by a henchman of the chiefs, and it took only partial effect, slicing off the villain's right ear. Then they closed, Chang-Wo and Taru, and there was a desperate affray, both struggling on the ground, for though the Manchu is big and extraordinarily powerful, my man was a younger man in those days, and had no match as a wrestler in the whole Japanese army. Unluckily he was struck on the head by the same man as had warded off his blow from Chang-Wo, and before I could come to his assistance the Manchu scrambled to his feet and disappeared in the darkness. He was one of the few who got away. We wiped out almost his whole band. As I expected, he had been about to torture to death the half-dozen Japanese whom they had brought as prisoners from the ambush. We had two hours left out of our twenty-four."

"And what is Chang-Wo doing now in Tokio?"

"I do not know; though I could make a guess. I had heard little of him since the war. But he is still the chief of his band of brigands; and we have every reason to believe that he is in Russian pay. But he is no longer in Tokio. As soon as Taru told me of his meeting in the Park, I sent men on the Manchu's track. He had disappeared; and I think he will not again be seen in our towns: his absent ear would make him now too conspicuous."

One day, not long after Bob had thus learnt the story of Chang-Wo, Kobo was more than usually busy. Telegrams reached the house in quick succession, and the ladies, though they betrayed no anxiety, showed by little indications that might have escaped a less interested observer than Bob that an important moment had arrived. Few outward signs of affection passed between Kobo and his family, but it was easy to discern how thoroughly his wife and daughter were wrapt up in him, and how they all doted on his only son, a boy at school in England. It was Wednesday, February 3. Bob was seated with the ladies waiting for Kobo to appear at the mid-day meal. He came in at length. The ladies rose upon their knees and made him a profound obeisance. He was dressed in European costume; in his hand he held a telegram.

"For you, Mr. Fawcett," he said gravely.

Bob took the envelope, tore it open, and read:

"You are requested report yourself Admiral Togo at Sasebo."

It was signed by the secretary whom he had seen when he called at the government offices in Tokio.

"I am summoned," he said to Kobo.

"Yes. I will accompany you. Let us finish our meal."

Bob was so much excited that he found it hard to eat. The others were outwardly as calm as though nothing had happened. The many courses were brought in as usual by the smiling musumés. Bob made a pretence at partaking of them all, but he was glad when the meal was over, and his host announced that rickshaws would be at the door in half an hour. It seemed an age. The moment of parting came. Bob bade farewell to O Kami San and O Toyo San, thanking them with a full heart for the hospitality they had shown him, then mounted to his place. Kobo San followed him. There was no hand-clasp, no good-bye kiss; wife, daughter, the musumés bent to the ground in the lowliest of obeisances; and as the coolies started to run down the hill, Bob looked back and saw them all at the door, still with smiling faces, and heard in their pretty, unstressed accents the soft, long-drawn-out word of farewell:

"Sayonara! Sa—yo—na—ra!"

Chapter IV
Six to One

A Newspaper Paragraph—Scenes by the Way—Mistaken Identity—A Warm Corner—A Modern Miracle—Yamaguchi

The train rattled down to Tokio, cutting at intervals through the magnificent avenue of cryptomerias, at such a headlong pace that Bob feared every moment lest it should jump the rails and end his career before it had begun. But he reached Tokio whole in limb, and, taking leave of Kobo San at the station, hurried to his hotel. After making his preparations, he found that there was an hour or two to spare before the train left for the west, and went into the reading-room to look at the papers, which he had not seen during his absence. There he encountered a dejected group, comprising his ship-board acquaintances Mr. Morton, Herr Schwab, and Monsieur Desjardins, together with a few other Europeans and a couple of Americans, all evidently correspondents.

"Hullo!" shouted Morton. "Thought you were at Hong-Kong by now. I wish I were!"

Morton's loud voice, and the atmosphere of the hotel, struck Bob with a curious sense of incongruity after the quiet of his recent sojourn at Nikko.

"What! You don't like Japan?" he said with a smile.

"Humph!" grunted Morton. "Precious little of Japan we've seen, boxed up here, asking questions, getting no answers. Haven't sent the *Post* a decent stick of copy since I came. Everything leaks out in London before we get it here. That wretched legation in Knightsbridge don't give us a chance. We might as well be in Kamschatka. But what have you been doing?"

"I've been to Nikko!"

"What! Finding ranges?"

"Yes," said Bob; "mountain ranges."

"You say ranges," broke in Herr Schwab instantly. "I hafe new batent kitchen range, save 95 per cent fuel. I can quote you—"

He stopped in stolid wonder at a general chuckle from the group. Morton, evidently scenting information, followed up his clue.

"I suppose you're out of work like the rest of us. Jap motto: 'No foreigners need apply'. They've had shoals of applications."

Although Bob had not been definitely warned to keep his business secret, he felt that he was not entitled to make any premature disclosure.

"Well, anyhow it's a pleasant enough way of spending a holiday," he said. "There's plenty to be seen."

"My word! yes," said Desjardins. "I am in enchantment. De Japanese, dey are adorable. Deir politesse, it is exquisite; dey tell you everyting, but vis a charm—everyting, except vat you vant to know."

"You are right," said Mr. Jacob T. Vanzant, war commissioner of the *New York Eagle*. "I flattered myself I could raise a column of red-hot news out of a dumb waiter, but it would be easier to make the Egyptian sphinx talk than to draw one of these smiling, affable young slips at the foreign office. But it's war, gentlemen; there isn't a doubt about that. Listen to this."

He took up a fortnight-old copy of the *San Francisco Argonaut* lying at his elbow.

"Our fellow-citizens will learn with regret that since the fifteenth current the location of Mrs. Isidore G. Pottle and her niece has been involved in obscurity. When our esteemed contributor's usual letter failed to reach our offices, we cabled enquiries to the Russian commandant-general in Manchuria, and received in response the following communication: 'Mesdames priées de faire retour via Port Arthur; disparues il y a deux jours'. We have every hope that in spite of the unsettled state of Manchuria Mrs. Isidore G. Pottle's magnificent energy and determination, which have been strikingly evinced in the palpitating series of letters that have appeared in the *Argonaut*, will ultimately ensure her safe return to her native city."

"But I do not onderstand," said Herr Schwab, "vherefore ze egsentricity of your Mrs. Bottle shall be a cause of var."

Mr. Vanzant smiled, and proceeded to explain that if the Russian authorities had not had serious grounds for believing that hostilities were impending, they would have had no occasion to interrupt Mrs. Pottle's projected journey across Korea to Seoul, and thus curtail the programme she had set herself to perform when she left San Francisco on her trip round the world.

"Very ingenious," remarked Morton; "but if that's all you've got to go on, seems to me you're raising a skyscraper on a very slight foundation."

"I presume, sir," retorted the American, "you have not met Mrs. Isidore G. Pottle."

Desjardins immediately wanted to know all about the adventurous lady, and an animated conversation ensued, in which Bob took no part. Remembering the telegram screwed up in his pocket, he had felt a certain constraint while Mr. Vanzant had been giving his reasons. Conscious that he was not a diplomatist, and fearing lest in an unguarded moment he should let drop information the mere hint of which would be telegraphed to every part of the world, he took an early opportunity of slipping away.

"Zey are civilized? Ach! zey buy nozink. Ruskin, zey vill not read him; batent mangle, zey vill not look at it. Vy, ven I vas in ze Congo State viz Mr. Burnaby, ze blacks zey buy eferyzink: pins, lawn-mower, lexicon, hair-oil—" These were the last words Bob heard as he left the room, and the last he was destined to hear from Herr Schwab for a considerable time to come.

At ten o'clock that night he quietly left the hotel, and was drawn in a rickshaw, with his slender kit, to the Shimbashi railway-station, *en route* for Sasebo. He had a long journey before him, but he had no idea of how long it was actually to be. Many times during that night and the next day his train was shunted into sidings, to allow the passing of trains bearing troops to the western ports. During the hours of darkness he slept soundly, but with the morning light he awoke to the fact that things were happening. At the stations, where refreshments in neat little boxes were brought to the passengers, he saw crowds, sometimes melting away, sometimes gathering, with looks of intent eagerness on their faces. At one station, which was thronged, he saw the actual departure of a train overflowing with the trim little Japanese soldiers. He was struck by the air of joyous confidence that marked their bearing, and the look of pride with which the women and children on the platforms bade them farewell. There was none of the frenzied enthusiasm and the bitter grief which he had noticed in the crowds that sped the British soldiers on their way to South Africa five years before; there was no kissing or hand-shaking, no hanging on the necks of the departing warriors, no impeding of their movements as they entrained, no tearful last words. A few shouts of "Banzai! Banzai!" as the train moved off, and then the throng dispersed in perfect order and decorum, to hide their sorrow, perhaps, in the seclusion of their own homes. Bob was much impressed by the scene; it was like the departure of a band of Crusaders in the great days of old.

He was glad enough when, after a journey of some thirty hours, he at length reached Sasebo, the naval station where he understood the Japanese fleet was lying. Leaving his portmanteau at the railway-station, he enquired of the station-master the way to the harbour, and was courteously informed by him, in the few English phrases he had at command, that the distance was not great. Always desirous of seeing as much of the people as his opportunities allowed, Bob decided to make his way to the harbour on foot, and declined the offers of the rickshaw coolies who stood waiting to be hired in the station-yard. A regiment from Southern Kiushiu had recently detrained, and the crowd that had assembled to greet them was dispersing, as Bob passed out, with the same general orderliness that he had remarked at the stations on the line. But in this case a few among the patriots had been indulging somewhat too freely in saké, and once or twice Bob moved aside to give a wide berth to knots of roysterers who seemed inclined to claim the whole roadway. As he passed a group of half a dozen young men whom he took to be students, he heard the word "Orosha", which he remembered as the Japanese equivalent for "Russia". This was followed by a string of remarks which by their tone were clearly of no complimentary character, but which were as clearly aimed at him. In anticipation of his long, cold journey, Bob had put on his long frieze ulster that covered him from his heels to his ears, and a deer-stalker cap that was very comfortable if not very elegant. His tall figure thus costumed, his fair hair and blue eyes, were sufficient to give him the appearance of a Russian to half-drunken patriots, who in the circumstances of the time were not likely to be well-disposed towards their national enemies.

Bob did not look round; he smiled a little at the thought of being taken for a Muscovite. "Never knew I was a handsome fellow before," he thought. Walking more quickly and more directly than the noisy students, he expected to pass out of their sight in the course of a few minutes. But he was somewhat disconcerted to find that the party quickened their steps behind him; the abuse became louder and more continuous; and even the quiet, orderly portion of the crowd, now thinning in the dusk, began, as he could see, to regard him with some suspicion. He was aware that the less educated Japanese do not draw fine distinctions in the matter of foreigners, and remembering what he had learnt in Nikko from Kobo, and still more from his servant Taru, of the outrages which Europeans had suffered at the hands of infuriated Japanese not many years before, he felt some apprehension of what the end of the business might be. It was hopeless to attempt to conciliate the youths by announcing his British citizenship, for his whole stock of Japanese words consisted of the names of a few common things, and the mere attempt to address them might increase their irritation. Thinking to shake them off, he turned suddenly down a narrow side street, leading, as he supposed, in the direction of the harbour. The houses at the sides were little one-story affairs built of wood; their fronts, removed all day, had been replaced for the night; no lanterns hung at the entrances; the one street-lamp was not lit; and the whole thoroughfare was deserted, except for two Chinamen who were proceeding in the same direction as Bob, about two hundred yards ahead.

He had scarcely turned the corner when he felt that he had made an unwise move, a feeling confirmed in a few moments, for the group of students, gaining courage from the fact that the eyes of the more sober section of the crowd were no longer upon them, followed him into the narrow street with louder and more threatening cries. Bob was annoyed; he had nothing to gain by a street row; but while he instinctively quickened his pace he took a tight grip upon a knobbed stick of cherry-wood presented to him by Kobo at Nikko, preparing to turn instantly on his pursuers if they attempted to close in upon him. He began to recognize that sooner or later there would be a rush, and though he was pretty sure that by incontinently taking to his heels he could distance the little fellows with ease, and suspected that this would probably be the wisest course, he could not bring himself to run away from a mob of students whom he overtopped head and shoulders, especially as his flight must be witnessed by two Chinamen.

Within a minute his anticipations were fulfilled. There was a yell and a sudden rush behind him. Quick as thought he stepped sideways into an angle between the latticed entrance to a shop and a low palisade that stood out a couple of feet from the wall, enclosing some architectural ornament, and faced the angry students. There were six of them, all armed with sticks, and they made at the solitary foreigner in a body. Fortunately for Bob, they could not reach him from behind; his left was partially protected by the railing; and as they surged forward they impeded one another's movements. Had it not been so, Bob's experiences in the Far East would have been closed there and then, for the Japanese are the finest fencers in the world, and singlestick-play is with them a favourite pastime.

Raising his stick to defend his head, Bob received upon it the simultaneous strokes of the three foremost of his opponents, which almost beat down his guard. But he had a wrist of iron; he had not served an apprenticeship in an engineering shop for nothing; and he instantly retaliated with two rapid sledge-hammer blows with his left fist, which felled two of the Japanese to the ground. The rest were for the moment somewhat staggered; they knew single-stick, but were not prepared for this peculiarly British variation. With characteristic pluck, however, they recovered themselves almost before their comrades had reached the ground, and undeterred by the fate of their vanguard, the others, going to work a little more cautiously, closed in towards the tall, erect figure of the foreigner. Keeping out of arm's reach, they tried to rain their blows on Bob's head. Their sticks rattled upon his; one sturdy little Japanese got in a heavy blow on his left wrist that put one arm out of action, while another at the same moment dodged in under his guard and seized him by the throat. With a great muscular effort Bob, dropping his stick, now useless to him, shortened his arm and struck his assailant behind the ear, at the same time raising his wounded arm to protect his head and making a dash forward to break through the ring. The grip upon his throat relaxed; the Japanese, falling under Bob's weight, was borne to the ground, but as he fell he seized Bob by the foot, and with a violent jerk tripped him up. As he dropped he received two or three blows on the back and shoulders; then he was overwhelmed by the weight of the three remaining Japanese, all striving to get at him at the same time. He felt that he was in a desperately tight place; afterwards he remembered that his sensations strangely resembled those he had experienced at a critical moment in a certain memorable soccer match between his club and an eleven of Clydebank riveters.

But before the assailants could distinguish between Bob's form and that of the half-senseless Japanese entangled with him, an unlooked-for diversion occurred. There was the soft pad of felt soles, inaudible to Bob and his enemies; two or three resounding thwacks on the craniums of the panting Japanese, and in a twinkling Bob was on his feet, breathless, hatless, speechless, returning as best he could the courteous salutations of two grave, silent Chinamen. Four Japanese were limping down the street, two others still lay senseless on the ground. The Chinamen were the same two figures Bob had seen immediately in front of him as he entered the thoroughfare, which was still deserted, all the inhabitants having gone down to the harbour, save one old ship's carpenter who had tottered to his shop-front, attracted by the sound of the scuffle.

"It is very good of you," said Bob, gasping. "I'm much obliged to you, I'm sure."

The younger of the two Chinamen, apparently a merchant, shook his head and smiled deprecatingly, from which Bob gathered that he did not understand English. The other, evidently a servant, preserved an impassivity of countenance such as only a Chinaman can command. Bob was at a loss how to express his gratitude; but the dignified merchant, waving his hand to signify that the affair was a mere nothing, bowed ceremoniously and continued on his way.

Bob picked up his hat and stick, dusted his coat with his hand, and felt his wrist to make sure that no bones were broken. Then, thinking it wise to return to the principal street and proceed to the harbour as directed by the station-master, he retraced his steps.

"I wonder where I have seen those two Chinamen before," he said to himself as he walked on. "Was it at Hong-Kong, or Shanghai?"

Down the long street, strangely quiet. Bob wondered what had become of all the people. The secret was ere long disclosed. He came to the quays. There were people everywhere; men, women, children, soldiers, sailors, crowded together in picturesque disorder. Out on the waters of the harbour there was a throng of shipping scarcely less dense. Nearer the shore, sampans, junks, transport vessels of all descriptions, the smaller craft hurrying this way and that, loaded with goods, loaded with men. Farther out, many twinkling lights, making curious fairy-like patterns in the deepening gloom. There Bob got his first vague glimpse of the fleet.

He looked, and wondered, and thought. Those silent forms, lying so peacefully amid the reflections of their lights—how soon would they fulfil their destiny as deadly instruments of destruction? What an amazing object-lesson in the history of nations! Forty years before, Japan, socially and politically, was as remote from western civilization as the peoples of Europe in the middle ages. Now she possessed, and, as she had proved in the China war, could make the fullest use of, the most complex engines evolved by western science. Bob recalled the tales told him by Kobo of Japan during his own childhood, and was conscious of a transformation more marvellous than the most fantastic of fairy lore. The ships were amazing enough, but what of the men? Every vessel bore its complement of officers and engineers trained to the highest point of efficiency, with perfect command of the myriad delicate details of these marvels of mechanical invention. They were the sons of men who had swaggered about the streets of Yedo in strange attire with their double swords, the terror of the despised peaceful folk, or, clad in mediæval armour, had swelled the trains of great daimios who came in from their distant fiefs to pay an enforced annual visit to the capital. The crews! they sprang from peasants, artisans, and menials who for generations had been forbidden to wear arms, and were supposed fit for little else than to be hewers of wood and drawers of water for their proud lords and lordlings. Yet, as the China war had proved, now that the awakening had taken place, this despised and unconsidered class had shown a daring, a martial spirit, a capacity for heroism, no whit inferior to that of their officers, the descendants of daimios and samurai whose very life was war.

The blare of a bugle woke Bob from his reverie. From the crowd at the end of the quay rose a shout of "Banzai!" which was taken up by the throng all around, and swelled by the echo from the walls of the arsenal. The last boatload of soldiers had just left shore for one of the transports. It was time for Bob to go on board. Soon he was being punted along in a sampan, which threaded its way slowly among lighters, tugs, and innumerable small craft, clear of which it came at length to the war-ships. The *Mikasa* was easily singled out; there was a short parley with the officer of the watch, and Bob, mounting the side, was ere long conducted to the presence of the admiral in whom Japan's highest hopes were centred.

Keen eyes, a grizzled pointed beard, a quiet self-possessed manner, a low pleasant voice—it was these that gave Bob his first impressions of Admiral Togo as, enveloped in his thick greatcoat, he greeted the young Englishman. Many years had passed since he trod the deck of the *Worcester* as a cadet: years in which he had seen the building-up of the great navy that now lay obedient to his single word. He spoke excellent English, and in a few sentences acquainted Bob with the situation that had called for his services. The fleet was about to sail; war might break out at any moment; he needed someone at hand in case the range-finders, on which so much would depend, should require checking or adjusting.

"You are in an exceptional position, Mr. Fawcett," he said. "We are not enlisting the services of foreigners; but the mechanism of the range-finder being of a special character, it was thought well to have on the spot some one from its original makers. I should point out to you that your services may be required on any vessel of the fleet at a moment's notice, and your duties may lead you into very grave peril. We are at the beginning of new experiences in naval warfare; there may be terrible things in store for us. It is right to warn you, so that you may not go blindfold into danger. It is for you to say whether you accept the position."

"Thank you, sir," replied Bob. "I've been sent out to do a certain work, and I can only take things as they come. I'm delighted to have the chance of seeing service on your magnificent vessel."

Bob's manifest eagerness provoked a faint smile from the admiral.

"Very well, then, I'll send for your baggage and hand you over to Sub-lieutenant Yamaguchi; he has not long left Glasgow and knows English well, so that he will no doubt prove an acceptable mess-mate. He will see that you get a berth, and look after you generally."

In a few moments Bob was being convoyed by the sub-lieutenant, a little fellow of five feet two, to the wardroom, where he was introduced to several other officers. Some of these had more than a smattering of English, and their courtesy and air of good fellowship would have made a more self-conscious stranger than Bob Fawcett feel at home. He spent a delightful evening in their company, and went to his bunk with vague expectations of things to happen next day.

Chapter V
A Fleet in Action

War—Nearing Port Arthur—In the Night Watches—The First Blow—A Battle of the Giants—In a Box-battery—A Rescue

Next morning Bob, in Yamaguchi's company, made a round of the fighting admiral's flagship. The youngest of four sister vessels, the *Mikasa*, launched at Barrow only four years previously, had a displacement of some 15,000 tons, a tremendous armament, and armour-casing varying from four inches to more than a foot in thickness. Forward and aft were two pairs of 12-inch breech-loading guns, mounted in barbettes encased in fourteen inches of armour. On the main-deck were ten 6-inch quick-firers, mounted on the "box-battery" system in an armoured citadel, the latest device of the naval architect to afford protection at once to the ship and to the crews fighting the guns. Bob already had some knowledge of armour-clad vessels, having more than once been sent by his firm to install range-finders in British ships, but never before had he enjoyed the opportunity of examining a vessel of the *Mikasa* type, now being adopted in the British navy.

For an hour or two he was busy on the navigating-officer's bridge, examining the complicated apparatus of the range-finder. The difficulty of regulating this ingenious piece of mechanism is due to the unequal expansion of the metals of which it is made. Obviously it was impossible to test its accuracy until a shot could actually be fired at a given range, but Bob saw that all its adjustments were satisfactory, and had an interesting discussion with the navigating officer, whose duty it would be, when the vessel went into action, to call the ranges for the gunners below.

While this was going on, Bob was too much occupied to notice the signs of increasing activity in the harbour. The *Mikasa* was surrounded by the other vessels of the fleet—battle-ships and cruisers; torpedo-boats and torpedo-boat destroyers formed an outer circle of wide extent. In the inner harbour no fewer than seventy transports were lying at anchor, and since early morning many of these had been filling up with cheerful crowds of Japanese soldiers and immense bales of stores, carried on heavy-laden sampans and lighters from the quays. While Bob was walking round the vessel with Yamaguchi, he suddenly noticed the wireless-telegraphic operator make his way quietly to the bridge where Admiral Togo stood talking with the captain. The man saluted, and handed the admiral a paper. The latter moved a little aside to read it, then spoke a few rapid words to the captain. A few minutes afterwards a number of flags were flying from the masthead, answering signals were run up on the other vessels, and a general movement was visible throughout the fleet. On the *Mikasa* all was activity. Bob noted with admiration the precision with which every man on board, without hurry or bustle, went about his allotted duty. The captain on the armoured conning-tower, with bells, speaking-tubes, and telephones all round him, issued orders which were carried out as instantaneously as though he were touching the responsive keys of an instrument. On all the other vessels similar activity prevailed. The fleet was preparing to sail. Moving with the ease of living beings in their native element, the several vessels fell gradually into their settled place in the line, and then, the *Mikasa* leading, steamed slowly out towards the open sea.

It was a moment never to be forgotten. Bob did not know whither the fleet was bound, nor on what enterprise, but he was certain that its departure was the first step in a carefully-arranged scheme, and his heart throbbed with the excitement of knowing that, happen what might, he was to be there, a spectator of, if not a participant in, events that might change the destiny of the world.

Negotiations between Russia and Japan had been broken off. Every man on board knew that, and recognized that this was inevitably the prelude to war unless Russia should do what no one could imagine her doing— yield. The sudden order to sail indicated that Admiral Togo had received instructions to deliver, or at least to threaten, a blow at the enemy. More than this no one knew. A Russian squadron was lying at Chemulpo, the port of Seoul, in Korea; another, the strongest fleet Russia had in Eastern seas, was at Port Arthur; a third was at Vladivostock, far to the north. The Russians were known to be filled with vast contempt for the "dwarfs"; they would surely not allow their insignificant enemy's fleet to approach their much-prized harbours without first meeting them on the seas; and it was with the expectation of a terrible fight, ship against ship, that the Japanese went out fearlessly towards the unknown.

Out into the sea, due westward, sailed the fleet, the *Mikasa* and her sister ships proudly riding the waves, the smaller vessels driving their bows through the water and rising like dripping seals from each encounter. The battle-ships kept line behind the leader, each holding on her course with unerring accuracy; and as they moved majestically on amid the surrounding cruisers and torpedo craft, they seemed to Bob like ocean leviathans accompanied by a brood of young.

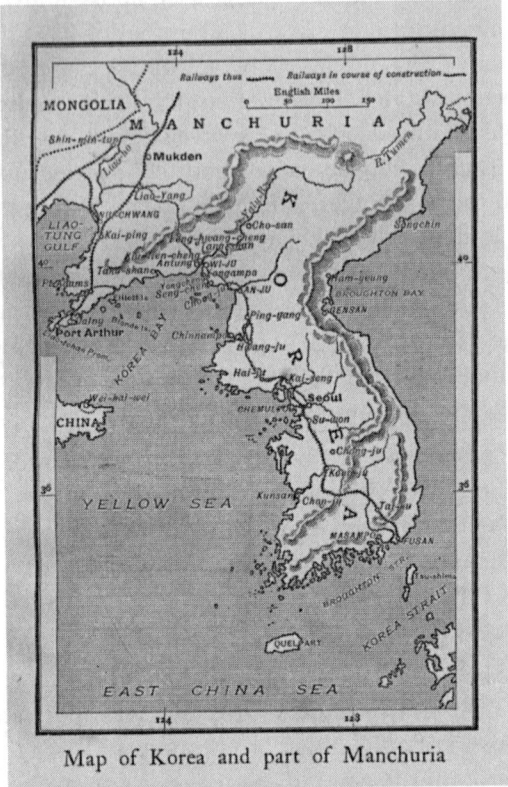

Map of Korea and part of Manchuria

Map of Korea and part of Manchuria

In the dusk, soon after passing between Quelpart and the southern extremity of Korea, Bob noticed that part of the fleet had disappeared. He remarked on the fact to Sub-lieutenant Yamaguchi.

"Yes," he replied; "some of the vessels have gone off northwards, to Chemulpo probably."

"Where are we going, then?"

"I don't know, but I should guess to Port Arthur—the place the Russians robbed us of nine years ago."

"Well, I hope that if there is to be any fighting we shall have first shot. What are the chances?"

"Port Arthur is nearly a hundred miles farther away than Chemulpo. If the Russians come out from Chemulpo, Admiral Uriu is bound to open the ball. But you needn't envy him that. Port Arthur is the nut to crack; the Russians have been spending heaps of money on fortifications, and, of course, if we can get past their fleet we shall have to bombard. Then you'll see what our gunners can do: and you'll come in there with that range-finding instrument."

"But you'll have to fight the Russian fleet first. You can't expect what we call in England a walk-over, you know."

The Japanese smiled.

"Come and have a game of 'go' in the cabin," he said.

Bob had already been initiated into the intricacies of 'go', the Japanese equivalent of chess. He played, and took a beating with a sang-froid that the self-contained Japanese themselves could not excel.

Now the *Mikasa* altered her course and steamed N.N.E., passing outside the Mackau Islands, and thence across the Yellow Sea to the Shantung promontory. Early on the afternoon of the next day the fleet had come within six hours' easy steaming of Port Arthur. It was bitterly cold, but the sea was smooth and the air clear, and Bob, who had borrowed a telescope, often swept the horizon in eager search of any sign of Russians, expecting that they would be scouring the Yellow Sea to get the earliest possible intimation of a Japanese attack. No war-ship was to be seen; only a few Japanese junks were sighted beating up against a brisk south wind, making for Kiauchau or the Yang-tze ports.

Suddenly, at a signal from the flagship, the squadron slowed down until the vessels had only steering-way; and the order was given to clear for action. With wonderful celerity the men moved hither and thither, stowing away wooden bulk-heads, mess-tables, benches, and other inflammable articles of furniture, to avoid the risk of a conflagration on board as the result of bursting shells. The decks were drenched with water and sanded; some of the seamen filled the boats from their hoses; some stacked coal around the bases of the funnels; others hung canvas screens round the Maxims and the smaller quick-firers. Ammunition hoists were rigged, the guns were cast loose, and hammocks were heaped around the conning-tower to protect this vital centre from flying splinters. Below decks the torpedo crews were busily overhauling the tubes, while the gunnery staff were preparing fuses and seeing that shells were collected in readiness for hoisting.

Watching these preparations, careful not to get in the way, Bob wished with all his heart that he could have taken an active part instead of being a spectator merely. If, as seemed probable, a night attack was in question, there would be little scope for the range-finder, and in any case he himself would not be required unless the instrument failed, which from his examination he thought unlikely. But the circumstances in which he found himself were so novel, that even though he could do nothing, the anticipation of what he might see warmed his blood and filled him with excitement.

Dusk fell; once more the vessels went ahead, steaming at half-speed. "We shall be within fighting range of Port Arthur before midnight," said Yamaguchi confidentially to Bob. The orderly confusion of the preceding hours had now given place to a quietude which was even more impressive. The *Mikasa* seemed to be pervaded by a tense expectancy, officers and men stood in silent watchfulness, and when they spoke it was in low tones, and disconnectedly. Admiral Togo stood with Captain Igichi and the navigating officer on the conning-tower, whose top had been removed; and Bob felt that every man on board had unbounded confidence in his cause, his admiral, and himself.

The vessels showed no lights. In the growing moonlight they glided along like monstrous ghosts. Only the phosphorescent gleam of the huge waves thrown up by their bows gave indication that these were no unsubstantial fabrics, but huge bulks of metal forcing their way, by favour of the toil and sweat of self-sacrificing engineers and stokers far below decks, against the resistance of the mighty element.

As the fleet drew moment by moment nearer to the great port, the strain became intense. Conversation had entirely ceased; the deep silence was scarcely broken, it seemed, by the hollow throb of the engines. All eyes were strained to pierce the distance, to catch sight of the enemy that now, surely, could not be far away, and the first intimation of whose proximity might be the explosion of a torpedo hurling the vessel and every soul on board to destruction. Suddenly, on the port quarter, appeared the lights of four vessels steaming in the same direction as the fleet towards Port Arthur, the gleam from whose lighthouse had for some time been distinctly visible. A ruse was being practised on the Russians. The vessels were Japanese torpedo-boats, making direct for the harbour, in the expectation of being taken for scouting vessels of the Russian fleet. Would the trick succeed? The *Mikasa* glided on.

It was now past ten o'clock, and in the distance the heights above Port Arthur appeared a black ridge against the faintly moonlit sky, throwing deep shadows on the waters of the harbour. Between the *Mikasa* and the roadstead several small black spots could be seen dotting the surface of the sea. The four torpedo-boats crept gradually closer; they came unsuspected upon the outermost vessel of the Russian fleet. Suddenly the sounds of three muffled explosions, at intervals of a few seconds, vibrated through the air. Bob held his breath; this was the beginning of things: what had happened? In a moment, from the far distance, came the rattle of machine-guns, followed by the deeper boom of quick-firers, growing in volume until it seemed as if the whole armament of the Russian fleet was engaged. On board the *Mikasa* there was the clang of a bell. The vessel slowed down, then stopped; the other battle-ships followed her example; and as search-lights flashed from the Russian vessels and the forts, cutting brilliant white cones through the lesser radiance of the moon, Bob caught a glimpse for the fraction of a second of the low hull of a Japanese torpedo-boat speeding forward to discharge its deadly missile. Hard by was the vast bulk of a cruiser, and stretched in a long line in the roads lay a dozen other war-ships of varying sizes, from the huge *Petropavlovsk*, instantly recognizable by her monstrous form, to the few Russian torpedo-boats which alone seemed to be alert.

After a time the firing almost ceased; but the flashlights continued to make wild gyrations, and every now and then there was a renewed rattle of machine-guns from the Russian ships. Not a shot was fired from the Japanese fleet. In advance of the battle-ships the cruisers had steamed forward to support the torpedo-boats; but the general bombardment which Bob expected had not begun.

He was beginning to think that all was over, and wondering what had actually taken place, when a dull explosion broke the silence, followed by two other shocks. Immediately the Russian search-lights swept round towards the harbour, and the forms of the vessels were silhouetted against the illumination.

"They have got in behind them—under the shadow of the hills," said Yamaguchi in Bob's ear. The little Japanese was panting with excitement. "Caught napping, if ever enemy was! You see? They expected another attack from the open. Our boats have got between them and the harbour; if only it were morning light!"

It was as Yamaguchi said. Buried in the dense blackness cast by the frowning heights above the harbour, the Japanese torpedo flotilla had stealthily crept to the rear of the vessels lying outside. It was a stroke cunningly planned and boldly executed. On board the *Mikasa* men and officers waited eagerly to learn the result. They had not a doubt of its success. At length Admiral Togo received a wireless message from the admiral of the advanced squadron announcing that four Russian vessels had been struck by torpedoes, and as the news was circulated through the ship, the manner in which it was received impressed Bob with a sense of the confidence, and at the same time the self-restraint, of these allies of Britain. There was no excessive elation; not a cheer was raised; every man seemed to regard the event as inevitable. The fleet at once wheeled round and ran out to sea, so as to be at dawn out of range of the Russian batteries.

The sun rose very red over Korea; the south wind blew steadily, topping the swelling sea with snowy crests. On the far horizon could be descried three Japanese cruisers, and the lower hulls of several destroyers, stationed like watch-dogs on the skirts of the Russian fleet. Soon after eight the cruisers were seen to be approaching, and behind them appeared the funnels of several Russian vessels in chase. Admiral Togo immediately signalled his fleet to stand in to the support of the cruisers, and the crew of the *Mikasa* braced themselves in eagerness for the expected fray. A sigh of disappointment broke from them as they saw the Russians almost at once retire towards Port Arthur, and anchor under the protection of the batteries on the heights. Surely the enemy, whose every word and action hitherto had indicated supreme contempt of their opponent, would not lamely accept the previous night's attack without attempting a counterstroke. But it was not known on the *Mikasa* that Admiral Alexieff had devotedly informed his majesty the Tsar that two of his battle-ships, the *Retvisan* and the *Tsarevitch*, and the cruiser *Pallada*, had been so seriously damaged by the Japanese torpedoes that they now lay helpless in the channel, where in all probability they would remain ingloriously out of action for some time to come.

Bob wondered why the Russians seemed disinclined to run out and risk a fair and square fight in the open. Admiral Togo was not the man to wait for an invitation. Between ten and eleven the order to steam ahead was given, the fighting flag was hoisted, and the *Mikasa*, her collision mats on, led the way.

All hands were piped to dinner. Profiting by the experience gained when he commanded the *Naniwa* in the Chinese war, Admiral Togo wisely resolved to give his crew a good square meal before the action began. Bob went forward among the men, interested to see them dispose of their strange mixture of Japanese and European food, and to observe their cheerful demeanour. While he was with them a summons reached him to go to the gunnery officer on the bridge. He found that some slight adjustment was needed for the delicate mechanism of the range-finder, which occupied him but a few minutes. He remained by the officer's side, and looked eagerly through his powerful glasses in the direction of Port Arthur, which presently came into view, a long bent line on the horizon. The gunnery officer pointed out to him the entrance to the harbour, between a range of bluffs on the east and a low-lying peninsula running almost due north and south. He learnt the locality of the Huang-chin-shan fort and the Lao-mu-chu battery on the bluffs, and the approximate position of a series of fortifications on the island, commanding the entrance to the channel and the roadstead beyond.

Then, looking through the eye-pieces of the range-finder, he saw a line of Russian war-ships extended outside the harbour. The scale indicated that they were at least six miles distant. There were five battle-ships, six cruisers, a gun-boat, and seventeen smaller craft—destroyers and torpedo-boats. The mosquito flotilla was grouped close to the entrance of the navigable channel. Just beyond them Bob descried the funnels of three large vessels apparently aground. These were the victims of the night's operations—the vessels whose unhappy plight was soon to result in the removal of Admiral Stark from the command of the fleet his laxity had jeopardized.

It was a fine sunny day, there was a gentle swell on the surface of the sea, and the *Mikasa*, steaming eighteen knots, drew rapidly nearer to the great fortress. Bob, looking steadily through his glass, singled out the flagship, the *Peresviet*, on which he expected the *Mikasa's* attack would be directed. The gunnery officer's eyes were now riveted to the range-finder. At length, whispering "Three miles and a half" in Bob's ear, he touched an electric apparatus at his side. The clang of bells was soon afterwards heard, signal-flags were run up at the vessel's fore, and Bob distinguished a curious clinking sound from an invisible point below him.

"Twelve-inch breech swung open," said the gunnery officer quietly. "Keep your eye on the *Peresviet*."

Almost immediately afterwards there came to Bob's ears a strange hoarse cough; the vessel seemed to wince. A few seconds of suspense, then Bob saw a small puff of smoke beneath the bows of the *Peresviet*: a column of water rose high into the air, and as the wind separated its particles into spray, it appeared as if a shower of many-coloured glass were falling over the deck of the Russian vessel.

"Beautiful shot!" said the gunnery officer. "We must alter the range."

Before a second shot could be fired from the *Mikasa*, however, one of her consorts had followed her example, and Bob saw a patch of dirty smoke on one of the bluffs near the Lao-mu-chu battery.

"Hasn't got the range yet," said the gunnery officer. "Now for ours."

Again the coughing sound, again the staggering recoil, and the Shimose shell burst on the armour plating of the *Peresviet*, which was at once obscured by a cloud of dense black smoke. The bombardment had begun.

Only a few seconds after the *Mikasa's* second shot, Bob felt the air vibrate, and the sea around the vessel was churned white by shells fired from the Russian ships and the batteries on shore. Now also the other vessels of the Japanese fleet joined in the fray, manoeuvring with beautiful precision so as to present moving targets to the Russian gunners and baffle their aim. The din all around was appalling; guns of all sizes and species were making fierce practice against the enemy; Maxims rattling, quick-firers shrieking and wailing. A column of black smoke rose from the deck of the *Peresviet*, showing that she had been hit near the base of her forward funnel. Then, as the eager sailors learnt the success of the shot, Bob heard the first cheer of the day. Immediately afterwards a projectile whistled over his head, exploded in the air beyond the vessel, and threw a rain of iron into the sea, the splinters falling like stones cast by some giant's hand.

"Better go down out of harm's way, sir," said the Japanese officer.

Bob went down, not so much to be out of harm's way as to see the gunners at their work. He looked in at one of the box-batteries. The gun crew of six men were busy with the shells that came up from the magazines on the ammunition hoists; one was placed in the breech, behind his bullet-proof shield the gun-captain laid his vast weapon, the men flung themselves on their faces, and the shot sped away on its terrible mission. Then the breech was swung open, another shell was heaved into position, the sight was taken, and the vessel winced as the huge projectile flew on its way.

Hitherto the aim of the Russian gunners had been far from accurate; indeed, all through the fight their shells did little damage, telling only too clearly of insufficient practice at moving targets. But it was different with the gunners in the forts. As they got the range, shells hurtled around the *Mikasa*; and Admiral Togo at once signalled to the *Hatsuse* and the *Asahi* to turn their attention to the fort, and the concentrated fire of the three vessels was brought to bear upon it. So dense was the smoke now that Bob could not distinguish the effects of the shots. Indeed, he was almost dazed by the noise around him—the clang of bells, the crash of the guns, the din of the working engines. All the time the captain stood on the conning-tower calm and unmoved, telephoning his orders to the captains of the guns as though it was a case of target practice instead of deadly war.

Bob had seen nothing of Yamaguchi since early morning, and he wondered how the gallant little lieutenant was faring. So few shots from the Russians had actually struck the *Mikasa* that Bob had ceased to fear anything for his personal safety. He knew that Yamaguchi was captain of the crew of a gun in one of the starboard batteries, and stepping over a coil of hose placed in readiness for extinguishing any fire that might break out, he made his way along the deck to find his friend.

There he was, peering through his glass to watch the effect of the last shot from his gun. Bob stood unnoticed behind. A huge projectile had just come up on the hoist, and two men were steering it to its place above the breech. Suddenly, somewhere above his head, there was a whistle, a hiss, a sharp ringing noise, then a terrible crash, a blinding light, and volumes of yellow suffocating smoke. A shell had burst on the armour casing near the muzzle of the gun. Bob was flung heavily against the breech-block, which had been swung open to receive the shell. He was half stunned; there was a strange ringing in his ears; he gasped for breath, felt that he was choking, and believed that in a few moments he must lose consciousness. But it was not in his nature to give in without a struggle. Collecting himself with a desperate effort, he managed to grope his way, half-staggering, half-crawling, out of the battery, away from the terrible fumes that still filled the confined space, hanging a thick yellow mist over the guns and settling down like a blanket upon the deck. Away from the noisome stench he quickly recovered so far as to be able to think again. What, he instantly asked himself, had become of the gun's crew?—what had become of Yamaguchi? Men were now hurrying up from all parts of the ship, but before they could enter the battery Bob was ahead of them, peering through the smoke for signs of the luckless gunners. The mist eddied, caught by a gust of wind, and through a break he saw, prone on the deck, two of the gallant crew shattered beyond recognition. And there—yes, a little to the left of them, stretched on his face, to all appearances lifeless—there lay his friend Yamaguchi. One bound and he was at the lieutenant's side. He stooped to lift him, and though he husbanded his breath the deadly fumes lying low over the deck made him gasp and turn sick. He felt that his strength was again slipping from him, but exerting all the will-power of which he was capable he raised the inert body, stumbled with it across the battery, and fell with his burden into the willing arms of the sailors who were crowding to the rescue.

Bob rescues Yamaguchi

Bob rescues Yamaguchi

At the same moment there was a sudden cessation of the din. Admiral Togo had signalled the fleet to cease fire; the vessels wheeled round, and were soon running full steam ahead into the open sea. But signals, commands, movements, all escaped Bob Fawcett. Overcome by the deadly fumes from the exploded shell, he lay on the deck beside Yamaguchi, unconscious, ignorant that the first bombardment of Port Arthur was over.

Chapter VI
Helping-to-Decide

A Torpedo-destroyer—Sea Legs—At Chemulpo—A Recognition— Stopping a Runaway—Mystification

For nearly a week after his adventure in the box-battery Bob was laid up. The sickening fumes had upset his system, and the ship's doctor insisted on his remaining in his bunk until he was thoroughly recovered. His first question on regaining consciousness had been for Yamaguchi, and he was rejoiced to hear that the lieutenant, though slightly wounded by a splinter from the shell, had been rescued from the poison-filled battery just in time.

"He owes his life to your plucky action," said Captain Igichi warmly, when he visited him the day after the bombardment. "His wound alone would not have been serious, but another minute in the battery would have done for him."

Bob made light of the matter, and was embarrassed to find that he was regarded with even more warmth of friendliness than before. The Japanese officers did not overwhelm him with praise, courage was too much a matter of course with them for that; but though they said little, Bob felt that they now looked on him as one who had proved his right to their comradeship, and he knew that to a Japanese this meant a great deal.

He was no sooner fit for duty again than he was transferred to the *Mikasa's* sister ship the *Hatsuse*, whose range-finder was urgently needing attention. The standard on which the tube containing the telescope rested had been broken by the fragment of a shell, though fortunately the mechanism itself had been but slightly damaged. With the aid of the ship's clever artificers Bob was able to repair the injury in a very short time.

He remained on the *Hatsuse* for more than a fortnight, during which he witnessed the first plucky dash of the Japanese torpedo-destroyers on Port Arthur, the attempt by five stone-laden steamers to block the channel, and the second bombardment, in which the Japanese vessels received no damage. Then one morning he was unexpectedly transferred to a torpedo-destroyer which had been ordered to Chemulpo. He was there to place himself under the orders of Admiral Uriu, if that officer were still at the port.

There was a considerable swell on, but it was a calm, bright, cold day when Bob left the monster battle-ship, which scarcely felt the motion of the waves, for the tiny *Kasumi*, rolling and pitching beneath. A boat was lowered from the *Hatsuse*, and but for his experience in yachting on the lower reaches of the Clyde Bob might have had some qualms as to how he was to mount the rope-ladder let down over the side of the *Kasumi*. Though he failed to make the ascent with the nimbleness of a deep-sea pilot, he was on his mettle, and did not disgrace himself in the eyes of the crews of the *Hatsuse* and *Kasumi*, critically watching him from their respective vessels.

On reaching the deck of the destroyer he was as much surprised as pleased to meet Yamaguchi. He knew that the sub-lieutenant on his recovery had been promoted and appointed to a torpedo vessel, but until this moment he had been unaware to which. Their meeting was very cordial; Yamaguchi looked on Bob as his preserver, and Bob on his part was delighted to find that he was to make the passage to Chemulpo in company with one whom he already regarded as a friend.

Besides Yamaguchi, the officers on board were two sub-lieutenants, a doctor, and an engineer.

"We are fifty-five all told," added Yamaguchi, after introducing their new mess-mate.

"Where do you stow them all?" asked Bob in surprise.

"Come and see."

The lieutenant showed him first his own cabin, in the after part of the vessel—a room about ten feet square by seven high, with about as much accommodation as a small bathing-machine. Next to it was the ward-room, a trifle larger in area, in which Yamaguchi proposed that Bob should make his sleeping quarters on a small settee.

"It's half a mile too short for you," he said with a smile.

"I can lengthen it, or double myself up," replied Bob, who was indeed more than satisfied with his quarters when he saw the space allotted to the officers—four tiny cabins, each of which could have stood comfortably on an ordinary four-poster bedstead. Amidships were the engine-room and stoke-holds, shimmering with a white light from the furnaces, so intense that the stokers had to wear coloured glass goggles to preserve their eyes from blindness. The stokers, strong of arm and steady of nerve, looked like small demons from the Inferno as they kept cheerful watch on the gauges, cooped up as they were within the length of a man's body from the blazing mouths.

On the fo'c'sle forward were the conning-tower and the captain's bridge, with the *Kasumi's* single heavy gun—a twelve-pounder. Beneath, in a compartment about half as long again as a full-sized billiard-table, was the bed- and sitting-room of the crew; three rows of hammocks were slung along each side, one beneath another. In a heavy sea the whole deck, in spite of the steel breastwork on each side of the conning-tower was liable to be swept with water from end to end. Bob was not squeamish, but he shuddered as he imagined the conditions under which the crew spent their watch below. It was a lucky thing, he thought, that the Japanese require even less than the limited space indispensable to the British Jack-tar.

The *Kasumi* was rolling and pitching so inconsiderately when Bob boarded her, that in making his way along the deck in Yamaguchi's wake he had to cling to every available means of support. And yet the swell had only been sufficient to give a pleasant, slow, rocking movement to the *Hatsuse* he had just left. But it was not until the gallant craft began to drive her nose at speed into a head sea that Bob began to realize what life on a torpedo-destroyer really was. There was perhaps a little less roll, but the pitching was a revelation of what a boat can suffer without breaking her back. Bob clung to a stanchion, expecting every moment that the huge mass of water breaking over the fore-bridge and flooding the deck amidships would rend the vessel asunder. It seemed impossible that the hull, of merely egg-shell thickness, could survive the strain. The low bow slugged into a monstrous bank of green water. "Now she's done for!" thought Bob. But a moment later she was balanced giddily on the crest of the wave, and began to switchback into the abyss beneath. All the time the mighty heart of the vessel was throbbing strenuously; Bob caught himself counting the pulse with a kind of anxiety lest the engines should prove unequal to their task.

"How do you like this?" said Yamaguchi in Bob's ear.

"Pretty well; it's rather be-wild—"

He was choked by a shower of spray, which left him gasping.

"You'll soon get used to it," said Yamaguchi with a smile.

It was some hours, however, before Bob was sufficiently accustomed to the *Kasumi's* eccentricities to be able to move about with any freedom. He found meal-time in the little ward-room particularly trying. The food was served out in tins; the officers sat at the table with feet planted firmly on the floor, and managed to gulp their soup between the rolls of the vessel. But Bob was not sufficiently practised to time his movements properly. He would raise the tin to his lips, only to find that he opened his mouth on empty air, or that the soup made a premature sally and covered a considerable part of his face and clothes, a mere starvation portion entering at the proper gate.

There was an even more unpleasant experience in store for him when he turned in for the night. Do what he could he was unable to avoid being tossed off the settee, rolled under the table, and brought up with a jolt at the opposite side of the room. The most ingeniously-contrived breastwork of cushions proved of no avail; it might survive a roll and a pitch separately, but when the motions were combined it was incapable of the complicated resistance necessary, and Bob, just dropping off to sleep, found himself sprawling among his bastions and outworks beneath the table.

"Hang it!" he growled, groping upwards after one of these mishaps; "better stay where I'm chucked!"

He pulled his coverlets off, and making a bed beneath the settee and one leg of the table, managed to reduce the area of his gyrations by clutching the table leg whenever his equilibrium was in jeopardy.

It was a still, fair morning when, on awaking from his troubled sleep and going on deck, he saw before him the city of Chemulpo rising from the sea-front up a steep snow-clad hill. It looked very picturesque in the sunlight. The quay was crowded with Koreans in their strange black mitre-shaped caps and long tasselled coats; coolies trudging along under burdens pendent to yokes of forked sticks bound to their shoulders; greatcoated Japanese soldiers, just landed from the transports in the harbour, moving with a brisk purposeful alacrity. Brawny Korean boatmen were propelling heavy-laden sampans from the transports to the quay; children in blue padded garments were running about, watching everything with wide curious eyes, and getting in everybody's way.

But what attracted most attention and caused most excitement on the *Kasumi* was the sight of the wrecks of the Russian ships sunk after the action of February 8. In one case a part of the hull, in the other only the funnel and mast, stood up a little above the waterline in the harbour,—shattered remnants of the *Korietz* and *Variag*; and as the *Kasumi* steamed past, Bob had his first opportunity of seeing at close quarters something of the effects of modern weapons of destruction. But there was no sign of any Japanese war-ships; as Bob afterwards learnt, they had left harbour some time previously for an unknown destination.

Bob, in company with Yamaguchi, was punted to the quay in a sampan, and he could not but admire the dexterity with which the muscular boatman, standing in the bows, drove the tapering-prowed boat through the bewildering maze of small craft. There was no time to explore the town, for Yamaguchi at once made for the railway-station. He had told Bob that he was the bearer of a communication from Admiral Togo to General Kuroki at Seoul, and Bob, having nothing to do in Admiral Uriu's absence, was ready enough to accept his invitation to accompany him. Soon the train was bearing them over snow-covered flats, past rough huts, round the bases of the white hills, into the more open country, and finally over a broad ice-bound river to the terminus some distance from the walls of Seoul. There, instead of hiring a rickshaw as Bob expected, Yamaguchi hastened into the city through one of the arched and towered gateways, and passing up the crowded main street, boarded a small electric tram-car, in which the Korean passengers were as much at home as any European.

"Up to date, you see," said Yamaguchi.

"Yes; upon my word the Far East is going ahead. Fancy electric cars in Korea!"

"Japanese, my friend. Owned by a Japanese company; driver, conductor, all the employees are Japanese."

"A peaceful conquest of the country to begin with."

"Now I must leave you," said Yamaguchi, as they stepped out of the car. "You won't mind waiting for me for a few minutes?"

The few minutes lengthened themselves out to nearly an hour before the lieutenant returned, but Bob found the time short, so much did he see that interested him. He watched the people passing. Some of the men, he noticed, were hatless, and wore their hair long; others had short hair, and through their transparent flower-pot-shaped hats he could see a curious top-knot on their heads, the distinguishing mark, as he afterwards learnt, of the married men. One old man, as he passed, opened out a fan-shaped bundle of oil-paper which dangled from his belt, and tied it over his hat, which it served in the office of an umbrella against a light shower of snow then falling. Everybody wore huge padded trousers and a short bell-shaped coat with wide sleeves, and walked along on strange sandal-like shoes bound to the feet by many strands of paper cord. Scarcely any women were to be seen; the Korean ladies are kept secluded, and do not go out into the streets except at night. The few women whom Bob saw were almost hidden by their long green cloaks, with which they hastily covered their heads at the appearance of a stranger.

While waiting for Yamaguchi outside the pagoda-shaped house in which General Kuroki was staying, Bob saw a Chinaman come out, whom he instantly recognized as the younger of the two men who had so opportunely run to his assistance at Sasebo. On the impulse of the moment Bob stepped forward to speak to the man, but remembered suddenly that he knew no English. The Chinaman passed by without giving any sign of recognition. Soon afterwards Yamaguchi appeared, and, announcing that he found it necessary to remain in Seoul until the next morning, offered to show Bob some of the curiosities of the town. The rest of that day was spent in wandering through the broad streets and side alleys, blocked with wares encroaching from the shops, and crowded with noisy, dirty little children playing happily in the filthy gutters. Yamaguchi explained how greatly the city had been improved of recent years, chiefly through the energy of Mr. M'Leavy Brown, the brilliant Scotsman who had so long and so wisely held the administration of the Customs.

Next morning Yamaguchi again had an interview with General Kuroki. As he left the house with Bob, the Chinaman whom the latter had seen on the previous day came up in the opposite direction, and Bob thought he saw a faint sign of recognition pass between him and the Japanese.

"Who is he?" asked Bob, when the Chinaman had passed. "I saw him yesterday, and a month ago at Sasebo, and I can't help thinking I had seen him somewhere before that."

"All Chinamen are pretty much alike, don't you think?"

Bob saw that Yamaguchi had evaded his question and was not disposed to give any information. Such silence only piqued his curiosity, and as they went on he found himself speculating still more deeply on the identity of the Chinese merchant, and endeavouring to recall the circumstances of their first meeting, which had not been, he was sure, at Sasebo.

New transports had evidently just arrived, for the streets were filled with Japanese soldiers, guns, and baggage-trains, preparing to move up country. Bob noticed, at the entrance of a side street, a Korean gentleman of high rank, to judge by his rich dress, waiting on horseback for a troop of cavalry to pass. Beside him was a group of Koreans, apparently his servants, and among them a low palanquin, elaborately decorated, through the open side of which Bob caught a glimpse of a veiled lady. The bearers, two fine-looking coolies, in white robes and round hats, stood at the front and rear of the palanquin.

The cavalry trotted by, and Bob, as he walked after them, remarked with a smile to Yamaguchi that they were not very easy riders.

"That is true," replied Yamaguchi, "but in the mud and snow of Korea they'll prove more useful than your Life Guards."

They had barely gone a quarter of a mile up the street, when Bob noticed a sudden commotion among them. The horse of one of the rearmost troopers, startled by the sudden appearance at the end of an alley of a bull heavily laden with bundles of straw, began to prance and curvet, then wheeled round, bucked, and, throwing its rider, set off on a mad gallop down the street. Bob instinctively looked behind him to see what there was to check the animal's mad career. He saw that the Korean gentleman had resumed his journey, being propped up by a servant on each side lest he should topple over on his high saddle; with the palanquin and his servants, he took up almost the whole width of the street. By this time people were shouting, and the clatter of the horse's hoofs was coming ever nearer. With one consent the Korean's servants ran to the sides of the street, the palanquin bearers dropped their poles and left the conveyance in the middle of the road, while the gentleman himself struggled with his horse, which had been rendered restive by the ever-increasing clamour.

Nothing stood between the palanquin and the runaway steed but Bob and Yamaguchi. Clearly, unless the animal's progress was checked, in a few moments it would dash into the palanquin, and that, being constructed chiefly of bamboo and lacquer, was certain to be utterly wrecked, while its occupant would probably be killed, or at any rate seriously injured.

The danger of the situation was instantly manifest. Bob dashed forward a few yards to meet the advancing horse; then, having placed a sufficient distance between himself and the palanquin, he halted suddenly and stood full in the pathway of the runaway animal. It came straight down upon him at a mad gallop. As it passed Bob sprang slightly aside, and seizing its hanging bridle dragged on it with all his might. Fortunately it was a light horse, standing only some fourteen hands; but in spite of this Bob felt as though his arm were being wrenched from its socket as he clutched at the reins. He was dragged along and almost pulled off his feet; but Yamaguchi came to his assistance, and the frightened animal was brought to a stop within a yard of the palanquin. There it stood with heaving flanks and panting nostrils, quivering.

Bob retained the bridle, and was beginning to lead the the horse up the street towards his rider, who was more chagrined than hurt, when the Korean gentleman overtook him on foot. He was extremely agitated, and, making a low bow, began to pour out his thanks in the strange monotonous jerky language of the country. Yamaguchi, interrupting him, spoke a few words in the same tongue. The Korean stopped, made a still lower obeisance, and said slowly in a strange compound of colloquial English and journalese that tickled Bob's sense of humour:

"I thank you very much, hon'ble sir. You do me gigantic favour. You save my wife—better-half, by your daring courage. It was jolly close thing. Accept, hon'ble sir, my profound thanks."

Bob bowed his acknowledgments, but his embarrassment was rather increased when the polite Korean, untying one of several little bags of orange-coloured silk that hung at his waist-band and served him as pockets, produced a limp visiting-card, and handed it with another low bow to his benefactor. Bob thanked him, and looked in some perplexity at the incomprehensible hieroglyphics on the card.

"You do not understand?" said the Korean. "My name, hon'ble sir, is San-Po. I am—" He stopped and looked puzzled, evidently at a momentary loss for an English word. Then his brow cleared, and he added rapidly: "I am helping-to-decide in His Imperial Majesty's War Office. If, hon'ble sir, you do me honour of a visit in my house towards An-ju, I shall esteem it greatest hon'ble favour—jolly well pleased."

Yamaguchi was smiling, evidently enjoying the situation. He did not offer to help Bob out of his embarrassment.

"Thank you, sir," said Bob, "I am afraid I am not coming that way just now, but another time—perhaps—"

He finished the sentence with a bow, to which the Korean responded with a lavish acknowledgment of his condescension. As Bob turned to continue his journey with Yamaguchi, he became aware that Korean courtliness has its obverse. Though he did not understand the words, there was no mistaking the tenor of the vehement harangue which the gentleman was addressing to his absconding bearers, who had now slunk back to their poles.

"What in the world does he mean by helping-to-decide in the War Office?" asked Bob.

"Oh, the war minister, the Pan-Go, or decisive signature, has what you call under-secretaries, the Cham Pan, which means help to decide; and under them are the Cham Wi, which means help to discuss. Our polite friend is one of the Cham Pan. But it really doesn't matter, for the whole army is quite useless. It never fights."

"All shams together," said Bob with a smile.

"San-Po spent a year or two in England: entered at Lincoln's Inn, I believe: that explains his command of English."

"It's a fearful and wonderful mixture. Mr. Helping-to-decide is rather an oddity. I'd rather like to see him at home, though I don't suppose I should enjoy it so much as my visit to Nikko. I never had a better time than with one of your countrymen there, Kobo San."

"Kobo San!" ejaculated Yamaguchi, with an accent of surprise.

"Yes. Do you know him?"

"I've met him," replied the lieutenant shortly, with another change of tone. Bob looked at him, but his face was inscrutable.

Chapter VII
The Battle of the Destroyers

A Chance for the Destroyers—Flotillas in Action—Winged—Repairing Damages—To the Yalu

Yamaguchi's business in Seoul being completed, he lost no time in returning to Chemulpo. In default of other instructions, he decided to keep Bob with him, and half an hour after his arrival, the *Kasumi* steamed out of the harbour to rejoin the fleet. Its fringe came into sight some ninety miles south-east of the Liau-ti-shan promontory. Through his glass Bob saw a destroyer detach itself from the squadron and come rapidly towards the *Kasumi*.

"Coming to make sure who we are," remarked Yamaguchi.

When the identity of the new-comer had been satisfactorily established, the other boat ran up signals, from which Yamaguchi learnt the position of the main fleet. Two hours later the *Kasumi*, going at half-speed, sighted the cruiser squadron, and about five miles beyond them the forest of military tops belonging to the Japanese battle-ships. Running close up to the *Mikasa*, Yamaguchi went off in a boat to make his report to Admiral Togo, and returned in high feather at having been ordered to place himself at the disposal of Captain Asai, who was in command of three destroyers that formed the first division of the Japanese torpedo flotilla.

"What about me?" asked Bob.

"Not a word. The fact is, I forgot all about you. I didn't mention you, neither did the admiral."

"Out of sight out of mind," remarked Bob. "But I'm delighted to hear it, for now that I'm used to this cockle-shell's little eccentricities I'm perfectly at home. Is there any chance of your going into action?"

"Every chance, I should think. I fancy we're going to have another slap at the enemy."

"The whole fleet, you mean?"

"No I don't. I've an idea the admiral wants to see how we mosquitoes can sting. Feel jumpy?"

"Not in the slightest. There's nothing I'm more anxious to see."

"Well, it may be pluck, but I call it sheer ignorance. Here we are in mid-ocean, a mere egg-shell—you know that; but we've enough explosives in our magazines to send half London sky-high, and a single fortunate shot plumping into us would separate us all into our elementary atoms."

The desired order came sooner than was expected. Late in the afternoon of Wednesday, March 9, Admiral Togo signalled two divisions of destroyers to approach Port Arthur, the one division to watch the entrance while the other laid mines at various points along the coast. The former duty was allotted to Captain Asai's division. Darkness had fallen, and the sea was rolling high, when the two flotillas, followed at a considerable distance by a couple of cruisers, broke off from the rest of the fleet and steamed northwards towards Port Arthur. On the *Kasumi* there was none of the orderly bustle of clearing for action that Bob had observed on the *Mikasa*. A destroyer must always be ready. The ward-room and the warrant officer's mess were fitted up as hospitals for wounded; the trolley for bringing torpedoes from the magazine under the turtle-back deck to the tubes aft was tested along the rails; Yamaguchi had a short colloquy with the engineer; and then he went to his place on the fore-bridge, confident that all was right.

The flotilla opened up the lights of the port about midnight. The presence of the boats was soon discovered by Russian scouts, for at irregular intervals the guns of the forts tried long-range shots at them. Within a few miles of the port the divisions separated, the second steaming straight for the harbour, where it proceeded to lay mines from the mouth of the channel along the coast towards Dalny. Captain Asai's three vessels meanwhile cruised off the Liau-ti-shan promontory.

Bob remained all night with Yamaguchi on the bridge, finding it less chilly there than below. In spite of the blazing furnaces he had never felt cold so keenly as in the captain's cabin when he dived down the small circular hatchway to fetch Yamaguchi an extra jacket. At about three o'clock in the morning they began to run down the coast. There was a head sea, which broke in great masses over the fore-deck, the driving spray being carried high over the canvas screens surrounding the bridge. Dawn was just breaking when the look-out descried the low hulls of several destroyers far-off on the horizon. The intelligence was at once signalled to Captain Asai on the *Akatsuki*. From his bridge he soon discovered that the approaching vessels were six in number; obviously they could not belong to the Japanese squadron. The order was instantly given to attack. Everything was already prepared for immediate action; every man was at his post; and the three vessels, cutting at the rate of an express train through the heavy seas, bore straight down on the six Russian destroyers.

"It's long odds on the Russians," remarked Bob to Yamaguchi.

The Japanese shrugged. "They're not islanders," he said; "we're like you Britishers, sea-dogs from birth, and our seamanship is a trifle better than theirs, I fancy. Besides, we're probably better armed. A Russian destroyer only has three-pounder quick-firers besides its twelve-pounders. Their shots can pierce our egg-shell, of course, but our six-pounder shots will do far more damage to their interiors."

"Won't you use your torpedoes, then?"

"No. Dog doesn't eat dog: we keep our torpedoes for larger game."

"You are not using the conning-tower?" asked Bob, noticing that Yamaguchi showed no sign of leaving the bridge.

"No; it is better to take one's risk in the open. Those peep-holes are rather worrying when you want to have a good look at the enemy."

The three vessels were now in line ahead—steaming straight for the Russian flotilla, the *Akatsuki* leading, the *Kasumi* a quarter of a mile behind, and the *Asashio* making a good third at the same distance. Bob on the fore-bridge was tingling with exhilaration. All his faculties seemed to be braced up. He had no sense of danger, in spite of his knowledge that one lucky shot from the Russians might explode the magazine beneath him and destroy the ship and every soul on board. His strongest feeling was one of impatience. The vessel was bounding along at more than race-horse speed; yet it appeared to be going slowly, too slowly, and he felt he would have liked to cry "Hurry up! hurry up! faster! faster!"

Two minutes had passed since the order "Full speed ahead!" Then from the fore-bridge of the *Akatsuki* the six-pounder shrieked. From that moment Bob saw and heard nothing except what went on in his own vessel. Immediately after the *Akatsuki* had opened fire, Yamaguchi gave his first order. There was an ear-splitting report; the vessel seemed almost to pause momentarily in its career, like a racer pulled up on its haunches; and a second or two later Bob saw a cloud of smoke over the fore-deck of the leading Russian boat, which, travelling at thirty knots, instantly shook off the pall and emerged from it with one funnel completely shattered. Bob did not hear the explosion of the shell; the din from the *Kasumi* and the other Japanese vessels, and from the approaching Russians, was too great to allow individual sounds, except within a few feet, to be distinguished. Almost before he was aware of it, the two flotillas had met and passed; they were within a few yards of each other, so near that the faces of the Russian seamen were easily visible; but Bob afterwards remembered few details, for the actual time of transit could be measured by seconds. The vessels sped past at a combined speed of some sixty miles an hour.

As the *Kasumi* came abreast of the leading Russian boat, which had already received a battering from the *Akatsuki*, her twelve-pounder added a growling bass to the whining of the lighter guns, now firing at their maximum speed. At this moment a shot from a three-pounder struck the compass-box on the fore-bridge, just above the chart-room, and a few feet from where Bob was standing. A splinter from the bursting shell hit the gunner serving the six-pounder on the bridge; the man was killed in an instant; a comrade came imperturbably to take his place. Immediately afterwards a twelve-pounder shell carried away the ventilator of the aft stokehold, and a three-pounder, penetrating the hull as though it were of paper, exploded in the ward-room, severely injuring a man waiting there to receive the wounded. Then the rearmost vessels of the two squadrons passed, and the *Kasumi's* twelve-pounder astern got in a parting shell, which took effect apparently among the boilers of the Russian, for when the smoke from the bursting charge had cleared away, the vessel was seen to be enveloped in a vast cloud of steam. Bob was surprised at the small total effect of such vigorous firing on both sides, though he realized afterwards that at the rate at which the vessels were steaming it was still more surprising that the effect was so great as it was.

But the fight was not yet over. At a signal from the *Akatsuki* the Japanese vessels spun round almost within their own length, and started in pursuit of the enemy, now steaming at half-speed to cover the retreat of the damaged boat. The Russian flotilla was somewhat bunched; presumably the boats had been hard hit, and either their commander had no definite plan of action, or their mechanism had been so much damaged as to retard their movements. Two had turned, but three others were manoeuvring in a small space, hampering one another, while the sixth, the lame duck, was making the best of its solitary way in the direction of Port Arthur. Captain Asai was quick to seize his opportunity. Slightly altering his course so as to cut obliquely across the path of the Russians, he brought the whole of his port-side guns to bear upon the huddled enemy; then before the Russians had time to take advantage of the broad target offered to them, he reverted to the line-ahead formation, and bore straight down upon them.

This time the two flotillas passed at such close quarters that a man could have thrown a line from one ship to the deck of its opponent. They were moving at less speed than in the former encounter, and the effects of their mutual bombardment were correspondingly greater. For the first time Bob was conscious of a tremor, not of personal fear, but a reflex of the wild scene around. It seemed to him as if nothing could survive the hail of shells that screamed and whistled through the air, to burst with ear-splitting crash whenever one was fortunate enough to find its billet in the hull or upper works of the gallant *Kasumi*. One shell, apparently from a three-pounder, ricochetted off the turtle-back deck beneath the forebridge, and burst in the air about ten yards to starboard, the splinters breaking a hole in the aftermost funnel and knocking a corner off the compass-box that stood within a few feet of it.

"There goes our second compass. We have only the standard left," said Yamaguchi.

Almost at the same moment there was a crash just below the spot where Bob was standing. A twelve-pounder shell had passed clean through the chart-room without exploding.

"A narrow squeak!" said Bob.

"Yes; we'll give that fourth Russian a little pepper," replied Yamaguchi, his face lit with the joy of service.

He gave an order, and all the *Kasumi's* port six-pounders let fly at the Russian destroyer, several shells ploughing into her hull just above the water-line. Bob noticed the strained expression on the faces of the Russian seamen, and one vivid picture flashed upon his retina and was gone—the picture of a man, struck by a fragment of a Japanese shell, falling with outstretched arms across his gun. A few seconds more and the *Kasumi* again came abreast of the last vessel in the Russian line. She replied so feebly to Yamaguchi's skilfully-aimed broadside that it was evident she had already been severely handled by the *Asashio*, now leading. But as the vessels passed, a big Russian picked up a tin canister and hurled it with such good aim at the *Kasumi* that it fell on the platform of the fore-bridge between Yamaguchi and Bob. The latter instantly lifted it to throw into the sea, but Yamaguchi stayed his hand.

"There's no danger," he said; "it will not explode now. We'll keep it; I'll make you a present of it."

At that instant a three-pounder shell exploded in the aft stoke-hold, bursting a steam-pipe, and dangerously wounding one of the engineers.

"Poor Minamisawa!" said Yamaguchi, when he heard of it. "He was twice commended for gallantry during the attack on Port Arthur a month ago."

By this time the flotillas had again passed each other. But on turning once more to renew the fight, Captain Asai found that the enemy had had enough of it. They were steaming full speed ahead towards the harbour. The order was given to pursue; but the Russians had obtained too great a start to permit of their being overhauled before gaining the protection of their cruisers and shore batteries. The pursuit had necessarily to be abandoned, and the Japanese commanders turned their attention to making good the damage sustained during the action.

The full results of this spirited forty minutes' engagement were not known on board the *Kasumi* until some time afterwards. Near the entrance to the harbour two of the Russian destroyers were intercepted by the second Japanese flotilla. The Russians, battered as they had been, showed no lack of courage. There was a short, sharp fight, during which one of the boats slipped past the enemy and got away. The second, however, the *Stereguschitshi*, was not so fortunate. She fell a prey to a Japanese destroyer, and was taken in tow. But she was leaking badly; the tow-rope was snapped like a thread of cotton by a heavy sea, and, left to her fate, the *Stereguschitshi* went down.

Meanwhile the three vessels of Captain Asai's division lay for about an hour with only steering-way on, until the extent of their injuries should have been ascertained and as far as possible repaired. On the *Kasumi* two compass-boxes had been damaged, part of the fore-bridge carried away, one funnel breached, the chart-room almost entirely wrecked; but the most serious injury was the shattering of the steam-pipe, throwing one engine out of action. The other two vessels stood by while some repairs were being made; it was not safe to leave the *Kasumi* to face alone the risk of the appearance of the Russian cruiser squadron. The work was barely completed, indeed, when two cruisers, the *Bayan* and the *Novik*, the latter flying Admiral Makaroff's flag, steamed out of Port Arthur and ran down towards the three destroyers. But at the same moment a forest of military masts appeared on the horizon: the Japanese fleet was evidently coming up in support; and the two Russians, fearful of being cut off, retired, fighting at long range with the leading Japanese cruisers until they ran in under shelter of the forts.

"Another bombardment coming off?" said Bob to Yamaguchi, as the splendid battle-ships went by.

"Perhaps. The flagship is signalling us."

"What are the signals?"

"Nothing important; the admiral merely says he is satisfied with us."

The flush of pleasure was not on Yamaguchi's cheeks, but on Bob's. He remembered the historic "Well done, *Condor*!" and felt a sympathetic glow.

The battle-ships steamed past, and took up a position whence they could neither see the Russian vessels nor be seen by them. Depending on high-angle fire from their twelve-inch guns, they sent shell after shell into the town and harbour, the effect of their shots being signalled by wireless telegraphy from the cruiser squadron stationed round the point. The bombardment lasted for nearly four hours, during which several outbreaks of fire were seen in the town, and a distant explosion announced that a magazine had been blown up. There was but little reply from the Russians, and about two o'clock Admiral Togo, having accomplished his immediate purpose, retired, accompanied by the cruiser and destroyer squadrons.

Two hours later Yamaguchi was signalled to go aboard the flagship. It was blowing hard at the time, and seas were sweeping the deck of the *Kasumi*, tossing her about, and rendering the launching of her boat a matter of no little difficulty. By the time the little lieutenant reached the *Mikasa* he must have been drenched through and through.

"Well," said Bob, when he returned, "are you promoted again?"

"No; but you are."

"What do you mean?"

"The admiral has remembered you, that's all. This morning, being forgotten, you were at zero; you may be soon at boiling-point. I am to put you on board the *Yoshino*—if I can."

"Ugh! it won't be a dry passage. If you can, you say?"

"Yes; I am ordered to the mouth of the Yalu, and shall drop you on the way, if I can do so without losing time."

"In a hurry, then?"

But Yamaguchi made no reply. He was telephoning to the engine-room. In a few minutes the *Kasumi* was slugging through the sea, half-speed ahead, in a north-easterly direction. The wind increased to half a gale; huge seas broke continually with thud and swish over the vessel, and Bob did not relish the prospect of the swamping he must undergo if he were to reach the *Yoshino's* side. He was overjoyed when he saw that the distance between the destroyer and the cruiser squadron was increasing instead of diminishing. Yamaguchi had clearly given up the idea of putting him aboard the *Yoshino*. From his manner Bob had already guessed that the expedition on which he was now speeding was one of some importance, and when at length the lieutenant turned to him and said, laconically, "Can't waste time over you", his pulse leapt at the thought that he was still to remain on the *Kasumi* and share in whatever adventure there might be in store.

Chapter VIII
Cut Off

Secret Service—Yamaguchi Returns—A Quick Change—A Bleak Ride—On the Trail

For some time Yamaguchi was too intently occupied in navigating the vessel between the Elliott and the Blonde islands to concern himself with Bob. But when he was through the strait he left the bridge and went below to get something to eat. Then for the first time he told Bob what his mission was. He had been ordered to survey the coast-line of Korea Bay as far as the Yalu, to report on the state of the ice, and especially to examine the condition of things at the mouth of the river. If he could at the same time pick up any information as to the disposition of the Russian forces along the shore, so much the better; but though he might run any personal hazards, he was on no account to risk his vessel; in war time destroyers cannot easily be replaced.

"You're fixed up for ten days, you see," he said to Bob. "I'm to be back in that time, and you're bound to remain with me."

"You'll have to go ashore, I suppose," said Bob.

"Yes, if I can get through the ice. And I think I can. I've been this way before; I suppose that's why the admiral selected me for the job. Unless it's because one of our engines is out of action. The ice usually clings to the shore till some time after this, but just before we reach Taku-shan there's a spit of land where, by some movement of the currents, the ice is sometimes loosened; and if I'm lucky, there'll be passage-way for a boat, if not for the destroyer herself."

"I say, you'll let me go with you."

"Certainly not. I'm already one notch down through not being able to put you on the *Yoshino*, and I can't afford to report you gone for good."

"But why shouldn't I go where you go?"

"Well, for one thing, it's my job and not yours. The admiral has plenty of lieutenants, but only one Bob Fawcett! Besides, why take you into danger?

If the Russians catch me, I'm shot. Well, that's part of my work; but you—you'd be shot too, and an Englishman is worth—how many of any other nation?"

"Too many to count," said Bob smiling.

"Anyhow, you're twice as heavy as me, and nearly twice as tall; and another thing, you'd find it hard to pass for a Chinaman."

"Oh! you're going in for disguises, then."

"Yes, I shall stick on a pigtail; I won't be caught if I can help it."

"D'you know, I've an idea. Your mention of a disguise makes me wonder if that Chinaman I saw in Seoul wasn't a Chinaman after all. I saw him before at Sasebo with another fellow; there was something about them I seemed to know. D'you think they were really Japanese I had caught sight of in Tokio?"

"It's possible, of course; but I shouldn't jump to conclusions. Their disguise must have been pretty feeble if you saw through it after only a casual glimpse in Tokio."

"Ah! I've a good memory for faces. But let us go on deck, it's so horribly cold down here."

By this time the vessel had left the Elliott Islands some ten knots on her port quarter. Looking out in that direction, Bob drew Yamaguchi's attention to the masts of several vessels that stood up among the islands. The lieutenant smiled, but said nothing. Bob, in spite of himself somewhat annoyed at his friend's reticence, formed his own conclusion: the ships were probably transports landing men or supplies on the islands, or preparing the way for a Japanese army-corps in anticipation of a siege of Port Arthur.

Keeping well out in the bay, the *Kasumi* thrashed her way through a head-sea on a course north-east by east. Darkness came on, and loth though he was to go below and shiver, Bob at length was so tired that he had to turn in. He spent a by no means comfortable night. It was like sleeping under a blanket of ice. During the hours of darkness, in order to save coal, the *Kasumi* went at less than half-speed, and it was nearing dawn when she arrived off Taku-shan. All that day Yamaguchi kept her far out, so that she should not be seen from the shore, which was fringed with ice. The wind had dropped, leaving only a long swell on the waters of the bay. At nightfall the *Kasumi* ran in, careful soundings being taken at various points; and Yamaguchi found, as he had hoped, that the current had kept open a narrow waterway between Takushan and the island of Talu. Announcing his decision to go ashore, he went to the ward-room, and soon returned, transformed into a very presentable young Chinaman, drooping moustache, skull-cap, pigtail, and all. A boat was lowered, and the lieutenant departed, saying that he would probably return by daylight.

That was the first of several short expeditions Yamaguchi made at night to the shore. Bob could never induce him to speak of what he did, but noticed that he always appeared abundantly satisfied. On all these occasions the same plan was followed: Yamaguchi was rowed in the darkness as near to the shore as the ice-fringe allowed; he finished the distance on the ice; and the boat returned to the *Kasumi* until just before dawn, when it again went shorewards and brought him off.

Four days thus passed away, and on the evening of the fourth, when the *Kasumi* had come opposite the mouth of the Yalu, Yamaguchi told Bob that he was now going on the last of these night journeys, and hoped, on his return, to rejoin the fleet and make his report to Admiral Togo.

"I may be away longer this time," he said.

"Can't I go? Every time you have been away I have been in a perfect stew lest you shouldn't come back, and I find it all precious slow."

"Very sorry, but it's impossible."

"How long do you expect to be away this time?"

"I can't say, but I have three days' rice stowed away in my pockets. I hope I shall not be so long as that. You had better amuse yourself by playing 'go'."

"But what if the Russian fleet comes up while you're away? For my part, I don't understand a commander leaving his vessel like this."

"You are not the admiral, you see. I don't think you need trouble about the Russians. The Port Arthur fleet daren't come, and the Vladivostock one probably can't. Good-bye."

Two days passed away, and by the end of the second Bob was almost tired of his life; he had played "go" till he went nearly mad. He wandered all over the vessel, examining for the tenth time every nook and cranny of it, until he felt that he could have drawn plans of its construction from memory. He got one of the gunners who knew something of English to teach him a little Japanese—common phrases like *Nodo ga kawakimashita*, "I am thirsty", which to a Japanese is "throat has dried"; and "I am hungry"—*O naka ga sukimashita*, "honourable inside has become empty"; and "it is horribly cold"—*O samu gozaimasu*, "honourably cold augustly is", until he wondered whether it would be correct Japanese to say "I'll augustly punch your honourable head". But even such amusement as this palled; and to his own restlessness was presently added anxiety about Yamaguchi, for whom he felt sincere affection. At sundown on both evenings the boat went off towards the shore in accordance with the captain's instructions, but on both occasions it returned without him. On the third evening, Bob decided to accompany the boat. The sky was clearer than it had been for many nights past; the moon was rising, and whatever danger there had previously been of the boat being seen from the shore was now more than doubled. Bob felt anxious, and, as he sat in the bows, peered through his glass towards the snow-covered flats and low hills that stretch on either side of the Yalu estuary.

The sailors pulled in to the verge of the ice, then lay on their oars. Many minutes passed. The crew waited in silence, and as the moon rose higher and its rays were reflected from the snow, it became almost as light as day. The sea heavily lapped the sides of the boat and swished against the jagged edges of the ice; otherwise there was no sound.

Suddenly, against the white background, a small dark form was seen, apparently rising from the other side of a hillock whose contour was indistinguishable in the universal white. The object soon defined itself as a small man running, and at headlong pace. Bob stood up in some excitement, wondering whether this was Yamaguchi at last. Immediately afterwards he saw other forms appear upon the crest, and he drew in his breath sharply as he recognized that these were men on horseback. They came rapidly over the hillock, and began to descend towards the sea after the running figure. Bob raised his glass to his eyes; yes, the runner was Yamaguchi, and the horsemen wore the fur caps and carried the long lances of Cossacks. It was a race for life!

The hillock was nearly half a mile away. Between it and the boat lay an almost level stretch of mud flats, covered for many inches by recently-fallen snow, and fifty yards of ice, now of course indistinguishable from the land. Could Yamaguchi reach the boat in time? He had the start of his pursuers, but they were mounted, and, as Bob now saw, there were eight of them. It was almost impossible that the runner could escape. Yet it seemed impossible to help him. The seamen in the boat had rifles, but now that pursuers and pursued had descended the declivity and come to the flat, a shot, however well aimed, might hit the man it was intended to assist.

In one tense moment Bob seemed to live a lifetime. Then, with a cry to the men to remain where they were—which, not knowing English, they understood rather by the tone than by the words—he sprang over the side of the boat on to the ridge of ice. It creaked and sank under him, but he leapt on towards the shore, intent on assisting the flagging footsteps of the

Japanese, who was evidently near the end of his endurance. The ice crackled and groaned as Bob raced on. He reached the softer snow, and his pace was checked; he heard a shot from one of the pursuing Cossacks ring past his ear; he shouted a word of encouragement to the panting lieutenant, and then, leaping, floundering, staggering over the intervening yards, he caught Yamaguchi by the arm and turned to run with him towards the boat, feeling all the time that theirs was a hopeless case, for the foremost horseman, distancing his comrades, was now but a dozen yards away.

All at once a shot flashed from the boat. Bob heard a strange sobbing sigh behind him. A moment after he felt the impact of a heavy body, he was thrown violently on his face, and a riderless horse galloped madly on towards the sea.

Bob lay for a few moments dazed on the snow. The cold brought him to his senses. He heard several shots ring out, and lifting his head cautiously he saw four Cossacks galloping on to the ice, and three standing by the side of their horses, taking aim at the boat across their saddles. Then came the crack of ice beneath the horses' hoofs; loud cries of distress rose on the air as men and horses floundered in the water; and a fusillade continued between the dismounted Cossacks on the shore and the crew of the boat, which was now being rapidly pulled out to sea. Bob saw his opportunity; it might last but a moment, he had no time to lose. Rising to his feet, still dizzy from the blow, he saw a few feet behind him the outstretched body of the dead Cossack; his horse had returned and was now standing patiently by his side. He stooped down, quickly relieved the Cossack of his cap, cloak, and arms; then, going quietly to the animal, he sprang upon its back, saw at a side-glance that the surviving Cossacks were still occupied, and touching the horse with his heel, trotted away southward on a line parallel with the coast, towards a clump of trees looming black against the moonlit sky more than half a mile away.

Having arrived there, and being out of sight from the scene of his late adventure, he pulled up to consider his position. Yamaguchi, he hoped, was by this time well on his way to the *Kasumi*; if only he himself could remain in hiding until the morning, and the vessel were still lying off the mouth of the river, it might be possible then to get on board. All depended on whether the Cossacks who had survived the fray would notice his disappearance, and the fact that their dead comrade had been despoiled. That they would not do so was in both cases very unlikely. His only chance, therefore, would be to make his way southward, in the hope of coming upon the outposts of one of the Japanese forces which he knew had been landed in the country. That course would be attended with considerable danger. News of the recent incident was bound to bring a larger force of Cossacks upon the scene; parties of Russians would soon be scouring the country, not only to discover traces of the fugitive, but to keep an eye open for the torpedo boat destroyer. It was well-known on the Japanese fleet that Cossacks were employed to ride up and down the coast and signal the approach of hostile vessels, and these would scarcely fail to note and follow up the tracks of his horse in the snow.

"This is a precious fix to be in," he thought; and the more he reflected the more awkward his position appeared. The chance of getting in touch with the *Kasumi* was very remote, for if he emerged from hiding and went down to the shore he could scarcely hope to escape discovery by Russian patrols. On the other hand, if he hid during the day he would not be seen from the destroyer. Besides, the *Kasumi* was due to rejoin the fleet; and though he knew that Yamaguchi, if a free agent, would do anything to serve him, he knew also that, with a Japanese, duty came inexorably first, and it was vain to expect Yamaguchi to cruise about indefinitely on the chance of picking him up. Supposing he left hiding and rode towards the south, there seemed little likelihood of his reaching the Japanese lines. Their outposts were probably not less than a hundred miles away. Between them and him many detached parties of Russians were no doubt patrolling the country. Even if he escaped the Russians he might fall into the hands of the Koreans, and that would perhaps prove a case of out of the frying-pan into the fire. Much as the Koreans hated the Japanese, by all accounts they hated the Russians still more; and being mounted on a Cossack's horse, and wearing Cossack uniform, knowing, moreover, nothing of the Korean language, he would have short shrift if he stumbled among the natives. Yet another consideration. Both he and his horse must have food. A bundle of hay was tied to the latter, sufficient perhaps for one feed; and on rummaging in the saddle-bags he found a little black rye bread and a flask of vodka. But this was very precarious sustenance, and he would be forced under stress of hunger to enter a village within twenty-four hours at the latest.

Of all the dangers besetting him the prospect of being followed up by the Cossacks of Yongampo was the most immediate, and Bob shut his eyes to the other contingencies in order to provide against this. Obviously the farther he got from the scene of the fight the better. He rode carefully through the clump of bare trees southward, and, emerging into the open, set his horse at a sharp trot. The ground was covered with snow to a depth of several feet, and as the horse's feet sank into it slightly, he concluded that the frost was yielding. Guiding himself by the sound of the waves lapping against the ice on the shore, which creaked and groaned, and now and again broke with a sharp report, he struck along the coast in the direction, as he believed, of Seng-cheng. The Cossack's deep saddle was very comfortable, but he wished that the stirrups were lower: his knees were a good deal nearer his nose than he was accustomed to.

The moon was going down, but there was still sufficient light to show that, except for a few scattered clumps of wood, the country was very open, and he knew that in the daytime he could be seen for miles. As he rode, he therefore looked eagerly about in search of some hiding-place where he might spend the rest of the night in tolerable security. After some three or four miles he found that the country was becoming increasingly difficult. On his left the irregular hills rose more and more steeply, and he was forced more and more towards the ice. Warned by his recent experience of the Cossacks, he edged away until he reached at length the summit of a slope some distance above the sea. Great banks of cloud were looming up across the sea; the wind was rising, and the air had that incisive rawness that portends snow. To be caught in a snowstorm in this bleak latitude would be a calamity, and Bob looked more anxiously around for shelter.

Some distance above him he saw, outlined against a clear patch of sky not yet reached by the clouds, a large dark building, which from its size he thought must be a place of some importance. It was in shape unlike anything he had previously seen. As he looked towards it, he caught sight of the last horn of the moon apparently in the very centre of the building. Evidently the place was a ruin. Whatever hesitation Bob might have had in approaching an inhabited dwelling-house disappeared; he made his way towards it with some difficulty, the horse floundering through drifts which more than once threatened to engulf him. Arriving at the building, Bob found that it was the ruin of a large stone pagoda, probably at one time part of a monastery. The wind howled eerily through its dilapidated walls, but it provided shelter of a sort; and, what was more important, being situated on a slight eminence it would give him a good outlook in the morning, not only far across the sea, but also landward towards the mouth of the Yalu. In this lonely place, then, Bob determined to pass the remainder of the night.

His first care was to rub down his horse; then he gave it half the bundle of hay. Then he unstrapped one of the blankets from the saddle and proceeded to make himself as comfortable as possible. He swallowed a few mouthfuls of the bitter bread, took one sip (more than sufficient) of the burning vodka, and being tired out soon dropped into an uneasy sleep, from which, with the instinct of one accustomed to early rising, he awoke at the first pale glint of dawn. Rising stiffly to his feet, he again fed the horse, ate a little bread, and went outside to look round.

Northwards, in the direction from which he had come the previous night, he could see with the naked eye for several miles across the snow; and through his glass, which he had luckily brought with him, he descried what was evidently a small town—no doubt Yongampo. Over the whole white stretch intervening there was no sign of life. Looking then seaward, he saw a leaden sky, white-crested waves lashed by the high wind and breaking in angry foam on the ice—nothing more. There was not a speck on the sea. The *Kasumi* had left him to his fate.

"And I dare say Yamaguchi is even more sorry than I am," he thought.

Then he turned again to the land and swept the horizon with his glass. What is that? In the far distance, towards Yongampo, he discerns two dark specks. He gazes intently, his hands so numbed with cold that he can scarcely hold the glass steadily. The specks are growing larger. Both are approaching him, one coming southward in a straight line, the other making a trend somewhat to his right. For some minutes he gazes at them; the specks become masses, and gradually define themselves as bodies of horsemen. Doubtless they are Cossacks; it is time to be up and away.

Chapter IX
Chased by Cossacks

A View-Halloo—Cossacks at Fault—Bluff—Suspicious Hospitality—
On the Pekin Road—A Hill Tiger

The situation was desperate. One band of Cossacks was evidently
following the tracks of his horse, the other taking a short cut to head him off.
The Mandarin road from Pekin to Seoul could not be far away; the Russians
had probably assumed that he would ride in that direction, and acquainted
as they no doubt were with the neighbourhood, they would have a great
advantage over him. His only hope lay in his horse, which was fortunately
a good one, and in the pink of condition. He must ride, and ride, and ride.

Returning to the pagoda, he found that the horse had eaten the last wisp
of hay. He led it out, down the slope on the side farthest from the pursuers,
through a dip between two low hills; then coasting round a somewhat
steeper hill which hid the pagoda from sight, he judged it safe to mount, and
was soon cantering over the snow-covered ground. It was rolling country;
at one minute he was as it were on the crest of a wave, the next he would be
in a trough. The snow was soft, and the horse's hoofs left deep pits in the
yielding surface by which the course of his flight could be easily tracked.
Soon he lost sight of the sea, and had nothing by which to take his bearings;
the sky all around was one unbroken lead-gray. As he rode on, he saw with
misgiving that the hills were becoming lower and lower; he would be in full
sight of the Cossacks when they reached the heights he had just left. There
was no alternative but to push on. Of refuge there was none; the whole
country seemed to be desert, with no marks of human habitation except
here and there a native hut perched on the edge of a clump of trees, the
abandoned home of some wood-cutter.

Every now and then he reined up his horse and turned in the saddle to
see if his pursuers were in sight. Struggling up a long slope, and halting at
the top to breathe the animal, he saw before him an almost level stretch, and
behind him—yes, there they were at last, a band of at least twenty, who had
probably dodged round some of the hills which he had laboriously climbed.

He looked eagerly round; there was no way of eluding the pursuers. Should he set his steed at the gallop and try to distance them? That was a vain hope; it would exhaust his panting horse, and the Cossacks would wear him down, following untiringly upon his track like wolves. He must on again, and husband the animal's strength as much as possible.

Down the slope, then, he rode, the horse's breath leaving a trail of vapour in the cold air. The sky was growing blacker, the wind, which had been blowing in gusts, dropped; there was no sound but the soft glugging of the hoofs as they plunged into the snow. Suddenly Bob heard a faint shout behind him. He knew well what it meant; the Cossacks had reached the crest of the hill and seen him cantering before them. He looked over his shoulder; they were no more than a mile distant. In half an hour they would close in upon him; perhaps the second band had already come round upon his flank and was now ahead of him; for all he knew, he might have been riding in a circle. Still he must ride on. He quickened his horse's pace; some ten minutes later he heard the distant crack of shots, but as no ping of the bullets followed he guessed that they had flown wide. But the fact that the Cossacks were firing was ominous. They were accustomed to take flying shots from the backs of their steeds; at any moment a luckily-aimed bullet might hit him. He lay upon the horse's neck and called upon the beast to gallop. More shots, more shouts pursued him, but the sounds were fainter. The gap between him and the Cossacks must be widening; could the advantage be maintained?

He spoke encouragingly to the animal, which galloped along with wonderful sure-footedness. Suddenly Bob felt a damp, cold dab upon his brow, then another; he lifted his head, and gave a quick gasp of relief when he saw that snow was falling. The lowering sky had opened at last; in a few moments the rider was making his way through a dense shower of whirling snowflakes, which filled eyes and ears and shut out all objects beyond a hundred yards. By favour of this white screen he might yet escape.

To the left he saw a small dark clump of trees stretching up the hillside. Pushing on until he came level with the furthermost edge he wheeled round, struck through the fringe of the clump where the trees were thin, and ascended the hill at right angles to his former course, in hope that his pursuers, losing him from sight, might overshoot the spot where he diverged before they discovered their mistake. The blinding fall of snow must now be fast obliterating his tracks; to distinguish them the Russians would have to slacken speed; and the few minutes he thus gained might enable him to escape them altogether. But he dared not wait; the Cossacks, finding that they failed to overtake him, would soon cast back and probably scatter in the direction they would guess him to have taken, and how could he expect to elude them all? Walking his horse for a few minutes to allow it to recover breath, he again urged it on, hoping that his luck would yet serve.

The air was still thick with the falling snow; to follow a certain course was impossible. He rode on. Suddenly he heard a dull thud not far to his right; could it be the sound of the Cossacks returning already? Quick as thought he reined up behind a large tree, and peering round the trunk saw, through the whirling flakes, a number of shadowy forms flit past in the opposite direction to that in which he had been going. Mingled with the thudding hoofs came the muffled sound of voices. He could not distinguish the riders, yet he felt sure that they were his pursuers. Waiting till all sounds were quenched, he cantered slowly ahead, knowing now that could he but keep a straight course the Cossacks would be unable, while the snowfall lasted, to find his trail. But for an accident he was safe.

Safe, indeed, from the pursuers; but there were still dire perils to face. He had been riding hard for three hours; the horse had for some time been showing signs of fatigue; he had no food either for it or for himself, and he was himself ravenously hungry. He was in a wild, desolate, sparsely-populated region; should he encounter natives he would be taken for a Russian; he could not speak their language; even if his horse's strength held out until he reached an advanced Japanese outpost, he might be shot before he could make himself understood. Yet, unless he fell in with someone who would give him shelter and food, he and his horse alike must succumb to fatigue and cold, and he would have escaped the Scylla of Russian hands only to meet death from the Charybdis of the elements. Chilled, tired, hungry as he was, for a brief moment his mind was crossed by the shadow of despair; but he pulled himself together, shook the reins, straightened himself, and once more rode on.

It seemed to him that he was wandering on a vast white Sahara, or adrift on a wide sea without chart or compass. All at once, on his left hand, a hut such as he had previously seen from the sea-shore loomed up, like an excrescence from the white plain. He pulled up, dismounted, and led his horse towards the building. It was partially ruined. The doorway was too low to admit the animal, but going round to the back he found a large gap in the rough mud wall just wide enough to allow the horse to pass. Here at least there was temporary shelter for both man and beast. True, there was some risk of the Cossacks appearing even yet; but the horse could go no farther; while it was resting the snow-storm might cease, and with a lifting sky he might be able to take his bearings and strike out a definite course. Leading the animal into the hovel, he scraped the snow from its body, rubbed it as dry as possible with the cloths he unrolled from the saddle, and sat down on a billet of wood, cold, hungry, and depressed.

Thinking, dreaming, he at length fell into a doze. When he awoke, he noticed that the snow had ceased, and the sky was clearing. It was four o'clock. Rising stiff with cold, he went outside the hut and observed a streak of dull red on the horizon.

"That must be the setting sun," he said to himself. "I wonder if, guiding myself by that, I could by and by reach a village and get food. Poor old horse! I hope you are not feeling as hungry and miserable as I am."

He led the beast out and mounted. It was now freezing hard; the snow gave a metallic crunch under the hoofs as he rode away. Westward, towards the setting sun, must lie the sea; in that direction there was nothing to hope for. Northward were the Russians, southward the Japanese, but how far away? His course must be eastward, for sooner or later he must strike the high-road, and when once on the high-road he must in time reach a village. There would always be the risk of meeting Russians, but he could only chance that. Eastward, therefore, he set his horse. His advent in a Korean village would not be without danger; but one peril balanced another, and his plight could scarcely be more desperate.

He had ridden, as he guessed, some three miles farther across the valley, when suddenly, in the dusk before him, he descried a cluster of huts. "At last!" he said to himself with a sigh of relief. Here at any rate were people; where people were, there must be food—and food, both for himself and his horse, must be obtained, whatever the risk. The hamlet might harbour a Cossack patrol; but at this stage Bob felt that it was no worse to fall into Russian hands than to die of famine on the snow-clad hills. On the other hand, if there were no Cossacks in the hamlet, his own appearance in Russian guise would be sufficient to procure him supplies. The Korean as a fighting man was not, Yamaguchi had told him, very formidable, so that even if the villagers proved hostile he felt that he could manage to hold his own.

Taking the Cossack's pistol from the holster, Bob rode on boldly into the hamlet. To assure himself that it sheltered no Russians, he cantered right through the narrow street, then turned his horse and made his way to what appeared to be the principal house. Like all Korean villages of the poorer sort, this one was dirty and cramped, consisting of a few one-story houses of mud with thatched roofs. The street was now deserted; the few people who had been in it when he cantered through had scattered into their houses when they saw him turn, regarding him no doubt as the pioneer of a body of Cossacks. He dismounted at the closed door of the hut, and knocked. There was no reply; save for the bark of a dog the whole village was shrouded in silence. He knocked again, and a third time, still without effect; the fourth time he battered insistently on the door with his pistol. Then he heard a sound within; the door opened, and by the dim light of a foul-smelling oil-lamp he saw a very fat elderly Korean spreading himself across the entrance.

Bob knew no Korean, no Russian, no Chinese, and only a few words of Japanese. These he had perforce to rely on.

"Komban wa!" he said politely, giving the evening greeting.

The man snapped out something in gruff tones.

"Tabe-mono!" added Bob, taking a few Japanese coins out of his pocket. "Uma! Pan taberu daro!"

The Korean shook his head and began to jabber words incomprehensible to Bob. His meaning, however, was obvious; he was not inclined to supply the food for horse and man for which his visitor had asked. Bob was in no mood to brook reluctance or even dilatoriness. Raising his pistol and pointing it full at the man's head, he poured out a torrent of the first abuse that came to him, which happened to be phrases he had heard addressed to the referee at football matches in the Celtic Park. No Korean, as he had expected, could stand up against this. In a short time a feed of corn was brought for his horse; he tied the beast up at the door, and returning to the room sat down on the stone floor, awaiting food for himself, and wishing that the furnace in the cellar beneath were not quite so hot. The air inside the hovel was foul and suffocating, but a man can put up with a good deal of discomfort when he is starving, and Bob did not turn up his nose at the evil-smelling mixture by and by set before him. It was a dish of which the poorer Koreans are fond—a compound of raw fish, pepper, vinegar, and slabs of fat pork, and the odour was like mingled collodion and decaying sea-weed. He tasted it, tried to swallow a mouthful, found it impossible, and then, in a burst of scarcely feigned rage, demanded meshi or boiled rice, which he had reason to suppose would be at once more palatable and more trustworthy. This was in due course forthcoming, and with the aid of a spoon, the only one the house contained, he succeeded in disposing of a quantity of food which would have astonished anyone but a Korean. His host had now become cringingly polite. Bob questioned him, partly by signs, partly by means of his few words of Japanese, regarding the direction of Seng-cheng and the Pekin road. The former, he learnt, was 70 li (about 21 miles) over the hills, the latter 10 li due east. Thinking over the situation, he resolved to make boldly for the road, which he knew led direct to Ping-yang, and on reaching it to travel by night and rest in hiding during the day. Having made a hearty meal, with a moderate potation of a thin rice beer which he found very refreshing, he rose to leave, and offered the Korean a yen, which, as prices go in the country, was probably four times the value of what he and his horse had consumed. The man, with many bows and protestations, refused to accept payment. Bob insisted, the Korean resisted, and, pointing to a wooden pillow-block on the floor and a quilt hanging on a peg, tried to persuade his visitor to stay the night. This invitation was politely declined, whereupon the Korean in his turn became insistent, so that Bob grew suspicious. The man's refusal to accept money was no doubt an attempt to ingratiate himself with the Cossack patrol to which he supposed Bob belonged; his pressing invitation was capable of a less amicable explanation. Bob in his guise as a Cossack would never think of spending the night alone in a Korean village; if he fell asleep he might never awaken. Shaking his head resolutely, he made signs that he wished the remains of his meal to be put up for him in one of the lacquer boxes he saw in the room. This having been done with manifest reluctance by his host, he moved forward his horse, the Korean following him still with pressing entreaty. All the time that Bob was bundling up a supply of fodder for his horse the man stood jabbering at his side, but he withstood these persevering efforts to detain him, and was just about to mount his horse, when he saw dimly in the dusk, at the end of the street by which he had entered the village, a body of men whom even in the distance he recognized by their quaint caps and baggy clothes as Korean infantry.

Instantly he vaulted into the saddle. At the same moment he heard the bang-bang of rifles and a volley of shouts. His fat host flung himself flat on his face, and Bob galloped up the street, smiling at the ineffectiveness of the Koreans' aim, and wondering how long it would take them to reload. At a turn of the street, even more to their surprise than to his own, he came plump upon another body of Koreans marching in no great order in the opposite direction. Evidently a clumsy attempt had been made to surround him. There was no alternative. He dashed straight at this new body; they scurried like rabbits to the sides of the road, yelling with fright, and by the time they had recovered sufficiently to remember that they were soldiers of the emperor, Bob was out of sight.

Only a few minutes after Bob had thus routed a Korean detachment, two Chinamen rode in at the other end of the village. They were shorter than the average Chinaman; yet, mounted as they were on the high saddles usual in Korea, their feet nearly touched the ground at the sides of their diminutive and sorry-looking ponies. They dismounted at the door of the house that Bob had lately left, and then it could be seen that the younger of the two was dressed like a respectable Chinese merchant, the other being evidently his servant.

The merchant enquired of the Korean at the door what was the meaning of the sounds of firing he had heard.

"The soldiers were honourably shooting at a Russian," replied the man.

"Did he have his lance?" asked the Chinaman instantly.

"No; but a pistol."

"You are sure he was not a Japanese dressed in Russian clothes?"

"Yes; he was tall, his cheeks were red, his eyes were blue, his hair the colour of ripe corn; there is no doubt at all that he was a red-haired barbarian."

The merchant spoke a few words to his servant; then both remounted, and set off as fast as their Lilliputian steeds could carry them after the departed Cossack.

Bob meanwhile had been hastening on. During the day his horse had had nearly five hours' rest, and after its good meal was again comparatively fresh. Scrambling over the hills, in no little danger of coming to grief in the darkness, he at length struck the beaten track over the snow that alone marked the course of the high-road. It rang hard under the horse's hoofs; much heavy sled traffic must have passed over it—no doubt supplies for the Russian cavalry, scattered over the whole of Northern Korea. All the way as he rode, Bob was alert to catch any sound of approaching troops, but the highway was deserted; he met neither man nor beast. After covering about ten miles he thought it best to leave the road and strike off into the hills on his left, with the object of skirting round Seng-cheng, which he felt sure was occupied by a Russian force, large or small. Choosing a spot where the highway edged a clump of wood, he rode some yards among the trunks, dismounted, and then carefully smoothed over his horse's tracks on the snow, leaving no track himself by retreating in the hoof-marks. Then he plunged deeper into the wood, in a direction at right angles to the road, leading his horse in order to avoid collision with the trees, and hoping by and by to reach some woodman's hut where he might safely pass the rest of the night. A faint moonlight began to shine through the leafless skeletons, assisting his progress. After half an hour he came suddenly upon a somewhat extensive clearing, in the midst of which he saw a small cluster of huts similar to those he had left behind. He was about to turn sharply off to avoid them, when something in their appearance struck him as unusual. Leaving his horse, he advanced cautiously, and found that the huts were deserted and in ruins; the blackened thatch and mud told a tale of burning, and Bob surmised that here was evidence of a Cossack raid. After a little search he found a hovel that had suffered less than the rest. He easily broke a way through its wall for the horse, returned and led the animal in, barricaded the opening with debris from the other huts, and made himself as comfortable as he could by means of the cloak and horsecloths rolled up before and behind the saddle. Then, being by this time dead beat, he soon fell asleep.

Just as dawn was breaking, he was startled from his heaviness by the loud snorting of his horse. Springing up on his elbow, he saw in the wan light the animal, its ears thrown back, its eyes protruding, tugging at the reins by which Bob had secured it to one of the beams supporting the roof. It was panting, trembling, frantic with fear. Wide awake in an instant, Bob reached for the case containing his rifle, which he had worn slung over his shoulder and removed on lying down. Even as he did so the faint light filtering through the loosely-barricaded doorway was obscured. There was a thump and the crash of falling woodwork, and a heavy body, in the suddenness of its onset looking even larger than it was, sprang between him and the horse. A shrill scream of fright, followed instantly by a dull thud, then a deep growl, and Bob, though he had never heard it before, was in no doubt what the sound implied: it was the warning growl of a tiger after a kill. Stretched upon the inanimate horse, he saw in the uncertain light a huge tawny form. Its back was towards him; its tail was lashing the ground within a few feet of where he had lain; in a moment it must scent him. To gain the door, even had there been any prospect of safety in flight, he would have to pass immediately behind the brute, which at the sound would turn in far less time than he would take to rush past. The beast was still growling and lashing the floor. Bob remained still as death, in the reclining posture in which the tiger's entrance had surprised him. In a flash he saw that his only chance lay in one shot so well aimed as to kill or maim the brute; if he missed, nothing could save him; yet the slightest click or rustle would not escape its sensitive ears. Even as he raised the rifle to his shoulder with all his care, the tiger heard the movement and half-turned its head. But its head was still too much covered by the length of its body for Bob to risk a shot at its brain, and he knew that in the sudden volte-face that was now bound to come the movement would be so rapid that he might very easily miss. Instantly leaning forward, he brought the muzzle of the rifle within a foot of the animal's body at the region of the heart, and fired. There was a scream of rage, a convulsive twist of the huge body, a leap, and Bob was on the floor, beneath the tiger, unconscious.

Chapter X
The One-Eared Man

Mr. Helping-to-decide on Tour—Watched—The Tragedy of the Topknot—A Vampire—Mr. Helping-to-decide at Home—An Unholy Alliance—Cross-Examined

"How do you do, sir? I trust you enjoy excellent health and spirits."

These were the first words Bob heard when he came to himself. He was surrounded by a group of Korean soldiers, about whom there was nothing martial but the blood-red band in their hats. In the centre, just alighted from a palanquin, was a Korean in long white cloak and a hat like an inverted flower-pot; he was bowing and smiling with a mingled expression of amiability and concern. Bob recognized him in a moment; it was Mr. Helping-to-decide.

"Thank you, I'm rather shaky," said Bob looking round. "What has become of that brute?"

"Outside, sir. You stop horses; you stop tigers too. You kill him stone dead, sir."

"Did I really? The last I remember is an uneasy idea that the tiger was going to kill me. D'you mind giving me your hand. I feel rather giddy and battered."

With Mr. Helping-to-decide's eager assistance he rose to his feet and staggered out of the hut. There lay the tiger, a fine animal nearly twelve feet long. Beside it was the horse, whose skull had been broken by a single blow from the tiger's massive paw.

"I wonder I escaped," said Bob.

"A good, a famous shot, sir," said the Korean; "but you have a scratch, an abrasion, on your nob just where your hair begins."

"Have I? I am lucky it is no worse. But how is it I have the pleasure of seeing you here, sir?"

Then Mr. Helping-to-decide explained that he was on the way to his country house some fifteen miles distant. He had been sent by his government to watch the Russians at Seng-cheng, and had gone into the town with the full determination to let nothing escape his attention. But the Russians objected to being watched. They peremptorily ordered him out of their lines, and compelled him to disband his troops, allowing him to retain only the small escort which Bob saw with him. He was following his wife and family, who had preceded him along the road, when the sound of a shot had arrested his progress, and on searching he had found the tiger in the throes of death, and underneath it the inanimate form of the man to whom he owed eternal gratitude. If only he had been a little earlier he might have killed the tiger before it made its spring, and so have saved his honourable benefactor the bruises he was sure he bore on his body and the cut he saw on his head. Still, he hoped that he might some day have an opportunity of doing something in return for the Englishman's condescending kindness.

It was now several years since Mr. Helping-to-decide had eaten his dinners at Lincoln's Inn, but he spoke with extreme volubility, and was seldom at a loss for a word. Law lecturers, London landladies, leader-writers and cabmen had all assisted to form his style.

"Many thanks," said Bob. "Really you are too kind. I am very glad to have met you, as, knowing the country, you may be able to assist me to escape."

"Certainly, sir, with the greatest pleasure. If you will come with me, no wild beasts will dare to molest you."

"I wasn't thinking of wild beasts," said Bob with a smile. "I was thinking of Russians. The Cossacks are after me."

An instantaneous change took place in the expression of Mr. Helping-to-decide's features. He glanced round with a quick movement like that of a startled hare, and peered among the trees as though expecting to find a Cossack behind every one of them.

"I don't think they are here just now," added Bob, repressing a smile. He proceeded to give an account of the circumstances that had brought him to that spot, the Korean listening with gathering apprehension.

"This is a most astounding fix," he said. "The Russians are very hostile, very unkind. They are on all sides" (he made a wide sweep with his arm); "they will find you, and then, hon'ble sir, what in the name of goodness will you do? You are more than a match for a horse, you have considerable facility with tigers, but with a Russian—ah! that is ultra vires. Why, would you believe it?—they treat me, who help to decide in the War Department of his Imperial Majesty—they treat even me as if I were a dog! It is a jolly astounding fix!"

The little man looked so sincerely perturbed that Bob made an effort to keep a grave face.

"It is very kind of you," he said, "to feel so much anxiety on my account. After a short rest I shall be well enough to push on. I shall have to do so on foot, unless one of your men will sell me his horse. I could give him a bill on Yokohama."

"On no account whatever, hon'ble sir. I am still head over ears in your debt. Do I not owe to you preservation of my better half? Yes, by gum! Now, sir, if you will do me the honour to ride in my insignificant conveyance, I will have you transported to my humble roof, where the weary are at rest, and we can there enjoy sweet converse about via media in these awkward circs."

Bob did not much relish the idea of proceeding over the roads cooped up in the narrow space of a palanquin carried by coolies, but the Korean's anxiety that he should keep out of sight was so evident that he decided to accept the offer. He returned to the hut to fetch the Cossack's cap, cloak, and rifle, and his own glass, but when he reappeared with them, Mr. Helping-to-decide again looked startled and begged him to leave them behind. Bob yielded, except as to the glass. A Korean cap was found among the official's belongings, and with this perched on his head Bob crept into the palanquin, prepared to endure an uncomfortable journey.

Just as the party was about to move off, one of the escort approached Mr. Helping-to-decide, and, first humbly kow-towing, said something in a tone of supplication. The functionary explained. The men would like the horse; would he allow them to cut up the animal? Bob declared that he had no objection whatever; whereupon Mr. Helping-to-decide told the men that they might have the horse if they first skinned the tiger. A dozen men at once set to work, and in half an hour the double operation was performed; the dismembered horse was distributed among the escort, the tiger's skin was entrusted to the head coolie, and after this long delay the party resumed their northward journey.

As they left the group of huts, no one noticed two Chinamen crouching in a ruined cabin, within a few feet of Bob and Mr. Helping-to-decide. They had seen and heard all that passed since the arrival of the Koreans. When the party had finally departed, the Chinamen left their place of concealment, struck through the trees in a north-westerly direction, and presently reappearing on their little ponies, made off towards the Ping-yang road.

Mr. Helping-to-decide rode by the side of the palanquin, the top of which was lifted up, and showed himself anxious to keep up his guest's spirits by a never-ceasing flow of conversation, to which Bob listened with a fearful joy. He explained that the Koreans were deeply interested in the result of the war, for it appeared inevitable that the country must come under the dominating influence either of Russia or of Japan. They would rather have neither, but if it must be one or the other, they preferred Japan to Russia. But there was one particular grudge they had against Japan. It was due to Japanese influence that the Emperor of Korea, some years before, had decreed the abolition of the topknot and plunged the whole nation into despair.

"Dear me!" said Bob. "I should have thought it the other way about. The cultivation of the topknot must give you a good deal of trouble."

"Ah! You are a barbarian—excuse me, a foreigner; you do not understand. How should you? In your country what do they do to a man when he is grown up and becomes married?"

"I don't know that they do anything—except send in tax-papers, and that sort of thing."

"Well, in my country we wear cranial ornament—topknot to wit. In Korea the topknot is a sine qua non; without it a Korean has no locus standi: he is a vulgar fraction—of no importance. Let me inform you, hon'ble sir, a gray-beard, though of respectable antiquity, if minus a topknot, is to all intents and purposes a baby-in-arms. That is our Korean custom. Now, hon'ble sir, can you imagine our unutterable consternation, perturbation of spirit, nervous prostration, when an Imperial decree issues—every conjugal Korean's topknot shall be abbreviated, cut off instanter! There is dire tribulation, sore perplexity. All Korea plumps into the depths of despair. Besides, it is the height of absurdity. How, hon'ble sir, shall distinction henceforth be drawn between celibate irresponsible and self-respecting citizen with hostages to fortune? That is what we ask ourselves, and echo answers, how? I pause for a reply."

Bob, chuckling inwardly at Mr. Helping-to-decide's wonderful command of the English tongue, looked sympathetic, and said:

"It was very awkward certainly. But what happened?"

"At promulgation of decree I was residing at my eligible country house. By gum, I think, such humiliating necessity cannot embrace the Cham-Wi—hon'ble helping-to-discuss in his Majesty's War Office. Perish the thought! But, hon'ble sir, stern duty calls me to metropolitan city. I arrive at the outer gate. Lo! I am arrested, I the Cham-Wi, by guardian of the peace—copper, who stands outside with huge shears ferociously brandished. I make myself scarce—bunk. Alas! vain hope: a brawny arm seizes me from behind; one, two, the deed is done; my topknot—where is it? It is beyond recall. I am dishonoured. Behold me on my beam ends!"

The recollection moved Mr. Helping-to-decide almost to tears. Having recovered, he went on to explain that a domestic revolution soon afterwards removed the emperor from the influence of his evil advisers. The decree was abrogated; and since then the Koreans had cultivated topknots anew, and had again become honourable men.

In spite of this bad business of the topknot, Mr. Helping-to-decide was quite emphatic in his preference of the Japanese to the Russians, and he was glad to know of the successes of the former at Port Arthur. He was able to give Bob some information about the progress they were making in Korea. Their armies now stretched in a long front of some fifty miles, and were only waiting for the break-up of the ice to press forward to the Yalu. Between their present position and Wiju there were five rivers in all, which would require to be bridged, but this would give little trouble to the Japanese engineers, who were exceedingly quick and capable. They had also exact information of the Russian dispositions. Many Japanese, disguised as Chinese or Koreans, were constantly moving in and out among the Russians, carrying their lives in their hands. Several had been caught and shot, but more had escaped detection and brought valuable information to their generals. The Russians were doubly incensed at this because they were unable to play the same game. While the Japanese were perfectly at home in the country, and were moreover very skilful in disguising themselves, no Russian could easily pass for a Chinaman or a Korean, for even if his physique were not against him, his ignorance of the languages would prove a serious drawback.

"That makes me wonder what I am to do," said Bob. "I want to reach the Japanese lines, and the disadvantages of the Russian are disadvantages in my case also."

"You must come to my house; we will disguise you,—make you look quite the lady. Then you can ride in a palanquin to the south, and I will send trusty men to guide you and bring you o.k. to the Japanese."

Bob was not enamoured of the suggestion, and hoped that some other means would offer. Meanwhile, having no alternative to suggest, he said nothing.

Twelve miles of the journey had been accomplished, at a terribly slow pace, and three more remained to be covered, when an old and weather-beaten Korean riding a pony appeared rounding the shoulder of a hill not far ahead. He quickened his pace when he saw the cavalcade, and on meeting Mr. Helping-to-decide entered into grave conversation with him. Bob, watching the functionary's face, saw its expression become more and more agitated and alarmed. He came at length to the palanquin, and explained that the rider was the sergeant in charge of the village they were approaching, and had come to report that during the past few days a notorious Manchu brigand, in Russian pay, had been raiding within ten miles of the village under pretence of reconnoitring. He was a man whom the people had long had reason to dread. During the war in 1894 he had committed terrible atrocities in Northern Korea, and had since infested the upper reaches of the Yalu with a band of desperadoes, terrorizing a district several hundred square miles in extent. His head-quarters were supposed to be in a mountain fastness some distance beyond the Yalu. Before the outbreak of the present war the Russians had more than once attempted to extirpate his gang, but he had always proved too clever for them. They had now come to terms with him, and were utilizing his great knowledge of the country and his undoubted genius for leadership. He was a most accomplished linguist, speaking every dialect of the Korean-Manchurian borderland, besides having a good knowledge of Japanese, a smattering of Russian, and a certain command of pidgin English. In his early youth he had been a trader on the Chinese coast, but it having been discovered that he was in league with pirates, he had suddenly disappeared, being next heard of as ringleader of his desperate band of brigands. He was utterly unscrupulous, and the fact that he was now acting with the Russians only increased the gravity of the news that he was in the neighbourhood of Mr. Helping-to-decide's home.

The Korean was much depressed during the remainder of the journey, and spoke but little. He cheered up, however, when the village at length came in sight. It was evening; only women were to be seen in the street, for it is the Korean custom for the men to remain indoors after nightfall, and leave the streets free for their women folk. Mr. Helping-to-decide rode through the village till he came to the only house of stones and tiles which it contained, where, dismounting, he politely invited the honourable sir to deign to enter his contemptible abode. Bob was very glad to stretch his limbs after many hours in the palanquin, and, slipping off his boots at the door, found himself for the first time an inmate of a Korean house of the better sort.

He could not help comparing it unfavourably with the Japanese interior he had found so pleasant at Nikko. There was a striking lack of the simple grace of Kobo's house. The room to which his host led him was small and bare. The tiled roof was supported on a thick beam running the whole length of the house. In place of the spotless mats of Kobo's rooms there was a dirty leopard-skin and an expanse of yellowish oil-paper covering the whole floor. The walls were of mud and plaster, with sliding lattices covered with tissue-paper that also appeared to have been well oiled. One or two jars and a lacquer box completed the furniture.

He saw nothing of Mrs. Helping-to-decide. The evening meal was shared by himself and his host alone. The food brought in by the female servants was sufficient for a much larger company. It consisted first of all of some questionable sweetmeats; these were followed by raw fish, underdone pork chops, rice in various forms, radishes of gigantic size, and fruit, including dried apples and very tough and indigestible persimmons. Bob knew that he would be regarded as impolite if he refused to partake of all these dishes. He did his best, but found it difficult to swallow anything but the rice, in the cooking of which the Korean excels. His poor trencher-work was, however, put to shame by Mr. Helping-to-decide himself, who disposed of course after course with a gusto which would have amazed his visitor had he not heard extraordinary stories of the capacity of the Koreans in this respect. When the meal was over, Bob was not surprised to see his host fall asleep, and being thus left to his own resources, he rolled himself up in his cloak and a silk coverlet provided by one of the maids, and made himself as comfortable as possible on the floor.

He passed a most uneasy night. He had not been long asleep when he half woke with the feeling that his right side was scorching. He turned over sleepily, only to find by and by that the left side was even hotter than the right had been. Whatever position he chose, he could not escape this totally unnecessary heat, which, combined with the unpleasant odour from the oiled-paper carpet, made him wish he could go back to the cold ruined hut in which he had spent the previous night. The explanation was, that beneath the floor was a cellar in which a fire had been lit, and the coolie had piled on enough fuel to last through the night. This was a simple means of heating the house, but Bob could not help wondering whether a refrigerator would not perhaps form a more satisfactory bed-chamber than an oven.

He was glad when morning came, and Mr. Helping-to-decide, awaking from his heavy sleep, had sufficiently regained his senses to discuss ways and means. It soon appeared that the trusty Korean servant who was to have assisted Bob towards the Japanese lines was absent, having gone to keep a watch on the Manchu brigands. Mr. Helping-to-decide accordingly proposed that Bob should remain with him until the man returned, and impressed upon him the advisability of keeping within doors in order not to attract attention. Bob was by no means pleased at the prospect of spending even one day within these close walls, but seeing no help for it he submitted with a good grace.

It was a dreary time. During the morning he was left to himself, and to while away the hours he found nothing better to do than to look out, through a slit in one of the tissued lattices, at what went on in the street. But after the mid-day meal, Mr. Helping-to-decide proposed a game of "go", which Bob knew from previous experience might be spun out to any length. They were in the midst of the game, when there was a great shouting and hurry-scurry in the street; then the clatter of galloping horses. Mr. Helping-to-decide sprang up in agitation, and Bob, going to his slit, saw a troop of Cossacks headed by a tall Manchu galloping up the street, followed by a band of riders, whom from their features and habiliments he concluded to be Manchu bandits. Mr. Helping-to-decide stood in quivering helplessness. The horsemen reined up before his house; some of them went round it in both directions, and the terrified owner turned his white face to Bob and groaned.

When the house was surrounded, the commander of the Cossacks shouted something which neither Bob nor the Korean understood. But the cry was immediately repeated in the vernacular by the tall Manchu; he had dismounted and was approaching the house with the apparent intention of forcing an entrance through the sliding lattice.

"What does he say?" asked Bob.

"He says, hon'ble sir, 'Bring out the spy'," faltered Mr. Helping-to-decide. "This is indeed a critical moment. I am at a loss—flabbergasted. I am driven to conclusion it is all u.p."

The Manchu had now come to the wall of the house, and bellowed what was evidently a threatening message.

"'If the spy is not brought out instanter,'" translated Mr. Helping-to-decide, "'"he will conflagrate this residence and adjacent village, with incidental murder of inhabitants.'"

Mr. Helping-to-decide wrung his hands in impotent despair.

"I shall give myself up," said Bob.

His host's agitation at once gave place to polite admiration and a show of confidence at which Bob almost laughed. He recognized that it was no laughing matter. The ruined state of the hamlet in which he had met the tiger was clear evidence that the invader's threat was no empty one, and the tales he had heard of the Cossacks' brutality did not promise a pleasant experience to any prisoner who fell into their power. But Bob felt that he had no alternative. There was just a hope that as a British subject he would come off with a whole skin, but in any case it was impossible to let the whole village suffer through any weakness of his. He therefore pulled aside the lattice, stepped out, and with a bold bearing that ill-matched his inward quaking, delivered himself up to the enemy.

The Cossack captain sat his horse side by side with the Manchu a few paces in advance of his troop. As Bob approached, amid perfect silence, he noticed that the Manchu leant quickly forward and peered at him with an interest greater than the circumstances seemed to warrant. Something in the man's face was familiar to Bob, who, as the Manchu turned half round to speak to the Russian officer, saw that he had only one ear. He remembered him clearly now. He was the man who had been saved from drowning by the *Sardinia*,—the man from whom Bob himself had saved Kobo's half-throttled servant Taru in the Ueno Park. It was Kobo's old enemy, the Manchu Tartar, Chang-Wo. The discovery did not tend to reassure Bob, but for all his tremors at the dangerous possibilities of the situation, he knew that his only chance was to maintain an air of utter fearlessness, and no one could have guessed from his undaunted attitude that he felt he was in a very tight place.

The Cossack captain looked hard at him for a moment, then gruffly addressed him, presumably in Russian.

Bob shook his head, saying, in the best French he could command, that he was sorry he was not familiar with the Russian tongue. To his surprise, the Cossack did not understand him. Bob had believed that every educated Russian knew French, and such ignorance seemed to prove this officer a boor.

"So much the worse for me," thought Bob.

The Cossack said a few words to the Manchu, who bent over and began a catechism in pidgin English, interpreting each answer as he received it to the Russian. Bob was surprised: on board the *Sardinia* the man had professed to know no English. He had some difficulty at first in understanding the strange idiom, but the general purport of Chang-Wo's questions was clear.

"What-side belongey?"

"I am a British subject."

"What you pidgin?"

"I am in the Japanese service."

"What-for you Japan-side?"

Bob hesitated. It was not likely that the Manchu would know what a range-finder was. He made an attempt to explain, but the circumlocutions he had to use aroused the Manchu's suspicion, and he interrupted impatiently:

"What you hab catchee in Korea?"

"I was left behind."

"What pidgin makee you hab got behind-side?"

"It was my bad luck—an accident."

"What-tim' you hab catchee accident?"

"Three days ago."

"What-side?"

"Near Yongampo."

"Supposey you tellum allo 'bout it?"

"Well, I got mixed up in a fight between Cossacks and Japanese, and I was bowled over."

"Bowled over! What that say?"

"Hit, tumbled on the ground: savvy?"

"How hab got wailo?"

"On a horse."

"How horso belongey you?"

"Caught it."

"What-side horso this-tim'?"

"Dead."

"You come this-side sampan?"

"In a ship."

"What callum ship?'

"That I can't tell you."

"No savvy?"

"Oh yes, I know; but I can't say."

"What-for no tellum?"

"Because I'm in the Japanese service."

"What namee Japanese that-tim' Yongampo?"

"What do you mean?"

"Japanese belongey you come Yongampo. He namee—what?"

"I can't tell you that."

"What-for no tellum?"

"For the same reason as before."

"Muss tellum—velly soon."

"Very sorry; it's quite impossible."

"You belongey too muchee sassy. You no tellum, my hab got whip."

Bob gave him a look, but said nothing. The Manchu raised his whip and dealt him a sharp blow with the stock, which struck his shoulder, only escaping his head because he swerved suddenly aside as he saw it coming. The next moment the Manchu lay sprawling on the ground. Bob had sprung at him and hit him so heavily and unexpectedly beneath the jaw that he lost his balance and fell backwards over his horse's haunches. He picked himself up, and drawing his sword rushed at Bob, who stood with flaming eyes and clenched fists ready to defend himself. But the Cossack officer moved his horse a pace or two forward and interposed. He spoke a few rapid words to the Manchu, saying in effect that the prisoner was too valuable to be killed in a fit of temper; information could no doubt be got out of him in course of time; and meanwhile he should have a foretaste of the discipline awaiting him.

The Manchu gave way with a sullen scowl, and remounted his horse. Then the captain gave an order; a trooper dismounted, and came towards Bob with a narrow leather thong in his hand. Bob instantly guessed what was to be done, and seeing the utter vanity of resistance, he submitted quietly, while the thong was firmly bound about his right wrist and then knotted to the near stirrup of the captain's horse. Another order was then given; the whole troop set off at a trot down the deserted street, and as Bob was dragged by the side of the horse, the last object he remembered seeing was the pale, terror-stricken face of Mr. Helping-to-decide peeping through the broken lattice of his house.

Chapter XI
Tried and Sentenced

Under Escort—A Court-Martial—Leading Questions—The Bear's Claw

Bob's sensations were by no means agreeable as he kept pace perforce with the Cossack's horse. The trot, fortunately, soon slackened to a quick amble, or he must soon have been utterly exhausted. In spite of the cold, the exertion of walking fast, heavily clothed as he was, made him uncomfortably hot, and his physical temperature was matched by his mental condition. He was in a rage; not at being made a prisoner: that was only to have been expected: but at being tied up like a dog, reminding him of the curs he had seen chained to bakers' carts in French villages. Anger, however, was a mere waste of energy, as he soon saw; at present he could only make the best of a bad case,—keep up his courage and his pace without reminders from the evil-looking knout he saw ready to the Cossack's hand.

As he trudged along, two reflections were uppermost in his mind. One was that, having been captured and treated with indignity, he was justified in regarding himself now as a combatant; this gave him a little consolation. The other was, that in Chang-Wo, the Manchu, he had an enemy of a particularly dangerous kind. He remembered Kobo's story of him; and the knowledge that this same man was doing desperate work for the Russians in Korea was not reassuring. The Manchu had evidently recognized him as the stranger who had saved the little Japanese from his vengeance in the Ueno Park, and clearly bore him no good-will on that account.

The road was a difficult one, leading over the rugged hills. Darkness fell, and still the troop pushed on. At length, when Bob felt on the point of collapsing, they rode into a town or village of fair size, which, as he afterwards learnt, was Yong-cheng, on the Pekin high-road. He expected that now at least he would be allowed rest and food, but as soon as the Cossacks arrived at the place they took him before a Russian officer of some rank, apparently a lieutenant-colonel. When preliminary explanations had been given, the colonel ordered the prisoner to stand before him, and in peremptory tones began to question him in French. Bob's French was not very fluent, but he answered as well as he could, repeating the replies he had previously given. He refused to say who had been in his company before he made off on the Cossack's horse, and assured the Russian that he knew absolutely nothing of any communications that may have passed between this person and spies on shore. His persistence made the officer more and more angry, until at last the latter shouted:

"You're a liar! Tell me the truth, or I'll hang you on the spot."

"I have already told you the truth," said Bob quietly. "I don't know whom my friend may have met at Yongampo, and if I did, I could not tell you—surely you must see that?"

"You're an insolent puppy. A means will be found to loosen your tongue. I'll give you a night to come to your senses.—Take him away."

Bob, almost fainting with fatigue and hunger, was led away to a close and dirty hovel, where he was given a hunk of coarse bread and a fat sausage to eat, and there he remained in the custody of two Cossacks through the night. At sunrise, feeling stiff and dispirited, he was again taken before the officer, and again put through an interrogatory, a trooper standing at his elbow holding a knout ostentatiously in his view. But the colonel was again baffled; he received no more information than before; and at length, with a curse of impatience, he roared an order to his men. Bob expected the knout to be immediately applied to his back, but to his surprise he was led out into the open, and after a period of suspense he was ordered to mount a horse that was brought up. A few minutes later he was riding out of the village, a Cossack with cocked pistol on each side of him, and the Manchu in the rear.

The explanation of this change in his destiny was that the Russian colonel had not given up hope of obtaining information, and was sending him to General Sassulitch at Wiju, where perhaps he would be brought to reason. The Cossacks were ordered to guard him carefully, but not to ill-use him, and Bob was somewhat surprised, after what he had heard of the brutality of these reckless soldiers, to find that he was treated with some consideration. The whole of that day was occupied in the journey to Wiju. The country was hilly and rugged, and Bob realized, from the slow rate of progress of himself and his escort, that the transport of a whole army would take much time, especially in this winter weather.

At various points along the road parties of Russian soldiers were met with, but it was not until the three riders came within a few miles of Wiju that Bob had striking evidence of the Russian occupation. To the south of that frontier town large gangs of coolies were at work throwing up entrenchments under the direction of Russian officers. Bob was led close to a numerous party near the high-road, employed in excavating a shelter trench. Their sullen looks and reluctant movements indicated that they were forced labourers, and in the hands of several of the Russians Bob noticed ominous-looking whips. He was not surprised, for if they trusted to the efficacy of the knout in their own army and navy, it was unlikely that they would spare it in the case of Korean peasants.

Like almost all Korean towns, Wiju stands on a hill; on one side it overlooks a plain, on the other the river Yalu. Bob was glad enough when, entering its walls and passing up the long straggling street, filled with Russian soldiers, he was halted and dismounted at a house over which a flag was flying. He was prepared by this time for the worst. Several times on the way explanations on his account had passed between his escort and enquiring soldiers, and he inferred from their smiles and gestures that he must look for short shrift. He expected now to be placed on trial as a spy, or perhaps summarily disposed of without trial, probably after another attempt to extort information from him. But after an hour's detention in the house, during which he was given a scanty allowance of food, he saw the Manchu Chang-Wo enter and deliver a message to the officer in charge. He was immediately ordered out and made to remount; his weary journey was evidently not yet ended. His Cossack escort grunted their displeasure, and scowled at him with dark looks, while the Manchu, who again accompanied them, urged them to hasten their pace and complete their unwelcome task.

They rode smartly down the hill. Presently Bob saw in the dark the waters of what was no doubt the Yalu before him, banked by rugged bluffs on the other side. This, then, was the famous boundary river dividing Korea from Manchuria. On the Korean side the channel was still frozen over; but the current was deeper and swifter under the Manchurian bank, where it was hemmed in by a large island occupying a considerable part of what must be in time of flood the bed of the river. In this part of the river large blocks of ice were floating down with the stream. Bob had forborne to put any questions to the Manchu; he would have liked to ask now what was to be done with him, but on second thoughts he decided still to hold his tongue. But in the course of the long wearisome ride he distinguished the name Sassulitch more than once in a grumbling conversation between his escort and the Manchu, though he was not then aware that the owner of the name was a general of division.

It was late at night when they at length reached Antung, a low-lying town on the river-side; dark as it was, Bob could see that the place was substantially built. He was taken to a large go-down which had been transformed into a barracks, and locked up in a room by himself. He was very tired, and threw himself wearily down on the straw mattress spread on the floor, hoping that for a few hours at least he would not be interfered with. But he had barely fallen asleep when he was roused by a heavy touch upon his arm. Sitting up, he saw an armed Cossack holding a lighted taper. The man motioned to him to get up, and feeling more dead than alive he followed his guide out of the room, where he was joined by a squad with fixed bayonets, then through the streets, until he arrived at a large house more freely illuminated than any other, and guarded by a sentry. In a few moments he found himself in a lofty room, standing before a table on the other side of which sat a number of Russian officers. On the table were placed a few flaring tallow candles set in clumsy candlesticks, and a couple of circular oil-lamps resembling those of English railway-carriages. At each end stood a Russian foot-soldier with fixed bayonet. In conversation with one of the officers Bob saw the big Manchu, the one-eared Chang-Wo.

For some moments he stood there, the object of keen scrutiny to the officers, who stared at him with various degrees of curiosity, and with varying expressions on their faces. Then the officer who was evidently of the highest rank among them,—it was General Sassulitch himself,—motioned the Manchu aside and said a few words in Russian to the younger officer at his right. The latter at once addressed Bob, speaking in excellent English, with but faint foreign accent.

"Prisoner, you are charged with being a Japanese spy. You are English by nationality, it appears; what have you to say to the charge?"

"I am an Englishman, it is true, sir," replied Bob. "As to the rest, I am certainly not a spy."

"You had better give an account of yourself."

"My name is Robert Fawcett, and I am an engineer. I was sent out a few months ago by my firm, at the request of the Japanese government, to be at hand in case the range-finders on their ships required attention. The vessel on which I was happened to come to the mouth of the Yalu, and I had just landed when I was unlucky enough to be knocked over by a Cossack's horse, and when I recovered I thought the simplest way out of the difficulty was to make my escape on the animal; its master was dead. The horse was killed by a tiger. Since then I have been wandering about until I gave myself up to a troop of your men. I have nothing more to say."

This reply was interpreted to the other officers, whose manner of receiving it betokened for the most part blank incredulity. A few words were exchanged among them, then the interpreter spoke again.

"You shot the Cossack whose horse you stole?"

"No."

"Who did?"

"I don't know. He was shot from the boat."

"You were armed?"

"No; I had nothing but my field-glass."

"You are not a soldier?"

"No; I am an engineer."

"A naval engineer?"

"Not specially. I've no naval experience except what I have picked up."

"In what ships have you been?"

Bob hesitated for a moment. Then he reflected that there could be no possible harm in mentioning the names of the vessels in which he had served.

"In the *Mikasa* and *Hatsuse*."

"But neither of these brought you to Yongampo."

"No."

"What was the name of the vessel that did?"

Bob again hesitated. The *Kasumi* was engaged in secret service. It was impossible for him to know what might be the ultimate effect of betraying her identity. In so doing he would in any case associate her commander with the expedition to Yongampo. He made his decision.

"That, if you don't mind, I'd rather not say."

When this was explained to the officers they began to talk with some excitement, and one of them thumped the table. The interpreter continued:

"The general insists on knowing the name of the vessel."

"I am sorry, sir, but I can't tell you that."

"You know the consequence of refusing?"

"I'm not sure that I do," said Bob with a faint smile; "but in any case I can't tell."

A short consultation took place at the table, then the officer resumed his questioning.

"You had just landed from the boat, you say. Had you not been to Yongampo?"

"No."

"Who had?"

"I cannot say."

"Why did you land?"

"To help a friend of mine who was hard pressed by the Cossacks."

"Had he been to Yongampo?"

"I cannot say."

"Who was he?"

"I really cannot tell you any more about him."

"Whom had he been to see?"

"I do not know."

"Was he also an Englishman?"

"I really cannot answer that question."

"Do you speak Japanese?"

"No."

"Chinese?"

"No."

"What language did you speak in Yongampo?"

"I have never been in Yongampo."

"How long have you been in the country?"

"In Manchuria?"

"Don't prevaricate. How long have you been in these parts—Manchuria or Korea?"

"A few days."

"How came you to be on friendly terms with the native in whose house you were captured?"

"Excuse me, I gave myself up. As to your question, I happened to do a little service, quite accidentally, to the Korean gentleman, and he was more grateful than the circumstances really called for."

"When did you do him this service?"

"A week or two ago."

"Where?"

"In Seoul."

"What were you doing in Seoul?"

"Nothing—merely visiting the place."

Bob felt as soon as he had spoken that this, the literal truth, would certainly be scouted by his judges as wildly improbable. For some time, indeed, the officers had been showing signs of impatience. Worn out as he was, Bob held himself erect before them; he had replied to all his interrogator's questions in the same self-possessed and courteous manner; and while one or two of the Russians seemed impressed by his bearing, the majority were growing more and more angry as they saw how barren was the examination. They now formed a group about General Sassulitch, and discussed the matter in excited tones. Then the Manchu was called up and questioned, and from his gestures Bob guessed that he was making very positive assertions. The discussion continued for some time; then the Manchu was again dismissed, the group separated, and the young officer standing beside General Sassulitch said:

"Prisoner, the officers of His Majesty the Tsar here assembled cannot accept your denials. You were found within our lines; you were undoubtedly associated with a Japanese who landed from some vessel to enter into communications with a spy in Yongampo; we have a witness here who declares that he saw you in Tokio, then in Seoul, and recently in Yongampo—"

"Pardon my interrupting, sir, but that is false."

"Denial is useless. Our evidence is positive. By your own confession you were concerned in the serious loss inflicted upon a troop of Cossacks during the pursuit of the fugitive, who in all probability was yourself; you confess to have made your escape on the horse of a Cossack killed at that time; and you were captured at the house of a Korean who is suspected on good grounds of sympathy with the Japanese. There is no doubt in the mind of the court that you are a spy; your claim to British citizenship cannot be accepted as any palliation of your crime; the court condemns you to the penalty of a spy: you will be shot."

Bob flushed slightly. There was a silence, then at a sign from the officer the two soldiers at the end of the room approached him. He gave a quick glance along the table; noticed one officer leaning forward on his arms, his handsome face wearing a quizzical smile; another lolling back in his chair with an air of boredom; a third rolling a cigarette as though the matter were of complete indifference to him; the general, stern and inscrutable, in the midst. Then, between his two guards with fixed bayonets, he was marched to his prison.

It was a longer walk this time. He was not taken back to the go-down where he had expected to pass the night, but to a tower or keep built on the wall by the riverbank. It was now too dark to see anything clearly; but as he was led into the building one of his guards struck a light, and as he mounted the narrow stairway to the fourth story he noticed several padlocked doors, showing that here were other prisoners besides himself. He was taken into a small room at the top of the building, a thick rug was thrown in after him, the door was slammed, bolted, and padlocked, and he was left to his meditations.

Chapter XII
At Midnight

Waiting—A Russian Offer—A Farewell Letter—What the Case Held—
Kite-flying Extraordinary—Prison-breaking—Free

Bob was so exhausted that he fell asleep at once, notwithstanding the gravity of his position. When he awoke some hours after daylight, he found some black bread and a plate of preserved beef and a jug of vodka by his side.

"To keep up my courage," he said to himself. He was hungry, and the bread and meat soon disappeared; but he found the vodka too fiery for his palate, and wondered if he would be allowed some water. He was to be shot, of course; when would that be? Shot! For the first time the reality of last night's scene forced itself on his mind. He had been so tired, and so strung-up in the determination to say nothing that would betray Yamaguchi, that the matter as it affected himself had not troubled him. But now—the thought of death struck him for the first time. It was a strange idea. He was well and strong; rather stiff and cramped, indeed, but that could easily be cured. Yet in a short time he was to be dead. He could not realize it; on board the Japanese vessels, in the poisonous box-battery on the *Mikasa*, on the *Kasumi's* shot-pelted deck, the idea of death had never been present to his mind. The oddness of it struck him most of all. It seemed absurd that he should die, and for what reason? His explanations had been too simple to be believed! He thought over the past days; there was nothing in his actions he could have altered, even if he had known that death was to come so soon. "Well, it can't be helped," he concluded. "I only hope I sha'n't funk it at the end."

Life was so vigorous in him at present, that he looked round his narrow room in an instinctive quest for some means of escape. It was about twelve feet square. The outer wall was of stone, some eighteen inches thick, pierced by a single unglazed splay window, narrowing from twenty inches broad on the inside to seven on the outside. The bottom of the window was about three feet above the floor, and it extended upwards for about an equal distance. Below it, embedded in the wall, projected a narrow platform about a foot high, which, Bob guessed, was intended to accommodate a watchman or possibly a marksman, for the tower had evidently been built as a watch-tower. Clambering up into the window-recess, Bob looked through the open slit, and saw that it commanded a view across the river, which flowed past at a depth of some eighty feet. The water-course was obstructed by ice; to plunge into it was impossible.

Returning to the floor, Bob noticed that the inner walls were of brick, comparatively new in contrast with the mouldering stonework of the outer wall. He concluded that at one time the whole story had formed a single chamber, and that it had been partitioned off recently, though in all probability before the advent of the Russians. The door was of massive make, and hung on ponderous iron clamps; it opened inwards, and there was no keyhole on the inner side.

"Things look black," thought Bob, as he convinced himself that there was no means of escaping from his dungeon. He tramped up and down with bent head, idly speculating on the scenes the old tower must have witnessed. How often in bygone days, he wondered, had Chinese, Korean, or Japanese flotillas passed under its walls up and down the Yalu? What romances might be woven about the spot, going back into ages long anterior to ironclads and machine-guns! He wished he knew something of the history of these far Eastern countries, and was resolving to look it up on the first opportunity when he suddenly remembered that he was to die, and the remembrance brought him to a stand-still and gave his imagination pause.

Looking again through the narrow opening, he saw in the distance a troop of Cossacks picking their way across the hills. He watched them with idle interest as they gained the summit and disappeared at a trot over the crest. He followed them in fancy; they were soldiers going perhaps to their death; and he wished that he too might meet with death in some active, heroic way, instead of tamely as the target of a firing-party. He was drawn from his reverie by the entrance of a soldier with a plate and jug. The man set the food down on the stone platform and left without a word.

Alternately pacing the room, sitting on the platform, or listlessly looking out upon the river, Bob passed the rest of the day. He saw no ray of hope. The room was bare; it contained nothing but his rug; everything had been taken from him; he had not even a penknife with which to while away the hours, as many a prisoner had done before him, in scratching initials or diagrams upon the walls.

"I wish they'd hurry up," he said to himself restlessly.

But the long day passed, and he was not summoned to his doom. At night he was given another meal. He was standing when it was brought him, and he moved towards the open door, without any hope of escaping. Outside, by the dim light of the lamp carried by the man inside, he saw another soldier armed with a rifle. The way was effectually guarded. He spoke to the man, asking when his execution was to take place. The man shook his head, evidently understanding not a word. The door was shut, bolted, and padlocked, and he was again left alone with his thoughts.

Next morning the soldier who brought him his food was accompanied by the officer who had acted as interpreter at his summary trial two nights before.

"Is my time up?" asked Bob almost eagerly.

"Not yet. The general will allow you another chance. Tell me what you know of the Japanese spies in Yongampo and of the Japanese with whom you landed, and the general will spare your life and keep you as a prisoner of war until peace is signed in Tokio."

Bob looked at the officer in silence.

"Come, why be obstinate? It isn't much to ask of you, and if you're an Englishman and a non-combatant the Japanese are nothing to you."

"You think I'll adopt that plea?" said Bob, with a touch of scorn. "No thank you. You've treated me as a combatant; very well, I've told you all I mean to tell you."

"You'll think better of it by and by. You've a day to think it over."

"I've thought it over."

"Well, think it over again. You'll come round, never fear."

The officer smiled as he went out. Bob spent the rest of the day in tramping his cell, which was very cold, looking out of the window, and wishing that they would not prolong his suspense. He expected to receive another visit from the officer before night, but saw no more of him until breakfast-time next morning.

"Well," said the Russian as he entered, "have you taken my advice?"

"No."

"Still obstinate! Your execution is fixed for to-morrow morning—the general gives you a long rope first, you see."

"That's a pleasant jest."

"Well, it's a pity for a young fellow like you to be so absurdly obstinate. You've only to mention a couple of names and give us a few particulars about men who can't possibly be of any interest to you, and—"

"Excuse me; I am in the Japanese service."

"Nonsense, you're an Englishman. What have you in common with the race of venomous conceited dwarfs who have dared to measure themselves against the might of an empire like ours?"

Bob stood with his hands in his pockets looking at his tempter.

"They may be all that you say, though, as far as the war has gone, it scarcely becomes a Russian to say it; but you, sir, ought to know perfectly well that, whatever they may be, it is impossible for me to betray them. I can't say any more; and I'd really be obliged to you if you'd drop the subject. Your general has decided that I'm a spy. I'm not a spy, but I can say nothing more to convince him. He has made up his mind, and so have I. You said to-morrow morning?"

The officer looked at Bob with mingled annoyance and admiration.

"What folly!" he exclaimed. "I can't but admire your constancy, but I'm sorry for you. Yes, to-morrow morning, at dawn. You needn't imagine you'll be let off, the general is determined."

"Very well."

"You can tell the man who brings you food if you change your mind."

"I will—if I do!"

The officer turned away. As he was going out at the door, Bob took a step forward, and spoke, with a little hesitation, and in a different tone.

"One moment. Could you do me a favour?"

"What is that?" asked the Russian quickly.

"Send me pencil and paper and an envelope. I have some friends at home—my father and mother—I should like—"

"I understand. You shall have the writing materials."

"And you will see that the letter is sent off?"

"Yes, yes; but it will not be necessary. Think over it." And he hurried away.

It was some time before Bob touched the food that had been brought to him. He was tired of waiting for the end. He longed for life; yet if he was to die, he wished it over and done with; the attempt to overcome his determination, the appeal to his self-interest against his honour, wearied and troubled him. For a time he tramped restlessly up and down, thinking gravely; then, catching sight of the food, on the stone slab, he reflected that he could meet his fate better fed than fasting, and he set-to with a will upon the ample supply of beef and black bread and tea, which he had asked for instead of vodka. After a while, however, he again fell into a fit of abstraction; he ate mechanically, musing on many things. Breaking one of the hard-crusted loaves, he saw a glitter like that of a golden coin buried in the bread. For a moment his curiosity overcame the gloom into which his long pondering had thrown him. He picked the bread away from the strange intruder, and discovered that what he had taken for a coin was the end of an empty cartridge-case.

"How did it get there?" he wondered, holding the case before him. He remembered how puzzled King George had been to account for the presence of the apple in the dumpling, and laughed aloud.

"No doubt about the bakery this bread came from," he thought. "Well, better a cartridge-case than a beetle."

He was seated on his rug by the wall opposite the window, where he was farthest away from the cutting wind that had been blowing in all the morning. Raising his arm, he shied the cartridge-case at the narrow opening; it struck the wall at the side of the recess, fell on the sill, and rolled down the slight inward slope on to the floor.

"Wretched bad shot!" remarked Bob to himself and the four walls. Then with a sudden start he remembered what was to happen on the morrow. He shuddered involuntarily, and dreaded the possibility of flinching when he stood actually face to face with death. Yet why should he flinch? He remembered the fearless manner with which the Japanese went open-eyed into mortal peril. He thought of Kobo's serene, unperturbed manner. Was it for him, an Englishman and a Christian, to show any more fear? The question answered itself, and he fell into a quiet reverie.

Thus passed some hours; how many he could not tell, for his watch had been removed. He was roused by the entrance of a man with writing materials. Receiving them silently, he sat and pondered. What could he say to the old folks at home? He wrote a full account of all that had happened since his last letter, then tore it up. His letter might be opened by the Russians; he must not give them any information. At last, with a full heart, he penned a few words intended for his parents' eyes alone. Then he sealed the letter, and placed it in his pocket to give to the officer at the last moment.

He felt now cramped and chilled, and, rising, began to pace the floor, walking from door to window and back from window to door. As he did so, his eye lighted on the cartridge-case. At first he merely glanced at it and passed on; then, spying it again, he looked a little longer; the third time he began to feel some curiosity and interest; the fourth time he stooped and picked it up, wondering again what strange chance had brought it into so unlikely a resting-place. To whom had it belonged? Whose rifle had fired it? How had it come into the bakery? What careless fingers had worked it into the dough? What a strange irony of fate, that a case once filled with an instrument of death, should now be choked with bread, an instrument of life!

"A bad match!" he thought. "Out with you!"

He felt for his penknife to scrape out the bread from the case, then remembered that his jailer had removed it. What was he to do? Feeling by force of habit in his waistcoat pocket, he came upon a little hole in the lining, and pushing his finger through, he touched a single lucifer match that had found its way down. He enlarged the hole, took out the match, and began to prise the caked flour bit by bit from the cartridge-case. He was, glad of any little activity that would enable him to kill time. Soon a little heap of crumbs lay on the sill of the window-recess. Then, drawing the match once more from the case, he saw that this time it had impaled, not a crumb, but a piece of some white fluffy substance.

"What is this?" he thought, and with growing curiosity inserted the match again. More fluff came out; it appeared to be cotton wool.

"Very odd!" he mused. He wetted the end of the match and inserted it again. A little more of the wool adhered, but the next time the match came out bare. He pushed it in again; but though he held it with the extreme tips of his fingers, it touched nothing.

"Empty at last, I suppose. Yet it didn't touch the bottom of the case. I wonder if it is empty."

He turned his back on the window and held the case up so that the light fell into it. But it was too narrow for him to see anything, supposing anything were there. He held it vertically, and shook it. Something fell from it, and rolled across the floor of the room. It was like a pea. Bob stooped and picked it up. It was a pea—no, it was a small pellet of paper!

Quick as thought Bob slipped it into his pocket, glancing instinctively towards the door and then to the opening in the wall. There was no one to see him. He smiled and took the pellet from his pocket. Unrolling it with infinite care, he found that it was a slip of very thin rice-paper, and on it— yes, in small letters, faintly traced in Indian ink, he saw the words:

"Be at window above river at dusk to-night."

That was all; there was no address, no signature. Yet, looking again at the writing, Bob felt that he had seen it somewhere before. Where? He could not remember, and as he stood trying to recall, he heard the heavy tread of his jailer in the passage outside. Instantly he slipped the paper into his pocket, flung the cartridge-case far out into the river, and was walking up and down when the soldier threw open the door and entered with his second meal.

That afternoon seemed to Bob interminable. He paced up and down like a caged lion, waiting for the dark. He wondered who the writer of the message was, what it implied, what possible plan of deliverance was in contemplation—for surely it must mean that someone was planning on his behalf. Many times he gazed out of the window, searching the whole vista from the horizon to the river below, knowing all the time that during the daylight nothing would be done, yet looking and looking again. The hours passed slowly, lingeringly. As night began to shadow the hills he ceased his restless walk and remained fixed at the recess in the wall. The sky darkened, his outlook shortened; he lost sight of the hills, at length he could not see the opposite bank. He leant forward in the recess, till his head touched the sides of the outer opening. The wind was fresh and cold, but he heeded nothing. His eyes tried to penetrate the dark until he felt that they were almost projecting from his head. Thus he waited, waited, and shivered, looking, listening, seeing nothing, hearing only the slow gurgle of the river as it rolled down between its frozen borders, and the creaking and grinding of the ice as the floating masses met, and parted, and met again.

So the hours passed, and Bob began to lose heart. Was the message a Russian trap? Yet what could it gain? Was it genuine, but his unknown correspondent had been prevented in some way from keeping the implied appointment? A bugle-call struck his ear; and when its echoes had died away the world relapsed into the same silence, save for the occasional bark of a dog, the dull noises of the ice-laden stream, and the sighing of the wind over the snowy wastes beyond. It became colder; the wind blew more and more keen; and at length, his limbs cramped, his fingers numbed, Bob had perforce to move, and lift his rug from the floor and wrap it round him.

What was that? His hearing was now so acute that he fancied he could have heard the world roll round. What was it? A rustle in the dark; a faint rustle outside the window, like the scraping of a bird's wing against the wall. He strained his eyes; stars were glimmering cold and clear, but there was no moon, and he saw nothing. Again, the same rustle. He tried to grope near enough to the opening to thrust forth his head, and his shoulders stuck; it was impossible, unless—yes, by turning on his side he could wriggle himself to the slit, and he put his head out sideways. Something touched his face, with the cold, filmy touch of a spider's web. He put out his hand; it was gone. Would it return? He waited. Again the same insubstantial contact; and now he seemed to see, against the starlit sky, a gossamer thread. He clutched at it, but it eluded his fingers and disappeared. He waited again, how long he knew not, but it seemed an hour; then the thin line scraped along the outside of the wall until it reached him. He grasped at it, almost fearing to touch it lest it broke and floated away. He held it, and drew it towards him. It was a thin silken cord!

He wriggled back slowly through the recess into the room, holding the cord with gentle firmness. As he pulled it, he felt that only the upper part yielded; the lower part was fixed or held below. He drew the upper string towards him, feeling as if he were playing a fish. For a few moments it came unresisting, then there was a sharp tug, as though the captured object, whatever it was, was making an effort to escape. Suddenly the resistance ceased; even in the darkness the opening in the wall was darkened, and with a somewhat disconcerting scrape against the wall Bob hauled in a large triangle of paper stretched on a light bamboo frame. It stuck in the opening. He had once more to crawl into the recess, and with some difficulty he coaxed the pliant framework through the narrow aperture. It was done. The bent rods sprang back to their former shape, and Bob at last understood what had been puzzling him. It was a kite!

All was now plain; the rustle, the elusive string, the reluctant captive. He remembered how interested he had been at Tokio, in watching the dexterous kite-flying of boys and men; in Japan, as in China, it is more than a pastime: it is an art. The string was attached to a kite, and the person flying it was below. He tugged gently at the cord as a signal that the kite had reached him, and instantly he felt that the line was loose. His pulse beat high. Cautiously he hauled in the slack; foot after foot it came through his hands; would the end of it never come? Yes, here it was; the silken cord was tied to a stretch of twine, and this—how long it was!—to a thicker rope. With eager care Bob drew this last up hand over hand; it was knotted at intervals, and as he pulled he felt the weight increase. At length it resisted his pull, yet gave slightly when he pulled again. Crawling again to the aperture, never letting go his hold, he found that the entrance was barred by a bundle, apparently of cotton waste. By turning this longways he found he could draw it through. No precaution, he perceived, had been neglected; the soft wrapping had deadened any sound.

Hastily untying the bundle, he found by the touch, for it was too dark to see, a chisel, a crowbar, and a hammer faced with flannel. He needed no prompting. It was impossible to loosen the stones in the time he had at his disposal. He knew not, indeed, what the time was; but it must be late, and if he did not escape before daybreak his doom was sealed. The stones of the wall were large blocks firmly cemented, and though the cement at its surface showed signs of crumbling, it was no doubt strong inside. All that he could do was to chip away a few inches on each side of the window, so as to enlarge the space sufficiently to admit of the passage of his shoulders. At the edges the stone was greatly weathered, at the farther end of the recess it was already peeling off. If he could widen the opening by some five inches, he thought it would be possible for him to squeeze through.

This had flashed through his mind in a moment. He started work instantly. Beginning at the outer right edge of the aperture, he applied the chisel to the stonework, and was delighted to find that by the mere pressure of his arm it came away in flakes, which fell to the ground eighty feet below. Working quickly, he had soon scratched away an inch of rotted stone for a distance of two feet along each edge of the opening. But as he went on, he found that the stone was becoming harder; it was necessary to exert more force. It would take long to chip the stone away as he had seen masons do. How could he shorten the labour? Cautiously working with the chisel, he slowly bored a hole two inches deep in the wall, at about the same distance from the outer edge. Then inserting the crowbar, he pressed upon it in an outward direction with all the strength he could exert in his cramped position. To his joy the stonework gave way, and pieces fell with a sharp clatter upon the ground. He waited anxiously, wondering whether any of his guards would have heard the sound. All was silent. Feeling with his hand, he found that the stone had broken irregularly, leaving a jagged surface, and this he proceeded to trim with the chisel. He went through the same double process on each side of the opening.

At last, after hours of work, when muscles of hand and arm ached unendurably, and his whole body felt bruised from lying so long on the hard stone, he thought that the opening must be large enough. Tying one end of the rope to the crowbar, he paid the other out. A slight tug below told him that it had been received: his unknown helper was still in waiting. Then he tied his rug to the twine, and let it gently down. This, too, being caught, he placed the crowbar horizontally across the window on the inner wall, turned on his side, and began to wriggle out of the opening feet foremost, always holding firmly to the rope. Had his work been successful? The question forced itself upon him as he moved painfully towards the outer air. Alas! half-way through he stuck; his jacket and vest were riding up into a ridge; it would increase the more he struggled; he must return to the room.

It was more difficult to get back than it had been to wriggle out. With a great effort he worked his way along the recess, and had just reached the floor of the room when his foot kicked the chisel, and it sped with a clatter across the floor. Immediately afterwards he heard a step in the passage. His jailer must have detected the noise, and would certainly come to discover its cause. It would be impossible to strip off jacket and waistcoat and wriggle out before the man entered, discovered his flight, and gave the alarm or perhaps cut the rope. With a sinking of the heart Bob listened. Was he to fail at the last moment? Perhaps the man would not come in after all. But no; the steps halt at the door; there is a light in the crack below. Bob hears the man fumbling for his keys; a key is inserted in the padlock; the bolt is drawn. By this time Bob, with lightning decision, is behind the door. It opens heavily on its rusty hinges, and half the room is lit up by the dim lantern carried by a Siberian infantryman, who peers into the room, and seeing nothing to his left, advances a few paces to light up the other half. At this moment Bob springs at him like a tiger. One crushing blow beneath the jaw, and the Russian falls backward like a log, his lantern clattering to the floor and being instantly extinguished.

Two seconds passed, seconds crowded with the most rapid thinking hard-pressed prisoner ever accomplished. The noise would draw the man's comrades from below. They must be kept out at all costs. But even if they were excluded, the soldier might be only stunned, or perhaps dazed, and would recover in time to cut the rope. There was nothing at hand with which to tie him up, no time to cut a piece off the rope and retie it to the crowbar. He might kill the man, but the thought was banished the same instant that it occurred to him. Two seconds; then, even as he heard the shouts of men and the trampling of heavy footsteps far below, Bob stooped, lifted the ponderous figure, and, with a strength of which he would not have believed himself capable, hurled him out into the corridor across the head of the staircase.

Bob surprises his Jailer

Bob surprises his Jailer

Then back into the room. He slams the door, picks up the chisel, and drives it with the hammer between the heavy oak and the floor. Off with his jacket, off with his vest; he rolls them up and forces them through the window. Everything must be dared now! Then feet foremost into the window-recess; out, out, grasping the rope; his legs are through, his body follows. Is the gap wide enough? He jerks himself on; it is a tight fit; his shoulders are through; he is dangling in the air, his arms almost forced from their sockets. Down he goes, hand over hand; his feet find the rope; he hears the clamour of blows on the door above. Down, down, faster and faster, the strain upon his muscles increasing with every foot of distance; down into what seems an immeasurable gulf. His feet touch the projecting sill of a window; he finds a momentary relief; then down again into space; there can be no delay, even for a moment. At last, panting for breath, his hands sore and bleeding, Bob feels a pair of arms supporting him; he loosens his grip of the rope, and falls half-insensible to the ground. But only for an instant. He sees as in a mist the outlines of two men, who drag him to his feet. The next moment, as though impelled by some higher will, he is racing down the frozen bank between the two shorter figures, over the creaking ice, towards the middle of the stream. Shouts pursue him, reflections of lights dance before his dazzled eyes, a shot is fired, there is a babel along the walls. Hauled up on the ice lies a small sampan. One of his supporters half pushes, half hurls Bob into it, then both urge it over the sagging ice into the stream. The edge gives way, the sampan slides with a glug into deep water, the two men leap on board with the agility of panthers, and the light craft bounds forward on its way to the sea.

Chapter XIII
Ah-Sam

A Silent Journey—An Old Friend—Circumstances Alter Cases—Enter
Ah-Sam—A Manchurian Inn—Held Up—Chinese Receipts

Not a word was said as the sampan floated down the river. For some
minutes Bob was too much amazed to take in anything beyond the mere fact
that he had escaped from his prison; his brain was in a whirl; the events of
the last few hours seemed a dream. He crouched in the boat, covered by the
cloak thrown over him by one of his rescuers: his outer garments had been
left at the foot of the tower. But collecting himself by degrees, he noticed
that one of the men stood in the bow with a long pole fending off the spars
of ice that jutted out into the stream, while the other lay almost horizontal in
the boat. Both were Chinamen, as he judged from their pigtails. There was
floating ice on all sides, and the progress of the sampan was a succession of
bumps. Sometimes it came to a stop, and the curved bow was pushed on to
a large floe by the pressure of ice behind. But the man with the pole knew
his work. A touch here, a push there, or a vigorous shove sent the light
craft on its way again; and all the time the second Chinaman lay motionless,
saying never a word.

Meanwhile the noise of alarm and pursuit from Antung struck Bob's
ears, and his thoughts were divided between wonder concerning the
identity of his preservers, the strangeness of their intervention, and anxiety
lest it should after all prove vain. He heard a deep bell booming, the blare
of bugles, the shouts of men: by and by from the right came the sound of
galloping horses. At this moment the man in the bow dropped silently into
the boat beside his comrade, and the vessel was left to take its course. It was
scarcely more than level with the surface of the water, and must have been
invisible in the dark night at the distance of a few yards. Even if it were
seen from the bank, the horsemen dared not approach the waterway owing
to the rotten state of the ice: all that they could do was to fire at it, with no
certainty of aim. Gradually the sounds from the shore diminished, and at
last died away; the Chinaman resumed his work with the pole, and floating,
jolting, stopping, jerking forward again, the sampan went safely on its way.

Still not a word had been spoken. Bob wished that one of the two figures would say something, no matter in what language. He had a strange longing for the sound of a friendly voice. But even when, two hours after their flight from Antung, the second Chinaman at last raised himself from his prone position, he gave the first an order by signs, not by words. With a combined push the two men drove the sampan with a swish and creak upon the ice on the right bank, where it remained stationary. They leapt overboard. At a sign from the second man Bob followed them; both then pushed the boat back into the stream, watched it for a moment as it circled irresolutely in the current, and then, as it gained its head and bounded more buoyantly on its way, they set off rapidly in a direction at right angles to the river, the second man now leading, and Bob making the best of his way with his companion.

Every now and then the leader paused to get his bearings, and altered his direction to right or left with little hesitation. At one point, when they came to a beaten track, he motioned to the others to remain where they were, and went ahead alone. In a few minutes he returned, and the silent march was resumed. The course led from the river-bed over country that became more and more hilly, and Bob was almost dropping with fatigue when, after walking rapidly for some eight or nine miles as he guessed, they came almost suddenly upon a high wall. Skirting the wall, they reached a gate, giving access to a courtyard. The gate was locked; the two Chinamen assisted Bob to climb it; a dog barked, but was instantly silenced by a sharp exclamation from one of the men mounting immediately behind Bob. Before them stood a low farmhouse, with still lower structures adjoining, which Bob found later were pig-styes and cow-byres not very different from similar appurtenances of farms at home. One of the Chinamen tapped twice at a window-frame latticed and filled with paper; there was no reply; he rapped again, twice, but slightly louder. In a moment a glimmer appeared within; a movement was heard; the frame was drawn aside, and against the dim light of a small bowl-lamp the form of a Chinaman was outlined. The moment he distinguished the features of the man who had tapped, he closed his fists, pressed them together against his chest, and bowed almost to the ground.

The three entered; the movable window-frame was replaced. Then one of the Chinamen turned suddenly to Bob, held out his hand, and with a smile and a bow said in careful clear-cut tones:

"I am glad to meet you again, Mr. Fawcett."

Bob stared at him in amazement. He recognized him now as the younger of the two Chinamen who had rescued him from the drunken students in Sasebo, who knew no English, and whom subsequently he had seen in the streets of Seoul. But though this was what he saw, the voice, the accent, the manner, reminded him of another person, not a Chinaman, but the Samurai who had been his host in Nikko. Grasping the outstretched hand, he said, with a gasp of amazement:

"Kobo!"

"Rokuro Kobo San," corrected the voice of Taru.

"Pardon me, sir; you will understand that I am—"

"A little taken aback, Mr. Fawcett? Yes, I understand. But you must be very tired and very hungry. You will permit my friend here to give you some food, and provide you with a jacket, then we can talk more at our ease."

In a few moments Bob, clad in a new silk jacket, was resting his weary limbs on a wadded quilt unrolled on the floor, eating with a good appetite and without enquiry the dishes placed before him. Kobo shared his meal, at the same time entering into explanations.

"You have no doubt guessed," he said, "that both myself and my servant Taru are on secret service. Our Japanese system is very elaborate. It has been most carefully organized since the Chinese war. No quarter of Manchuria has not been surveyed by our agents; many of the inhabitants are in sympathy with us, many of them are in our pay."

Bob glanced at their host.

"No," said Kobo, smiling, "he is not a Chinaman; he is a Japanese, like myself."

"But he has a pigtail!"

"So have I! Mine, however, was assumed a few weeks ago, its hold is precarious; our host's is natural, it was grown for the purpose. We have seen this war coming for ten years; and two or three suffice for the growth of a pigtail, if one sets about cultivating it in earnest. Our friend, with hundreds more, was sent over to settle in this country; some have cultivated the pigtail and become good Chinamen, others with equal success have devoted themselves to the topknot and are passable Koreans."

"Your motto is 'thorough'," said Bob admiringly.

"Yes, even to the loss of our heads. You see now why I was unable to recognize you in Sasebo and Seoul, though I half believed that in Seoul at any rate you recognized me. I could say nothing. There are Russian spies also in all parts of the country, and a single incautious sign might have compromised me and led to my discovery and suicide."

"Suicide!"

"Of course. Any Japanese would kill himself rather than do harm to his country's cause."

"Evidently one might never know when one is meeting a Japanese. May I ask—is Mr. Helping-to-decide a Japanese?"

"No, no," returned Kobo, laughing outright. "He is a real Korean; he means to help, but he never can decide. Now I want you to tell me how you met him; indeed, to give me a full account of what has happened to you. I have a reason for asking."

Bob rapidly sketched an outline of his adventures since he left Japan.

"Yes," said Kobo, when his story was ended. "Of course I learnt from Yamaguchi in Yongampo that you were with him. I heard of the fight on the shore; I did not know you had so thoughtfully come to Yamaguchi's assistance; in fact, I followed you as a Cossack despatch-rider until you killed your first tiger—"

"You knew that!" exclaimed Bob in surprise. He had said nothing about that incident.

"Yes, I came in at the death; that is to say, I was present when Mr. Helping-to-decide came upon the scene, and having satisfied myself that the man I had been following was not a Russian, I resumed my journey northward. I was proceeding to Feng-huang-cheng when I heard that you had fallen into the hands of Chang-Wo—an old enemy of mine, as you know—and had been sentenced to death. I came back at once to Antung. Fortunately the baker who contracts for the Russians' ammunition-bread in Antung is a Japanese agent. He discovered the place of your imprisonment, and bribed one of the Siberian guards—an easy matter, I assure you—to see that a special loaf was delivered to you. The rest you know; and let me say, you did your part much more rapidly than I had supposed possible."

"It was really extremely good of you to—"

"Not at all, not at all," interrupted Kobo; "it was my duty—in the circumstances."

"In what circumstances?"

"They had sentenced you to death. You will understand my position. If I had been perfectly sure that, with the prospect of death before you, you would have acted as you did—refused to give them any information,—it would have been my duty to go straight to my destination."

"I should have been shot?"

"Undoubtedly. Personal considerations are immaterial. Only reasons of state can override reasons of state. Another time—let us hope it will never occur—I need not trouble; I can go on my way—now that I know you are to be trusted."

This gave Bob something to think about. It was a view that had not struck him till then. He could not but recognize that it was strictly logical. One life was of no account compared with the vast national issues at stake. Kobo could allow nothing to delay him but the public service. Logical as it was, however, Bob had somewhat of a shock when it was brought so nearly home to him that Japan, if not the world at large, was governed by logic; and though he had a passing pang at the thought that Kobo, after a few days' knowledge of him, was not convinced of his trustworthiness, his soreness was a good deal relieved when he remembered that but for Kobo's caution he would now be lying in a Russian grave.

"Now, Mr. Fawcett," said Kobo after a pause, "you no doubt feel the need of a good sleep. But I will ask you to wait a little longer, while we discuss your future movements. It will soon be daylight, and I must then be gone; I must continue the journey you have twice unwittingly interrupted. You cannot, of course, accompany me. I do not wish to carry you into danger, nor can I endanger my mission by being encumbered with you. On the other hand, you cannot remain here, for Chinese houses, as you see, are not built for secrecy, and you would certainly be discovered ere long by the Russians. It will be best for you to make another attempt to reach our lines. You must go alone; I would willingly lend you my servant Taru, but that I myself require him. But our host here has a Chinese servant who is familiar with the country; he will act as your guide."

"Does he speak English?" asked Bob.

"Yes, pidgin English; indeed, he considers himself an accomplished linguist. As to your route, it will be dangerous to attempt to cross the Yalu anywhere between Antung and the sea. The Russians will naturally be on the alert, the more so because of the recent appearance of destroyers off the coast. All the fords between Antung and Wiju will be narrowly watched. When they discover the sampan they will probably connect it with your escape, and suspect that you have taken the shortest way to our lines. Your best course will be to go northward and make a circuit as soon as it is safe to do so."

"But will there not be a danger of meeting Russians northward also? I can't pass for a native, unluckily."

"Not as you now appear, but we can alter that. I think your guide had better travel as a carter; you will go as his man. Our host will dye your hair and stain your face and dress you as a Korean."

"But I shall never be able to manage the topknot."

"True, but that will not be necessary. Being unmarried, I presume—"

"Certainly."

"You will not require a topknot, which is the monopoly of the married men. Your hair is sufficiently long for you to pass as a bachelor, which, you will take care to remember, is an inferior and ignominious condition. As a further precaution, you had better pretend to be dumb whenever you encounter people. Your guide should, I think, set off with his cart in the morning towards Tang-shan until he finds an opportunity of crossing the main road. In order not to attract attention you follow at night, and do not join the cart until it has crossed. If a strange Korean were seen leaving this house it might arouse suspicion, and the fact might be reported by spies to the Russians. Your further course must be determined as circumstances dictate, and may safely be left to your guide. I think all is arranged, then; it only remains to introduce the Chinese boy to you."

Kobo said a few words to their host, who called in a loud tone. In a few moments a stout little Chinaman appeared, salaaming as he entered the room. His round hairless face was impassive, his slanting eyes looked intelligent, and he kow-towed profoundly when Kobo briefly introduced him.

"This, Mr. Fawcett, is Ah-Sam. Ah-Sam, Mr. Fawcett is an Englishman; he does not speak Chinese; you will be able to turn your knowledge of his language to account."

"My speakee Yinkelis first-chop so-fashion," said the Chinaman, giving Bob some qualms as to the possibility of using this dialect of English as a means of communication.

Kobo then proceeded to explain to Ah-Sam in his own language the scheme of action he had arranged. The Chinese listened gravely, nodding his head from time to time. When his instructions were concluded, he went off silently to prepare for his journey. Kobo then gave Bob detailed particulars of the road he was to follow on the next evening, and finally bade him farewell.

"I hope I shall see you again," said Bob after warmly thanking him once more for his rescue.

"I hope so. We cannot tell. Good-bye!"

Bob slept for many hours. When he awoke he had to undergo a long process of disguising at the hands of his host, from which he emerged completely transformed in complexion, appearance, and dress. His hair from light-brown had become black, his cheeks sallow. He wore the Korean national costume—huge cotton trousers padded with cotton wool, tied round his waist with a long tasselled ribbon; a short bell-shaped coat, also padded, with long sleeves; padded socks, in which the ends of the trousers were tucked; and paper shoes, fastened to the feet like sandals. These last were much more durable than they appeared. He wore no hat, but as it was cold, and there was a prospect of snow, he was provided with a large umbrella on a bamboo frame that fitted the head, so that in case of need he might carry some means of protection.

At nightfall he left the house with his host, who offered to accompany him until he overtook the cart. Both were mounted on small Korean ponies. After three or four hours' riding over snow-covered hills they struck the high-road, and leaving this at an angle in a north-easterly direction, they ascended into another low chain of hills, and in about two hours reached a small village. Here, as the Japanese host had anticipated, they found Ah-Sam awaiting them in an inn. The Japanese then took his leave, and Bob was left to his new guide.

The aspect of the inn was not very inviting. Bob's nose as he entered was assailed by the strong smell of pork and vegetables stewing in two huge cauldrons, one on each side of the door. The place consisted of one room, about forty feet long, with a low platform called a k'ang running the whole length of the wall, covered with dirty matting, sheep-skin coats, pedlars' packs, and miscellaneous frippery, with a score of rough labourers and carters lolling on them, eating, drinking, and smoking a very pungent tobacco. The k'ang, Bob found, covered the heating apparatus of the place, and was, in fact, a kind of flue. The middle of the room was occupied by what appeared to be a rough altar, but which turned out to be a kitchen-range—an oblong brick structure about three feet high, hollow in the centre, with an arched covering pierced with holes, above which various cooking pots were placed during the evening.

As Bob entered, Ah-Sam came from his perch at the end of the k'ang nearest the door, putting his finger to his lips. Bob suddenly remembered that he was to feign dumbness. He therefore made no reply to the remarks addressed to him, presumably in Korean, by the boy, but submissively accepted a bowl of soup, the mere odour of which was nauseating. He went through the forms of eating, but soon gave it up, and making a virtue of necessity, settled himself to sleep at the cleanest part of the k'ang, picked out for him by Ah-Sam.

At daybreak next morning they set off, and Bob had his first experience of riding on a Manchurian cart. It was rather more unpleasant than jolting in a four-wheeler over the cobbles of the Glasgow streets. The framework of the cart, about fifteen feet long by four wide, rested on a huge axle-tree between two wooden wheels whose iron tyres were more than an inch thick. There were no springs. On each side ran a low wooden rail, intended to support so much of the load as overlapped from the body of the cart. There was a small pony in the shafts, and in front of it six mules three abreast, attached by long hempen ropes to iron hooks in the framework. The mules had neither bit nor bridle; they were guided wholly by the driver's voice and whip, the latter twelve feet long in the handle, with a thong of equal length, and so heavy that both hands were required to wield it. Ah-Sam sat on the front of the cart, and gave Bob a place behind, where he helped to balance the vehicle on its two wheels. The cart was but lightly loaded; it contained a few empty sacks, some fodder for the animals, a supply of food, and a couple of spades. Beneath the framework, cunningly hidden between the wheels, there were two rifles and a good stock of ammunition.

Bob had had no little difficulty in remembering that he was dumb. After their meal in the inn that morning Ah-Sam had roughly ordered him to make himself useful and help to harness the mules, pouring out upon him a torrent of Chinese which Bob judged from its tone to be highly abusive. He went submissively enough to work, but being new to the job fumbled a good deal, and was several times on the point of asking how this or that was to be done. But he always caught himself up in time, turning what he intended to say into such inarticulate grunts as even a dumb man can utter. When, however, the inn and the village were left behind, and no human being was in sight, he thought it safe to throw off his restraint, and ventured to address a question to Ah-Sam in the front of the cart. He found the Chinaman's pidgin English at first rather difficult to understand, but after half an hour's conversation had gained sufficient familiarity with the idiom to get a fair idea of the man's meaning. He learnt that the talk in the inn had been of two matters: first, the great entrenchments which the Russians were making around Antung and Kiu-lien-cheng; and secondly, the annihilation of a Cossack detachment by a band of Chunchuses, the bandits of the country, some distance away in the hills.

"Russians belongey allo muchee mad," said Ah-Sam. "He say catchee killum allo piecee Chunchuses, galaw!"

Bob was about to ask for particulars of the Chunchuses, when, from round a corner, appeared a native driving a laden ox. Ah-Sam instantly put his finger to his lips, reminding Bob of his dumbness. When the native appeared, Ah-Sam stopped for a talk. This occupied some time; then the teamsters parted and went on their several ways. The route followed by Ah-Sam was rather a foot-path than a cart-track; and but for the snow, which filled the ruts and formed a fairly hard and even roadway, it would have been impassable for wheeled traffic. As it was, the progress of the cart was very slow and toilsome.

About mid-day they came to a dip in the hills where Ah-Sam decided to halt, take a meal, and feed his team. This done he remounted to his place, Bob sprang on to the tail of the cart, and the slow journey was resumed. But they had barely begun the ascent of the upward slope when from the left, across the snowy waste, a troop of horsemen were seen galloping rapidly towards them. The riders soon defined themselves by the bright yellow of their uniforms as a sotnia of Cossacks. Ah-Sam at first affected not to notice them, stolidly driving on; but turning his head at length in response to their loud shouts, he drew rein, muttered a warning to Bob and an order to run to the head of the team, and sprang from his perch in time to make half a dozen rapid kow-tows before the Cossacks reached him. He continued his obeisances as the captain of the troop roughly addressed him in Chinese, but suddenly stood erect and began to expostulate in voluble yet obsequious tones when, in response to an order, two of the Cossacks dismounted and approached the cart with drawn swords, evidently with the intention of cutting the traces. Bob, holding the head of one of the mules which was plunging excitedly, of course understood not a word of the colloquy; if he had known Chinese he would have heard the captain curtly inform Ah-Sam that the mules were required for the Russian service, and Ah-Sam's protest that they were already engaged in that service. He had just delivered, he said, a load of millet and forage stuffs to the honourable contractor to the honourable governor of Antung, and was on his way back to a farm at Kuan-tien to fetch another load. If the honourable captain took his mules, he would be unable to fulfil his commission. The roads, as the honourable captain saw, were so bad that with his team, small enough as it was, he was already behind time. He needed more mules, not less; he had begged the honourable contractor to give him three more, but none were to be found. His strong and capable assistant had been taken away to work in the Russian trenches, and he had been forced to hire at the last moment a big, loutish, dumb fool of a Korean, who could do nothing but eat, and who at this moment, as the honourable captain saw, was an absolutely useless, incapable, soft-muscled —

He was interrupted by a general hullabaloo among the mules, which, unused to the handling of a European, were kicking and plunging and threatening to involve the whole team in an inextricable tangle. Stretching his arm, Ah-Sam flicked two or three of the mules with his long whip, roundly abused Bob, and, apparently in ungovernable rage, struck him also with the lash, which cut through the wadding of his trousers and caused him to utter a smothered growl, at which the Cossacks laughed with enjoyment.

The mules having been reduced to order, Ah-Sam returned to face the captain, kow-towed again, and repeated his story. The Russian had already countermanded the order to his men, and was clearly hesitating. He was a good-tempered-looking fellow, thought Bob,—a young clean-limbed captain, picturesque in his long silver-ornamented coat and astrakhan cap. Interrupting Ah-Sam's shrill sing-song of protest, he demanded to see the receipts which the muleteer doubtless possessed if his story was true. The Chinaman instantly produced a number of papers from a bag tied beneath his coat, and handed them to the captain, who examined them carefully. They were unmistakably receipts, in proper Chinese form, and recognizing that he might get into hot water with the authorities if he delayed the procuring of the supplies so urgently needed, he at length said that he would be satisfied with three of the mules, and when these had been unyoked, gave the Chinaman permission to proceed.

Before he rode off, however, he asked, as by an afterthought, a question which appeared to be incomprehensible to Ah-Sam, who looked puzzled, then asked a question in return. The captain smiled as he explained to his lieutenant what the Chinaman had said; both laughed heartily; then the word was given, and the troop rode off in the opposite direction to that from which they had come.

Bob had been waiting for an opportunity to tackle Ah-Sam on the matter of the whip. While it was well, no doubt, to keep up their character as master and man, he had a suspicion that the Chinaman had laid on with unnecessary vigour, perhaps to experiment on the quality of the foreigner he was escorting. When, therefore, the Cossacks were safely out of earshot, Bob went forward and sat beside Ah-Sam.

"What was the Russian laughing at?" he said.

"Ch'hoy! He say, hab my see one piecee Yinkelis man what lun wailo? My say, what likee Yinkelis man my savvy tiger, bear, monkey, hairy Ainu; Yinkelis man belongey likum he?"

"Oh! And I suppose you hit me with the whip to make it quite clear that I was not an Englishman. You hit me like this, you know."

Bob suddenly rose, took the Chinaman's whip, and gave him a smart cut. Ah-Sam yelled.

"He hurtee velly muchee," he said, rubbing the place.

"Yes, I know. If we meet any more Russians, perhaps you can prove I am not the runaway Englishman without using your whip."

"My no hit massa no mo'e; my member plenty too muchee, no fear!"

Chapter XIV
Mrs. Isidore G. Pottle

Fair Captives—Pidgin—Among the Chunchuses—Seeking Cover—A Breathing Space—A Picnic

The travellers pursued their journey without incident through the rest of the day. Occasionally they met a native with whom Ah-Sam exchanged a few words, and in these conversations he learnt that the Russians were in great strength between them and the river, and had impressed hundreds of Manchurians to work on the fortifications. This forced labour was by no means to their taste, and many of the inhabitants were therefore in hiding, so that the travellers need not be surprised at the comparatively deserted condition of the country through which they passed. From this information it was clear that to turn southwards would be dangerous as yet. Ah-Sam accordingly drove on in an easterly direction, making long detours to avoid climbing the hills, which became higher and higher as they advanced. They spent the night in a solitary inn, smaller than the first, and fortunately less crowded. Early on the following morning they pushed on again. Ah-Sam told Bob that they were now passing beyond the region which he knew intimately. He had only a general knowledge of the country, and must trust to passing wayfarers to keep him in the right way.

So that day passed. On the next, Ah-Sam thought that they had probably by this time turned the Russian positions on the Yalu, and might safely take a southerly course. The country was very wild; the hills were higher and more precipitous than those in the district already traversed. But there were signs of spring. The snow was thawing in the valleys and the less exposed parts of the hills, and the ice of the streams they crossed was rotten, the cart often crashing through. But these being shallow hill rivulets, no harm was done; the only inconveniences were the having sometimes to cut a way to the opposite bank, and the strain on the mules in drawing the heavy cart over the rocky beds and up the rugged slopes. It was easier to make progress at early morning or late at night, for then the snow was still crisp and the ice still solid.

About mid-day they were slowly following the valley of a stream somewhat broader than those hitherto encountered, hoping that it would bring them out some distance up the Yalu about the neighbourhood of Sukuchen. As they proceeded, they came almost unawares upon a remarkable cleft in the hills to their right—a wild and rocky gorge, strewn with irregular masses of rock small and large, and narrowing as it led upwards to a sparse clump of trees at the top. Even in broad daylight it formed a dark forbidding gully, the hills rising sheer precipices on either side, showing masses of granite too steep even to give lodgment to the snow. From a point high up, a thin waterfall plunged over the crags and wormed its way down among the boulders. The travellers stopped for a few moments to observe the scene. Suddenly Ah-Sam pointed upwards: on a ledge of rock almost at the summit, near a narrow fissure, he had descried the form of a bear motionless on its haunches. Following the Chinaman's outstretched finger, Bob at last made out the distant form. For a moment the instinct of the British sportsman prompted him to attempt to stalk the animal, but even as he looked it suddenly disappeared, and he remembered then that as a menial Korean he would have cut an absurd and outrageous figure in pursuit of a bear.

He was still regretting the impossibility of obtaining the skin, when he was startled by the sound of a high-pitched voice coming from some spot ahead of them. The valley here rounded a prominent bluff; no human form was to be seen. Before he had quite collected himself he heard the voice again; it was a woman's voice, speaking in accents of distress, or at least excited remonstrance, and he fancied that it had a very British ring. Springing from the cart, and bidding Ah-Sam follow him quickly, he hurried on ahead, turned the bend, and saw before him, hastening up the slope, five persons, two of them little more than a hundred yards away, the other three at a somewhat greater distance. He was amazed to see that two of the five were ladies, in European costume. The nearer was a young lady, tall, in a costume of grey tweed; her right wrist was in the grasp of a native. The farther was a lady of maturer years, equally tall, very stout, wearing a heavy sealskin jacket, her bonnet awry, her arms pinioned by two natives who were urging her along. The captors were obviously Manchus; they wore the pigtails, the wide-brimmed hats, cotton blouses and loose pantaloons common to the country.

It was from the elder lady that the cries had proceeded and were still proceeding. They were not cries of fear or appeals for mercy, but rather outpourings of wrath and indignation. Her head was being shaken vigorously from side to side, threatening to dislodge her already disordered head-gear. She was evidently not merely protesting, but resisting with all her might, and as she dwarfed the men in both height and breadth, she was giving them no little trouble. The younger lady was causing no such commotion. She was walking quietly by her captor's side, unresisting, saying nothing, accepting the situation resignedly.

Bob took in these details in a few seconds. Then, without counting the odds, he rushed forward, fumbling in the slit of his wadded pantaloons for the pistol he carried there. In the soft snow his footfall made no sound that was not smothered by the unceasing denunciation of the stout lady, and the Manchus were too much occupied with their captives to be alive to the presence of strangers. Bob noticed that the man leading the younger lady held in his right hand a musket or rifle. Making rapidly up on him, Bob stooped just as the Manchu at last heard his tread and was turning, snatched the weapon from his grasp, thrust it between his legs and tripped him up. Then without waiting he dashed on, came within a few feet of the Manchus by the time they had contrived to face round, the lady still struggling between them, and pointing his pistol full at the head of one of them, shouted in English:

"Hands up!"

A Korean Knight-errant

A Korean Knight-errant

The very sight of a Korean with a pistol in his hand was enough to throw a Manchu bandit off his balance. The Koreans are a soft, inert, unwarlike race; even their soldiers are never known to fight; and yet here was a Korean, without a topknot and therefore of no social account, actually pointing a pistol and uttering a menace which sounded all the fiercer because it was in a language never heard in these parts from Korean lips before. Bob did not give the bandits time to recover from their amazement. Rushing up to them he sent one spinning over with a right-hander, and wrested the weapon from the other. The large and indignant lady being now released, struck this man smartly over the head with her umbrella, and then, marched down the hill to meet the younger lady, who was coming rapidly towards her with an air of mingled astonishment and relief. Behind came Ah-Sam, who had left his team at the foot of the slope, and was driving before him, in cowed amazement, the Manchu who had held the girl. For a moment it seemed as if the three Manchus, trusting in their numerical superiority, were inclined to retaliate, but there was something in Bob's manner that warned them in time, and they slunk away, muttering curses Manchurian but unmistakable. As they did so, the elder lady stood watching them with menace in her mien, her left hand clasping the hand of the girl now by her side, her right retaining a determined grip of her umbrella. Bob meanwhile walked slowly down the hill towards her. He was a little out of breath, and a great deal astonished. His lips twitched with amusement at the sight of the elder lady, so large, and so unconscious of her disarray, like a ruffled hen in her attitude. The girl seemed partly to share his feeling, for he detected a slight twinkle in her dark eyes as they met his. When the Manchus were out of sight, the elder lady's features relaxed, and becoming aware that the stranger to whose intervention she owed her release was within arm's length, she turned to him and said quickly:

"You speakee English?"

"Yes, madam."

Before Bob could explain himself further, the lady, with a capacious sigh of relief, said:

"That's a comfort, Ethel. Now I guess we shall find a track out of this horrid country." Then, in the pidgin English of literature, she added, addressing Bob: "You plenty muchee goodee Chinee boy. Me givee you heapee thankee—plenty muchee cashee. You belongee this country?"

"No, madam——"

Again his explanation was forestalled.

"Me wantee go Seoulee. You savvy Seoulee?"

"Yes, madam. I—"

"You takee us rightee there—can do?"

During this interrupted monologue the younger lady had shown signs of increasing embarrassment. With flushed checks she half interposed between her companion and Bob, touched the lady's arm, and said quickly:

"Auntie, don't you see?—you are making a mistake; this gentleman is not a—"

"Is not what?" said the lady, putting up her eye-glass, and adding with some asperity: "Then what is he?"

"Let me introduce myself," said Bob, bowing. "My name is Fawcett—an Englishman, at your service."

The lady put up her eyeglass and stared with unfeigned amazement, exclaiming under her breath:

"A Britisher! Well, of all the extraordinary—You will excuse my surprise, Mr.—Fawcett, I think you said? The circumstances are so remarkable. I fear I owe you an apology, but really—" she turned to her companion and began to tie her bonnet-strings—"it just beats anything."

Here Ah-Sam, who had been hovering restlessly in the background, came up and said:

"No tim' belongey this-side, massa. Plenty Chunchu man come this-side chop-chop, makee big bobbely, supposey catchee, he killum allo piecee massa, two-piecee girley, Ah-Sam all-same."

"What does the man say?" asked the lady, staring at the Chinaman as at some strange animal.

"He says that we must not remain here. The men, Chunchuses apparently, threatened to return, and if they do—well, we shall all be in a very awkward fix. Perhaps if you would let me know who these people are—"

"Why certainly. My niece and I are doing Asia. We got as far as Mukden, and there the Russians tried to stop us—said it would not be safe, war was expected. I told them it was all nonsense. They insisted; I persisted. They set a guard over us—free citizens of the United States. Intolerable! We slipped away; naturally;—bribery, of course; very disgusting, but the only way. We struck east for Gensan; got among the hills. Our Chinese guide lost his way, or pretended to, and we were snapped up by a party of brigands, who figured that we spelt dollars, and have kept us with them ever since."

"Then you are Mrs.—Mrs. Isidore—?"

Bob hesitated, endeavouring to recall a name that for the moment eluded him.

"I guess you're on the right track," replied the lady with a look of surprise. "Pottle—Mrs. Isidore G. Pottle; though it beats me how you happened on my name."

Bob then explained that he had learnt of Mrs. Pottle's disappearance from the columns of a San Francisco paper at Tokio. But he cut explanations short, looking anxiously in the direction in which the brigands had disappeared, and parried the questions which he saw Mrs. Pottle was eager to put, by asking for information as to the strength and position of the band. The three men he had seen belonged to a gang of some sixty or seventy, whose last camp was about a mile distant from that spot. Mrs. Pottle was uncertain of the exact number, for it differed from day to day, and that morning the whole band had ridden away with the exception of the three in whose hands Bob had found the ladies, and a few left to guard the camp. Such absences were common. They lasted sometimes only a few hours, sometimes for several days. The brigands were all mounted, and when the camp was changed the ladies were always sent on foot in advance, since nothing on earth would induce Mrs. Pottle to ride pillion on a wild horse behind a wild man. The brigands had done them no harm; they were well fed with atrocious food. Mrs. Pottle said she thought there could be nothing worse than a Russian hotel till she met the Chunchuses. Their Chinese guide had decamped with everything they possessed, including Mrs. Pottle's purse, though she still had her cheque-book, note-book, and umbrella.

"I am not alarmed for myself," said Mrs. Pottle in conclusion; "I am an old traveller, tough, seasoned. But dear Ethel—this is her first tour, and though the poor child bears up well, I am terribly afraid these hardships will ruin her constitution, and then I shall not be able to look her poppa in the face."

"Auntie, I am quite well," said the younger lady, who indeed looked, as Bob thought, the picture of health, with her fresh cheeks and bright eyes. "I am only afraid that your nerves will break down."

"Nerves! I never had any. But Mr.—Fawcett, I think?—what are we to do?—Well, of all the—a Britisher, and in Korean dress!..."

Bob asked the ladies to walk down the hill while he took a look round. He really wanted a few minutes to think over the situation alone. He was beset by perplexities. Difficult as his own position was, it was doubly difficult now that he had someone else to think of. It was most embarrassing—to have to act as squire of dames in such a clumsy, ridiculous costume. Mrs. Pottle's state of mind, he could see, was unmixed amazement; but her niece evidently had a sense of humour. "If she wasn't so confoundedly pretty!—", and then Bob caught himself up, and bent his mind to the problem before him. If the brigands returned in force, he could hardly hope to escape them. If he did, it might be only to fall among another gang: brigandage is an organized profession in Manchuria. Supposing he escaped all danger on that side, he might encounter Russians, and though he himself might pass unmolested as a dumb Korean in company with a Chinese carter, the presence of two ladies in European dress would awake suspicion and provoke the most dangerous enquiries.

Yet he could not leave the ladies: that was out of the question. He secretly suspected that the portly and strong-minded Mrs. Isidore G. Pottle was capable of brow-beating and scaring any number of Manchus or Russians, but her niece!—He looked again at the trim figure.

"That white tam o' shanter makes her—h'm! ... What in the world are we to do, Ah-Sam?" he asked of the Chinaman, who had remained at his side.

"My no can tinkee. One piecee velly largo woman; he makee plenty bobbely; one piecee littee girley, he too muchee fliten, evelyting makee cly-cly, galaw! Supposey you hab larn fightee pidgin, you no can cham-tow allo velly bad tief-man, all-same."

This speech fell on deaf ears, for in the middle of it Bob caught sight of several horsemen in single file far up the hillside in front. Noticing that his eyes were fixed on some distant object, Ah-Sam turned in that direction also, looked hard for a moment, and then exclaimed:

"Chunchuses! Bimeby allo come this-side. What can do? Catchee killum one-tim'."

Now that danger was actually upon him, Bob prepared instantly to meet it. In a flash he remembered the gully he had passed recently with Ah-Sam, and recognized that it was the nearest, indeed the only, defensible position within reach. It was so narrow that, near its summit, it might be held, he thought, by a few against a host. He at once ordered Ah-Sam to turn the cart and drive it as quickly as possible back to the spot where the waterfall emptied itself into the stream, and then up the steep, rocky gorge. In a few minutes the team was plunging through the broken ice at a great pace. Nothing but a Manchurian cart could have stood the strain. It was flung about at all angles; it cannoned against rocks, now one wheel, now the other disappearing in mud or snow; but it survived every shock, and drawn by its four sturdy beasts with Ah-Sam at their head, it groaned and creaked on its upward course until it reached an abrupt twist in the gorge about three hundred yards from its lower extremity.

Meanwhile Bob had led the two ladies diagonally across the hillside by a shorter route than that taken by the cart. Mrs. Pottle bravely panted along, making tremendous exertions under her thick sealskin jacket to keep pace with Bob, who assisted her with his arm. Her niece stepped along as lightly as a doe, her cheeks flushed with excitement, and her wavy black hair escaping in disorder below her white tam o' shanter.

Gaining a point above the bend at which the cart had just arrived, Bob saw that the stream flowed around a huge granite boulder which had slipped, apparently at no very distant date, from the almost perpendicular cliffs above, blocking up the greater part of the already narrow defile. Here Bob shouted to Ah-Sam to stop and wedge the cart between the boulder and the opposite wall of the ravine. Looking round, he saw, some fifty feet above, to the left of the stream, the cleft near which the bear had been seated. It was visible now as a fault in the rock, a few yards across. The fissure narrowed towards its base, and from it a shelf of rock ran horizontally outwards, meeting the stream at an acute angle about a hundred yards from where Bob stood. Beyond this junction the gorge rapidly narrowed, and became extremely steep. Leaving the ladies to rest, Bob climbed up the rocky bed to explore, and found that after a time further progress was blocked by a perpendicular wall that rose sheer two hundred feet.

Returning, he reassured the ladies with a word, and then took Ah-Sam with him down the gully. The mouth, some thirty yards wide, was jagged and strewn with rocks, and formed so eminently defensible a position that Bob hesitated whether to attempt to hold it or to retire at once to the still more difficult post behind the cart. It would be a hazardous matter to turn his position; before this could be effected he could inflict severe loss on his assailants. But in a few moments he gave up the idea of holding the lower ground. To begin with, he had no desire to come to blows if a fight could be avoided, for, apart from the risk of being overpowered by the Chunchuses, there was the likelihood that the sound of shots would bring the Russians on the scene. They must be in great force no more than twenty or thirty miles away, engaged on the Yalu entrenchments, and firing in the hills would almost certainly be heard by scouting parties. If the Russians came up, the Chunchuses could disperse with their accustomed celerity, but Bob would be unable to save himself unless he were prepared to abandon the ladies who had so strangely fallen under his care. They would no doubt be well treated if entrusted to an officer of rank; but if the Russians happened to be an ordinary troop of Cossacks, Bob doubted whether he might not as well leave the ladies to the Chunchuses as to them. First of all, at any rate, he had the Chunchuses to deal with. He hoped that when they saw how strongly he was posted behind the cart and the boulder they would draw off. In any case, Ah-Sam's forethought had stocked the cart with enough provisions to last through a siege of some days, and in view of that contingency it was wise to do what he could to strengthen his position still further.

The distant specks on the mountain-side had disappeared. Slowly scanning every portion of the horizon, neither Bob nor Ah-Sam saw any sign of life. They retraced their steps towards the boulder, halting now and then to roll down the steep slope such loose rocks as might give cover to an attacking force. The ladies met them as they reached the cart.

"Well, Mr. Fawcett," said Mrs. Pottle, "did you see anything way down there?"

"Nothing. But if those were your friends the brigands, we shall have them upon us in half an hour."

"Oh! what shall we do, then? You had some plan in bringing us here?"

"Yes. Ah-Sam and I are going to fortify ourselves; it is our only chance."

"Good gracious! They have guns, and I've only my umbrella!"

"We have our pistols and a couple of rifles."

"Against a hundred, perhaps. Still, two determined men, behind rocks—could you spare a pistol for me?"

"If necessary, but I hope we sha'n't have to fight. They will probably tire of besieging us here."

"A siege! But, my dear boy, we can't stand a siege without food, and I confess, Mr. Fawcett, I am hungry. Really, I must eat, and I will say this for the brigands: they did give us food, of a sort."

"Ah-Sam has plenty of food—of a sort," said Bob, smiling. "And perhaps, Mrs. Pottle, while we are doing what we can to strengthen the position, you won't mind preparing a meal."

"Of course not. If only I could get a cup of tea!"

"Ah-Sam has tea, and rice, and millet, and a few other things."

"The dear man! But a kettle?"

"He has a pot, and an oil-lamp, anu plenty of matches."

"A treasure! Let us have the things, and I will turn up my sleeves and set to work. There is water in the stream. Ethel, my love, we shall have a cup of tea for the first time in six weeks. Come and help me."

Bob admired Mrs. Pottle's spirit. Leaving the ladies to themselves, he assisted Ah-Sam to unyoke the team and drag them higher up the ravine, where they tethered the animals to the trunks of some overhanging trees, and supplied them with fodder from the cart. Then, with some difficulty, they pushed and rolled some of the smaller boulders in front of the vehicle, arranging them in such a way that loopholes were left between them covering every part of the approach. The position was now such that the little party was effectually concealed from the road below; but Bob knew that their presence could not remain undiscovered, for the cart and the animals had left very distinct traces in the snow and mud.

Everything possible having now been done, Bob went once more to the mouth of the gully to reconnoitre. There was as yet no sign of the brigands. He was still looking out across the hills when Ah-Sam came up, carrying a pot of rice.

"Chow-chow allo leady, massa," he said. "My fetchee chow-chow this-side; ch'hoy! women boilum tings, spoilum tea; China boy no can dlink it; too muchee stlong for China side; no allo plopa; Yinkelis man hab got numpa one tummy; can dlink anyting."

"I'm afraid we do make it too strong. But I'll explain to the ladies; you shall have some made specially weak for you. Stay here and keep watch while I get something to eat, and come back at once if you see any sign of the Chunchuses."

"Allo lightee, massa. My hab catchee plenty chow-chow. No fear!"

Bob returned to the ladies.

"Come, Mr. Fawcett," cried Mrs. Pottle. "I've just finished my fourth cup. Capital tea, even without cream and sugar. But I don't understand your man. I thought Chinamen liked tea, and I gave Ah-Sam a particularly strong cup. He was positively rude—used most sinful language, and actually threw it away. You must be thirsty; now do drink this, and here is some rice—chow, your man called it; I thought that was the Chinese for dog?"

"Yes," said Bob with a twinkle, "or any other form of food."

"Disgusting!" exclaimed Ethel. "Surely it is not true?"

"I'm afraid it is. Fido is quite a standing dish in China."

Mrs. Pottle looked horrified.

"I wonder," she said reflectively, "what that stew was they gave us yesterday?..."

Her speculations were broken in upon by the sight of Ah-Sam running up the gully.

"Massa," he cried, "my look-see plenty piecee Chunchu come this-side chop-chop, galaw!"

Chapter XV
Fortifying the Gully

Stopping a Rush—The Trappers Trapped—Allies—A Manchu Marksman—A Sighting Shot—Building a Barrier—Velly Good Fighty Man—Ah-Sam at the Front

Mrs. Pottle grasped her umbrella as Bob sprang up, leapt over the boulders, and hurried to the mouth of the ravine. In the distance, to the right, he saw a band of mounted men, about sixty in number, easily recognizable by their nondescript dress and long lances as the redoubtable bandits of Manchuria. They disappeared in the bend of the valley. Again they emerged into view, now only a quarter of a mile away, heading straight for the gully over the trail of the cart. Bob hurried back to his place behind the boulders, and took the rifle handed him by Ah-Sam, who retained the other.

"You won't kill them if you can help it, will you?" said Ethel, whose cheeks had become a little pale.

"Nonsense, Ethel," interrupted Mrs. Pottle; "don't be sentimental. I don't wish them any harm, but—"

She did not finish the sentence, for at this moment the horsemen arrived at the mouth of the gully, and halted, evidently in some hesitation, as though fearing a trap. Their leaders spoke together for a few moments; then the whole band dismounted, and, leaving their horses in charge of some of their number, began to climb up the gorge. Bob felt that it was high time to check them.

"Call, Ah-Sam," he said, "and tell them that if they move another step forward I fire."

"Hai yah!" shouted the Chinaman. The little man had a shrill piercing voice, and his exclamation brought the bandits to a sudden halt two hundred yards beneath. He then gave them in Chinese Bob's message, and as he spoke, they strained their eyes upward as if to pierce the barricade. There was a short consultation among them, and then one of them advanced a step and shouted a reply.

"What does he say?" asked Bob.

"One piecee Chunchu say-lo, 'Come this-side, ha-loy! he no killum China-boy, two piecee girley; massa fightee man, he catchee ling-ch'ih'."

"What's that?" asked Bob.

Ah-Sam looked puzzled; his vocabulary was evidently for the moment at a loss. Then he said:

"Ling-ch'ih he killum velly velly slow; he cuttee slicee allo littee piecee: velly long-tim' die-lo galaw!—velly annoying!"

Mrs. Pottle gathered the gist of what Ah-Sam said, and burst forth in great indignation.

"The fiends! I will not allow it. They are arrant cowards. Drive them off. They were frightened of my umbrella. You shall not fall into their power through us. Drive them off!"

Bob considered for a moment. If by delivering himself up he could have ensured a safe-conduct for the two ladies he might have taken the risk; but he was not at all sure that his surrender would satisfy the bandits, incensed at the loss of the prisoners, for whom they expected a good ransom, and at the rough treatment dealt out to the three men. On the other hand, by putting a bold face on it he might scare them off, especially in view of the presence of Russians in the neighbourhood.

"Tell them," he said, "that we refuse to surrender. If they move forward, I fire."

Ah-Sam translated the message. There was another short consultation; then with a shout the bandits rushed up the steep gully straight at the barricade. Mrs. Pottle still grasped her umbrella and walked to and fro in high indignation; Ethel sat with clasped hands, her lips firmly pressed together, her eyes fixed upon Bob.

"Don't fire!" said Bob to Ah-Sam. Resting his own rifle between two boulders, he took careful aim at the foremost of the attacking party, who presented an easy mark as he came directly towards the barricade. He did not wish to kill the man, being anxious not to drive the brigands to extremities; yet it was necessary to teach them a lesson. Seizing a moment when the man's pace was checked by an awkward rock, Bob fired. It was a well-aimed shot, at about a hundred yards' range, and took effect where he intended, in the lower part of the man's leg. A howl of pain announced that the shot had told. Mrs. Pottle exclaimed "There!" with a note of satisfaction; her niece gave a little gasp; neither could see that the man had fallen like a log.

"One piecee hab catchee hot!" muttered Ah-Sam.

The wounded man howled and howled again, and as the others halted in hesitation, Bob thrust the barrel of his rifle conspicuously through the loophole. Next moment the whole band turned tail, and bolted down the slope, leaving their injured comrade behind them, and not pausing until they were out of sight round the corner of the gully.

"Allo lun wailo chop-chop," said Ah-Sam.

"But the poor wounded man!" exclaimed Ethel, starting up. "He must be in terrible pain."

"Nonsense!" said Mrs. Pottle. "He is not killed if he can howl like that."

Ethel got up and looked through an interstice between the boulders, while Mrs. Pottle proceeded to give Bob her views on the situation. Minute after minute passed; there was no sign of a renewed attack by the Chunchuses. Mrs. Pottle brewed more tea and talked on; Ethel moved restlessly about, starting up whenever a groan was heard from the wounded man, and looking more and more concerned as she saw him more than once make a futile attempt to reach his friends. They did not come to his assistance. He tried to crawl down the rocky slope, but each time fell back with a groan, and at last lay perfectly still. Bob had watched Ethel's movements, and saw, though she said nothing, that she was becoming uneasy about the wounded Manchu. He would undoubtedly bleed to death if something were not done for him; his friends were unwilling to face the marksman up the slope. Bob wondered whether he ought to run the risk of going down. Between his boulder and the man there were many rocks which would afford cover for the greater part of the way. If he reached the man, the Chunchuses would probably hesitate to fire lest they hit their comrade; and it had become apparent to Bob that one reason, probably the strongest, why they had not developed their attack was that they feared to bring their enemies, the Russians, upon the scene. At last, unable any longer to resist Ethel's mute plea, he rose, bade Ah-Sam cover him with his rifle, and, crossing the barricade, made his way as quickly as possible down the gully, dodging from rock to rock.

The last dozen yards were open ground, fully exposed to the attack of the Chunchuses. He ran across them, and stooped to the wounded man. At the foot of the gully several of the Chunchuses now showed themselves and watched his proceedings. He first tied his handkerchief round the injured limb, then lifted the man and turned to make his way back. He took two steps, then staggered; the man was heavy, and the necessity of carrying him in a horizontal position, in order to check the flow of blood to his wounded leg, made him a cumbrous burden on so steep an ascent. Bob was doubting whether he would be able unaided to bring the man into safety, when Ah-

Sam appeared. He had marked the difficulty, and, seeing that an attack from below was for the time improbable, had run to his master's assistance. Together then they carried the Chunchuse up the gully, and carefully lifted him over the barricade, and Bob was rewarded by a grateful glance and a murmured word of thanks from Ethel, who at once bent down to assist the man. Mrs. Pottle, for all her outward truculence, had a kind heart. Protesting all the time that it was ridiculous to waste sympathy on a brigand, she lent her niece willing aid, and soon the limb was well bandaged, and the man was supplied with food and tea.

By this time the Chunchuses had congregated about the mouth of the gully, where they stood discussing the situation with some excitement. Bob guessed that the appearance of a Korean capable of fighting, in company with a Chinaman of courage and assurance, had somewhat astonished them; and though it was impossible for Ah-Sam to hear what they were saying, it was not difficult to guess that they were divided in opinion, some being inclined to renew the attack, others to seek a compromise. It was Bob's policy to wait. Suddenly the colloquy below was interrupted; there was a sound of galloping horses, and immediately the Chunchuses were scattering, seeking cover behind boulders at the mouth of the ravine. Behind them came one or two of the men they had left in the road in charge of the horses. For a few moments there was wild confusion, a clamour of mingled shouts, the clash of arms, the stampeding of horses. A shot rang out, the babel ceased, and a man was seen hurrying up the gully, holding a piece of torn and dirty rag upon his musket.

"Tell him to stop," said Bob to Ah-Sam when the Chunchuse had come within fifty yards of the barricade.

"What is happening now?" asked Mrs. Pottle, endeavouring to peep over a boulder.

"Please go back, Mrs. Pottle," said Bob earnestly. "I don't know what may happen yet. It appears to be a flag of truce."

"I decline to have any parley with the brigands," said Mrs. Pottle decisively; "I firmly decline. They are outlaws, and—"

"Auntie, Mr. Fawcett wishes to speak to the man," interposed Ethel mildly.

The emissary had stopped at Ah-Sam's bidding, and was now speaking rapidly in answer to the Chinaman's questions. His features wore an anxious look. From Ah-Sam's translation of his speech, Bob learnt that the commotion he had recently witnessed was due to the sudden appearance of a mixed force of Russians and Manchus, who had ridden up in two parties, one from each side of the valley, and closed in upon the Chunchuses at the gully's mouth. Sheltered by the large scattered rocks, the brigands were able for the moment to keep the Russians at bay; but at any moment their position might be rushed. They knew that they could expect no mercy from the Russians, and they were now in a terrible dilemma: on the one side the Cossacks, on the other the armed men, they did not know how many in number, behind the barricade. Between two fires they would be utterly annihilated. As a counsel of desperation the flag-bearer had come to beg the leader of the party more favourably posted to admit the Chunchuses behind his entrenchments, where they might make common cause against the Russians.

This was a critical moment which Bob had not foreseen. Obviously there was little time for deliberation. Though no more shots had been fired, he had no doubt that the Russians were only awaiting a favourable opportunity for swooping on the band of Chunchuses, and after they had been disposed of it would not be long before he too, with his companions, must fall into their hands. The ladies might be safe with them, of course; but he himself durst not appear; they were hunting him for his life. It was thus impossible for him to remain neutral. Recent events had in fact made him a natural ally of the Chunchuses. They might be brigands, but they were at the same time patriots, fighting on their own soil against an alien invader. Their methods were not perhaps commendable from a western stand-point, but the Russians themselves, as he himself had seen during his wanderings in Korea, were not always too scrupulous. There was only one consideration that made him hesitate, and that was, would the sudden friendliness of the Chunchuses last after the pressing danger was past?

Bob was not long in making up his mind.

"Tell them," he said to Ah-Sam, "that I will help them if they will help us in return. If they succeed in beating off the Russians, they must afterwards help us to cross the Yalu and come safely within the Japanese lines. Will they do that?"

"My talkee, massa."

Ah-Sam put the case to the man, who stood impatiently awaiting Bob's decision. The answer was voluble, and accompanied by gestures which to Bob were very mysterious. Ah-Sam explained that the Chunchuse had at once accepted the offered terms, and had emphasized his promise by swearing by the graves of his ancestors that he would make his words good.

"Is he to be trusted?" asked Bob.

"Oh yes. He one piecee head man; he talkee velly good; he velly muchee aflaid joss angly, spoilum allo piecee Chunchuses this-tim', supposey no do what he hab say do. He allo lightee, massa."

"Very well. Tell him I will see what can be done."

"What are you going to do, Mr. Fawcett?" asked Mrs. Pottle. "I strongly object to have any dealings with the brigands, and I declare—"

"Auntie," interposed Ethel gently, "don't you think we had better trust to Mr. Fawcett to do what he thinks best?"

"Well, I wash my hands of the whole business. China boy, fetchee more water from the streamee; we wantee makee more tea."

Thanking the girl with a glance, Bob sprang over the barricade, and, with a parting order to Ah-Sam to remain with the ladies, set off to join his late enemy. At the mouth of the gully he found that the Chunchuses had taken up positions behind every available rock. They were somewhat tightly packed, and as some of them moved from their places to meet their returning leader, and for a moment left cover, the Russians began to take snap shots at them from the crest of a hillock about six or seven hundred yards away. One man was hit just as Bob reached the band. There was a reply from several of the Chunchuses; but it was clear that they were hopelessly outranged. Their muskets did indeed carry the distance of the Russian position, but with no accuracy, and as the Russians were careful to present no considerable target, they were unlikely to suffer any loss.

Peering cautiously round the edge of a boulder, Bob looked across the valley in the direction pointed out to him. At first he could see nothing; then, on the crest of the hillock, he saw one or two moving objects which by and by resolved themselves into the caps of men on the other side. He wondered why the Russians, armed as they were with good weapons, did not advance boldly to the attack; but the explanation soon suggested itself. The horses of the Chunchuses having been stampeded, escape for the latter was impossible. The Cossacks recognized that they had them in a trap, but were disinclined to throw away lives by coming to close quarters in broad daylight with a strongly entrenched enemy. At nightfall, however, the odds would be all in their favour. They outnumbered the Chunchuses by at least two to one; under cover of night they could easily rush the position through the wide gaps between the boulders; and in a hand-to-hand fight their superior numbers were bound to tell. Bob had no doubt that they would defer their attack until night, and that was a serious danger to be provided against.

He was still watching the hillock, wondering how many men were encamped on the farther slope, when he noticed a dark shape rise upon the crest. Its outlines were clearly visible in contrast with the snow-covered ground, and in a moment Bob recognized the form as the head and shoulders of a Manchu. The man had apparently just spread his cloak before him, for he bent down face forwards, until only his head was visible, a dark motionless patch at the summit of the hill. A minute or two passed, then Bob saw a faint puff of smoke just below the crouching Manchu, and immediately afterwards a metallic "splat" was heard on the rock close to Bob's elbow. The man had evidently posted himself with the object of taking pot-shots at any of the Chunchuses who incautiously afforded him a target. His rifle was a good one, and that he was a good marksman was soon proved, for a second puff of smoke was followed, not by the sound of a bullet striking the rock, but by a howl of pain from one of the defenders, whose arm, overlapping the edge of the rock behind which he stood, had been pierced by the Manchu's shot. Only half a minute later, a third shot was even more accurate; a man's head showed above a rock, and with a suddenness that startled everyone he fell back, dead.

The movements which had exposed the defenders to the aim of the Manchu marksman were partly due to the impatient rage of the Chunchuses at their inability to retaliate. Bob saw that a succession of such incidents would destroy their nerve and demoralize them. He was himself a good marksman; at eight hundred yards he had more than once scored a possible on the butts at Darnley; and the sight of the dead man by his side banished his last feeling of compunction at taking an active part. Removing his cloak and cap to reduce his height and bulk as much as possible, he cautiously made his way to the boulder at which the Chunchuses were least huddled. As he ran across a few yards of exposed space, bullets pattered all around him; a man at the edge of the boulder for which he was making raised his hand to his cheek, and withdrew it covered with blood; a splinter of lead or rock had inflicted a slight jagged wound. The man looked at his hand with stolid indifference, and wiped it on his coat. It was evident that there were other marksmen on the crest of the hill, though only the Manchu was in sight. This incident had the curious effect of steadying Bob's nerve, and when he reached the boulder he was able to take a quiet look round.

A few feet to the right there lay an isolated rock much lower than the one whose shelter he had gained. Throwing himself flat on the ground, he crawled slowly forward, and noticed when he came to the smaller boulder that, still farther to the right, and a little in advance, there was a yet smaller rock, the lateral interval between the two being so narrow that he thought it unlikely he could be seen by the Russians if he used it as a peep-hole. It turned out as he surmised. He found that, while himself invisible, he commanded a view of about one-sixth of the space occupied by the Russians. As he looked, he saw that the Manchu who had been so troublesome had disappeared; the line of the hill-crest was unbroken. Bob feared that the man had escaped him, but in a moment he caught sight of his head and shoulders again, at a point somewhat to the left of his former position. He lowered himself as before, and bent forward on his elbow, waiting a favourable opportunity to test his marksmanship. The moment came; some incautious Chunchuse had no doubt exposed himself, for Bob saw the Manchu lift his rifle in the attitude of taking aim. He was destined never to pull the trigger. From his first movement Bob had covered him; while he was still aiming, the crack of a rifle was heard in the gully, and the Manchu's head fell forward, his rifle forming a dark streak on the snow. So instantaneous had been the effect of his shot that Bob was for the moment doubtful; but it was impossible to mistake the attitude of the inert form on the hillside. The man was dead.

The fact came home to Bob with a sort of shock. A soldier in the heat of battle has no time to reflect; his duty is to shoot straight and keep his nerve. But this single shot had not been fired in the rush of fight; it had scarcely caused his nerves to tingle more than in a keenly-contested musketry competition at home. For the moment he felt guilty as though he had committed a crime, and, rifle in hand, stared spell-bound at the prostrate figure. Then he was startled from his reverie by the sound of a hail of bullets whistling through the air and pattering on the rocks, and around him the discharge of a dozen antiquated pieces within the space of a few yards filled the air with the pungent smell of war.

After some minutes the din ceased. For an hour afterwards the firing was merely spasmodic. Bob was confirmed in his conclusion that the Russians were only putting in time until nightfall. Knowing that it would be impossible to hold the wide gaps at the mouth of the gully against a rush of superior forces, he saw that sooner or later the Chunchuses would have to take refuge higher up; but he was anxious to defer this movement, and cast about for some means of at least inflicting a temporary check upon the enemy. The Chunchuses themselves were making no preparations for the changed conditions that must arise, and being ignorant of their language, Bob was unable to consult with them. He therefore called Ah-Sam to his side, and through him asked the leader of the brigands what he proposed to do. The man replied that when night came he meant to retreat up the gorge behind the barricade; his men were too few to hold their present position; they would be overwhelmed at the first assault. Bob pointed out that it was bad policy to retire within their inmost defences except as a last resource. Cooped up in the narrow space, above, they would be in desperate straits if the enemy found a means of climbing the hills and taking them in the rear. The man at once answered that the hills were unscaleable. Nobody had ever been known to ascend them from this side. He was ready to make a stand at the mouth of the gully if it were possible, but the honourable stranger himself saw that it was out of the question.

Bob considered for a few moments. Dusk was creeping on, and if anything was to be done it must be done quickly.

"Tell him," he said at length to Ah-Sam, "that if he and his men will do what I ask them, we can make this position very strong. It will not take longer than about half an hour."

The Chunchuse at once agreed, and Bob proceeded to explain his plan. As soon as it was dark enough he proposed to send out ten of the best-armed and most skilful marksmen in skirmishing order to a distance of a hundred yards beyond the mouth of the gully, with orders to give instant warning of the enemy's approach. Twenty of the rest were to act as a reserve behind the boulders. There were some thirty men left; these he proposed to divide into squads of five, and they were to roll or drag towards the entrance of the ravine the loose boulders that lay scattered along the banks of the stream above. The reserve meanwhile would load the muskets of the whole body, and hold these in readiness for instant use at various points, to which the workers would hasten, each to his appointed spot, at the first alarm.

The suggestion was immediately approved by the leader, and received with eagerness by his men when it was explained to them. Since Bob had appeared on the scene, and especially since he had shot the Manchu on the hill, the brigands had regarded him with a good deal of respect. When the country had become sufficiently dark for their movements to escape the notice of the Russians, the plan was immediately put into operation. Bob himself superintended the work of the thirty. Under his directions they rolled and dragged the rocks downward, blocking up the gaps at the foot of the ravine. The task was arduous and unequal. Bob added a man to a squad at one point where the stone to be moved was unusually heavy, taking one from a neighbouring squad that happened to be less taxed. During the first quarter of an hour the work went on at a great rate. There was a good supply of manageable boulders near at hand, and the men were encouraged when they saw a continuous breastwork beginning to fill the gaps which had appeared to them indefensible. But as the nearest stones became used up, the task grew in difficulty, for higher up the ravine the boulders were larger and required much greater exertions to move them. It was becoming colder as the darkness increased, but the ground was as yet not sufficiently hardened to be slippery, and the huge masses of rock often sank into holes and were obstructed by irregularities in the ground, so that the half-hour had long been exceeded before the breastwork was finished. The task, however, was completed at last. The new barrier was rough and uneven, but promised to be quite adequate to its purpose.

There was still no sign of the enemy. No doubt they were waiting until they might suppose the defenders lulled to security; perhaps they were having a meal in preparation for their attack. As the idea struck Bob, he asked whether the Chunchuses had any provisions with them, and was alarmed to find that they were almost foodless, their supplies having been on their horses' backs. They carried in their wallets no more than one day's food. This was unfortunate; it might prove a calamity. The coming struggle was likely to be severe, and the brigands, however much inured to hardship they might be, could not fight well if they were hungry. Bob advised the men to husband their little stock as much as possible; he feared that nothing could be spared from what Ah-Sam had brought in the cart, and already foresaw the ultimate destiny of the little Chinaman's team.

Recalling seven of the scouts outside, leaving three still to keep a vigilant look-out for signs of the advancing enemy, he leant on the breastwork, and peered out into the darkness, wondering whether anything had been left undone. As he looked at the few yards of snow-covered ground still visible before him, an idea suddenly flashed across his mind. Calling up Ah-Sam, he sent him to bring his four spades from the cart. Removing a small boulder at one extremity of the barricade, he borrowed a spear, went outside to a distance of ten paces, and with the spear drew a line across the mouth of the gully parallel with the barrier. Four feet beyond this line he drew another parallel with it, then returned within the defences. In a few minutes Ah-Sam came back with the spades, and Bob was astonished to see that he was accompanied by Ethel.

"I have brought you some tea," she said; "it will refresh you. Auntie is very anxious to know what you are doing. I could hardly persuade her not to come and see."

"It is very good of you. Please go back, Miss—" He paused. Mrs. Pottle had omitted to mention her niece's surname. He saw a faint smile in Ethel's face.

"Auntie never stands much on ceremony," she said, "and she has taken you quite for granted. My father's name is Charteris."

"Do, please, go back. The Russians may be upon us at any moment, and you will be in danger. Tell Mrs. Pottle that we are doing our best. Ah-Sam, go back with Miss Charteris, and remain with the ladies."

"My no likee go that-side," protested Ah-Sam. "My velly good fighty man; my no tinkee—"

"Come, Ah-Sam!" said Ethel.

Ah-Sam looked from one to the other, then without another word, but with a very downcast countenance, he walked behind the girl up the hill.

Bob had no difficulty in making the Chunchuse leader understand by signs that he required the services of four spademen. These were at once forthcoming—four strapping fellows, who soon showed by the way they handled their implements that before they became brigands they were husbandmen. He set them to dig a trench between the parallel lines he had drawn, placing one man at each end, and the other two back to back in the centre, with orders to work towards their comrades at the fastest rate of which they were capable. After five minutes he relieved them by another squad, and while these were working it struck him that if the Russians attacked suddenly, and the diggers tried to scramble over the barrier, they would come directly in the line of fire and either lose their lives or cause the loss of precious time to the firing party. He therefore removed a small rock at each end, and when he sent out the next relieving squad he gave them express orders to make for the barrier, each man for the gap nearest him, if the alarm were given. The men worked so energetically that in a short time a trench four feet broad and two deep stretched across the entrance to the gully. The men were then withdrawn. They joined their comrades in disposing of the scanty rations at command. All being now in readiness to meet an attack, the scouts also were recalled, and Bob, feeling that he had done all that he could, sat down to rest and await the event.

The time dragged slowly on. The whole band maintained almost absolute silence; no sound was to be heard save the rush of the stream. Waiting in the dark, all his senses on the alert, Bob wondered whether the enemy had drawn off. It was unlike them so to do; the Russians were implacable where Manchurian brigands not on their side were concerned. The existence of these armed bands within their lines was at all times a serious menace. The whole population, save for parties of hired desperadoes, was hostile to the Russian cause. If in the coming conflict with the hosts of Japan the Russians were beaten, the news would rapidly spread through the country, and each isolated band of Chunchuses would become the nucleus to which thousands would flock, harassing the retreating army, and threatening a catastrophe like that which befell Napoleon's grand army in its retreat from Moscow. It was therefore most unlikely that the little force of which Bob now found himself the virtual commander would be left unmolested. The Russian captain had much to gain with his superiors by extirpating the band.

Bob was turning things over in his mind, when suddenly Ah-Sam made his reappearance. This was somewhat surprising. The average Chinaman has no stomach for a fight; he will die at his post if need be, but as a rule he shows no dissatisfaction at being ordered to the rear. Bob had expected that Ah-Sam would be more than glad to have the opportunity of remaining in safety with the ladies.

"What are you doing here?" he demanded. "I ordered you to remain above."

"My savvy, massa. My velly muchee aflaid largo piecee woman. She say my come back chop-chop bottom-side; massa want gib orders allo piecee Chunchuses; no can do supposey China-boy no this-side helpum talkee. Littee piecee missy say all-same; my no can stay topside no longer, galaw!"

Bob already knew Mrs. Pottle well enough not to be surprised at her taking a different view from his own. The fact that Ethel Charteris had acquiesced in her aunt's command to Ah-Sam to return showed that she was in no fear; and reassured on this score, Bob reflected that certainly Ah-Sam would be very useful, even indispensable, to him.

"Very well," he said, "keep close at hand, and we'll see what sort of a fighting man you are when the time comes."

Bob turned his back on the gully, and once more looked earnestly into the darkness. He therefore did not see the look of gleeful satisfaction on the quaint face of his henchman, nor hear the chuckle he uttered as he sat down to wait beside his master.

Chapter XVI
Hemmed In

The Deadly Breach—Yinkelis-fashion—Chang-Wo is Surprised—Short Commons—Enfiladed—On the Ledge—The Ammunition Question—Chang-Wo Disappears—Footsteps

The minutes passed. The air grew colder. Only the dim flickering of the stars threw a faint light over the scene. One or two of the men had fallen asleep; the rest waited, some stolidly, some restlessly, for the expected encounter. Bob remained at the breastwork, intently watching.

At length one of the men who had been out as scouts whispered hurriedly to the leader; he had heard a slight sound from the distance. The sleepers were roused; every man stood to arms; all were on the instant doubly alert. After the first rustle there was an extraordinary stillness; the watchers seemed scarcely to breathe. Bob heard nothing, but in a moment the scout whispered again. The Russians were coming! Through Ah-Sam the message was passed from the chief to Bob. Ten minutes passed in tense and breathless expectancy, then there came a sound which every man behind the barrier heard. It was the clash of wood against steel; one of the enemy had stumbled and clumsily allowed his weapon to strike that of a comrade. No other sound followed. The enemy were evidently advancing with extreme caution, hoping, as Bob conjectured, either to surprise the Chunchuses, or at any rate to approach sufficiently close unseen to carry the defences with a rush.

In a whisper Bob bade Ah-Sam repeat a caution he had already impressed upon the chief. Not a man should fire until the word was given. The reserve were to withhold their fire altogether until the enemy had reached the wall, or until their comrades had reloaded. Another period of waiting, shorter; then the crisp footfalls of a body of men creeping over the freezing ground were distinctly heard. Suddenly, about thirty yards away, a dark mass of figures came into view; there was a low word of command, and the whole body of Russians and Manchus sprang forward with a yell in which every dialect was represented from the Danube to the Yalu.

Would the obedience of the bandits be equal to the strain of waiting for the word? Bob had hardly time to wonder, for the enemy had swept over the first twenty yards dividing them from the rocky breastwork; behind it, all was silent. Then as if by magic the mass seemed to melt away; the attacking party had, as Bob expected, failed to see the shallow trench; the first line stepping into it fell headlong, the second tripped over them, and next moment the majority of the men were floundering affrighted on the snow-covered ground. Then Bob gave the word. The muskets roared, and bullets fell thick into the midst of the struggling heap immediately under the muzzles of the defenders' weapons. An awful cry ascended from the heaving mass. It was impossible to distinguish what was going on, for the men upon the ground were a tangled medley, some trying to regain their feet and flee from the spot, others writhing with wounds, too badly hit to rise, a few pressing madly forward to the breastwork, which they strove to scale. Then the reserve opened fire; the clamour was redoubled, and the survivors turned their backs, and, jumping or scrambling over their fallen comrades, fled amazedly away into the darkness.

Yells of exultation and defiance burst from the throats of the defenders, now at last able to give vent to the feelings pent up during hours of silent waiting. The leader was eager to spring across the breastwork and slaughter the wounded wretches, whose groans were heard as the tumult subsided. Bob hauled him back by main force, and ordered him to send out a few scouts to discover whether the Cossacks were within striking distance. Learning soon that the enemy had all retreated beyond the hill, he posted five men at intervals about four hundred yards out to keep watch, and proceeded to attend to the wounded. Among the defenders only one man had been hurt by the bayonet of a gallant Russian, who had come right up to the wall and fallen dead beneath a Chunchuse bullet. But in and around the trench there were twenty-eight prone forms, and of these Bob soon saw that eleven had keen killed outright. They were partly Russians, partly Manchus. As Bob went along the trench, carefully examining the survivors in turn, he came upon one lying on his right side, and groaning. He turned the man over, and started—even in the dim light he fancied he recognized his features. Thrilling with expectancy he went to the man's other side and stooped to him. Yes, the right ear was gone; it was without doubt the Manchu, Chang-Wo! Bob rose, and calling to Ah-Sam, bade him carry the wounded man within the barricade; he himself followed, wondering at the strange fate which had connected him with the Manchu ever since his arrival in Japan. He was perplexed as to what could be done for the rest of the injured, whose moans gave him many a pang. He was in no position to deal with them—he had no surgical appliances, no food; yet he could not leave them to perish miserably. What could he do? A thought struck him. Why not deliver them to their own friends? It might be difficult; neither party could trust the other; but he was determined that it should be attempted, even though the Russians regarded it as a trap.

With Ah-Sam's assistance he explained the matter to the leader of the Chunchuses, whose name, he learnt, was Sing-Cheng. The man was wholly at a loss to understand Bob's object. He had acquiesced unwillingly in the order not to butcher the wounded, partly because he knew they would probably die of themselves if left. But that they should actually be given up, living, to their comrades, seemed to him a foolish proposal. Why had they been shot if the effects of the bullets were to be disregarded?

It was no time to explain. Bob, indeed, felt that it might be a difficult task to reconcile such opposites in a Chunchuse mind. He merely asked Ah-Sam to say that it was his wish, and that he had a good reason for it. A colloquy ensued between Ah-Sam and Sing-Cheng. Then the former turned to Bob and said:

"He say velly well, massa, but no can tinkey so-fashion. He say massa plenty good fightee man. Can makee place velly stlong, shoot allo lightee. He tinkey one piecee Yinkelis topside man. He no savvy what-for massa helpee spoilum Roshians. Ch'hoy! He do what massa say this-time."

"Very well," said Bob.

It was necessary to send a message to the Cossack commander. He could not entrust a verbal message to a Chunchuse; he could not dispense at present with Ah-Sam. He must write his proposal, and he had neither paper nor pencil.

"No doubt Mrs. Pottle will have both," he said to himself.

Leaving instructions with the Chunchuses to keep a strict look-out, he hurried up the gully. The ladies must have been alarmed by the firing, and he could fulfil his errand and reassure them at the same time. He spoke to them before he reached the inner barricade, and, when he arrived, found them standing within the line of boulders, ready to meet him. Even Mrs. Pottle was subdued; the terrors of the past half-hour had shaken her. He noticed that she grasped her umbrella.

"Oh, Mr. Fawcett!" she exclaimed; "what has happened?"

"We have beaten off the Russians—once," Bob replied quietly.

"You are not hurt?" said Ethel, leaning towards him, her face very pale.

"No; only one of our party is injured—very slightly. Don't be alarmed. I don't think we shall be troubled any more to-night. I came to borrow some writing materials. Some of the enemy are badly wounded, and I want to send a message to their officer asking him to carry them away."

"Oh, how thoughtful of you! Auntie, a leaf from your block-book. Here is a pencil."

Mrs. Pottle tore a leaf from the book in which she had noted down her impressions of travel in the East, and gave it to Bob.

"Come back soon, Mr. Fawcett," she said. "I am very nervous. That horrid shooting keeps throbbing in my head."

Promising to return if possible, Bob hastened down to the breastwork, and on a boulder, by the light of matches struck for him by Ah-Sam, he wrote in French to the Russian officer. Explaining that he was unable to tend the wounded, he suggested that six men at a time should be sent unarmed to carry them off; he would guarantee their safety. Meanwhile he held one of the wounded men as a hostage.

He despatched the note by a scout, who, venturing about half-way to the Russian position, called aloud for someone to come out and meet him. After some delay a Cossack cautiously approached and received the note. Half an hour elapsed, during which his communication, Bob surmised, had been discussed in the Russian camp; then a Manchu came forward and told the messenger in his own tongue that the terms were accepted. If treachery were practised, the Russians would hang every man caught in the gully. Bob smiled when Ah-Sam translated the message. He knew that, treachery or no treachery, hanging or worse would be the fate of any prisoner; there was no mercy for the Chunchuses.

It took more than an hour to remove the wounded, whom Bob had had carefully carried to a distance of a hundred yards from the breastwork, in order that his defences might not be too closely inspected. When the last had disappeared, Bob went to the spot where his wounded prisoner had been laid. Chang-Wo had now recovered consciousness. He was suffering from a severe scalp wound, which had already been roughly dressed. At Bob's orders Ah-Sam struck a match and held it close to the Manchu's face. He blinked and scowled, then stared at Bob for a moment with a very puzzled expression; he was clearly trying to reconcile the features of the man before him with the Korean dress. Then he glared; a look of rage and chagrin darkened his villainous face. Bob saw that he was recognized. The Manchu attempted to rise, but fell back and groaned. Bob said never a word to him, but giving orders that he should be made as comfortable as possible, he arranged with the chief to keep half the men on duty during the night, while the others rested; and then with Ah-Sam he returned to the ladies in the lonely refuge above.

Mrs. Pottle in his company soon regained her self-confidence, and insisted on a full account of the fight below. Bob told her as much as he thought she should know, and all the time Ethel, like Desdemona, hung upon his words.

"You cannot hoodwink me," exclaimed Mrs. Pottle at the conclusion of the story. "It was you planned it all; I know it was. I have been six weeks with the Chunchuses, and they've no brains. If it had not been for your quickness, Mr. Fawcett, we should have been bound to the Russian cart-wheels by this time."

"Oh no!" returned Bob. "But I must not conceal from you that we are still in a difficult position, Mrs. Pottle, and it is not too late for you still to escape all danger by seeking safety with the Russians."

"I positively refuse; I will not hear of it. I have had enough of the Russians. Besides, what could they do? It appears to me that they've overreached themselves in undertaking to conquer Japan. And mercy me! I don't want to be sent back via Siberia! No, Mr. Fawcett, I'm nearer my country here, and here I shall stay—to the bitter end!"

"But Miss Charteris—"

"She has no wish apart from mine, and of course where I am she must be."

"Well, Mrs. Pottle, you know the position. I will do my best. Now I think you should try to get some sleep. You have had a most exhausting day, and will be quite done up."

"Oh, I couldn't sleep a wink. I should dream. No, I must get the China boy to boil some water; tea will keep us awake. Ethel, my love, you are not sleepy?"

"I think I am, auntie. I think I could sleep now I know that—that—"

"That what? Well, well! Ah-Sam, fetchee cloakees, ruggies, anythingy, from the cartee; missy wantee go sleepy."

But it was Bob who brought all the available wraps from the cart, and made a comfortable couch on the rock for the ladies. After all, it was Mrs. Pottle that fell asleep first. She slept calmly through the night, though she declared when Bob made his appearance that she had scarcely shut her eyes.

The night had passed peacefully. Bob himself had not dared to slumber, for fear lest the attack should be renewed. When morning dawned, he saw the Russians in their old position on the hillock. An occasional shot when one of the garrison exposed himself showed that they were still on the alert, but hour after hour went by and no attack in force was made. Thinking over the situation, Bob could not but conclude that the enemy were either bent on starving him out, or had sent for reinforcements. As nearly as he could judge, their original strength had been some eighty Cossacks and sixty Manchus. At least thirty men must now be subtracted as dead or incapacitated, and as it was likely that many who had escaped after the night attack were more or less badly hit, it was natural that they should hesitate before again approaching the fatal gully.

With either of the two alternatives, Bob recognized that the prospects of the garrison were anything but good. The food question had confronted them the night before; if the Russians persisted in a blockade they would soon be face to face with starvation. There were so many mouths to feed — the ladies first of all, for whom the supply of rice and millet in the cart might suffice for a few days. There was almost nothing for the brigands, who, in fact, had already skinned and cut up Ah-Sam's pony. Ah-Sam had only sufficient fodder in the cart to last his mules two days, even at the most economical rate, and there was not a vestige of herbage in the neighbourhood.

Bob kept as much as possible out of Mrs. Pottle's reach during that day. She had a most uncomfortable habit of asking pressing questions that he found it impossible to evade. But at nightfall she had an opportunity of making the enquiry on the matter that had troubled her all day — this very matter of food.

"We have done very well," she said. "Ah-Sam's rice is excellent, and his millet cakes passable, though I can't trust him to make the tea. But what have you had, Mr. Fawcett? You have not shared in one of our meals to-day."

"No, I shared with Ah-Sam."

"But what did he have? He refused to take any rice or millet."

"He shared with the Chunchuses."

"Yes, but that's what I don't understand. They had nothing left yesterday: where did they get food to-day?"

Bob hesitated, but knowing that the truth must come out sooner or later, he at last said:

"We had a little beef—horse-beef, in fact; very like the real thing."

Ethel shuddered. Mrs. Pottle gasped, then cried indignantly:

"I am ashamed of you, Mr. Fawcett. I am not thinking of the poor beast. It is a shame to deceive me. You could have had rice: I would have boiled it for you myself."

"But, my dear Mrs. Pottle, we don't know how long we may be cooped up here; and if I used your rice you would be reduced to eating the mules."

Mrs. Pottle looked at him. Her plump cheeks turned a little green. Then with a forced laugh she said:

"Well, by all accounts I've eaten worse. I don't say I relish mules, but if it comes to that—"

"Don't worry, auntie," interposed Ethel. "There is still some rice left. Mr. Fawcett will find a way out of this difficulty, I am sure."

Bob privately wished that he felt anything like the same assurance. Two days passed, during which his anxiety did but deepen. No movement was made by the Russians. This fact only increased his uneasiness, for it was a proof that the worst of the position had yet to be faced. One of the mules had been killed and cut up; Bob found, indeed, that the Chunchuses were almost reckless in their consumption of the flesh, and he had to impress upon Sing-Cheng the necessity of putting them on fixed rations. At best the fare was meagre; the animals were hardy and muscular, but with no superfluous flesh; and what flesh there was was not too wholesome without vegetable food. The men ate their scanty rations without grumbling, but they objected to the feeding of Chang-Wo; in him, indeed, Sing-Cheng had recognized an enemy against whom he bore an old-standing private grudge. He was for killing the Manchu out of hand; he reeled off to Ah-Sam a long and passionate account of the evils he had done. But Bob insisted that the prisoner must be fed exactly as themselves, and kept him bound hand and foot to the cart.

On the third day, shortly after dawn, Bob was disconcerted to find that the enemy had achieved what Sing-Cheng had declared to be impossible. Shots from a point high up the cliff on his left told him that in some way, probably by making a considerable detour, the Russians had gained a position whence they could enfilade his encampment behind the boulder. The new danger to which he was exposed was soon brought home to him. The enemy, themselves for the most part under cover, began to pick off the Chunchuses, while their comrades on the hill in front kept up a hot fire which showed that escape in that direction was impossible. The unfortunate garrison were placed in a desperate plight. If they shifted their ground to avoid the flank attack they exposed themselves to the enemy on the hill. To neither could they make any effective reply. In the first place their arms were ineffective at the range, and secondly, the Russians had all the advantage of cover. Bob himself, with his more accurate rifle, managed to put *hors de combat* one or two of the enemy who exposed themselves; though he dared not shoot as often as opportunity offered, for his stock of ammunition was small, and it was necessary to husband it.

As his men dropped one by one he recognized at length that the position was untenable. He must withdraw them behind the barricade above, which was protected by the contour of the hill from the marksmen on the cliff. But this raised the question, what was he to do with the ladies? There were two reasons against their remaining where they were. First, seventy Chunchuses huddled in the small free space behind the barricade were scarcely fit company for them; secondly, they themselves would be in the way if the Russians pushed home an attack. Both Mrs. Pottle and Ethel had up to the present borne the stress of the situation with good heart, and under Ah-Sam's tuition had become adepts in the cooking of rice and millet, which, with tea, brewed in diminishing strength daily, was their only sustenance. Bob did his best to disguise from them the full gravity of the position, but felt all the time that they must see the hollowness of his assurances.

While he was wondering what to do for the best, his eye lit on the fissure in the rock above which had attracted his attention when he first came along the road. Was it deep enough, he wondered, to afford protection to the two ladies? At the mouth it was exposed to the enfilading fire of the Russians, but if it extended for any considerable distance into the rock, it might form a place of refuge. He resolved to explore it. It could only be approached by the shelf of rock that abutted on the mountain stream, and this for the greater part of its length was sheltered from the enemy. But there was a strip of some twenty yards lying in the interval between two shelving rocks, and this was quite open. It would be a case of running the gauntlet. He looked round in final search of another way; there was none; he must himself take the risk.

But it was necessary first to ensure the safety of his little force during his absence. He therefore withdrew the greater part from the wall at the mouth of the gorge, leaving only a dozen men, who were protected from the fire of the Russians on the heights by a projecting spur of the hill. These being the best marksmen could probably hold the enemy in check for a time, but Bob ordered them to withdraw behind the upper barricade if the Russians, realizing the weakness of the defending force, should at last attempt a rush. Meanwhile the men he had withdrawn were set to construct with boulders a small fort high up the gorge just under the waterfall; this would form excellent vantage ground in case the Russians occupied the lower portion of the gully.

These arrangements having been made, Bob left the ladies in charge of Ah-Sam and started on his hazardous expedition. Knowing that the fissure, if of any considerable depth, must be quite dark, he took with him a torch improvised out of a piece of sacking smeared with mule fat, and a box of matches. He climbed over the intervening rocks, turned a corner, reached the ledge, and walked along until he came to the exposed portion, where he halted for a moment. Then, springing forward like a sprinter, he dashed over the narrow shelf at the imminent risk of stumbling and falling to the rocky bed of the stream fifty feet below. He was seen by the Russians on the hill, and in the few seconds he took to complete the passage he heard a patter of bullets on the rocks, and one or two even followed him as he gained the opening and plunged in. But he had escaped unhurt, and safe in the fissure he paused to take breath and to light his torch, reflecting that he would run double danger in coming out, for the Russians would doubtless be on the watch for him.

Making his way into the cleft, he found that it was broader than he had expected. After about twenty yards it took a sudden curve to the left, and then widened into a jagged irregular passage some four yards in breadth, and of varying height. At one moment, torch in hand, he had to stoop to avoid a sharp edge of rock; a little later the passage was at least twenty feet high. He had penetrated as nearly as he could judge for about fifty yards, when his steps were arrested by the faint sounds of firing behind him, and he hurried back. As he approached the opening the sound became so loud and continuous that he felt sure a stiff fight was in progress. Keeping close to the less-exposed wall of the cleft at its mouth, he saw from his elevated position that the Russians were at last making the long-expected attack. From the hill a hot fire was being brought to bear upon the mouth of the gully, while a number of the enemy were just emerging from round the hillside to the right, being protected from the fire of the dozen Chunchuses by the boulders. They were making for the right extremity of the barrier, a point which it was impossible to defend because of the direct and rapid firing from the hill.

Clearly the twelve men gallantly holding their own at the mouth of the gully were in danger of being cut off. Bob only took a second or two to recognize the urgency of the case; then, springing on to the ledge at the mouth of the cleft, he rushed along it at breakneck speed, and owed his safety to his quick movements, for before the Russians caught sight of him, occupied as they were with keeping down the fire from the barrier beneath, he had covered several yards, and the snap shots they then took flew wide of the mark. Arriving at the corner, he shouted to Ah-Sam below an order to recall the men from the breastwork. The command was instantly given, and the brigands, running like cats from rock to rock, scrambled up the gully and flung themselves pell-mell through a small gap left for them in the barricade above, one or two of them being hit by Russian bullets. The advancing enemy at once occupied the far side of the abandoned breastwork, and opened fire on the upper defences; but when a few attempted to cross and move up the gully the fire of the Chunchuses proved too hot for them, and they hastily retreated.

Except that the defenders were now driven into a more confined space, the general situation had from the Russian point of view improved but little. The Russians dared not press forward up the gorge, for it had been so thoroughly cleared of boulders for the construction of the barricades that it was almost wholly devoid of cover for an attacking force. The double entrenchments above were even stronger than the breastwork below, and could only be carried at a terrible cost.

By this time Bob had clambered down among his men. Unpleasant news was in waiting for him. Through Ah-Sam the brigand leader informed him that the men's ammunition was running short; they had only an average of five rounds a man remaining. This was an irremediable misfortune. Only one course was possible. All the available ammunition was collected and distributed, principally among the twenty best shots in the band. Ten of these men were stationed at the barricade by the carts, and ten in the fort recently constructed higher up the gully. The remainder of the garrison were given one round apiece, and this was only to be used on an emergency. They were to make no attempt to reply to the fire of the Russians. Bob stationed himself by the cart where Chang-Wo was still bound, and fired a shot at intervals whenever an incautious member of the attacking force presumed on the general silence of the besieged and emerged from cover. More than once his shots took effect, and as a result the enemy became more cautious, keeping well behind the shelter of the rocks, and settling themselves to establish a strict blockade.

Thus the day passed. At the approach of night, Bob for the first time informed Mrs. Pottle of the place of safety he had found for her and her niece. The strain of the siege was beginning to tell on the elder lady, who quite meekly accepted Bob's proposal, and prepared to climb with him to the cleft. He was as much pleased as surprised to find that Ethel became cooler and more self-possessed as her aunt grew more nervous. When she learnt of the new habitation in the heart of the rock she was eager to visit it; clearly the romance of the situation appealed to her more strongly than the danger.

Bob did not care to risk lighting his torch. It was therefore a task of no little difficulty for him and Ah-Sam to conduct the ladies along the narrow ledge to the mouth of the cleft. But the passage was successfully made, and Mrs. Pottle, panting for breath, heaved a sigh of relief when she found herself seated on the sacks placed by Ah-Sam within the entrance. Then Bob lit his torch, and by its light the ladies saw the rugged sides and roof of their new abode.

"You must leave me the torch, Mr. Fawcett," said Mrs. Pottle. "I cannot be left in this gloomy place in the dark."

"I will give you the materials for one," said Bob, "but it will be unwise to keep a light constantly burning. The Russians would see it from their hill, and I don't want them to frighten you by firing shots into the cleft."

"But in the morning," said Ethel, "we shall want to communicate with you. Will it not be dangerous for you to come and see us if the opening is exposed to the Russians' fire?"

"We will guard against that," said Bob. "Ah-Sam and I will pile up some boulders at the opening, and at the edge of that shelf of rock, and then we shall be pretty safe. And for your own security here I have brought a pistol; use it on the least provocation. Either I or Ah-Sam will be near at hand; when we are not on guard at the barricade we shall get a little sleep in a recess round the corner, just before the ledge begins; we shall hear you if you call."

"Well, Mr. Fawcett," said Mrs. Pottle, "I guess you're a real nice boy, and if we get out of this alive I don't know how I shall be able to show my gratitude. Anyhow, your name shall be known throughout the United States, from Texas to Oregon. Ethel, will you take the pistol or shall I?"

"You have your umbrella, aunt," replied Ethel with a sly look at Bob.

Leaving the ladies to settle the point between themselves, he returned to the edge of the gully, and succeeded in obtaining a few hours' sleep. He was awakened by the voice of Ah-Sam addressing him urgently.

"Topside piecee Manchu no belongey no more this-side," said the Chinaman. "Hab gone wailo other-side, galaw!"

"Gone?"

"Lun wailo chop-chop, massa; my no can find he."

"How did that happen? What was the sentry doing?"

"One piecee man gone dead."

Bob hurried to the cart, and found that it was indeed as Ah-Sam had said: Chang-Wo had escaped. The cords that had bound him to the cart lay loose; they were uncut. On the ground beside them lay the dead body of one of the Chunchuses; he had been stabbed to the heart. No one could give any information of the escape. The sentry had been changed at intervals according to Bob's instructions; no sound had been heard during the night; the Manchu had somehow managed to free himself from his bonds and stolen away in silence. Bob was vexed, even more at the slackness of the guard than at the disappearance of Chang-Wo, and he did not fail to point the moral in a serious talk with Sing-Cheng, who for his part was almost beside himself with rage. Nothing could be done, the Manchu was gone. Bob wondered whether their paths would ever cross again.

That day also passed, and still the Russians had made no sign. Bob chafed at their inactivity. Apparently they were determined to starve the garrison out. They might have been waiting for reinforcements, and the fact that none had arrived seemed a proof that the general advance of the Japanese army towards the Yalu had given the Russian staff other matters to think about. How long could the defenders hold out? The pony and one mule had already been eaten; there was no food for the other two mules, and they must soon be killed to appease the men's hunger. For the ladies there still remained a quantity of grain that might be eked out with great economy for two or three days, but the supply of fuel was failing. Ah-Sam had hitherto found scattered billets of wood in the shape of branches fallen from the trees high up the cliff and inaccessible from below. There was still the cart, and it was evident that ere long that must be broken up.

That night Bob took a spell of duty at the lower barricade, leaving just before three o'clock in the morning to snatch a rest before dawn. He had just dropped off to sleep when he was startled to wakefulness by the sound of a shot. His resting-place, as usual, was the end of the ledge leading to the ladies' bower, as Ethel had called it, and the sound seemed so close to him that he knew at once it must have proceeded from Mrs. Pottle's pistol. Hurrying along the ledge as quickly as possible in the darkness, his footsteps were heard by the ladies, and Mrs. Pottle cried out to him to come to their assistance. The mouth of the cleft was in pitch darkness, the night being cloudy; but Bob struck a match, and saw Mrs. Pottle standing with her face to the interior, holding the pistol in her right hand, and with her left pushing Ethel behind her ample form.

"What has happened?" asked Bob anxiously.

"I have shot something. Take care; there may be another, there may be hundreds. I will fire again. Listen! do you hear footsteps?"

All three held their breath. There was not a sound. Bob picked up and lit the torch, and advanced in front of the ladies, throwing a faint illumination on the irregular roof and walls. Nothing was to be seen.

"Perhaps it was a bird," said Bob.

"Not at all, Mr. Fawcett. It was a man, I know it was. I was lying awake, thinking, and listening to dear Ethel's breathing, when I heard a footstep. I jumped up; I heard it distinctly; then a sort of grunt, like a man clearing his throat; then I saw a pair of eyes shining—"

"Oh, Aunt Jane, how could you in the dark?"

"My dear, I did; and to prove it, when I fired the pistol the eyes disappeared, and you woke up, and you yourself heard footsteps, several footsteps, going quickly away into the interior."

"I did seem to hear footsteps," said Ethel, "but I was so scared that—Oh, Mr. Fawcett, I don't like this dark place. We don't know who may be in it."

"But I went a good way through it before I brought you here, and saw nothing."

"Depend upon it, there's another entrance," declared Mrs. Pottle, "and the Russians were coming to attack us this way. If I had not been awake we should all have been murdered. I think I frightened them, I know I did; but they will come back. Mr. Fawcett, you must bring up your men and drive the villains out at the other end."

"It is extraordinary. I cannot think that is the explanation. Russians would not have run away at one pistol-shot. I must go into the interior and explore. Ah-Sam, go and bring me another torch."

The Chinaman had followed in Bob's footsteps. He soon returned from the encampment with a torch, which he lit at Bob's order.

"You will stay here with the torch till I return," said Bob.

"No can do," declared Ah-Sam. "My walkee behind-side massa, look-see iniside. Supposey massa catchee Rosha man; ch'hoy! what for China-boy stop wailo? One piecee man catchee you, he killum—sartin."

"Nonsense. You must guard the ladies. Do not follow me unless I call you. I will be as quick as I can," he added to the ladies.

Then taking one torch in his left hand and a pistol in his right, he advanced cautiously into the cleft, leaving the ladies standing with joined hands.

Chapter XVII
A Night Reconnaissance

A Council of War—Looking West—Light—The Face of the Cliff—
Scouting—A Question of Navigation

Bob had not walked many yards along the rough floor when he heard a slight sound ahead. Thrusting his torch well forward, he advanced with great caution, feeling some anxiety now he had the evidence of his own ears that Mrs. Pottle had not been dreaming. If by any chance one of the enemy had found his way to the cleft, Bob felt that he himself would be at a great disadvantage, being seen while the other was unseen. "But I am in for it now," he reflected; "it would be as dangerous to retire as to advance." He was so intent upon watching the space in front of him that he stumbled more than once over the rocky, uneven floor of the cavern. At every few yards he stopped to peer more carefully, and to listen; always he saw nothing, always heard the sound of a light footfall ahead. Fearing that his quarry would escape him he hurried his pace; there was a corresponding acceleration in front; he hurried still more, so did the other; until Bob, his uneasiness now banished by set determination, was pushing forward at the utmost speed the rough ground permitted.

Now he heard the sound of heavy breathing, and a scurrying noise as of more than one person in full flight. Stumbling, falling, scrambling on, Bob dashed in pursuit; he must know at all costs what this new peril might be. At length, at a point where the roof shelved downwards, he caught a glimpse of a dark form not many yards in advance; it was immediately lost in shadow, then again it was discovered by the torch. He did not venture yet to fire, but sprang forward to reduce the distance between himself and the hurrying form. He was gaining on it; its pace appeared to be slackening; he called on it to stop, or he would fire. Suddenly the form disappeared, sinking as if into the floor. Bob took a couple of steps, and then started back with a thrill of terror. He felt wind upon his cheek; the torch flared more brightly. He had emerged from the cleft; beneath him yawned a vast empty blackness. He was on the brink of an abyss. At that moment he heard from below a heavy thud, and started back from the edge with a sudden feeling of faintness. Then he became aware that his torch could be seen from far around, and flinging it upon the ground he stamped out the flame.

Recovering from his momentary vertigo, he crawled cautiously to the brink of the precipice. There was nothing to be seen, save where a thin streak of still unmelted snow in a crevice a few yards below made a grayish patch on the black. He rose, picked up the torch, relit it when he had retraced his steps for several yards into the cavern, and made his way back to the other end.

"Well?" exclaimed both the ladies in a breath, as they saw him in a circle of light some time before he reached them.

"We have been so much alarmed about you." added Mrs. Pottle. Ethel gave a sigh of relief.

"There was something, or somebody," said Bob quietly.

"A Russian?"

"I don't know. Whoever he was, he is gone. He fell over a precipice at the far end."

"Oh, how dreadful!" exclaimed Ethel. "Mr. Fawcett, you are quite pale. Did you—is there—"

"Don't be alarmed," said Bob. "I have been right through the cavern now. It is open at the other end; and to make sure that you are not startled again, Ah-Sam and I will build a barricade across the cavern, so that it will be impossible for anyone to reach you from the rear. When it is light I will explore again, and find out who the intruder was."

"I hope you killed him outright," said Mrs. Pottle.

"I could not fire. He was gone before I knew, and—"

"And you nearly followed him! Oh!" Ethel covered her face with her hands.

"You are pale, Mr. Fawcett," said Mrs. Pottle. "What would I give for a little brandy! I really cannot allow you to risk your life any more. I should never forgive myself if I led you into any harm. As soon as it is light, I will give myself up to the Russians; I will indeed, I am quite resolved; this cannot go on any longer. I see how selfish I was; but for us women you could have got away."

Mrs. Pottle's declaration had on Bob the effect of a tonic. He smiled as he saw the lady grasp her unfailing stand-by—her umbrella.

"I don't think it would have been so easy," he said. "I hope you will give me another chance. We have got on up to the present better than I dared to hope; we need not talk of surrender just yet."

"Besides, auntie," said Ethel, "you wouldn't go when Mr. Fawcett gave you the choice, and it isn't fair now that—"

"There now, that'll do. I am outvoted. I will stay as long as there is any tea, but when all the tea is gone I shall take that as a warning from Providence, and then, Mr. Fawcett, I shall give myself up, and plead with the Russians for your life."

With Ah-Sam's assistance Bob collected the loose rocks within the cleft and made a rough barrier across the narrowest part of the cavern. Then he returned to his post and slept, leaving the Chinaman on guard.

After a distasteful breakfast of mule's flesh and tea, Bob again made his way through the cavern. Counting his paces, he found that it was about one hundred and fifty yards in length. Just before the farther opening it narrowed considerably, so that there was little more than room for two men to pass through abreast. At the mouth it emerged on the side of a sheer hill-face nearly two hundred feet above the ground. Standing just within the cleft, Bob was to a large extent sheltered from view from the open by a jagged spur jutting out from the cliff, a piece of rock that had apparently offered greater resistance to denudation than the surrounding surface. He approached the edge of the precipice, and throwing himself on his face, peered over.

The first object that caught his eye, wedged in between two rocks near the foot of the precipice, was the body of a large brown bear. It was almost with a gasp of relief that Bob realized that the object of his chase was not a human being. In a flash he remembered the bear which he had seen squatting at the side of the gully when he passed the entrance a few days before.

"What an ass I was not to remember it!" he thought.

Then he blamed himself for allowing the ladies to take up their quarters in the cleft; before he had thoroughly explored it. The bear had evidently used it for his winter's sleeping-place, and had been alarmed at the disturbance of his domain. He now lay stone dead, having fallen sheer for about sixty feet and then rebounded from a slope on to the rocks beneath.

Looking up, Bob saw that the weather-carved cliff stretched for at least three hundred feet above him. On his left he observed that the hill-face bent round; beyond its outline he saw an extent of undulating country bounded by snow-capped hills. He wondered what was round the corner; the mouth of the gully must of course be in that direction, and not far away.

He remembered that the general trend of the cavern had been towards the left; it must form one side of an irregular triangle, of which the gully and the hill-face were the other sides.

What bearing would this discovery have on the situation in which he and his strange allies found themselves? He had barely asked himself the question when he saw a Cossack in the distance, riding at speed as if directly towards him. Coming from the west, he had probably brought news or orders to the leader of the Russian besiegers. Bob watched the rider draw nearer and nearer, and then pass from his sight to the left behind the jagged rock. Then he turned and retraced his steps through the cavern, thinking deeply as he went.

Nothing happened to break the monotony of that weary day. The Chunchuses, pent up in their narrow quarters, became restless and irritable, and Bob feared lest they should quarrel among themselves. They resented the short rations on which they were kept, and looked hungrily on the one remaining mule, which, poor beast, seemed so wretched in its mute famished condition that Bob ordered it to be shot. More than once, as he pondered over things, he wondered whether it might be possible for the garrison to slip away through the passage he had discovered, but always he had to reject the idea as impracticable. Even if they succeeded in descending the precipitous cliff in safety, they could not hope to get clear away; for the Russians would soon discover their absence from the gully, they would be pursued, and the enemy, being mounted, must infallibly run them down. Nothing was to be gained by such a hazardous attempt; there seemed no alternative but to wait on.

The position was one of great strain and responsibility for a youth whose powers of endurance and of organization had never yet been put to so severe a test. But it is in circumstances of difficulty and danger that a man shows of what stuff he is made, and the manner in which Bob braced himself to his task won a good deal of admiration from the ladies. Though his sunken eyes and lined face showed how severely he was being tried, he was always cheery, always hopeful, keeping his anxieties to himself, and ever ready with plausible reasons why his companions should not despair. Mrs. Pottle sang his praises all day long to Ethel, and Ethel listened and said little.

Next morning Mrs. Pottle, who had taken charge of Ah-Sam's stock of grain-food, reported that it was coming to an end. The tea would last perhaps for two days, she said; but there was no fuel save what could be got by breaking up Ah-Sam's cart. Mrs. Pottle, in spite of herself, was evidently hankering after something more substantial than rice. She began to drop hints. Mules and oxen were both four-footed, she said; there was a great deal in custom; after all, one couldn't say unless one tried; and so on. Ethel only shuddered. But one mule would not last for ever. What could be done? It seemed to Bob that they must all either starve or submit. More than once during the day he went through the cavern to the farther end, and anxiously scanned the limited horizon—with no defined purpose or expectation of help, for from that direction help could only come to the Russians. He was surprised, indeed, that the enemy had not already been reinforced. The Cossack who had ridden up on the morning of his discovery of the bear had no doubt carried instructions from head-quarters. The only conclusion to be drawn was that the Russians were too fully occupied with the Japanese on the farther bank of the Yalu to spare troops for the purpose of wiping out a band of Chunchuses. The Cossack captain, however, had clearly received orders to keep his quarry cornered, either until he starved them out, or until a further force could be sent to his assistance. Such a force might arrive at any moment.

Even while Bob had the possibility in his mind, he saw, clearly defined on the sky-line on the farther side of the valley, a small band of mounted men approaching at a walking pace. The group was too small to be of any avail as a reinforcement, and Bob was wondering who the new-comers could be, when, as they drew nearer, he noticed among them one man on foot, walking with a strangely awkward gait. Intently watching him, he had in a few moments the explanation of his awkwardness: he had his arms tied behind him. Evidently he was a prisoner—some luckless Japanese scout or spy, perhaps, who had fallen into the hands of a Russian patrol, and was now being marched off for summary trial. Bob compared his own case with that of the Japanese, almost to the advantage of the latter, and watched him with mixed feelings until the edge of the hill hid him from sight.

Glancing down, he saw the dead bear still jammed between the rocks; but there was a change in its appearance. Pieces of its fur had been torn away; apparently it had been mauled by some prowling beast of prey. Bob shuddered as he realized what a fate he had himself escaped—when suddenly a thought came to him. The bear had fallen headlong down the precipice. Was it possible that he himself might make a safe and leisurely descent, and, under cover of night, reconnoitre the Russian position? At the back of his mind there was a dim outline of an idea that brought a flush to his cheeks and a light into his eyes. He turned sharp round, hurried through the cavern, and, stopping only to answer a remark from Mrs. Pottle, sought his faithful Chinaman, Ah-Sam.

During the next hour the two were busily engaged at a secluded part of the gully, making the traces from the mule-cart into a long knotted rope, with three loops at intervals, formed of the collars of the animals. There was not enough to construct a ladder, but Bob hoped the rope would prove long enough to let him down from the mouth of the cavern on to the slope, whence the descent to level ground would be easy. When it was complete, he took the only shaft of the cart which had not been demolished for fuel, returned to the cavern, and, evading Mrs. Pottle's eager questions, went quickly with Ah-Sam to the farther end. At the point where the cleft narrowed just before opening out on the hill-face they placed the shaft across from side to side, and then firmly attached the rope to it.

It was not safe to do anything more in the daylight. During the afternoon Bob at last yielded to Mrs. Pottle's entreaties, and related the story of his adventures up to his meeting with her.

"It just beats anything!" exclaimed the lady at its conclusion. "Why, Ethel, what a story it would make!"

"I don't think of that, auntie."

"Well, why not? My pen is rusting for want of work. What do you think, then?"

"I think it is all very strange, and very wonderful," said the girl with a blush. "And very encouraging to us. Mr. Fawcett has come through so much. And I should just love to see that Japanese gentleman,—Kobo, did you call him?"

At dusk Bob returned with Ah-Sam to the farther end of the cavern and let the loose end of the rope dangle down the cliff-side. It fell short of the top of the slope, the spot from which the hapless bear had rebounded, by a distance of apparently some ten feet. On to level ground the drop would have been easy, but on to the slope it might prove fatal to Bob as to the bear. There being no more rope available, only one thing could be done: the length of rope in the cleft above, some four or five yards, must be reduced. Ah-Sam untied the end and reknotted it to the shaft, using less of the rope; then, carefully examining the fissure, Bob discovered that the shaft was just long enough to be jammed vertically between a depression in the floor and a projection in the roof, about a yard from the mouth. When this had been done, he found that the lower end of the rope just touched the slope beneath.

"Allo velly good, massa," said Ah-Sam with an air of satisfaction.

"Yes. Now may it soon be dark. I am going down; you will remain here, and if you feel a tug on the rope, that means that I am coming back."

"My savvy; my no wailo; no fear!"

Waiting until all was dark, Bob let himself over the edge, and by aid of the loops, in which he was able to stand upright, thus resting his arms at intervals, he climbed easily down. When he reached the slope he found that the upper portion of it was steeper than it had appeared above, and he was glad the rope was long enough to enable him to steady his steps down the first few feet. Then he dropped to a sitting posture, and moved cautiously on hands and heels to the bottom. So careful was he to avoid making a noise, by displacing a loose stone or striking the rock too heavily with his boots, that it was nearly ten minutes before the descent was completed.

When at last he rose to his feet, he looked around to take his bearings if possible. Fortunately the clouds that had obscured the sky for some nights past were gone; there was no moon, but a faint radiance from the stars, by which he saw that there was nothing to serve as a landmark save the two upright rocks that framed the mangled body of the bear. Carefully noting the position of these in relation to an irregular fissure in which there still lay a drift of snow—all snow on the surrounding hillside being now melted— he turned his back on the steep cliff and skirted round the rugged spur that hid the mouth of the cavern from observers below. This spur, though only a few yards wide at the summit, increased in width as it approached the level until it measured fully fifty yards at the base.

Groping his way slowly among the loose stones and boulders that had fallen from the rocky face of the hill, he struck somewhat to the right, away from the mouth of the gully, knowing that there the enemy would be alert to prevent the besieged from breaking through. His object was to gain the open ground and then to make a circuit of the Russian position.

After a time the less frequency with which he encountered boulders showed that he was passing into the open valley. Suddenly he became aware of a dull glow in the distance on his left. He was unable to see whence it proceeded, but, as it was doubtless due to a camp fire, it was necessary to take double precautions lest his figure should be thrown up in relief against it and thus become visible to the Russians on the hill, if any chanced to be there. Inclining still more to the right, he almost turned his back to the faint light, and took a direction which he calculated would bring him to the extreme left of the hilltop position first held by the enemy. This post, he guessed, was probably left at nightfall and resumed at dawn, but it would be unwise to run the risk of passing between it and the glow he had noticed; he must make his way round it.

Pausing a moment, he scanned the sky above him for a bright star by which to set his course, then set off again, counting his paces. In daylight he had estimated that the summit of the hill was nearly half a mile in a straight line from the mouth of the gully; the distance would be greater over the uneven ground, and still greater from his starting-point. Every now and then he stopped to listen and look round. When he had counted some three hundred paces, the source of the glow at last became visible. On his left there were two fires some distance apart, with a few men moving about them, standing out for a moment black against the glow, then appearing red as they passed to the side, then vanishing altogether. From the position of the fires Bob guessed that they stood just under the hillside on the far side of the gully. There could be no doubt that they marked the site of the enemy's camp; and they were so near the barricade that if the besieged ventured to make a sortie they would not only have to reckon with the force on duty at the mouth of the gully, but also with a flank attack from the main body encamped a few yards away.

In the darkness it was impossible for Bob to tell when he had reached the summit of the hill. But he stopped at intervals to look back, and when he found that first one then the other fire gradually disappeared from sight, he judged that between them and him the brow of the hill intervened. At this point it was necessary to take another star as his guide. Turning now to the left, almost at right angles with his former course, he plodded warily on, skirting the hill not far from the summit, the fires appearing and disappearing with the inequalities of the crest. Though he kept eyes and ears keenly alert for sound or sight of the enemy, he neither heard nor saw any trace of them except at the camp fires. Continuing his course as nearly straight as he could, he came at length opposite the farthermost fire; then he turned again to the left, and moving with still greater caution, he made straight towards it. He was now descending a gradual slope. The fire was burning low; backed by the slope he thought he might venture still nearer; so, dropping on all-fours, he crawled for some distance over the ground, sodden with melted snow, until he stopped at length within some eighty yards of the fire. A little in front of him he heard the gurgling of the stream from the gully running across the face of the two camps. In the dim glow he saw by their dress that the occupants of the camp opposite him were Cossacks; the other camp was clearly that of the Manchus. He threw a glance round the position; a little in advance of him, to the right, he descried a number of dark forms, which he soon concluded were the picketed horses of the enemy. Two sentries were on duty, walking to and fro some forty yards from the outermost row of tents, and meeting about the middle of the exposed face of the camp. Beyond, Bob caught a glimpse of the figure of a Manchu patrolling in the same way opposite his camp. The Manchus' horses were not at the moment in sight, but a sudden replenishment of the fire caused a bright flame to spring up, making Bob lie absolutely motionless and almost hold his breath, at the same time throwing up the figures of the horses tethered just under the hill.

He had now learnt all that was possible about the enemy's position. As soon as the fire had died down again he might retrace his steps. He lay still on his face, waiting, letting his eyes range at random, when suddenly he gave a violent start. A little to the left of the horses, beside a tall bare sapling, stood a man whom he perceived, as he looked more closely, to be bound to the stem. He wore the dress of a Chinaman. The fitful flame from the Manchus' fire cast a lurid light upon the face of the prisoner, and with a feeling of dismay Bob recognized him: it was Kobo!

It flashed upon him at once: this was the prisoner he had seen among the fresh band of Manchus that morning. Kobo had been captured at last. His doom was sealed—unless he could be rescued. Bob almost sprang up in his excitement. How could he make his presence known to his friend? By his bearing he saw that he was awake. If he could communicate with him perhaps some means of effecting his escape would offer. Kobo had dared much for him—to Kobo he owed his own escape from the spy's fate; how eagerly would he do something in return for Kobo!

He lay watching, thinking, hoping that by some lucky chance he might be enabled to approach the prisoner. He dared not move. The minutes flew by, the fire was sinking; in a few moments it would again be replenished, and his position again be imperilled. He saw not the shadow of an opportunity of assisting Kobo. For the present he must give up the idea. Crawling back slowly and stealthily he reached a point where it would be safe to rise. Then, finding the star by which he had steered his course, he made his way toilsomely, reluctantly, up the hill again.

This time he took a shorter circuit inside his first track, and on the nearer slope of the hill, until he came to a spot which he thought must be opposite the opening of the cleft. But how could he make sure? If he swerved too far to the right and blundered upon the breastwork at the entrance to the gully his life was not worth a moment's purchase, and the safety of his party would be fatally jeopardized. Pausing in his incertitude, he bethought him of the fact that the enemy's watch-fires might be used to determine his rightful course. So long as they were out of sight, obviously he would be in no danger of coming upon the breastwork, though he might find himself perilously near it if he happened to hit the spur at the mouth of the gully. Fetching a wider circuit he abruptly altered his direction, looking anxiously at the fires in the hope that they would by and by be concealed from him by the prominent spur. It was a long time before either disappeared, and more than once he feared lest, after all, he had turned too early to the right. But at length first one, then the other, was hidden from his view, and against the penumbra of their glow the spur stood out dark upon his right. He gave a sigh of relief, and stopped for a moment to wipe the perspiration from his brow.

He steered now towards a point somewhat to the left of the bluff's jagged outline, until he came close beneath it. Then he turned sharp to the left, to find the slope up which he must climb to reach the fissure. For some minutes he stumbled about. The night was darker than ever, but he knew that his general direction was right, for the ground became rougher and the loose stones more numerous. At last, close at hand, he recognized the tall twin rocks imprisoning the bear. Swarming up the steep slope on hands and knees, he came to the top, and stretched out his right hand, moving it from side to side to feel for the dangling rope. He touched it, caught it, gave it a gentle tug. He felt it tighten. Ah-Sam had faithfully remained at his post above. Then with straining muscles he scrambled up; he reached the fissure and Ah-Sam's welcoming hands.

"My tinkey Roshians hab catchee," said the Chinaman.

"Not yet, Ah-Sam. Pull up the rope, then follow me back to the ladies."

Soon darkness and silence brooded upon the rugged hillside. The blinking stars saw nothing; no sound broke the stillness save when at midnight a hungry wolf came padding to the foot of the slope, and snarled as he fixed his fangs in the carcase of the bear.

Chapter XVIII
Rushing a Cossack Camp

Panic—To the Yalu—Hill Paths—Historic Ground—An Introduction—A Man-Hunt—First Aid—Approaching the Ford—Mrs. Pottle Decides

At dead of night, the eyes of a lynx, but none other, might have seen a rope dangling heavily from the mouth of the fissure high up the cliff. If the animal had not been scared away, it would have seen a dark form in cautious silence climbing down the rope—a man, with a rifle slung upon his back. He reached the slope and waited. A few moments afterwards a second man followed, and, guided by the first, arrived at the foot of the slope, interrupting the supper of the half-gorged wolf. The first man returned to the summit, and met a third man descending, whom he stationed half-way down the incline. These movements he repeated until he was able, without descending himself, to pass each new-comer down from hand to hand. When fifty men had thus descended, and were assembled on the level, the first man led them with the same silence and caution among the fallen boulders until they came to open ground. Then he halted, and stationing his companions some three paces apart one from another, took from his pocket a long piece of thin twisted cotton and passed it down the line, each man gripping it with his left hand.

Taking the end of the cotton in his own hand, the leader moved forward, followed by the rest, along a track approximating as closely as possible to that which he had taken some six hours before. Every now and then he gave a slight tug at the line; his followers at once stopped, while he took stock of his surroundings. He came to a spot whence he expected to obtain a view of the enemy's camp. It was almost invisible, for the fires were very low. Skirting the farther side of the hill-crest, the long queue of men at length reached the utmost horn of the crescent track. By the leader the forms of the Russian sentries could be dimly seen pacing to and fro. Counting off ten men from the right of the line, he left the remaining forty in position before the Russian camp, and proceeded with the ten to a point under the hill some distance farther on in their course. Then creeping forward, he waited till the nearest sentry's steps began to recede, then stole on again, still holding the cord, his men still following, until he came within a few yards of the sentry's beat. Just as he reached this spot his foot struck against some obstacle; he staggered, recovered himself with an effort, and stooped to discover what had checked his progress. It was a prostrate body. Instantly he clapped his hand upon the fallen man's mouth, lest he should cry out. Something in the touch suggested a suspicion. He placed his hand over the man's heart; it had ceased to beat.

The next moment he himself was prone upon the ground, and the ten men with him did as he did, and lay side by side, motionless. The sentry, suspecting nothing, tramped back along his beat, came to the end, wheeled round, and once more receded. Bob rose to a stooping position, and, followed closely by his ten, crept forward across the sentry's track towards the tethered horses. From one there was a whinny, from another a snort as the men approached; otherwise not a sound. The silent ten passed round the animals, coming between them and the hill. Suddenly there sounded a cry, the challenge of a sentry. Instantly Bob fired his pistol and dashed forward towards the smouldering fire, which he stirred with a kick into a bright blaze. A moment later there was a shout, a clamour, a babel from the end of the camp. The firing of the pistol had been the pre-arranged signal for a rush by the forty. It was instantly obeyed. The Russians, half-awake, struggled to their feet, to find one force between them and their horses, and another, a larger shouting band, sweeping upon them in front. In wild confusion and affright they ran this way and that; many made no attempt even to seize their rifles; they broke towards the mouth of the gully, their flying forms making admirable targets in the firelight.

Meanwhile Bob hurried towards the tree to which he had seen Kobo bound, fearing lest some undesigned shot should do him mischief. To his amazement the prisoner was gone. There was no time to speculate upon his disappearance. Without a halt he dashed forward, his ten men following with loud cries in his track across the low shelter-tents, cooking utensils, abandoned rifles and lances, and the various impedimenta of a small camp. The raiders met with almost no resistance, and the Russians, as they fled in panic towards the barricade, swept through the startled Manchu camp and carried its occupants with them. The men stationed on the breastwork at the mouth of the gully stood to arms, bewildered by the sudden outcries and onrush; but when they were suddenly attacked from the rear by the small force of Chunchuses Bob had left in the gully, they also broke and fled with the rest outwards across the low hills, pursued in the darkness by the exultant brigands. At Bob's orders Ah-Sam, the first of his ten, shouted to the Chunchuses to return; nothing was to be gained by pushing the pursuit farther. But the command was vain; only three or four answered to the summons, the rest were intent upon paying off old scores.

Amid the rout the Manchus' horses had stampeded; but the better-trained animals of the Cossacks remained, and over these Bob set a guard. Then he had the camp fires replenished as beacons for his own men, and awaited their return. In twos and threes during the next half-hour they straggled in. They brought no prisoners; but through Ah-Sam Bob learnt that many a Cossack and many a Manchu lay between the camp and the hill. Already Bob had collected some ninety rifles abandoned by the fugitives, and set men to gather what ammunition they could. Scattered as the enemy now were over the face of the country, most of them without arms, all probably without horses, rushing blindly onward in the dark, he felt that little was to be feared from them. His principal danger was lest a reinforcement should be on the way to join them, or lest the news of the surprise or the appearance of the stampeded horses should bring up in hot haste some Russian force in the neighbourhood.

It was imperative that the victors should make good their retreat as soon as possible. They had captured enough horses to mount the whole force, and in the camps had been found a sufficient supply of food to last for several days. Ordering the men, through Ah-Sam, to carry into the gully all that they could lay hands on, and to lead the horses up through gaps in the barricade, Bob went to find Sing-Cheng, to discuss the situation with him.

As he reached the breastwork there was brought to nim a wounded Manchu, who had been discovered hiding behind the rocks. Bob at once set Ah-Sam to question him, enquiring specially about the Chinaman whom he had seen tied to the tree. He learnt that, two days before, Chang-Wo had come into the camp after escaping from the gully, and had a long conversation with the Cossack captain. He had then ridden away eastward. During his absence the Chinaman had been brought in, and as there was reason to believe he was a Japanese spy, he had been tied up until he could be conveyed to head-quarters. The Manchu was amazed to hear that the prisoner had escaped. It was incomprehensible.

When Bob with some difficulty found Sing-Cheng, and asked him what he advised, the man replied that he had no fear of the Russians, but he did fear Chang-Wo. He was a very great man, very powerful, very cunning. A vast number of Manchus were at his beck and call; his fastness lay only two days' march in the hills. It was surprising that he had not already brought his bandits in overwhelming force to storm the gully. Bob suggested as a reason that a large Russian reinforcement was expected. There was little chance of booty if the Chunchuses were overcome, and Chang-Wo would prefer that the Russians should bear the brunt rather than risk losing a considerable number of his own men. The chief admitted that this might be the reason; but he pointed out that Chang-Wo, his own capture rankling in his mind, would have a strong personal interest in the destruction of the garrison of the gully. If he had gone to his headquarters to fetch more men, he might at any moment arrive on the scene, with a force numbering anything from three to five hundred. Clearly no time must be lost in getting beyond his reach.

Bob asked whether Sing-Cheng was ready to fulfil his promise to escort the party across the Yalu. The man professed his eagerness to do so, if the honourable foreign gentleman would lend him his continued assistance. He himself felt that he was in a dangerous predicament. If he went westward he would run the risk of falling in with the Russians; if eastward, he would almost certainly meet Chang-Wo. Northward the way was blocked by high hills. The only possible course lay to the south, and that led direct to the Russian positions on the Yalu. But he knew of a difficult and little-used path over the mountains by which they might travel. It would bring them out at a point where the river might be forded, and where such Russian troops as might be in the neighbourhood would probably be merely small detached forces engaged in watching the fords and passes. Bob enquired whether the man was sure of the way. The man replied that he knew every step of it.

"Then we will chance it," said Bob. "Ah-Sam, tell him to get his men in order, ready to start the moment there is light enough to see the way. I will go and prepare the ladies."

Mrs. Pottle almost flung her arms round Bob's neck when he appeared.

"My dear boy," she exclaimed, "we have been in a terrible state of alarm about you. What have you been doing?"

Bob gave her a brief account of the rushing of the enemy's camp—successful even beyond his highest hopes.

"Why, there!" said the lady at the conclusion of his story. "I told you, Ethel, that Mr. Fawcett would prove equal to the occasion. Mr. Fawcett, you are lost as an engineer, you ought to be a soldier. When we get within reach of the telegraph, I shall wire a full account of you to my paper, and I guess there'll be a competition for your services in some capacity or other in my country."

"Auntie, Mr. Fawcett must be very tired," said Ethel. "Is there any tea left?"

"Of course. Dear me, how thoughtless! Mr. Fawcett, you shall have a cup of tea in five minutes."

"And you will explain to us what is to be done next, won't you?" added Ethel.

At the first streak of dawn a long cavalcade stole out of the gully. The brigand chief led the way, mounted on a strong Korean pony. Behind him came half his men; then the ladies, for whom side-saddles had been improvised; after them the remainder of the force, all on horse-back. Sufficient provisions had been found in the Russian camp to give them all the good meal so much needed. Bob rode at one time ahead with the chief, at another with the ladies, who were in high spirits now that the tension of the last few days was relaxed. He was with them as they rode past the scene of the midnight sally, and endeavoured to distract their attention from the terrible evidences of the fray.

Sing-Cheng led the party across the crest of the hill on which the Russians had first posted themselves, and struck off in a direction approximately south-west. As they rode, a chain of mountains came into view in the distance, the foot-hills beginning about three miles off. The cavalcade made towards a dip in these hills, and after covering several miles of rising ground, approached what appeared to be an almost perpendicular wall of rock. Not till they came within a few yards of it did the strangers see a possibility of penetrating the apparent obstruction. Taking his course unerringly, the chief led them in single file along a narrow giddy footpath zigzagging up the face of the cliff. The horses had much ado to keep their footing, but they were used to the mountains and carried the whole party up without mishap. At the worst of the road Bob and Ah-Sam both dismounted and led the ladies' horses; the former guessed from Mrs. Pottle's look of terror as she rounded awkward corners and skirted sheer precipices, that her passion for travel would be cooled for many a day.

After half an hour's difficult climb the fugitives reached a height whence they obtained a distant prospect of the late battle-ground, spread like a map in the bright sunlight behind them. Then they turned a bend in the path, and the scene was shut from their view. The chief still led on among rugged hills, with no sign of habitation. At one time they were at the bottom of a ravine; an hour later they were toilsomely scaling the steep face of a cliff, which from the base appeared impossible to climb. The horses were fresh when they started, and plodded along steadily. Except for short intervals for food and rest the march was continued uninterruptedly till dusk, and then Bob and Sing-Cheng selected a strong position for camping—a spot sheltered from the wind, that blew colder towards night. Sentries were placed around the camp, but the hours of darkness passed without alarm. There was as yet no sign of pursuit.

Next morning the march was resumed, and continued through similar inhospitable country until about three o'clock in the afternoon. Then, just as the riders were climbing what appeared to be the highest peak they had yet met with, the chief came to a sudden halt, sprang from his horse, and made signs for the rest of the party to follow his example. He said a few words rapidly to his men; then, beckoning Bob and Ah-Sam to accompany him, went forward cautiously on foot towards the skyline just above.

As they gained the crest, a fine panorama opened before them. At a distance which Bob roughly guessed at five miles, they saw a broad river crossing the plain from east to west, at one point broadening into the semblance of a lake dotted with islands. Hills of varying height shut off stretches of the river at intervals. On the other side the chief pointed out a cluster of dwellings just discernible amid a light ground haze.

"Wiju," he said.

Bob looked at the town with interest, remembering his unpleasant associations with the place. Below, to the left, between the spectators and the river, which it shut from their view, was a steep eminence which the chief called Hushan.

"He callum Tiger Hill," explained Ah-Sam.

"What is that?" asked Bob, pointing to a smaller river on their right, winding among the hills and disappearing behind Tiger Hill in the direction of the Yalu.

"Ai-ho," said the chief.

Beyond the Ai-ho, between that river and the Yalu, was a town which, though it appeared larger than Wiju, Bob judged to be somewhat smaller in reality, for it lay much nearer to his point of observation.

"Kiu-lien-cheng," explained the chief, in answer to Bob's mute question. Bob remembered that this place had played an important part in the China war. It was, moreover, the scene of Kobo's exploit, when his company had the honour of being first in the town. Beyond Kiu-lien-cheng on the river, but shut from sight by intervening hills, lay Antung, a place of bitter memories to Bob. Looking towards Wiju he could see small black moving bodies, which were no doubt companies or regiments moving about the town; and beyond it, he descried a long line of carts filing towards it from the north. He scanned the whole landscape with interest and care. The first great operation in the Japanese land campaign must obviously be the crossing of the Yalu; it would probably take place within the next few weeks, with the beginning of spring. Where would the decisive action be fought? If the Japanese army attempted to effect a crossing anywhere in the country outspread beneath him, they would have indeed a hard nut to crack. The rugged country to the north of the Yalu seemed to offer ideal conditions for defence, and Bob was convinced that the Russian engineers would have taken full advantage of the natural features.

"A very strong position, Mr. Fawcett."

The words so exactly corresponded with his unspoken thought that for a moment he was scarcely aware that they had been uttered by another. Then he turned with a start, saw that Ah-Sam and the chief had their rifles up and their fingers already at the triggers, and, following their upward gaze, noticed the figure of a short, sturdy Chinaman between two rocks above his head. Even as he looked Ah-Sam dropped his rifle and said something to Sing-Cheng, and with a second glance Bob understood. He went forward eagerly with outstretched hand.

"Kobo San! You don't know how glad I am to see you," he said warmly. "Are you all right? How in the world did you escape?"

"I will tell you," replied Kobo. "But, pardon me, I am terribly hungry. Have you a little rice to spare?"

"Ah-Sam," said Bob, "run back and ask Mrs. Pottle to prepare a meal for a friend of mine. You shall have something in five minutes. Upon my word, Kobo San, I am glad to see you. I hoped you had got away safely, but the uncertainty—"

"You seem to know of my capture."

"Ah! The tables are turned this time. I am only sorry you didn't give me the chance to rescue you. But come, let me take you to the ladies. They will be delighted to see you."

"Pardon me, did you say Mrs. Pottle?"

"Yes; do you know her?"

"She is at present the subject of diplomatic correspondence between the United States and Japan," said Kobo, with a smile. "She is the widow of Mr. Isidore G. Pottle, I presume; I knew him."

"How strange! But come, you must be famished."

Kobo walked slowly down the incline. Bob noticed that he limped.

"Are you hurt, sir?" he asked.

"A slight touch in one foot."

"A sprain, perhaps. This is very rough walking."

"No, it was a Manchu bullet."

"Good heavens! You must be in terrible pain. Let me help you."

"It is nothing—a scratch."

But Bob knew from the manner in which he set his foot upon the ground that the hurt was not so insignificant as Kobo would have him believe. Fortunately a few yards' walk brought them to the spot where the rest of the party had halted.

"Mrs. Pottle, let me introduce a friend of mine—Rokuro Kobo San."

Kobo bowed, and Mrs. Pottle, throwing a hasty glance over his costume, jumped to a conclusion, and said cordially:

"Very muchee gladee meetee you, sir."

"I am indeed honoured, madam," returned Kobo, bowing again ceremoniously with impassive face. Bob and Ethel had instinctively turned aside to conceal their amusement; and Mrs. Pottle, with a surprised and startled glance at the supposed Chinaman, began haltingly:

"I beg your pardon—but—"

"I am a Japanese, madam. I think I once met your esteemed husband, Mr. Isidore G. Pottle."

"Well!"

Mrs. Pottle was too much amazed for further words. To cover her embarrassment; she ordered Ah-Sam with a flourish of her umbrella to bring the food he had been preparing, and Kobo fell to with avidity, explaining that he had eaten nothing for nearly two days. When he had satisfied his hunger, explanations were exchanged. Kobo's story, told in his quiet unemotional way, made a strong impression upon the ladies, Mrs. Pottle frequently exclaiming, "It's wonderful! It's wonderful!"

At Liao-yang, he explained, he had made a discovery that promised to be of great importance to his government. It was worth risking something to convey the news with all speed to General Kuroki, and he decided to take the shortest cut, the main road through Feng-huang-cheng, Kiu-lien-cheng, and Wiju, frequented though it was, trusting in his disguise as a Chinese merchant to escape detection. To guard against accident, he had sent his man Taru with an oral message by way of Yongampo, hoping that in any case he would succeed in crossing the Yalu near its mouth.

Provided with unexceptionable papers, he himself had journeyed without interference until he had come some distance beyond Feng-huang-cheng. Then, however, he was overtaken by a party of two Cossacks and three Manchus, who stopped him and put him through a close interrogation. One of the Manchus caught him by the pigtail, and, being, dissatisfied with his replies, gave that ornament a vicious tug. It came away in his hand.

The Manchu's suspicions were redoubled, though it is not unusual for a Chinaman whose locks are scanty to wear a false pigtail. Kobo was made prisoner, and carried with the party, who struck off eastward from the high-road into the hills. From scraps of their conversation he gathered that they had been sent to bring help to a Russian force, he could not tell how large, which was bent on routing out a band of Chunchuses entrenched in a mountain fastness, but that they had been unsuccessful in their errand, the Russians being unable to spare troops for the purpose. The men discussed among themselves the result of their failure. Clearly it would be necessary for the chief of the Manchus to send for men from his own head-quarters three marches away, a course which for some reason or other they supposed he would be reluctant to adopt. But Chang-Wo, as they named him, had sworn to exterminate this particular gang of bandits; they had for long been a thorn in his side; and he had now additional reasons for his venomous hatred of them, for they had captured him and held him a prisoner until he escaped by slipping his bonds and killing a sentry.

Kobo was brought into the Russian and Manchu camp and carried before the officer. Chang-Wo happened to be with them. He instantly recognized the Japanese he had so good reason for hating, and demanded that he should be put to the torture. But on being asked for his reasons, he had shown by his own admissions, reluctant as they were, that the prisoner was too important a man to be summarily dealt with; his vindictive wishes had been overruled by the Cossack captain, who resolved to carry the Japanese to Feng-huang-cheng as soon as the Chunchuses were disposed of. In his eagerness to wreak vengeance on his old enemy, Chang-Wo resolved to fetch reinforcements from his stronghold and hasten the final discomfiture of the Chunchuses, and set out the same day.

"But how did you escape?" asked Bob. "I saw you tied to a tree."

"We had an agent in the Manchu camp," replied Kobo quietly. "He cut my ropes after dark, and I slipped away. There was a commotion immediately afterwards; but it was dark, no one could find me."

Bob remembered the dead Manchu whom he had stumbled upon outside the Russian camp. Evidently this was Kobo's agent. He had met his death through rescuing Kobo; and Kobo spoke coldly of a commotion!

After his escape, Kobo had pushed on eastward during the night, and at dawn was several miles from the scene. He continued his journey until mid-day, and then had the ill-luck to be sighted by a band of Manchus—the men whom Chang-Wo himself was bringing towards the Russian camp. Instantly the whole band of four hundred were at his heels. For three hours they chased him among the hills. Being mounted, sometimes they had the advantage, at others their horses were only an encumbrance. But Kobo was faint with hunger and fatigue. They gained on him slowly but surely. The nature of the country did not give him an opportunity of eluding them. More than once they could easily have shot him, and that they did not do so indicated that Chang-Wo had ordered that he should be taken alive, reserving for him, doubtless, a slower and more horrible death. At last he was almost run down; Chang-Wo and half a dozen men were but a short distance behind him, leading their horses up a rocky path too steep and rugged for them to ride. Kobo knew that as soon as they were able to remount he must be overtaken; capture seemed inevitable. He looked round anxiously, almost despairingly, for a means of escape. On the far side of the ravine he was skirting he saw a rocky ledge jutting out, approaching within a short distance of the path he was travelling, then receding again. The sight was as a ray of hope. To leap across the chasm involved a terrible risk; the descent between ledge and ledge was a sheer hundred feet, and if he missed his footing he must be dashed to pieces. In a moment he took his resolution. Collecting his remaining strength he jumped. His feet lighted on the projecting ledge. For an instant he swayed, and his life hung in the balance—an inch forward, an inch backward, would mean life or death. The crisis was but momentary. He stumbled forward, he was safe.

Meanwhile the pursuers were hastening up the opposite path. They came to the spot whence Kobo had made his desperate leap; and though Chang-Wo stormed and cursed, not one of them would face the risk. To reach their quarry in any other way would involve a long detour, meanwhile he every moment increased his distance from them. Then Chang-Wo raised his rifle and fired. His shot struck Kobo in the foot.

At this point of the story Ethel rose quietly and slipped away.

In spite of the wound, Kobo had tramped on until dusk. He had had no food, he had travelled almost without rest for a whole day and night, yet he could not afford to delay. Until he reached the Japanese head-quarters he would be in constant danger; and it was a matter of the most urgent necessity that he should give to General Kuroki the information he had gained. He rested for a few hours, cold, hungry, in increasing pain. He bandaged his injured foot as well as he could, then with morning light set off again.

"I count myself fortunate that I met you, Mr. Fawcett," he said. "You can perhaps assist me with a horse. I must press on, there is so much risk that my servant Taru will fail to get through."

There was no complaint—no further reference to his wound. He showed no curiosity as to how Bob had known of his capture, nor as to the strange company in which he found him. His mind was entirely possessed by anxiety lest the news should not reach his general.

Unnoticed by Bob, Ethel had now returned, carrying a tin can belonging to Ah-Sam filled with water. She said a few words to Mrs. Pottle, and that lady at once came forward.

"Now, sir, will you allow me to attend to your foot? You cannot go on like that. Kindly take off your shoe."

Mrs. Pottle's manner was not to be denied. In a few minutes she had deftly bandaged the wounded foot, winning a very courtly speech of thanks. Then Kobo was given one of the led horses, and the whole party moved forward, taking care to avoid the risk of being seen on the skyline. As they rode, Bob gave Kobo an account of his experiences since they had parted at the hut some ten days before, and Mrs. Pottle found an opportunity not only to praise Bob's skill and resourcefulness, but also to enquire into the circumstances in which Kobo San had met her late husband, Mr. Isidore G. Pottle.

The course of the party was now due east, parallel with the Yalu. Sing-Cheng was anxious to strike the river at a ford known to him, several miles above Wiju. It was not likely to be held in strength by the Russians unless the Japanese were close up to the river, which seemed improbable. It might be guarded by a small detachment; in that case the whole party must be prepared to make a rush and take their chance. In the evening they met two Manchu peasants, whom they eagerly questioned in the hope of obtaining definite information; but nothing could be got from them. Kobo suggested that as a precaution it would be advisable to keep these peasants with them. Accordingly they were forced to accompany the party during the rest of their march.

At dark they encamped in the hills within about two miles of the ford. No fire was lighted, and the utmost silence was enjoined. Bob did what he could for the comfort of the ladies, who showed wonderful pluck and spirit under the long strain they were enduring. Double guards were posted to provide against the chance of surprise during the night. The repose of the camp was undisturbed. Nevertheless Bob was very anxious. He walked restlessly around the camp, listening, peering, reflecting. Kobo insisted on taking his share of duty, allowing Bob to snatch a little sleep. He too was restless, and appeared frequently to strain his ears in the attitude of closest attention. Mrs. Pottle and Ethel slept soundly through the night—for the first time, they said, since their flight from Mukden. The knowledge that Korea was now so near at hand had given them renewed hope of at length reaching safety, and, great as was their confidence in Bob, they seemed to have gained additional assurance from the presence of Kobo, whom Ethel in particular looked at with admiration and awe.

During those hours of darkness, in a depression of the hills little more than a mile away, lay Chang-Wo, with four hundred of his Manchu braves. Only the accident of a convenient camping-ground had led him to halt just in time to miss discovering the fugitives' camp. Even now an incautious shout, a flicker of light, an accidental shot sounding in the still air of these mountain solitudes, would bring him down upon his quarry like a beast of prey. Neither Bob nor Kobo so much as suspected the proximity of this ruthless foe; yet his presence was reflected in their strange uneasiness.

In the dark hours before dawn, Bob and Kobo discussed the situation with the brigand chief. All were agreed that if the ford was to be rushed it must be as soon as day broke. About an hour before sunrise, therefore, the camp was roused in complete silence, and the party moved cautiously towards the Yalu. The same order of march was observed as had held since their departure from the gully, except that Bob and Ah-Sam now rode in front with Sing-Cheng, leaving the ladies in Kobo's care. For half an hour they marched on; then Bob, whose anxiety increased as they drew nearer to the river, suggested that two or three should go forward on foot in advance of the rest, to make sure that the coast was clear. On second thoughts he decided to go himself in company with Ah-Sam and the chief. He informed Kobo of his intention. The Japanese at once assented, and said that he would halt the party until Bob returned.

The three then stole forward. The sky to their left was just faintly alit with the dawn when they heard the rush of water before them. Following the track which the chief knew well, they came at length to the river, at a point about half a mile below the ford. There was not yet light enough to reconnoitre farther without danger; they therefore took shelter behind a clump of bush and waited for a few minutes. Then they went forward again, with still greater caution, all their faculties alert.

Almost immediately an alarming surprise broke upon them. A few yards beneath them they saw a Russian outpost. A little farther on, encamped near the bank of the river, was a large Russian force, consisting chiefly of cavalry, but including several infantry regiments, and a still larger force occupied the farther bank. Nothing but the fact that the Russians feared no enemy behind them had saved Bob's party from falling into their hands. Even now it was only too clear that the fugitives' case was desperate. It was hopeless to attempt the ford. With some thousands of Russians on each side of the river, scouting parties would doubtless be out in all directions. The presence of Russians in such force seemed to indicate that they were being driven across the Yalu by the advance of the Japanese, so that it would be impossible to get over the river lower down. On the high road through Wiju, moreover, the main body of the Russian army was probably in full retreat. Russians would be swarming in all directions. What was to be done? The chief looked at Bob with dismay. Had they come so far only to be captured after all?

"Let us go back to the others," said Bob quietly.

Kobo received the bad news with the calmness that characterized him. He put a few sharp questions to Sing-Cheng, then turning to Bob said:

"There is another ford, he says, higher up the river. He knows the path to it. It is difficult, more precipitous even than the one by which we have come. But we must take the risk. I advise, however, that the ladies should go forward under escort, and claim the protection of the Russians. Among so large a force they would enjoy a security that could not be expected in the case of the small party with Chang-Wo's band."

Bob looked round. The ladies were at a little distance. Both showed signs of the hardships they had recently endured. Mrs. Pottle was thinner; her cheeks were lined and careworn; the aggressiveness of her attitude had quite disappeared. Her niece was not so much altered; but Bob had noticed with anxiety the growing paleness of her fair cheeks, the strained look in her eyes. He went up to the two, and in a few words explained the difficulties of the situation, concluding with the recommendation that they should follow Kobo's advice. For a few moments Mrs. Pottle wavered; she looked at Ethel with a tremulousness all the more pathetic because so foreign to her.

"Auntie," said Ethel, "I think we ought to remain with Mr. Fawcett. I am sure we shall get through. We are nearly there. What a pity to give up at the last!"

"Yes," returned the elder lady emphatically, "you are right. It is good of you, Mr. Fawcett, but we cannot hear of it. We won't be bundled over to the Russians. We are ready to go with you: when will you start?"

Chapter XIX
Sound and Fury

Across the Yalu—Kobo gives Counsel—A Monastery—A Buddhist Settlement—Big Bobbely—An Attack at Dusk—A Pyrrhic Victory—Boanerges—A Despatch—"A Terrible Curse"

In a few minutes the whole party set off to retrace their steps, riding for a short distance over their tracks, then striking off in a new direction under the leadership of Sing-Cheng. But the difficulties of the march were even greater than the man had indicated. At almost every step the party were confronted by a new danger. The path was so rugged that riding was impossible. All had to dismount and lead their horses. A single false step might carry horse and pedestrian over the edge of a precipice and dash them to pieces hundreds of feet below. Bob thought his hair would have turned white with the anxiety of watching over the ladies, guiding them at every turn, diverting their attention whenever the path led over more than usually dizzy eminences. They struggled on with heroic determination; and Bob spared them the knowledge that before the day was out two of the Chunchuses in the long line had missed their footing and fallen headlong to their death.

Struggling on painfully, the party covered nearly twenty miles that day, encamping at nightfall on the north bank of the river. The chief was eager to cross by the ford at once, but Bob was unwilling to risk the dangers of a crossing in the darkness, and without having assured himself that the Russians were not here also. Before it was light he stole down with Sing-Cheng to reconnoitre. There was no sign of the enemy; and at daybreak the whole party started with unutterable gladness to complete, as they hoped, the last stage of their journey.

Before they reached the river one of the Manchu peasants who had been captured, seizing a favourable moment, felled the man in charge of him and scrambled down an almost perpendicular declivity. A dozen shots followed him before Bob could interfere to stop the fusillade. The sound of the shots echoed and re-echoed over the hills; they must be heard by any Russians who happened to be in the neighbourhood, and if heard they would certainly bring the enemy upon the track. For several miles Bob turned at intervals anxiously to look back; there was no sign of pursuit. But, unknown to him, ten minutes after the unfortunate incident a Manchu had galloped up to the spot where the firing had taken place, and there, hidden behind a rock, had watched the disappearing tail of the procession. His fierce eyes lit up as he looked. In a few moments he was galloping back. The Manchu was Chang-Wo.

The cavalcade crossed the river. It was a question of the direction they should take. There were probably Russians between them and the Japanese lines, it would therefore be well for them to strike south-east in order to give the enemy as wide a berth as possible. Bob pointed out that this would probably cause the loss of a day; but Kobo replied that he would rather lose one day, or even two, than run the risk of his information never reaching General Kuroki. Bob noticed that the safety of himself or of the party never entered into Kobo's calculations. With him it was merely a weighing of advantages, with the sole consideration how best his news might be delivered.

On the south side of the Yalu the fugitives saw on all hands traces of the Russian occupation. Almost every village had been sacked and burned; the country was for the most part deserted; the few Koreans who were seen wandering in disconsolate helplessness about the sites of their ruined homes scuttled away in terror when Bob's cavalcade approached. They were evidently afraid lest the party should be a band of raiders come to capture and destroy the little that the Russians had left.

No precaution was neglected to save the party from coming upon the enemy unawares. Pickets and supports were thrown out in front and rear, and the pace was regulated by the careful reconnoitring of the advance guard. The march continued for six or seven hours, and then was interrupted by a short halt to rest and feed the horses. About one o'clock, shortly after they had started again, one of the men in advance galloped back with the news that he had seen a force of Cossacks crossing the line of march from east to west about a mile ahead. Word was at once given to halt again, in order to allow this body time to pass out of sight. Bob, accompanied by Sing-Cheng and Ah-Sam, went forward, and, taking his stand behind a rock so that he could not be seen, looked out, and saw the troop of horsemen, plainly Cossacks by their yellow facings, winding among the hills, apparently striking across from Chen-seng, as the chief explained, higher up the river, to Wiju. In a quarter of an hour they would have disappeared, and it would be safe for the fugitives to continue their advance.

Bob was just returning with this good news to his party, when he was met by a messenger hastening to tell him that a large force of cavalry had been seen coming up behind, and were at the present moment no more than two miles away. He put his horse to a gallop, debating within himself, as he rode, what to do in face of this new emergency. For a moment he felt oppressed by a sense of despair. The events of the past fortnight had put a great strain upon him, and the present dilemma, coming at a time when he had hoped that all was safe, was almost overmastering. But collecting his thoughts he tried to look the situation squarely in the face. If he pressed on, he ran the risk of bringing upon him the Cossacks whom he had just seen out of harm's way. If he hesitated, he must assuredly be overtaken by the cavalry behind, which in all likelihood would turn out to be Chang-Wo's band. There was danger either way. He had not made up his mind how to choose between the two alternatives when he reached the rest of his party.

"What are we to do, sir?" he asked Kobo, after telling him of the direction in which the Cossacks had disappeared.

"I advise an immediate advance," replied the Japanese, whose serenity always had a bracing effect upon Bob. "If the Cossacks see us, they may mistake us for Manchu allies of theirs. We shall at any rate be a mile and a half farther on our way before they discover us; while if we wait and allow the horsemen behind to overtake us there is bound to be firing, the shots will bring the Cossacks down upon us, and we shall be hemmed in between the two bands. In any case we must make up our minds that both parties may chase us, but the Cossacks at any rate will not carry the pursuit far, knowing as they must do that our army cannot be far away."

The soundness of Kobo's advice was self-evident. The word was at once given, the little party set off at a trot, and in a few minutes had crossed the path of the Cossacks, easily discovered by the trampled slush. Some time elapsed before they came in sight of the rear files of the departing enemy. These had their backs to them, and the horses' hoofs making little sound in the soft earth, the Cossacks rode on in ignorance of the riders behind them. It was soon clear that no immediate danger need be feared ahead. If Bob's party could elude the horsemen in their rear they might yet make good their escape. Every step increased their distance from the Cossacks, whose course they had cut at right angles. As soon as it appeared that there was no risk of being heard, Bob gave the order to gallop, in the hope that if they had not already been sighted by the riders behind, they might either escape their notice altogether or gain a sufficient lead to make pursuit vain.

But it was soon evident that the pursuit had already begun. Riding in the rear of his party, Bob looked back at a point that promised a good view of the country, and saw that the horsemen were urging their steeds at a pace much more rapid than the horses of his own party were capable of. Half an hour later he judged that they were only a mile away; in another half-hour they might overtake him. Already some of his party were beginning to drop behind; he knew what their fate must be if they were overtaken by the enemy, and he rode up beside Kobo to consult him.

"We cannot go on much longer," he said. "Our horses are almost knocked up after their hard work. It seems to me that our only chance is to find some defensible position and make a stand."

"I agree with you, Mr. Fawcett," said Kobo. "To find such a position in this country will not be easy. There are no gullies or defiles, as you see. I have already asked the chief if he knows of any spot that we could hold; he cannot help us. But we won't give up hope."

"No. And look, sir, I believe there is a chance after all."

He pointed eagerly to a rocky spur a little in front of them, somewhat to the right. Following his outstretched forefinger, Kobo saw four white-clad figures standing there, apparently watching the approaching bodies of horse.

"Monks!" he said. "You are right; where there are monks there will certainly be a monastery. Let us hope it is near at hand."

"There it is!" cried Bob; "farther up the hillside, among the trees. I see the roof. We had better make for it."

Kobo assented, and Bob instantly swung round to the right, and began to lead the party down the steep slope which separated the path from the still steeper slope on which the monastery stood. As soon as the monks saw his intention, they turned tail and began to scamper up towards the building. Bob shouted to them, urging his tired horse in advance of his party, scrambling as rapidly as possible over rocks and tangled shrubs, and breasting the opposite hill. The more he shouted the faster ran the monks. If they reached the monastery before him they might shut their outer gates. Urging his horse still more vehemently with whip and voice in an oblique direction to the path taken by the monks, he came to a wall; the gateway was open; he dashed through into the courtyard up to the main door of the temple enclosure just in time to thrust the handle of his whip between the post and the door as the monks were shutting it against him. Bringing his horse sideways to the door, he made the animal push it open, though the monks did all in their power to keep it shut. Other monks from within came to the assistance of their fellows, but by this time Sing-Cheng with some of his men had reached Bob's side; the monks were overwhelmed; Bob pushed his way in, followed by the rest of his party, and the last man had only just come within the wall when the foremost ranks of the enemy came surging up the hillside.

Bob shouted to Ah-Sam to conduct the ladies to a place of safety, then ordered the men to dismount and line the wall that stretched across the neck of the crag. Immediately afterwards he gave the command to fire, and the volley emptied several saddles among the assailants. The leading files halted indecisively, but the next moment a big Manchu, whom Bob recognized even in the distance as Chang-Wo, dashed up the slope on a fine white horse, and with yells of fury called on his men to follow him. They responded with a shout, and galloped forward, discharging their rifles. But the wall was too high for them to jump, approaching, as they did, up a slope, and the movements of their horses on the rough ground spoilt their aim. Bob saw that if his garrison behaved with ordinary steadiness he could defeat any attempt at direct storming, and he knew that since their defence of the gully his men had lost whatever dread they might formerly have had of Chang-Wo and his band. They fired again at the word of command; Chang-Wo himself was powerless to hold his men together; they had all the disadvantages of the position, and turning their horses' heads the survivors dashed down the slope at the imminent risk of breaking their necks. Seeing that nothing could be done, Chang-Wo, raving with baffled rage, followed them, narrowly escaping a bullet from Kobo's rifle. The Japanese, whose wounded foot prevented him from standing with the rest, had dragged himself to the top of the wall when the enemy surged up, and fired at them as calmly as at target practice. But he was so weak that he could scarcely hold his rifle steady, and it was to this physical weakness that Chang-Wo owed his escape.

Two or three minutes had been enough to decide the fight. The bodies of twenty of Chang-Wo's men and several horses strewed the slope. Except for two men with slight flesh wounds Bob's party had suffered no hurt. Looking at the retreating enemy, Bob thought it unlikely that they would make another attempt on the position for some hours to come. It was now nearly dusk. He left a portion of his band at the wall to be on the watch against the Manchus, who had now disappeared round the base of the hill, then went to assist Kobo into the monastery, and to find out what manner of place it was into which he and his party had thus unceremoniously intruded.

It had evidently been at one time a very extensive settlement. Besides the temple, a large rectangular structure of wood, with a tiled double roof and curved eaves, there were several smaller buildings, the dwelling-places of the abbot and monks; but the majority of these were much dilapidated, only two or three being kept in repair. The temple itself was richly decorated, with an elaborate altar ornamented with beautiful carvings and a lavish display of gilt and colour, and several figures representing various incarnations of Buddha. Everything was spotlessly clean, showing evidence of reverent care on the part of the white-robed monks.

Mrs. Pottle and her niece had been taken to the abbot's house, and when Bob came to them the former was voluble in praise of the tidiness of her surroundings. To find a roof over her head once more was sufficient comfort in itself; but the abbot, as soon as he learnt from Kobo that he had nothing to fear from this strange intrusion, had already shown great attention to his visitors. Bob learnt that the inmates of the monastery at present numbered sixteen, six of whom, however, had gone to a distant town to purchase stores. They had been expected back all day, and it was for them that the monks had been looking when Bob caught sight of them so opportunely. If they arrived now they would find themselves shut out; and the abbot, when he learnt that the leader of the besiegers was none other than Chang-Wo, wrung his hands at the prospective fate of his monks, for the Manchu was well known all over the country, and his name struck terror into all who heard it.

Bob asked to be taken through the settlement. He was anxious to see what possibilities of defence it afforded. Its size was a serious consideration. The stone wall that ran for about ninety yards across the neck of rocks was loose and crumbling, in some places ruinous, having clearly been used as a passage-way instead of the main gate. The spot was fortunately inaccessible from the rear, which was protected by steep rocks; but in front, except for the clear space up which the Manchus had made their futile charge, the hill-face was on both sides dotted with chestnuts, pines, and other trees, together with a tangle of immense ferns and shrubs, affording complete cover to the enemy if they mustered courage for a planned attack.

In the course of his round, Bob learnt a very disconcerting fact. The well on the crag from which the monastery had in old days been supplied with water had failed for several years past. The monks were too poor to dig a new one; too characteristically indolent also, as Bob surmised. They were content to fetch their water as it was required from a mountain stream that ran at the foot of the hill. At present, while their stock of provisions was fairly large, they had only a few gallons of water in their tanks. This news reminded Bob of the horses, who in the excitement of the recent fight had been overlooked. After their long march they were in urgent need of water, and Bob saw that it was necessary to get a supply before the investment became stricter. Questioning the abbot through Ah-Sam, he found that the stream could be approached under cover of the trees, and there was just a chance, if the enemy had retired to some distance round the bend of the hill, that a quiet sortie for water might pass unobserved. He therefore, as a preliminary precaution, sent three men down as scouts to discover what the enemy were about.

While they were gone he returned to the abbot's house, and found that Mrs. Pottle was making merry over the discovery of a gramophone of immense size in one of the apartments. The abbot explained that the instrument had been left in his charge some time before by a high Korean official fleeing southwards before the Russian advance. He knew nothing about its use; indeed, had left it severely alone; it looked to him a good deal like an instrument of war, and was entirely out of place among his peaceful community.

"He tinkum makee velly big bobbely," explained Ah-Sam.

"No doubt," said Bob to Mrs. Pottle with a smile. "He would probably feel somewhat alarmed if he heard some of our popular music-hall songs coming from the bell. I think we might respect his feelings, don't you?"

"Why certainly, Mr. Fawcett. He seems a nice old gentleman, and it would be a pity to shock him. But, my dear boy, what is to become of us? Shall we ever get away from those horrid Manchus? I blame myself now very much for not following your advice and throwing myself on the mercy of the Russians, for without us women hampering you I am sure you could have got away in safety."

"Never fear, we shall get through in time," said Bob. "We have Kobo San with us now, and he is a tower of strength in himself."

"The very look of him gives me courage," added Ethel. "What a brave man he must be! He has never complained once of his wounded foot, and I am sure it must hurt him terribly."

"Yes; I am much interested in him," said Mrs. Pottle. "He is so close, so silent; a strong man, if I am not mistaken. Where did you meet Mr. Kobo?"

"I will tell you all about it—but here come my scouts," replied Bob. "What have they discovered?"

He learnt that they had seen nothing of the enemy, save for half a dozen whom they had noticed riding away to the south-west.

"Possibly to bring assistance," he thought, though on reflection that seemed hardly the quarter in which help could be obtained. He sought out Kobo, who was resting in one of the other houses, and asked his opinion.

"No doubt they have been sent by Chang-Wo to be on the look-out against the approach of a Japanese force. It is clear to me that Chang-Wo will not retire without an attempt to reduce the monastery, especially as he knows that I am here."

"But you think it would be possible to fetch water?"

"Certainly, if it can be done very quietly."

Bob at once went off to make the necessary arrangements. He first sent a number of the Chunchuses down the hillside to a clump of trees on the right, some distance below the wall, to cover the water-carriers and take the Manchus in flank in the event of a sudden assault. Then, under guidance of one of the monks, he himself with twenty men stole out to the left. He stationed the men at equal distances apart down the slope, then started six buckets along the line. As these were filled they were passed up from hand to hand, and returned in the same way when empty to be filled again. Within the walls the monks received the full buckets as they arrived, and emptied them into a large tank behind the temple. The work was done as quickly and quietly as possible, but every now and then one of the men as he moved up the slope to the man above him struck the edge of his bucket against a rock, causing a sound that could hardly escape attentive ears. Such accidents could not be avoided, but at last they occurred so frequently as the men grew tired that Bob thought it time to make good a retreat. Just as he was giving the order, there was an outburst of yells from lower down the slope, and some hundreds of Manchus on foot came surging upwards. Seizing the muskets that lay ready to their hands Bob's men made a break for the wall, the enemy only a few yards behind them. From the Chunchuses in the clump of trees there was a sharp discharge of musketry, but it was ineffectual to check the rush, which had evidently been prepared with some skill, or the movement could scarcely have been unobserved by Bob's scouts.

It was now nearly dark, and as the men of Bob's party scrambled in hot haste over the wall they were in imminent danger of being shot down by the excited garrison in mistake for Manchus. Bob was glad that he had been able to leave in command so cool and experienced a warrior as Kobo. As he vaulted over the low wall, pursued by a Manchu, he heard Kobo's clear voice, incisive amid the tumult, addressing the Chunchuses in their own tongue. Not a man of them fired his piece: it was clear that Kobo had ordered them to await his command. At last, just as Bob, unrecognized in the darkness, had followed the last of his men across the wall, he heard Kobo give a sharp order. There was a rush of Chunchuses to the wall; they had stood some paces back in order to allow their comrades room to get across. Muskets and rifles flashed all along the line; and the cries of wounded men mingled with shouts of rage and defiance as the whole mass of the enemy swarmed up to the low breastwork.

There was no time for the defenders to reload; the fading light barely allowed man to see man; snatching up their long spears they stood resolute to meet their foes. Seventeen of the men who went out with Bob had returned in safety. For a few moments they were too breathless after their scramble to take a hand in the fight; but with Ah-Sam's help Bob collected them into a compact body and held them as a reserve. He succeeded but just in time. Scarcely thirty yards away a mass of yelling figures, led by a tall man armed with a bayonet, swept through a gap in the wall. Others followed; the space beyond was choked with advancing forms. With the instinct of seasoned warriors the Manchus felt that at this point the defence was weak. Pointing to the furious crowd, Bob, having learnt the word from Ah-Sam, ordered his men to fire. There was a burst of flame; every shot told in the dense throng; and while they were at a momentary recoil Bob led his men headlong into the thick of the mêlée. He could never afterwards recall any details of the ensuing fight. He only remembered Kobo limping at his side, the grunts of the combatants, the reek of gunpowder, an occasional sigh or groan as a man dropped to the ground, felled by the stock of a musket or transfixed by a spear. But it was his charge that turned the scale in the quarter where the attack was fiercest. Suddenly the pressure relaxed; a tremor of panic seemed to pulse through the enemy's ranks; and a moment later the space in front of the wall was clear of the enemy.

He was almost inclined to rub his eyes, so sudden was the change. He looked round for Kobo, but could not see him. His first feeling was one of relief for the sake of the two ladies whose fortunes had been so strangely linked with his own. But he could scarcely hope even now that all danger from Chang-Wo and his ruffians was past. The accounts he had had of that warrior gave him little expectation that even a third or fourth rebuff would turn him from his purpose of vengeance. In the silence that followed the repulse—a silence unbroken even by cheers from the victors, for the men were exhausted—he wondered whether another attack was immediately to be feared. He looked again for Kobo, but in vain. Then he called up the chief and Ah-Sam, and told them to place pickets down the hill to watch the enemy. The rest of the men he bade to tend the wounded, among whom he feared that Kobo would be found. It was now quite dark, but he hesitated to use torches, lest they should draw the fire of the enemy and facilitate another assault. After some minutes an exclamation from Ah-Sam announced that Kobo was found. He was pinned to the ground beneath a huge Manchu. Bob had him carefully lifted and carried to the abbot's house, where the ladies, who had awaited the issue of the fight in nervous dread, were only too glad to find relief for their emotions in active tendance. Kobo, unconscious from a blow on the head, was placed in their hands. Under their care he soon came round, but found himself unable to rise. The wound in his foot had reopened through his recent exertions; it was clear that he suffered great pain, but he was smiling when he said to Mrs. Pottle:

"Thank you, dear madam. I am a battered wreck, I fear, put hopelessly out of action."

Kobo might still advise, but evidently the whole weight of the active defence was now to fall on Bob. He went out to take stock of the situation. He found that twelve of his men had been killed outright, and twice as many wounded. Doubtless the Manchus had suffered far more heavily, but their losses were unimportant, so greatly did they outnumber the garrison. Another assault, pressed with anything like the determination of the last, must drive the defenders from the wall into the temple and the dwelling-houses, all flimsy wooden buildings useless as fortresses against a greatly superior enemy. Yet Bob felt sure that another attack would be made. Chang-Wo could not afford to wait. The Japanese advanced-guard must be drawing ever nearer, and might come up at any moment. The assault might not be made during the night—the Manchus had painful experience of the perils of darkness—but it must certainly be expected at dawn. With scarcely more than half his force left, Bob felt that the wall must be abandoned. Was it possible in morning light to do anything that would materially strengthen his position?

Perplexed and almost despondent, he went back to the abbot's house to consult Kobo. As he entered, it happened that the light from a small oil-lamp was reflected in his face from the polished brass of the gramophone. With its wide bell-shaped mouth projecting upwards it bore a certain resemblance to a mortar. Bob was not surprised that the abbot had mistaken it for a piece of ordnance, and he caught himself idly wishing that it were indeed a heavy gun of some kind. Kobo saw his look, and with a smile gave voice to Bob's unuttered thought.

"Unfortunately, it only discharges words," he said.

Bob stood stock-still. An idea had struck him—an idea that, even as his intelligence seized on it, amused him by its whimsicality. Why not? Before now, in the history of the world, a speech had proved more effective than the heaviest artillery. Kobo and the ladies watched with curiosity the changing expressions on his face.

"Where is the abbot?" he cried.

"My lun chop-chop find he," said Ah-Sam. It was some time before he returned; he had found the venerable man prostrate before the high altar in the temple, intoning with constant genuflection a formula of which even he had no notion of the meaning—the mystic words Na-mu-Ami Tabul, handed down through generations from the time when Buddhism was a spiritual power. Ah-Sam had not dared to interrupt; he knew that the abbot would not heed an interruption. Only when his prayers were finished did the old man rise and accompany Ah-Sam, and Bob saw that his eyes still bore the rapt, far-away look of devotion. A few questions and answers passed; then Bob sent for Sing-Cheng and several of his men, and asked them whether they had ever seen an instrument like the one before them. They looked solemnly at the gramophone. Not one gave an affirmative answer.

"Do they think Chang-Wo or any of his men has seen such a thing?" he asked.

"He say no ting likum belongey this-side no tim'," interpreted Ah-Sam.

"Ask him whether one of his men has a fine loud voice and can curse well."

"He say one piecee man hab got velly big loud sing-song; he one tim' bonze, hab got sack cos he velly bad bonze, makee plenty too much bobbely in joss-house. He can do swear first-chop: topside galaw!"

"The very man!" exclaimed Bob, unconscious of the broad smile with which Kobo was now regarding him, or of the look of mystification on the faces of the ladies. He got the chief to send for the whilom Buddhist priest who had been expelled from his monastery. While waiting for the man to appear he examined the gramophone; saw that it was in order and ready for use; and found, as the abbot's reply to his questions had led him to expect, that there were several spare cylinders for taking records. As he moved about, too intent on his proceedings to notice anything around him, a light dawned on Mrs. Pottle.

"Well, I never!" she exclaimed in a loud whisper. "The boy's a right-down genius, Ethel; I told you so."

Ethel put her fingers to her lips, as the messenger returned, accompanied by a bullet-headed scowling individual whom Bob had already remarked as one of the most determined of his fighters. The man looked somewhat suspicious of the company, still more when Ah-Sam explained why he had been sent for. He had never been asked to curse professionally before. But he brightened, up when he at last understood that his powers of denunciation were to be employed against the enemy. He was touched on a point of personal pride, and declared that his curses had no match in all Manchuria. Bob invited him to curse the Manchus as loudly and venomously as he was able, and the bonze was soon launched on a full tide of invective which, though in a strange tongue, Bob felt to be quite overpowering. Ah-Sam explained to him afterwards that every one of the enemy had been signalized by a special curse, embracing not only himself but his ancestors for a thousand years. The man wound himself up to such a pitch of frenzy that he was quite oblivious of the fact that he was yelling, by Bob's careful manipulation, full into the brazen mouth of the gramophone, whose whirring was wholly smothered by his virulent bellow. Kobo was silently laughing; the ladies tried not to look shocked; Ah-Sam nodded his head and beamed approval, though he was as ignorant as the man himself of the true inwardness of the situation. The capacity of the cylinder was exhausted long before the unfrocked bonze; he was streaming with perspiration when he at length drew his lurid declamation to a close. And he went away a happy man when Bob thanked him fervently, assuring him that such terrible cursing would no doubt avail where all else had failed.

After an interval, Bob took the gramophone to the remotest corner of the settlement, where, shutting himself up in a disused house, he tested the instrument under a covering of blankets. Satisfying himself that the latest record was effective, he got Ah-Sam to carry the machine into the open space in front of the gate. He formed a connection between it and the abbot's house by leading a thread of strong silk from it beneath small rocks into the courtyard. Having proved that the connection was complete, he sat down to wait for the onslaught of the Manchus, which he expected to take place as soon as morning dawned.

No one thought of going to sleep that night. Mrs. Pottle wrote diligently in her note-book, and Bob, without neglecting any precautions for the guarding of the camp, found several opportunities of conversation with Ethel. In a far corner of the large hall Kobo spent several hours in writing alone. By and by he folded the paper, and beckoned Bob to his side.

"I hope much from your device, Mr. Fawcett," he said. "It is a clever idea of yours—to turn the superstitions of these people to account. I think you will succeed. But you must use your success without me. I am so useless that I should only be an encumbrance to you. But my information must not be lost; I have therefore written it down here, and I give you this paper, and entreat you, when you get away, to deliver it as speedily as possible to our general."

"But what will become of you?"

"I shall remain here. Perhaps Chang-Wo will not trouble about me after you are gone. If he finds me—well, I shall then kill myself, as many of my ancestors did; but my life belongs to my country, and while there is any chance of living to do service, I shall not take the extreme step."

"But the Manchus will torture you if they catch you."

"That is likely enough. It is the fortune of war."

"I cannot agree to it," said Bob flatly. "I will not take your despatch unless you make an effort to escape with us. In any case I cannot leave the rest of the wounded to fall into Chang-Wo's hands, and you, Kobo San—no, I certainly shall not go without you."

Kobo endeavoured to induce Bob to change his mind, but finding him obdurate, he at length unwillingly consented to share the fortunes of the rest of the party. As it was now drawing towards dawn, Bob had the horses saddled in readiness to seize the moment when the gramophone should have done its work, and one of the animals was specially fitted up for Kobo, with a rest for the wounded leg. Then he went the round of the defences, giving the men instructions how they were to act.

At the wall, as dawn stole over the sky, stood Bob anxiously waiting. It was still half dark when he saw the enemy cautiously approach. They had conceived too great a respect for the defenders to attempt to take the position at a rush; for they were unaware how much the garrison had been reduced in the combat of the previous night. They took every advantage of cover, flitting in the half light from tree to tree and clump to clump until they had come within a few yards of the walls. Then they halted, puzzled apparently by the strange stillness and the seeming desertion of the position. Bob himself was hidden by an angle of the wall; not a man of the garrison was to be seen. For all the Manchus knew, the defenders might be crowding under shelter of the wall. Bob saw a man climb a tall birch from which the greater part of the settlement could be seen. Discovering from his perch no sign of the Chunchuses, the Manchu shouted excitedly to his comrades, and they rushed forward all along the line. The central body at once came upon the gramophone, which stood lifting its great brazen mouth towards the rising sun. From his secret nook Bob saw them recoil; they evidently took it to be a gun of some kind. Then, finding that nothing happened, and no doubt reflecting that a gun needs a man to fire it, some of the bolder among them approached the instrument cautiously and walked round it, keeping at a safe distance. The rest were now hidden by the wall, under which they crouched until they should receive the command to burst into the courtyard.

Bob felt that the moment had come. He pulled the silken cord, and saw the Manchus nearest the instrument start and look round in apprehension. They heard the preliminary whirring. Then, though the mouth was pointing away from him, Bob could hear in the still morning air the first few words of the bonze's speech. The Manchus stood as if spellbound; one or two edged towards the trees. What was this incredible thing? They looked in alarm at one another; no man but themselves was in sight; it must be from the seeming gun that this voice proceeded, calling down upon them and their ancestors the most terrible defilements and atrocities. This strange monster must be in league with the devils against them. The blatant voice from the gramophone rose louder and louder; curse rolled upon curse, shaming Ernulfus for ever; the passionate tones rose higher and higher towards the peroration, till they became a shriek. The Manchus did not wait for the end. With one accord they bolted under cover; anathema remorselessly pursued them through the trees, over the rocks; and before the bell emitted its final howl the scared enemy had rushed pell-mell down the hill, round the bend, and out of sight.

Chapter XX
Herr Schwab Gomblains

Heavy Odds—War and Commerce—Dead Sea Fruit—A Handicap—Kuroki—Mrs. Pottle is Indiscreet—A Parting

The moment the last of the Manchus disappeared round the bend, Bob gave the order to mount. He knew that though for the moment scared out of their wits by the mysterious voice, they would soon recover when they found it was after all a voice and nothing more. Further, he was disturbed by the absence of Chang-Wo. That redoubtable warrior had not been among the discomfited throng; he had not come within hearing of the anathema; it was scarcely likely that he would relinquish his purpose for an unknown cause. Bob therefore got his little party into order. Mrs. Pottle with her niece and Ah-Sam led the way down the hill, accompanied by half a dozen of the best of the Chunchuses, all mounted on the fastest horses. They went down on the opposite side from that taken by the Manchus, and Bob gave orders to Ah-Sam to conduct them with all possible speed in the direction of Ping-yang. Mrs. Pottle pleaded to be allowed to ride with the main body, but Bob explained that the presence of ladies would prove a source of weakness to him, and that they might do good service by pushing on and sending, if possible, a Japanese force to the relief of the others. Bob had wished also to entrust Kobo's despatch to Ah-Sam for delivery to the Japanese general, but Kobo replied that though the Chinaman had proved a loyal and devoted servant, he preferred that Bob himself should retain the message.

"It is to your courage, presence of mind, and resource that the safety of the party is due," he said, "and I know that if anyone can carry the message through, it will be you. One word only: if you should be wounded, pass the despatch to someone else. If that is not possible, destroy it, for though I wrote in Japanese characters the Russians would no doubt get someone to read them, and it is of vital importance that they should know nothing of what I have written. I still hope to see the general myself and give him my news; but I am very weak, and I fear that I may not be able to keep up with you."

Scarcely three minutes after the ladies and their escort had disappeared down the hill the main body followed. A dozen unwounded men rode in advance; then came the wounded with Kobo; then a few men bringing up the rear to give warning of pursuit. Nothing was seen of the enemy as the band moved downwards and struck off to the south in the track of the ladies. The necessity of sparing the wounded caused the pace to be very slow, scarcely more than four miles an hour; but as hour after hour passed, and still no enemy appeared, Bob began to think that the scare had been so effectual that the Manchus had utterly lost heart.

Suddenly there reached his ears a shout of alarm, followed by several rapid shots, and he saw his advanced guard galloping back upon the main body. A quarter of a mile behind them, round the brow of the hill, came Chang-Wo dashing along at the head of a hundred yelling Manchus. They must have made a circuit with the intention of heading off the fugitives. To evade them was impossible; only one course was open, and the odds were all in favour of the enemy. Bob had scarcely forty men left, but spurring his horse towards the Manchus, he waved the spear he had caught up at the moment of departure, and called on the chief and all the unwounded men to follow him. So great was the confidence with which he had inspired them that they obeyed instantly. Uttering strange guttural cries little resembling a British cheer, they set their horses to the gallop. There was no attempt to secure a regular formation, but in this respect the enemy had no advantage; they came, each man for himself, a scattered group. The ground was rough and strewn with stones, but the riders on either side gave no heed to the horses' footsteps; they had eyes only for each other. In a few seconds the two parties met in the shock of battle. Bob, slightly in advance of his men, rode straight for Chang-Wo, whose head, he noticed, was bandaged; he had been wounded in the fight at the monastery. The Manchu carried a long Chinese sword, with which he parried the thrust of Bob's spear; but before he in his turn could make an offensive stroke, Bob was past him, and, shortening his weapon, had driven it through the Manchu immediately behind. At the same moment he heard a great shouting in front of him, and even as he wondered whether this portended a reinforcement of the enemy, he felt a stinging blow upon the head, staggered, lost grip of the reins, and, falling upon his horse's neck, was thrown violently to the ground.

"It is an outrage! I, Hildebrand Schwab, say it. It vill be a casus belli, sure as a gun, between Gairmany and Japan. Vizout doubt I vill send a telegram to our kaiser, who is in Berlin. I let you know I am a beaceable Gairman sobjeck; notvithstanding vich I am arrested, my liberty is in constraint, my dignity—the dignity of a Gairman sobjeck—is alltopieces. It is, I say it, monstrous; it is onbearable; it is a zink zat I nefer, nefer oferlook!"

Bob was gradually aroused to full consciousness by Herr Schwab's loud voice in bitter complaint. A soft, polite, bored Japanese voice replied:

"The hon'ble correspondent must know that hon'ble correspondents are not allowed beyond Ping-yang. It is plainly written in the instructions issued by his excellency the general for the guidance of hon'ble correspondents, and I regret to say that the hon'ble correspondent has only himself to blame."

"Instructions! You say instructions! Donnerwetter noch einmal! Vat are ze instructions? Ze instructions are to do nozink, see nozink, say nozink. Vat is zat for a kind of var gorresbondence? I rebresent ze *Düsseldörfer Tageblatt*. I am instructed to agombany ze Japanese field-army. Zey are my instructions—nozink else!"

"I regret I cannot allow the hon'ble correspondent to proceed."

"Vell zen, I brotest; I emphatically brotest. All ze same, I ask you to agombany me backwards to ze next village. Business are business. Zere I make vun deal viz a nice Korean gentleman vat give me order for gomblete set *Brockhaus Encyglobaedia*. But zere vas ozer zinks: I ask you agombany me back till I gomblete my business."

"I regret it is impossible. I must return as rapidly as possible to Chong-ju. The hon'ble correspondent will kindly excuse me."

The Japanese officer turned away, leaving Schwab to retrace his steps in sullen and indignant rage. Bob was amused. A moment later the Japanese came into the hut where he was lying, and finding him awake and conscious, asked how he felt.

"Pretty shaky. I am glad to find myself in Japanese hands. Tell me, did Miss Charteris—did the ladies get in safely?"

"Yes. Two ladies rode into my camp this morning with a Chinese attendant, and told me that an English gentleman was hard pressed by a gang of Manchus. I sent the ladies on to Chong-ju, and rode out to assist you. Fortunately I came up at the critical moment. You had apparently just been knocked off your horse. The Manchus did not wait to receive us. You have had a very nasty knock, hon'ble sir."

"And Kobo—"

"Kobo San! What do you mean?"

"Did you not find him?" Bob started up anxiously. "He was with us. He was wounded. Surely you helped him to escape?"

"I am very sorry, sir. I heard that a wounded Chinaman belonging to your party was missing—presumably captured by the Manchus. I had no idea that he was a Japanese disguised, still less that he was Kobo San."

"The ladies said nothing of him?"

"Nothing. They were exhausted with hard riding, and much agitated. They mentioned no name but your own."

Bob lay back in mute hopelessness. Kobo had fallen into the hands of his enemy! Something must be done to save him. Bob dared not think of the nameless tortures he might suffer at the cruel hands of Chang-Wo.

"How long ago did this happen?" he asked.

"Six hours ago. It is now five o'clock."

"Can't you do something to help him? You know him—how valuable he is to your country. Surely something can be done."

"I regret more than I can say. I would do anything possible for Kobo San, but I must obey orders. I should have pursued the fleeing Manchus had I not been instructed not to advance beyond a certain line. Kobo San will know how to die for Japan."

Bob could say no more. At that moment he almost wished that he could exchange places with Kobo. He knew that Kobo himself would meet his fate with the serenity that characterized his every thought and action; but the knowledge that so brave and heroic a man, when safety was in sight, should have fallen at the eleventh hour into the clutches of his vindictive and merciless enemy, was a bitter disappointment.

The two companies of Japanese infantry who had rescued Bob and his party occupied a small adjacent village that night. Herr Schwab had to submit to the further indignity of being kept under guard. In the morning Bob, who had recovered somewhat from his blow and subsequent fall, asked to be taken to see the implacable correspondent. He found Herr Schwab busily writing.

"No, it is not var gorresbondence," said the German, without looking up, "it is business; so you, Mr. Japanese, vill besokind as leave me in beace."

"And how *is* business, Mr. Schwab?" asked Bob.

"Vat!" said Schwab, turning with a start; "do I see Mr. Fawcett? It is vonderful, it is incredible! I am glad indeed to meet vat I may viz bermission call a friend. My heart is fery heafy. It is years since I make a so disastrous journey. Vat hafe I done? Nozink. My egsbenses—vere are zey? I do not bay vun shilling in ze bound. My embloyers—zey regard me as colossal humbug. I write letters—yes, dree golumns ze day: 'Imbressions of Japan', 'Views in Korea', 'A Gairman at ze Front'; and zey vire me, four shillings ze vord, 'Gife us var news'. Var news!"

Herr Schwab laughed bitterly.

"Vat can ve know of var news? Zat is vat I ask. Zere vas myself, Mr. Morton, and Monsieur Desjardang, viz ozer gorresbondents—var gorresbondents!"—(Herr Schwab again laughed bitterly)—"at Ping-yang, sixty miles away from ze var. Ze Japanese declare it is great concession ve are allowed so glose—so glose! And ze regulations—potztausend! scarcely dare ve look towards ze nort. It vas heartbreaking—veek after veek pass by; our egsbenses run on."

Bob looked as sympathetic as possible.

"It must have been very rough. Still, you managed to get away apparently."

"Yes, sir. I egsblain to my friends it is onbearable. For myself, if I do not gife ze Japanese ze slip I get ze sack. I offer my friends to agombany me; ve share egsbenses. But Mr. Morton he say somezink about 'blay ze game'; Monsieur Desjardang he talk about ze vord of a Frenchman; but I, Hildebrand Schwab, I retort 'business are business'. So I take off ze vite band vat Japanese red-tape seal on my left arm, and ze same night I am on my vay to ze Yalu. I suffer much hardship, but do I murmur? No; I book seferal orders for Schlagintwert Gombany. But, sir, as you see, I am again in bondage. Vile I am making deal viz Korean excellency, whom I meet on tour of insbection, lo! ve are surbrise by Japanese. Ze order for ze *Conversationslexicon*, I hafe it; but ze order for ze bianola, zat is gombletely gone lost."

Herr Schwab's gloom was depicted in his features, when suddenly an idea seemed to strike him. Laying his hand confidentially on Bob's arm, he said:

"Stay, all is not lost. If you, Mr. Fawcett, can conclude ze transaction, I shall hafe great bleasure to bay you fipercent commission. Ze gentleman is San-Po of ze Imperial Korean Var-office: you vill find him vizout difficulty. Fipercent, Mr. Fawcett!"

Bob had started in surprise at hearing the name of his friend Mr. Helping-to-decide. At the same moment, looking out of the hut, he saw a cavalcade passing the door. At the head rode a high Korean official—a well-remembered figure, with the regulation hat, topknot, and white baggy garments. Mounted on a diminutive pony, his feet almost touched the ground, and his equilibrium was maintained in the customary Korean manner by two sturdy attendants, who supported him on either side. No sooner had Schwab's eyes lighted on this rider than he started forward with an exclamation, saying to Bob:

"Vizout offence you vill permit me to vizdraw my brobosition: egsguse me."

He rushed out in unwieldy haste, wresting from his pocket a capacious note-book as he ran. After him darted a nimble Japanese sentry in full cry. Bob chuckled as he watched the scene. Mr. Helping-to-decide, hearing a guttural hail behind him, half turned upon his saddle (on which Bob recognized the skin of the tiger he had killed), and seeing that he was pursued did not stay to decide why or by whom, but whipped up his pony in haste to escape. Swaying from side to side, he was held up with difficulty by his two supporters, and unsteadily turned a corner, followed within a couple of yards by the lolloping form of Herr Schwab, who in his turn was, but a yard or two ahead of the Japanese.

An hour or two later the whole detachment moved out towards Chong-ju. Bob was provided with a pony, from whose back he saw Schwab trudging disconsolately along in charge of two little Japanese infantrymen. The white band, with his name and the name of his paper in red Japanese characters, was again bound to his left sleeve, labelling him "war correspondent".

On arriving at Chong-ju, which was crowded with Japanese troops, Bob enquired first for Mrs. Pottle and her niece, and learnt that they had already departed under escort for Anju. His next question was for the headquarters of General Kuroki. Learning that these were at Anju, he explained to the officer in command that he had important information for the general, which he had been instructed to deliver personally, and asked to be allowed to proceed at once. The colonel in charge suggested that Bob might give him the information, which he would then forward. He thought Bob looked hardly fit to travel farther on horseback, and there were no carts to spare. But Bob was determined that he would confide Kobo's paper to none but General Kuroki himself, hoping to be able to induce the general to organize a rescue-party on Kobo's behalf. He accordingly rode on with a small escort, and arrived at Anju on the Seoul road late at night, and dead beat.

Fatigued as he was, he at once sent a message to the general asking the favour of an interview. Within half an hour he was in the presence of the commander-in-chief. He felt a little nervous as he looked at the great soldier. General Kuroki was somewhat taller than the average Japanese. His face was deeply bronzed, his hair and moustache gray and bristly. The sternness of his features was relieved by a humorous twinkle in his dark eyes as he glanced at Bob, who felt that the general's undoubted strength of character was combined with tenderness and humanity. He handed him Kobo's small folded paper, and waited while he read it.

"I thank you, Mr. Fawcett," he said at length, refolding the paper and handing it to an aide-de-camp. "Kobo San's intelligence is of the highest importance, and I am greatly in your debt for having brought it to me at such risk. Kobo San does not say why he has not returned. Do you know where he is?"

"I am very sorry to say, sir, that he is a prisoner. He was wounded in crossing the hills, and I very much fear that he is now in the hands of Chang-Wo, the Manchu brigand."

"Indeed! That is deplorable. Tell me, please, all you know. You were, I think, with Lieutenant Yamaguchi in Seoul; I shall be glad to know of the circumstances which have brought you here. Sit down, you look very tired. Perhaps, indeed, you would rather wait till the morning?"

"No, sir, I would rather tell you now."

He proceeded to relate as briefly as possible his experiences from the time he last saw Yamaguchi to the final escape from the Korean monastery. General Kuroki listened without remark, a faint smile crossing his face when he heard of the novel use made of the gramophone.

"You have had a desperately hard time," he said at the conclusion of the story. "I had already heard part of the circumstances from the American ladies who came in some time ago. I can quite understand their warm praise of you. And, let me say, you are to be congratulated on your escape from the Manchu Chang-Wo; he is a desperate villain—an old enemy of Kobo San, as perhaps you know. But now tell me; you came through the mountains north of the Yalu; is the road practicable for guns?"

"It might, I think, with some labour be made practicable for guns for some miles up to the spot where we first struck the Yalu; but I don't think the path we subsequently followed could be so used."

"That path is marked, I think, tentatively on our maps. Look at this; that is the path, is it not?"

"Yes," said Bob, after a glance at the map unrolled before him.

"It would be of the greatest importance to us if it were practicable. Did any of the Chunchuses with whom you have been acting come in with you?"

"Unfortunately no, sir. I learnt that they slipped away immediately after we were relieved by your cavalry."

"They are free lances, and probably thought if they came in they would have to act under our orders, or more probably be disbanded. No doubt they are making their way back by devious paths to their old haunts in Manchuria. It is a pity they have gone. I should have liked to employ some of them as guides."

"May I offer my services, sir?" said Bob instantly. "I couldn't find my way back from here to the hills, but once there I think I could act as guide over the path in question."

"Thank you. I accept your offer at once. I must, of course, wire to Tokio for permission to employ you, as otherwise your duty would be to rejoin the fleet. I will do that at once, and the answer will no doubt come early in the morning. Now, Mr. Fawcett, I will not keep you longer. You need a thorough rest after your trying experiences: that knock on the head will trouble you for some days, I fear; but I hope a good rest will set you up again. My aide-de-camp will provide you with quarters—rough, but the best at my disposal. I shall send for you in the morning."

Only now that the strain was relaxed did Bob realize how desperately tired and worn he was. When he reached the lodging allotted to him, he dropped on to the bed just as he was, and fell fast asleep. It was nearly noon when he awoke. Ah-Sam came to his side, carrying over his arm a suit of clothes.

"My hab catchee tings for massa," he said. "Aflaid massa no can get iniside."

"Well, I can only try," said Bob with a smile. "Get me something to eat, Ah-Sam. Stay, where are the ladies?"

"He in house topside-pidgin man—velly nice. He go Seoul bimeby."

"Oh! Just run and tell them I'm here—"

"Allo savvy. My tellum allo 'bout massa long tim' ago."

"Ask them not to go until I have seen them, then get my breakfast."

"Allo lightee, massa. Littee missy wantchee look-see what—"

"Don't stand talking. Run at once, or they may gone."

"No fear! My savvy littee missy no can wailo 'cept—"

"Go at once!" shouted Bob, and the Chinaman fled.

About an hour later Bob, clad in a Japanese uniform, which left a good deal to be desired about the sleeves and the trousers, was conducted by Ah-Sam to the missionary's house in which the ladies had been hospitably lodged.

"My dear boy, how glad I am to see you!" exclaimed Mrs. Pottle, coming forward with outstretched hands. "We were afraid that you had not escaped from that dreadful brigand. If I had not had Ethel to take care of, I should certainly have ridden back myself—even with nothing but my umbrella that you make fun of."

Bob, from his knowledge of Mrs. Pottle, felt that the fair American was quite equal to that or any other hazardous adventure.

"I am glad indeed there was no occasion," he said. "I wouldn't have you come within fifty miles of that desperate gang."

"That would have been no worse, not a bit, for I haven't slept a wink worrying about you, neither has Ethel; indeed, the dear child has lost all her colour, as you see."

Bob looked at the younger lady, but found that her cheeks were warm with a charming little blush, which deepened as she avoided his glance.

"Oh, Aunt Jane," she said, "you really shouldn't exaggerate—I—"

"There now! I've done it again. I am always putting my foot in it. But all's well that ends well. You're here safe—but dear me, poor boy, you've lost your colour. We shall have to take care of you, I can see that."

"Oh, it's nothing," said Bob; "a rap over the head, that's all. I shall be right in a day or two."

"But you will let us do what we can," said Ethel. "We owe you so much, Mr. Fawcett, and there is so little that we can do."

Bob looked, as he felt, rather uncomfortable. Mrs. Pottle noted the fact.

"Don't go, Mr. Fawcett," she said with a smile. "There, I promise, you sha'n't hear another word of thanks. I knew it: you look quite relieved already."

Bob laughed, and the ladies joined him, while Ah-Sam looked on gravely, in evident wonder at what had caused the merriment.

"Can I do anything to help you on your way?" asked Bob. "I'm afraid I shall soon have to say good-bye."

The ladies looked at him in surprise.

"But are you not going to Seoul?" asked Mrs. Pottle.

"Not yet, I'm sorry to say. I have something yet to do."

"We are not in a hurry. We could quite well wait a day or two."

"It is not a matter of days, unfortunately. It may be weeks or even months."

"You are not going back?" said Ethel, vainly endeavouring to conceal her anxiety. Bob afterwards remembered that there was a tremor in her voice.

"Yes," he said, "I am going north again. General Kuroki thinks I can be of some use to him, and afterwards—well, I have to find my friend Kobo."

"But, Mr. Fawcett, surely that is quixotic," said Mrs. Pottle. "You could not hope to find him. Indeed, poor man! if that villain Chang-Wo has captured him, his life will not be worth a moment's purchase. Think of the risk you would run: it is terrible."

"Yes, indeed," added Ethel earnestly. "Please do not go. Think of—of your friends."

"Believe me, I will run no needless risks, but I must do what I can to find my friend or learn his fate. Remember what I owe to him."

"Yes, we ought not to forget that," said Ethel; "you owe him—what we owe to you."

She turned away. Mrs. Pottle put her arm about her niece's waist.

"Is it to be good-bye, then?" she asked.

Before Bob could reply, Ah-Sam, who had left the room for a few minutes, returned hurriedly.

"One piecee Japanee come fetchee ladies Seoulee side. Hab got horses; wantchee lide wailo chop-chop: topside fightee pidgin."

A few questions asked of Ah-Sam, and Bob explained to Mrs. Pottle that an officer was about to start on military business for Seoul, and the occasion had been seized to provide the American ladies with an escort. He would arrive within a few minutes. Bob despatched Ah-Sam with an answer, then turned to Mrs. Pottle.

"Yes," he said, "it is good-bye."

"But not for long," she replied with forced cheerfulness. "We shall stay, anyhow, two months at Yokohama, and you must come right along as soon as you can."

"Good-bye, Mr. Fawcett," said Ethel, giving him her hand. "We shall pray for your success. Good-bye!"

Chapter XXI
The Battle of the Yalu River

The Impossible—Stage Properties—Outwitted—The Battle Opens—
Russians at Bay—Yamaguchi's Experiences

"It is clear, Mr. Fawcett, that you have the bump of locality."

"I am not sure of that, sir. What I remember of these hills is due to
the Manchu Chang-Wo. We were continually looking back, expecting to see
him on our track."

"At any rate you seem to have brought away a remarkably vivid
impression of the country—fortunately for us. This path, bad as it is, has
saved us an immensity of labour, and—what is more important—time."

General Inouye pulled up his horse as he spoke, and looked back
upon the long line of troops zigzagging up the face of the mountain. The
blue uniforms of the Japanese soldiers showed up clearly against the bare
ochreous rocks of the hillside, offering a conspicuous mark to the enemy,
had the enemy been there to see. But these rugged, precipitous hills had
always been regarded as impracticable for troops; the Russians had no fear
of attack from this quarter, and had made no attempt to occupy them.

There was an unusually large prospect from the spur overhanging the
deep gully on which General Inouye and Bob stood side by side. Above
them the road disappeared abruptly round the face of the mountain;
below, it wound erratically down the boulder-strewn slope, here and there
plunging out of sight in a hollow, to emerge again, it might be hundreds of
yards lower down, as a narrow ledge on the face of a perpendicular crag,
on which the Japanese troops seemed in the distance like an army of ants
on the march.

These were the hills through which Bob and his party had made their
perilous journey some weeks earlier. They lay on the left flank of the Russian
army drawn up around Kiu-lien-cheng, and on the banks of the Yalu, to hurl
back the Japanese when they attempted to set foot in Manchuria. General
Sassulitch fondly hoped that these hills would afford a complete protection
to his flank: as the event was ordered, it was from them that he sustained

his most crushing blow. The Twelfth Division, known to the Japanese as the Sampo Shidan in consequence of its large equipment of mountain-guns, was chosen to make the hazardous passage, and to any troops of less endurance than the Japanese, the task might well have proved impossible; for they were not only required to cross a series of steep mountain ridges, but to do so within a very limited time, and to bring their guns with them. Bob watched the steady progress of the column with many a thrill of admiration, and with pride that he was privileged to bear a small part in this momentous movement. Burdened with its artillery, ammunition, and supplies, the column moved steadily forward; now crawling with infinite pains up almost perpendicular slopes, the willing little soldiers pushing, hauling, at times almost carrying the wretched horses and ponies groaning under guns, gun-carriages, or boxes of shell; then with no less strain staggering, slipping, sliding down the opposite face of the hill, to begin another climb in this unending series of bluffs and chasms.

The march had begun early in the day; it was now late in the afternoon, and Bob more than once saw General Inouye looking anxiously westward. They rounded the shoulder of a steep hill; half a mile or more ahead a small body of cavalry thrown out in advance had halted, evidently in doubt as to their further course.

"To the left," said Bob, answering General Inouye's unspoken question, "across that small spur, and straight up the farther slope."

The general translated the instructions to an aide-de-camp, who clattered down the hill at the imminent risk of his neck.

"You say, Mr. Fawcett, that in another hour we should open up the Ai-ho river?"

"Yes, sir. As far as I remember we sighted the river from the crest of yonder hill." Bob pointed, as he spoke, to a conical hill about two miles ahead, behind which the sun was now setting in a blaze of glory. Within the hour General Inouye and his staff had gained the crest of the hill, and were looking down on the noisy little river hurrying through a narrow valley to join the Yalu some miles below. On the far side of the stream was another range of hills, upon which, as General Inouye was aware, the main Russian force was concentrated. It was against these hills that the Twelfth Division would hurl itself at dawn on the following day.

Approaching the Ai-ho the hills became somewhat less rugged, facilitating the deployment of General Inouye's force along the left bank of the river. The Twelfth Division had arrived in good time at the appointed place; with guns unlimbered for action, it waited only for the word.

"Good-night, Mr. Fawcett," said General Inouye when they separated; "good-night, and thank you. You have rendered us a most valuable service—how valuable the events of to-morrow may show."

Bob spent the night in the bivouac of the staff. Even the prospect of the coming struggle failed to disturb his sleep. He had gone through too many experiences of late not to take full advantage of any chance of rest.

The position of the two armies that lay facing each other through the long summer night was in many respects an extraordinary one. The river Yalu is joined nearly opposite Wiju by the Ai-ho; above and below the confluence its channel is dotted with numerous large islands, between which the stream threads a tortuous and at times impetuous course. At the angle formed by the two rivers is Tiger Hill, a steep bluff jutting far out into the channel. Just below the hill runs the Mandarin road from Seoul to Pekin, passing from Wiju on the south bank, across two sandy islands connected by a ferry, and thence to Kiu-lien-cheng, on the Manchurian side, a short distance to the north of the river.

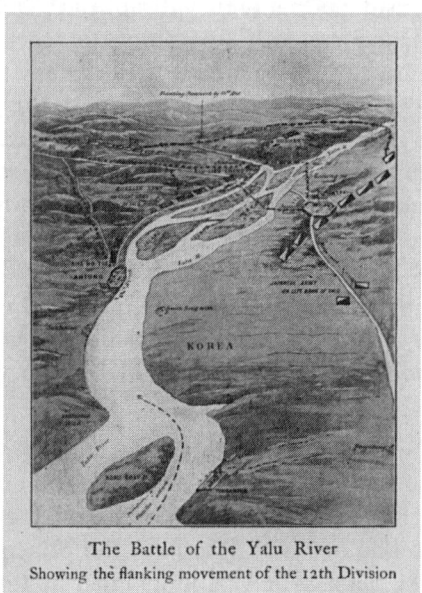

The Battle of the Yalu River
Showing the flanking movement of the 12th Division

The Battle of the Yalu River Showing the flanking movement of the 12th Division

The Russian front, before the development of General Kuroki's attack, extended from a point opposite Yongampo at the mouth of the Yalu to Sukuchin, some thirty miles up the river, and above Wiju. The main body was massed around Kiu-lien-cheng, the left wing having its outposts on

Tiger Hill and the islands in the river above that point, while the right had outposts on the larger islands opposite Wiju. A strong force was held in reserve at Antung.

On his ride up from Wiju Bob had been greatly puzzled by a series of huge screens of brushwood, matting, and stalks placed along or across the roadway. What object, he wondered, could they serve? It was not until he reached the high ground near the Yalu that their purpose became clear to him. He saw then that the heights on the Russian side of the river completely overlooked the lower hills on the Korean bank; in ordinary circumstances every movement could be observed from the Russian lines; the numbers and dispositions of troops, the construction of fortifications and batteries, could all be noted with the aid of strong field-glasses. From the Japanese point of view this was a serious weakness of the position. Secrecy is so essential a condition of the Japanese system of conducting warfare that General Kuroki was led to adopt a novel and somewhat extraordinary method of baffling the curiosity of the enemy. Looking back from a point of vantage near the river, Bob saw a force of blue-coated Japanese infantry marching to the front along the Mandarin road. Suddenly they disappeared behind a leafy screen, and though he watched carefully, expecting to see them emerge again farther along the highway, he was unable to detect any further sign of their presence. The incident recalled a conjuring trick of Mr. Maskelyne; and to the Russians beyond the river it must have been both puzzling and irritating. Thanks to this system of screens they could neither form an estimate of the strength of the Japanese opposed to them, nor make any likely guess as to the probable point of attack. Their position was one of extreme strength; but uncertainty regarding General Kuroki's movements largely discounted the advantages they enjoyed as a defensive force entrenched among rugged hills. Here and there, indeed, General Kuroki allowed them to obtain a hint of his arrangements; they snapped at the bait—with what result is now written in history.

It was nearly ten years since the Japanese Field-marshal Yamagata had forced the passage of the Yalu in the face of a Chinese army supposed to be impregnably entrenched in the positions now held by the Russians. The main crossing had been made opposite Wiju, but the principal movement was greatly assisted by the passage of a column higher up the river at Sukuchin. General Sassulitch must anxiously have asked himself whether the Japanese would or would not repeat this operation. Patriotic self-complacency probably suggested the answer. Was it likely that the Japanese would dare to repeat against a trained and disciplined Russian army the manoeuvre, necessarily hazardous, which they had risked against raw Chinese levies? Emphatically no. And in arriving at this conclusion the Russian general was assisted by an ingenious feint on the part of his opponent. With an openness that should have inspired distrust, General Kuroki collected a large amount of bridging material on the Korean shore at Yongampo and higher up the river opposite Antung, while a strong naval flotilla, comprising torpedo-boats, destroyers, and gun-boats, fought its way some distance up-stream, as though in support of a projected crossing in the lower reaches. To meet the expected attack in this quarter the Russian general kept a large body of troops elaborately entrenched in readiness at Antung, and allowed his attention to be diverted from the point thirty miles higher up, at which the first crossing had been made ten years earlier.

General Kuroki had completely taken the measure of his adversary. Having persuaded General Sassulitch to disperse his troops over an unnecessarily large front, he made careful dispositions to ensure a successful passage of the river at Sukuchin, and under cover of a flank attack from this quarter he proposed to pass the main body of his army across the island-strewn channel opposite Wiju. The Twelfth Division, entrusted with the flank movement, had easily driven away a small Russian force stationed on the right bank opposite Sukuchin, thrown a pontoon bridge across the river, and established itself on the right bank almost without opposition. The Russians made no attempt to correct their mistake, so convinced were they that the real danger lay towards the mouth of the river. Besides, were they not sufficiently protected by the chain of impassable ridges that stretched far inland between the Yalu and the Ai-ho? Yet it was across these impassable ridges that the Twelfth Division had orders to make its way, and establish itself on the left bank of the tributary stream in readiness for a general attack on the Russian position. This movement, as we have seen, was duly carried out. It was the eve of May-day.

A fierce artillery duel had meanwhile been fought between the Japanese batteries near Wiju and the Russian positions around Kiu-lien-cheng. In this battle of the giants the Russians were completely outmatched—another triumph of Japanese secrecy and prevision. Unknown to the enemy the Japanese had brought by sea to the Yalu a large number of quick-firers and heavy guns, and, most important of all, several howitzers. To these the Russians could only oppose a limited number of field-pieces. A movement of Japanese infantry towards the crest of the hills on the Korean side drew the fire of the Russian batteries and disclosed their position. They were at once answered by an appalling cannonade from the Japanese batteries. From the islands in the river, from the heights north and south of Wiju, the Japanese rained a murderous fire of shell and shrapnel upon the luckless Russian gunners. There was no escape, for they had not reckoned with the howitzers cunningly placed in pits on the islets beneath, and able to search the whole

Russian position with high-angle fire. The hills seemed to wilt under the storm; the earth was riddled, the very rocks were rent with the hail of lead and steel scattered by the bursting charges of the terrible Shimose powder. A thick pall of poisonous smoke hung over the devoted Russian batteries; nothing could live under this shattering bombardment. The Russians stuck to their guns like heroes; never certainly did soldiers deserve better of their country. But gradually their fire slackened, then died away: the gunners lay dead at their posts.

That night the Guards and the Second Division of the Japanese army were passed by two bridges across the river, and took up a position on the right bank, sheltered under the bluffs or in the hollows in the sandy bed of the stream. The Second Division had crossed somewhat below Wiju to an island on the far side of the channel, the Guards immediately opposite Tiger Hill. The Russians were now threatened with a frontal attack by these two divisions—the Second operating direct from the Yalu, the Guards across the mouth of the Ai-ho—while the Twelfth Division, higher up the Ai-ho, was ready to attack them in flank.

Bob was tingling with excitement when he awoke on the auspicious morning of May-day. The air was crisp and keen, but spring had come at last; spring, and with it the dawn of a new era for Japan. General Inouye's camp was early astir; the sturdy little soldiers, in their trim blue uniforms, went about their morning duties with quiet cheerfulness, ready to launch themselves at the word upon the grim hills opposite, where death, they knew, awaited some; glory, they hoped, all.

Too late the Russian general had realized his fatal error in allowing the Twelfth Division to march unopposed across the hills. Too late he had taken such feverish steps as were now possible in the attempt to retrieve it. He had withdrawn in haste a considerable force from Antung to hold the bluffs on the right bank of the Ai-ho, and hurriedly begun to throw up entrenchments. General Inouye smiled when he learnt of these tardy efforts to stay him; plans carefully thought out for years were not likely to be foiled by bustle at the eleventh hour.

Hardly had the sun risen when the battle was begun by a general outburst of artillery fire along the whole of the Japanese lines. There was no response from the enemy; it almost seemed as if the position were already deserted. But soon the order was given to the Japanese infantry to advance to the assault. The three divisions moved forward simultaneously. Bob could not see what the other two were doing, but he watched with tense eagerness as the Twelfth Division dashed down the hillside to the bank of the Ai-ho. A murderous rifle-fire was opened upon them from the Russian trenches.

But never a man faltered. Springing on nimbly, some taking what cover the ground afforded, others disdaining precaution, they reached the stream. They plunged in, holding their rifles and pouches above their heads, and forcing their way against the rapid current that swept along breast-high. They had now entered the zone of fire; the surface of the river boiled under the hail of Russian bullets; the turbid waters were red with Japan's best blood; but to Bob, watching intently from the hill above, the sound of their war-song came floating upon the morning breeze—

"Oh! it is easy to cross the Yalu river!"

and, with sublime and happy indifference, they struggled on.

Look: they are gaining the farther bank. At last—it seems an eternity!—the river is crossed. Up, up they scramble, scaling the bluffs in grim silence now. The air rattles with the crack of rifles, throbs with the thud of heavy guns. Men are falling fast, but the survivors are still pressing on, up the murderous heights, ever drawing nearer to the enemy on the crest. Bob, his whole body a-tingle, can bear his inaction no longer. He turns to a senior officer of the staff:

"May I follow them up, sir? I have nothing to do now."

"You had better stay with us," replied the officer with a smile, lowering his field-glass; "still, if you wish—"

Bob does not wait for second thoughts. He races down the hill, wades the river, and springs up the bluff in time to overtake the rear of the advancing line. What impels him he knows not; all he feels is that he must be there—there, at the supreme moment of the conflict. He gains the crest and looks eagerly ahead. Ah! the Russians are falling back, and back, and back; not in rout, but sullenly retreating to the next ridge, turning there at bay, occupying every post of vantage, and pouring thence their terrible fire. They will not wait, then, for push of pike? No; and when they have discharged their rifles they run again. Nothing stays the advance. The Japanese swarm up and over every new position, the enemy scurry like rabbits before them, and now, as the pace quickens, and the victors drive the fugitives up hill and down dale across these rugged pathless hills, the retreat becomes a rout, and the little soldiers raise a great shout of joy.

While the Twelfth Division had thus triumphantly performed the great operation entrusted to them, their comrades of the Second and Guards Divisions had pressed home their attacks on the Russian front. The whole of General Sassulitch's army was in full flight on Homatan and Feng-huang-cheng. General Kuroki had only a small force of cavalry to pursue the retreating enemy; he had to rely largely on the speed and endurance of his infantry, and they pressed on the heels of the Russians with a relentless activity which, in this mountainous country, no cavalry could have equalled. The guns, even the mountain batteries, specially equipped for speedy transit, were left miles behind, and three of the leading Japanese companies, having outstripped the rest of the pursuing infantry, found themselves terribly outmatched when the Russians at last turned at bay on the plateau of Homatan. The three companies of Japanese were suddenly confronted by a battalion of infantry and two battalions of artillery, strongly posted on the plateau; but with magnificent determination they stuck like bull-dogs to their grip, and engaged the enemy, holding them in fierce fight until reinforcements should come up. The Japanese had only their rifles to oppose to the combined artillery and musketry fire of the Russians. In the company to which Bob had attached himself three out of every four men were either killed or wounded, yet the gallant survivors stuck to their posts. Bob marvelled how he came unscathed through the hail of shot and shell; it seemed that the little force must be annihilated. Still the gallant remnant held on; and at length, when they were at their last cartridge, help came. Other companies of Japanese infantry swarmed up to the plateau. The Russian gunners, seeing that all was lost, wrenched the breech-blocks from the guns, hammered the sights, and broke the levers. Then came a terrible three minutes' mêlée, in which the bayonet did its murderous work. Most of the Russians died at their posts; three hundred were captured, together with the guns of the two batteries. It would be hard to say whether the fight at Homatan was more glorious to the victors or to the vanquished.

This was the last stand of the Russian army. The pursuit from this point was taken up by the small force of Japanese cavalry, and the wearied infantry, after an action almost unparalleled in military history, bivouacked on the field.

The officers of the company extended to Bob a hearty welcome to their mess; the menu consisted of the usual rations of the rank and file: rice, dried fish and pickles, washed down in water from a neighbouring mountain stream.

Bob was eating as heartily as the rest when he was startled by a familiar voice behind him.

"How do, Bob?"

He sprang up, and almost choked himself in the eagerness with which he welcomed no other than his friend Yamaguchi.

"Well—I'm—blowed!" he ejaculated, shaking hands so vigorously that Yamaguchi at length laughingly protested. "How in the world do you come here?"

"You don't bear me a grudge, then? I was very sorry; but I had to leave you with those Cossacks, you know."

"Don't mention it; I'm only too glad you got away safely—though, in truth, your dastardly desertion of me has landed me in a pretty pickle of fish. But I'll forgive you; I'd forgive anybody to-day. Isn't this glorious, old fellow? Did you see the fight?"

"I had a little part in it. We've been working in the lower reaches of the river. General Kuroki deluded the Russians into the belief that our main crossing was to be effected there. Sassulitch swallowed it whole. I had to land some men yesterday on a small island above Yongampo. We were stormed by the enemy. I withdrew the survivors in boats, and unluckily my boat sank and I was knocked over by a splinter from a Russian shell. They picked me up and carried me off to Antung, and then towards Feng-huang-cheng, but our cavalry came up and released me, and here I am."

"Got a bad knock?" asked Bob, noticing that his left arm was bound up.

"Oh no! a bit of the muscle torn away, that's all. But come, I'm sure you've more to tell than I have. I want to know what you've been about since you deserted the *Kasumi*."

Bob's story necessarily occupied a long time in the telling, but Yamaguchi listened with growing excitement, never interrupting until Bob came to the point where Kobo had rescued him from the tower.

"Ah!" said the Japanese. "You came across Kobo? I put you off the scent, didn't I? Of course it was he I was in communication with on those night expeditions from the *Kasumi*. But go on; your story's quite a romance."

Bob proceeded with his narrative. When he told how Kobo had been captured almost within sight of safety, Yamaguchi looked distressed.

"That's a national loss," he said. "We can't spare a man like Kobo San. That monster Chang-Wo will torture him—to wrench information out of him if he can—of course he can't—in sheer devilry at any rate. And the worst of it is nothing can be done for him—nothing."

"I'm going to try," said Bob quietly.

"You! You've had enough adventure, I should think, to last you a lifetime. You'll be made mincemeat of yourself if Chang-Wo gets hold of you."

"Nevertheless, I'm going to try. Kobo saved my life. I should be an ungrateful beast if—Well, it won't bear discussion. I shall see General Kuroki as soon as I can, and get his leave."

"You're a good fellow—upon my word, you are. I wish you luck. If another than Kobo were concerned I'd do my best to hold you back, but for him—I'd do it myself if I could. He's worth it. But I have to be off to Antung to-morrow, and then rejoin my ship. Shall we see you on board again?"

"I don't know. Perhaps—if I find Kobo."

Chapter XXII
A Dumb Chinaman

Sing-Cheng Vows Vengeance—At Head-quarters—Tracking the "Mountain Tiger"—Deaf and Dumb—A Hill Fastness—Tracked—Strategy—Chang-Wo's Way

General Kuroki's brilliant victory had been won at great cost. Such dash, such persistence, such fearless disregard of death had not perhaps been seen on any battle-field since the days when arms of precision were unknown, and the rival combatants fought man to man at deadly grips. The whole day after the battle was occupied in burying the dead and helping the wounded, and Bob, assisting in the sad work, saw many new signs of the invincible stoicism of his country's allies. Many a sturdy little soldier, though maimed beyond repair, accepted his fate and bore his pain without a murmur, his deepest hurt being in the knowledge that for the rest of the campaign, perhaps for the rest of his life, he would be unable to do further service.

Towards evening, as Bob with Ah-Sam passed over an outlying corner of the position, where there remained a number of prostrate bodies still uncollected, he fancied he heard a groan. He stopped and listened. In a moment he heard the sound again, faint, but distinct, less a groan of pain than the tired gasp of a man utterly spent. Over a comparatively small area lay some thirty bodies close together, and Bob saw by their dress that they were not Japanese, but Manchurian natives. Picking his way carefully through them towards the sound, he at length saw a white-sleeved arm move, and when he bent down, he found that, pinned beneath a cold body, lay a man still alive. The wounded man was soon released, and then Bob saw that it was the chief of the Chunchuses, Sing-Cheng, the man with whom he had spent his memorable fortnight of peril and adventure.

He was somewhat seriously wounded. Giving him a drink of water from his flask, Bob searched carefully the surrounding ground for any other man in whom life still remained. He found only one; the rest were dead. With Ah-Sam's assistance he then carried the chief into the Japanese camp, where his wounds were attended to, afterwards sending a couple of men to bring in his still more gravely wounded comrade.

Next morning Bob visited the chief, and was glad to see that he was already giving promise of a quick recovery. With Ah-Sam's aid he questioned the man, being curious to know what had become of him after the last desperate brush with Chang-Wo's Manchus. He learnt that the chief had struck due east with his band, marching through the hills to avoid both Russians and Japanese, and had forded the Yalu some fifty miles higher up. They had then made their way towards his village, intending to recuperate there and await a favourable opportunity for resuming their usual occupation of brigandage. But on arriving they found that Chang-Wo had been before them. Furious at his recent rebuff, he had slain every man, woman, and child in the place, including the chief's family, not one escaping to tell the tale. Without waiting longer than to learn from the country-people, who gave him the news, in what direction the Manchus had gone, the chief started on their trail, but lost touch, and had not found them until the afternoon of the day on which Bob discovered him. Chang-Wo had fallen upon him while he lay there in hiding; his men had been taken by surprise, and, as Bob saw, the band had been annihilated.

Bob was tempted to ask why the Chunchuses had been in hiding at that spot—-a place obviously of some danger. But he had a shrewd suspicion of their purpose. He had little doubt that both Sing-Cheng's band and Chang-Wo's had been hovering like vultures about the field, waiting for the fall of night to begin their work, when Chang-Wo had discovered his enemy and swooped down upon him with all the advantage of the first blow.

The chief's story had been many times interrupted by frenzied outbursts against his enemy. He himself would recover, he was told; he would live for nothing but to exact vengeance. His family were killed, the graves of his ancestors had been defiled, his band was exterminated; he was alone. But alone he would follow Chang-Wo to the ends of the earth, and when he found him, he would take such a terrible revenge that all Manchuria should shake with the horror of it.

Sing-Cheng's threats, made with a set grimness of determination, started Bob upon a train of thought. He himself had a strong motive for tracking down the Manchu brigand. It was Chang-Wo who had-captured Kobo; where he was, there Kobo, if he were still alive, would be found. To save Kobo was the dearest wish of Bob's heart; could he avail himself of the chief's thirst for revenge, and enlist his aid?

"Ask him whether he knows where Chang-Wo's haunt is," said Bob to Ah-Sam.

Years ago, the chief replied, he had himself been a member of the brigand band, when the stronghold had been in the hands of Chang-Wo's predecessor—an old wise chief, a man of matchless cunning and resource. This man had been treacherously assassinated by Chang-Wo, who had made himself the master of the band. For a time Sing-Cheng served under Chang-Wo, but he had left him, at the risk of his life, and pointing to a deep scar upon his neck he mutely indicated the reason of his leaving. Since then he and Chang-Wo had been bitter enemies, but Chang-Wo had always commanded the larger band, and Sing-Cheng had been obliged to keep out of his way. Now, however, come what might, he would soon or late take his enemy's life, though he lost his own. He knew his mountain stronghold; he would make his way thither, and wait like a tiger until the moment came for leaping on his prey.

"Where is this stronghold?" asked Bob.

It was three days' journey among the hills. It lay cunningly concealed in a wild region, accessible by only one difficult path.

"Then it can be surrounded?"

No, for on the other side it was protected oy a deep rocky gorge, through which ran a rapid torrent. Ascent from the gorge was impossible, because a wall of granite rose sheer for several hundred feet, and at the top indeed overhung the ravine, affording no foothold, even if it were possible to cut steps in the rock. On that side the fortress was impregnable; and even on the other, access was so difficult that any attempt to capture it must be hazardous in the extreme.

Bob left the man and pondered on the information he had obtained. Valuable as Kobo was, he could not hope that General Kuroki would send a force into hostile country on the poor chance of saving him. If Kobo was to be saved, it must be by some private enterprise. Bob wondered whether he could raise a force of Manchus and storm the place. He reflected that even if such an expedition proved successful, it might fail in the very object with which it had been designed; for Chang-Wo, the moment he felt himself in danger, would assuredly kill Kobo, if till then he had kept him alive. It was clear, then, that to win success in its main object, the rescue of Kobo, any expedition must be organized and carried through with secrecy.

Several days passed before Sing-Cheng had recovered sufficiently to move about freely. During these days Bob spent many anxious hours in thinking and thinking again. He consulted nobody. If Yamaguchi had been at hand, Bob would have discussed every detail of the problem with him; but he did not care to unbosom himself to strange Japanese officers, and he hesitated to go to General Kuroki himself until he could put before him a scheme that was reasonable and likely to command his approval. He put many questions to Ah-Sam and the chief—questions which sometimes puzzled them, and to which he obtained sometimes useless answers; but all the time he was fitting together the bits of information he obtained, and slowly outlining a plan.

At length one day he went to head-quarters and asked for an interview with the general.

"Well, Mr. Fawcett," said Kuroki on seeing him, "are you ready to rejoin the fleet?"

"Are there any orders for me, sir?" asked Bob anxiously. "I hope not."

"At present you remain with me—at my request. But why do you say you hope not?"

"Because I wished to be still at your orders, sir. I have been thinking about Kobo San. You remember, sir, he is presumed to have been captured by the Manchu brigand Chang-Wo; is there any chance of a force being sent to rescue him?"

"None at all. I answer you quite frankly. Useful as Kobo San has been and might still be to us, he is now, if Chang-Wo's prisoner, in a part of the country remote from my line of advance, and an expedition on his behalf is out of the question. Besides, it would be labour and time lost. His life would not be worth a moment's purchase if we made an attack in force on Chang-Wo."

"I had thought of that, sir. But I wondered, that being the case, whether you would allow me with my Chinese boy and a Chunchuse chief to go secretly to Chang-Wo's haunt, and discover if we can whether Kobo San is there and still alive, and communicate with him if possible."

"That would be a dangerous business, Mr. Fawcett."

"Possibly, sir; but I have been over the mountains before, and the Chunchuse knows the district well, and was in fact at one time a member of the same gang. I should like to make the attempt, for Kobo San has been a good friend to me."

General Kuroki smiled.

"Kobo San's public services are likely to weigh more with me, Mr. Fawcett. Before I say more, have you any definite plan?"

"My idea was for all three of us to go as Chinamen, with a story that our farm has been burnt down by the Russians, and that we are going to Gensan to find employment with an uncle of my boy Ah-Sam—a master stevedore there."

"But you don't speak Chinese?"

"No, sir; but I was a dumb Korean for a day or two, and it won't be any more difficult to be dumb in Chinese."

"True," said the general, smiling. "Well, you seem to have concocted a sufficiently plausible scheme. I will not stand in your way. You go at your own risk. I shall be very glad if you succeed; if you fail—"

General Kuroki gave him an expressive glance, which seemed to say that sympathy would in any case be vain, for failure would possibly involve death. Bob thanked the general and withdrew.

A day was spent in making preparations. Bob was carefully disguised as a Chinaman; the chief altered his dress somewhat, and did what he could to hide his scar; and both he and Ah-Sam got together a number of small portable Chinese objects such as might have been saved from the wreck of a farm. Then early one morning the party of three set off on foot. They carried no arms, except each a revolver concealed with a supply of cartridges in a special pocket in their baggy trousers. As Chang-Wo's haunt did not lie in a straight line between Kiu-lien-cheng, their starting-place, and Gensan, their ostensible destination, they struck at first north-eastwards, in order to approach the fortress from a direction that would lend colour to their story.

For two days they tramped on. Their account of themselves found easy credence at the hamlets where they stopped for rest and food, and Bob was secretly amused to watch the cleverness with which Ah-Sam feigned a sorrowful indignation to match that of the chief. On the evening of the second day they arrived at a village which, as they entered it, Sing-Cheng explained was a little more than ten miles from Chang-Wo's stronghold. They made their way to an inn, and Ah-Sam, who for safety's sake was allowed to be spokesman on these occasions, once more glibly repeated the story about the raided farm and the purpose of finding shelter with his uncle in Gensan. The landlord, an active little Chinaman, appeared to Bob to give the travellers an anxious warning, and as they continued in conversation, the other guests in the inn formed a group and took a voluble part. Bob sat upon the k'ang, wishing with all his heart that he could understand what was being said, but doing his best to keep up the semblance of being deaf and dumb by munching away at the food given him and letting his eyes rove round the room with a half-vacant stare.

He learnt later from Ah-Sam what the matter of the conversation had been. The landlord, on hearing of the travellers' destination, had expressly warned them against approaching too near the fortress of the Manchu brigand. His guests added their warning to his. They were for the most part peasants of the neighbourhood, and the manner in which they spoke of Chang-Wo showed how terribly they were afraid of him. They did not even name him directly, but referred to him in circumlocutions, calling him variously the Mountain Tiger, the Wild Man of the Hills, and the One-eared Devil. For ten miles around his haunt not a building was left standing. No stranger who penetrated within the zone came out alive. If an intruder was caught he was killed on the spot, and his corpse was chained to a post as a warning to others. The method of execution was the slow torturing penalty common in China; the victim was crucified.

There was special danger at the present time, for the Mountain Tiger had returned to his lair a few days ago, laden with booty obtained from the slain in a great battle that had been fought down the river. The Russians, the hated barbarians from the west, had been victorious, largely by the Wild Man's help; and as the landlord repeated this story, industriously circulated by the brigand's men, a deep groan was uttered by several of the company. Had he brought back any Japanese prisoners? asked Ah-Sam. There was none to bring, was the reply; all the Japanese had been killed save those who fled. But one of the guests mentioned that nearly a month ago a prisoner had been brought to the fortress—a small man dressed in Chinese garb, but really a Japanese, an old enemy of Chang-Wo's, and, it was whispered, a man of consequence. Woe to the enemy who fell into the One-eared Devil's hands!

Ah-Sam at once asked whether the prisoner was still alive, or had he suffered the penalty. Only a few days ago, was the reply, a man had come into the village from the stronghold, released from his duties by the return of his chief. For a fortnight he had been on constant guard, scarcely daring to sleep, for nameless tortures would have been his fate if he had allowed the prisoner to escape, or even if he had been found absent from his post. He had signalized his release from duty by getting drunk, and drunk he had remained ever since.

Ah-Sam affected the greatest alarm at hearing all this. With well-feigned nervousness he asked how the region of danger could be avoided. Where did it begin? Was it guarded?

Before these questions could be answered a new-comer entered the inn and demanded food. He was a tall muscular Manchu, of most forbidding countenance, and as he pushed his way through the group he gave a lowering suspicious glance around, and allowed his eyes to rest on the solitary figure seated on the k'ang. The conversation was stilled. The new guest wore the leggings and carried the fowling-piece of a Manchurian hunter. Having obtained his supply of food from the landlord he went to the k'ang, where he arranged a comfortable place for himself, and, squatting there, began to eat his meal in silence.

For a few moments the rest of the company conversed in subdued tones, making no reference to the topic that had engaged them when the new-comer entered. Once or twice this latter glanced round at Bob, who was within a yard of him, still looking listlessly about, and idly fingering a small metal image which was among the native objects he had brought with him. At length the man addressed a few words to him. Bob did not turn his head or alter his movements. The Manchu spoke to him again in still louder tones. Again Bob paid no heed; he felt the necessity of being doubly on his guard; the man for all he knew might be a spy in Chang-Wo's pay. A third time he was addressed, in still louder and more impatient tones. This time the landlord cried out that the young man was deaf and dumb, and half an idiot to boot. The Manchu gave a grunt, and shoved a huge mass of rice into his mouth, emptying the copper vessel in which it had been contained. Feeling that the man's eyes were off him, Bob watched him narrowly, wondering whether he would be satisfied with the explanation, and keeping a firm hold upon himself in case the man should suddenly put him to a test. His precaution was justified, for with a sudden movement the Manchu tossed the pan upon the floor, where it fell with a resounding clang, and at the same time swung round and fixed his evil eyes on the squatting figure not two yards away. Bob did not even start; he ceased fingering the idol and watched the pan as it rolled across the floor and came to rest; then he looked round with his empty stare, smiled vacuously, and took up the idol once more. The Manchu drank a heavy draught of rice-beer, then threw himself backward and was soon snoring.

Bob caught a look of approval in Ah-Sam's eyes. The stranger being asleep, the company resumed the conversation at the point where his entrance had interrupted it. Where did the dangerous region begin? Some three miles from that inn. It was impossible to enter it without being discovered; no one indeed wished to enter it; if some incautious traveller did intrude within its borders, his only wish, and that a vain one, was to make his way out. The reason of its being so carefully guarded was that once the Mountain Tiger had narrowly escaped being surprised by a sotnia of Cossacks, and he had determined never to be caught napping again. On the outer edge of the prohibited district there were patrols by day and by night, and surprise visits were paid to every hamlet in the neighbourhood. Within, at a distance of about two miles from the fortress, there was a series of posts about a quarter of a mile apart, and the ground between them was studded with innumerable and unexpected obstacles. One only path led to the stronghold, and upon this men were constantly encamped. These particulars had been learnt at various times from members of the garrison when they came out on brief spells of furlough, and neither the landlord nor the man who had spoken most could vouch for the truth of all the details they had thus picked up.

Ah-Sam enquired whether the obstacles mentioned completely encircled the fort. The question was answered by an old man who had hitherto taken little part in the conversation. There was no need, he said, for artificial obstacles on the farther side of the fort. He had been in it on one occasion many years ago, in the time of the old chief, and he knew therefore more about it than anyone present in that inn. Had any other of the company ever entered the stronghold? No, none had but himself alone. Sing-Cheng had just opened his mouth to contradict him when Ah-Sam gave a loud sneeze, the snoring figure on the k'ang stirred, and in the general rustle Ah-Sam whispered to the impetuous chief to be more carefully upon his guard. The old man continued, speaking in low tones and with a solemn air of mystery. On the other side of the fort, he said, was a ravine, so wide, so deep, so precipitous, that no other defence was needed. He remembered that, when he was a young man, one of the inmates of the fort had incautiously stepped too near the edge; he had fallen, and his mangled body was washed and battered by the foaming torrent until the vultures had picked his bones clean.

The incident impressed the company. There was a moment's silence. The snores of the prone figure on the k'ang had ceased. Then Ah-Sam asked again: Could the fort be seen from that village? No, it was too far away, said the landlord; but it could be seen from a low hill about nine miles to the south-east, the direction which he advised the travellers to take. But it was so distant that it looked scarcely larger than a hut upon the hillside. Ah-Sam said that he must get a glimpse of the stronghold next day; he had never before heard of such a terrible place, and he would like to be able to tell his uncle, when he reached Gensan, that he had seen with his own eyes the dread haunt of the Mountain Tiger.

The conversation dragged on for some time longer, turning upon the great struggle then in progress between Russia and Japan. Bob was thoroughly tired when at length the voices ceased, the evil-smelling lamps were put out, and the guests sought their several couches. He was burning with eagerness to learn from Ah-Sam what he had discovered; but it was too dangerous to attempt to talk to him in the inn, and he had perforce to wait until the morning.

Early next morning they purchased as large a stock of provisions as they could carry in their wicker-baskets, and set off towards the hill of which the landlord had spoken. Bob felt that the eyes of the people in the inn were upon them as they left. The late-comer of the previous evening stood at the door watching them with his furtive eyes. Ah-Sam, in obedience to a cautious whisper of Bob's, had made particular enquiries regarding the road to their alleged destination. The nearest village of any consequence, he had learnt, was about twenty miles distant, on the far slope of a range of high hills just visible against the morning sky. Towards this, then, the three took their course, in a direction that would lead some four miles outside the forbidden district of the Mountain Tiger. The country was rolling and sparsely wooded, becoming more and more broken as it approached the hills that stretched across the horizon from south-west to north-east.

When they were fairly away from the inn, Bob whispered to Ah-Sam that on no account must he or the chief look behind. Presently the path led them through a clump of trees, and Bob seized the opportunity to look back, from behind a trunk, along the path towards the inn. He was just in time to see, about a third of a mile away, the figure of a man scuttling along in their wake. Even in the distance Bob was almost sure that he recognized the beetle-browed guest who had so persistently addressed him in the inn. Again impressing upon his two companions the importance of not looking back, he set a steady but not hurried pace, and now that he was well out of earshot, got from Ah-Sam a full account of what he had learnt in the inn. They tramped on for two hours before resting on the slope of a low hill, which from the Chinaman's general description appeared to be the hill from whose summit Chang-Wo's fort could be seen. But, in order to avoid the appearance of curiosity, Bob called a halt some distance down the slope rather than at the top. Then pursuing their way after a short rest, still careful to show no suspicion of being followed, they gained the crest of the hill, and saw a wide expanse of country spread out before them. They did not pause now, but Bob, taking his observations as he walked, noted in the far distance to the left a bright spot against the dark background of a hill. It gradually defined itself as an extensive building perched on a precipitous spur. The intervening country was bare; and at two or three spots upon it he descried small moving patches, which he surmised to be bodies of horsemen. One of these patches, from its size consisting of from twenty to thirty riders, was much nearer than the others, and apparently heading in his direction. It was still very far away, and since it was not coming from the direction of the inn he hoped that the horsemen were not concerned with him. He would have liked to hurry his pace, but recognized that he would thus awaken the suspicion of the man behind, who, as he had perceived by a hasty glance some time before, was still following.

The situation was clearly somewhat awkward. If the horsemen were indeed coming on the track of the party of three, Bob suspected that they would not be satisfied with explanations, but would arrest them and carry them to the fortress for examination by Chang-Wo himself. In that case nothing could save them, for Bob at any rate must be instantly recognized. If they were not actually on his track, they might be set upon it by the Manchu coming up behind. It was important, at any rate, to know whether they were working in concert with that dogged pursuer, and Bob decided that his best course was to dodge the latter until this point could be cleared up.

What could be done? There was no time for making experiments; if the attempt at eluding the Manchu did not succeed at once, it would fail miserably and entirely. Bob looked anxiously around. For some distance the path had led over loose, rocky ground, alternating with small copses of hill trees where the rainfall had washed the soil into hollows. The copse nearest to the spot on which he now stood was a ragged clump of stunted pines, which in the late Manchurian spring had scarcely begun to show signs of new growth. In any case it would prove an insecure place of hiding, for it would be instantly searched by his pursuers. But half a mile farther on he spied a narrow watercourse zigzagging almost at right angles to the track. It was a mountain stream which had been so swollen by the frost and rains that it had cut a bed some feet deep in the face of the hill. Except where it crossed the path it was concealed by the shelving bank.

As Bob's eyes fell upon it, a sudden idea struck him. Hurrying his pace, he led the way towards it, and found that on the other side was a stretch of damp, mossy ground, leading up to an irregular group of rocks somewhat to the left of the path. These rocks were the lower fringe of a vast extent of broken country—a country of large boulders separated by narrow, tortuous fissures. Without telling his companions what was in his mind, he waded through the stream, the water of which was still icy cold, and stepped on to the wet, oozing ground. The two Chinamen followed him; the footsteps of the three left deep prints in the moss, filled instantly by water. They gained the rocks beyond; then Bob, instead of pursuing the same course, which would have been among the inhospitable boulders, turned sharp to the left, and describing a rough semicircle came back to the stream.

His followers tramped along behind him, saying never a word, wondering what his purpose was, and confident that this doubling on their track was not without some important end in view. Along the bed of the stream, the water rising almost to his knees, he made his way as rapidly as possible, crossed his former path, and continued his march for some hundred and fifty yards beyond, till he came to a spot where the bank on the right was low, scarcely above the level of the water. There he left the stream, and wading through a small swamp, bore continually to the right until he arrived almost at the path again, more than a hundred yards from the stream. He had thus made a complete circuit, and come to a point where the hillside rose steeply above the path and was strewn with several fallen trees uprooted or overthrown by the previous autumn's storms. Creeping forward with great caution under cover of the prostrate trunks and of the few standing trees which the elements had spared, the little party came to a spot almost immediately over the path, but completely screened from the sight of anyone below. There they lay in cold silence and waited.

Hardly more than two minutes passed when they heard the rapid shuffle of footsteps upon the stony path, and the hard breathing of a man. Peering cautiously over, Bob saw that it was their Manchu pursuer. He was moving with swiftness on his clogs, seeming uneasy at having lost sight of the party. He did not look up; indeed, he would never have suspected the hiding-place above him, for no one could have reached it directly from the path without being seen by him. Panting and perspiring, he had only just passed the concealed party, when Bob heard the clink of approaching hoofs, and a few moments later a group of riders dashed over the crest of a hillock some distance on the other side of the path and bore down immediately on the Manchu, who stopped, wheeled round, and stood waiting.

With a thrill of uneasiness Bob saw that the foremost of the horsemen was Chang-Wo himself. Sing-Cheng also recognized his old enemy; Bob heard him pant, and for a moment feared lest an incautious exclamation should betray him. But Ah-Sam was on the watch; he laid his hand on the chief's arm, and the man restrained his pent-up rage.

Chang-Wo rode up to the Manchu and eagerly questioned him. Bob was, of course, unable to follow their brief conversation, but from their gestures and demeanour—the man pointing along the path ahead, his leader's face gleaming with malignant satisfaction—he divined what its purport was. With a grunt of approval Chang-Wo rode on; his troop followed him. Bob counted sixteen horsemen. Then the Manchu, his features relaxing in the relief of a task accomplished, sat down contentedly beside the path, untied his wallet, and brought out a handful of dried fish, which he proceeded to devour.

The party in hiding waited on, cramped and chilled, not daring yet to rise. The man was only a few yards below them; they could hear the working of his jaws, the smacking of his lips, his grunts of appreciation; between the mouthfuls any movement they might make would assuredly be heard by him. Half an hour passed slowly by; once or twice Bob noticed that the man paused in his eating and looked somewhat anxiously in the direction in which the horsemen had disappeared; but hearing nothing, seeing nothing, he returned to his fish until his appetite was appeased. He had just retied his wallet preparatory to rising, when the sound of hoofs scattering the loose stones was heard. A few seconds later Chang-Wo dashed up, followed at a little distance by fourteen out of his sixteen men. He almost rode down the Manchu, who, having scrambled to his feet, stood in cowering alarm as the brigand chief pulled up his horse with a jerk, and rained down upon the man a shower of furious questions. Vainly the poor wretch tried to make reply; at the first word Chang-Wo shortened the long spear he carried, and with ungovernable rage drove it through him. The man fell without a groan. Then Chang-Wo, riding his horse over the prone body, roared an order to eight of his men, and with the remaining six galloped away over the crest of the hill.

Chapter XXIII
The Tiger's Lair

A Tramp by Night—A Distant View—Across the Ravine—The Cleft in the Gully—Scouting—Light and Shadow—Baffled—An Inspiration

Bob and his men still crouched behind their fallen log. Here indeed had been an expressive object-lesson in the methods of the Mountain Tiger. The sight of the dead man gave Bob a sickening sense of horror. Had his friend Kobo suffered a similar, perhaps a worse fate? Or was he still alive, with a more awful fate in store? As these questions suggested themselves Bob felt his courage renewed, his determination strengthened. Be the issue what it might, for Kobo he must and would dare all.

The eight men left by Chang-Wo had evidently been ordered to continue the search. They spread out fan-wise, and began to ride slowly in the direction in which the three fugitives had been last seen to be going. Bob watched them anxiously. Fortunately they spread from a point almost opposite to the hidden three. It did not occur to them that the fugitives had made a circuit, doubling on their tracks. They tried to find traces of footsteps on the ground, and drew gradually farther away from the hiding-place. As soon as the last of them had disappeared, Bob scrambled down to the path, followed by his men. He shuddered as he passed the dead Manchu; Sing-Cheng with no compunction stooped and rifled his clothes; then all three set off in the direction Chang-Wo had taken: there would be less danger in following him. Thus, keeping a sharp look-out, they retraced their steps for nearly two miles. Then, noting a patch of scrub on the left which offered a resting-place sufficiently secure from observation, Bob plunged into it, found it deeper than it had appeared, and decided to remain there for the rest of the day.

Night fell; the sky was clear and starlit, and taking the stars as their guide the party of three resumed their journey, following a course due south. All through the night they marched, eyes and ears alert, but seeing nothing save rocks and trees and their grim shadows, hearing nothing but the faint calls of wild beasts. At daybreak they were dead beat; their journey had been arduous, and they knew not whither their path would lead. Even Sing-Cheng was unfamiliar with this region.

At dawn they found themselves nearly at the top of a range of hills, which the chief recognized as being near the large village mentioned in the inn. It was wild desolate country; there were occasional patches of grass among the hills; on sheltered slopes mountain trees grew in clumps; but in those latitudes the signs of spring appear late, and the prospect had all the bleak dreariness of winter. Choosing a spot defended from the cutting morning wind by a wall of rock, they snatched a few hours' sleep, taking it in turns to keep guard; then after a meal they pressed on again, bearing to the east with the object of coming upon the fort from the side of the ravine. Bob hoped that Sing-Cheng could have led him direct to this spot, but when Ah-Sam asked him the Chunchuse said that he had never approached the place from this quarter, and could only guess at its whereabouts.

By and by they came to a stream of some size, flowing north and south. Bob guessed that this must be the stream that ran through the ravine; it gave him hope that he was on the right track. He looked along the surface of the water for the roughness that would indicate a ford. At that spot they crossed, tying themselves together with the straps of their baskets to prevent themselves from being swept away by the rapid current. Having crossed, they pushed on without a halt, up the left bank, and arrived somewhat late in the afternoon at an elevated spot, where they came suddenly in sight of the fort, a mile or more below them.

Sing-Cheng's eyes gleamed as he saw the stronghold of his enemy. He stretched his right arm towards the place and began to speak excitedly. Bob pulled him behind a rock. It was not unlikely that Chang-Wo among his many precautions had set a sentry to watch this part of the surroundings of the fort, even though the ravine rendered it unassailable from this direction.

Keeping well in cover, Bob himself took a long look at the stronghold that was now more important to him than anything else in the world. What he saw was an irregular fortress, probably a hundred yards in diameter, built on the edge of the ravine, which appeared a black strip in the distance. There were five flanking towers, two resting on the ravine, the other three disposed somewhat irregularly on the outer wall; this was evidently of considerable height. In the whole enceinte there was, so far as Bob could see, only one gateway, on the farther side. Allowing for his distance from it, and for the slight slope of the intervening country, he estimated that the ravine was wide; and from the general lie of the land, and his own experiences of the lower course of the river, he knew that it must be of great depth. On the near side of the ravine, almost exactly opposite the fort, he noticed that the edge was broken by a narrow cleft running at right angles to it. Beyond the fort the country was bare and rolling to the north, but to the west and south was much broken up by knolls and plantations of fir.

The gray stone walls stood out in clear relief against the background. Within the enclosure scores of figures were moving about between the low buildings; it was like an ant-hill for activity; and on the rising ground beyond the farther wall Bob descried more than one ragged encampment, confirming what had been told in the inn about the careful guard maintained on the only practicable line of approach.

As he took in these details, Bob realized with a new clearness how Chang-Wo had made himself a power and terror in the land. With such a fastness to fall back upon, and supported by a numerous band of desperadoes, he could defy Russian and Chinese alike; it was easy to understand that neither had been eager to try conclusions with him. The fort was so situated and so massively constructed that it might mock at any attempt at capture, short of a regular siege enforced by heavy artillery.

Yet it might be in this solitary mountain stronghold, the lair of the Mountain Tiger, that, dead or alive, Kobo San lay. As Bob let his eyes dwell on it with anxious care, he felt his heart sink within him. What had he come for? What could he do, with two helpers however willing, however earnest, to rescue Kobo if Kobo was indeed immured within those strong towers? How could he discover whether his friend was there? The strength of Samson could not tear down those massive walls; the wiles of Ulysses could not avail to win entrance through that single gateway; only an eagle could ascend from the depth of the ravine, and even had he eagle's wings he would ascend in vain. Why had he come on this wild enterprise? Now that he had seen with his own eyes, what remained to him but to acknowledge the hopelessness of his quest, and quit this region of tyranny and death?

Long he mused, weighed down by a despair more bitter than had burdened him when he lay under sentence of death at Antung. He felt a strange certainty that Kobo was there a prisoner, and alive; humanity, gratitude, affection combined to produce an intense longing to save his friend, yet even his longing was clouded by a sense of powerlessness, his activity seemed paralysed.

Ah-Sam had been watching him out of his slant expressionless eyes. For a time he stood by his master mutely, noting every shade of feeling that flitted across his tired face. At last he touched him lightly on the arm.

"Massa no can do not'ing. Allo wailo this-tim'."

Bob started as if stung. The words were but the echo of his own despair, yet they provoked him to almost violent repudiation.

"Impossible!" he said. "Nothing is impossible. We have ourselves done things people would have said impossible. At the gully—at the temple!

What has been done can be done again. I am going into the fort. When it begins to get dark I shall go and find out a way. We haven't come all this distance to go back without making an effort. We'll have a try, Ah-Sam,—a try, anyhow."

"Allo lightee, massa; tly, no fear."

In his cold unexcitable manner he told Sing-Cheng what his master had said. The man grunted approval; he saw no way of accomplishing their purpose; he did not care for that; the Englishman had scattered Chang-Wo's Manchus with curses from a brazen bell, and he was ready to follow the Englishman anywhere.

"That's right," said Bob heartily. "Please God, we'll find a way."

Till dusk he waited, thinking, puzzling. The first move must be to spy out the position—the surroundings of the fort, especially the ravine. He resolved that this was a task for himself alone; the risk of being seen would be trebled if he took his companions. He wondered whether the moon would give him light; without it he could discover little or nothing, with it he might himself be discovered. The afternoon had been cloudy; a high wind had swept dense cumulus across the sky; but the cloud mass had been broken, not continuous, and the fitful gleams he might expect if the moon rose would serve his purpose better than a steady shine.

It was not yet dark when he started, but sufficiently gloomy.

"Wait here till I return," he said to Ah-Sam. "If you are discovered, save yourselves as best you can."

He crept cautiously down the long slope. Shrubs, mounds, irregularities in the soil, gave him cover for a considerable distance. A belt of low trees apparently fringed the ravine; if he could gain that, he thought he would be safe. He came to it, passed through, and found that it did not extend quite to the edge of the ravine; a space of a few yards had at some time been cleared, but was now becoming overgrown with brushwood. He threw himself on his face, crawled behind a thick clump, and found himself on the brink. For a few moments he waited, wondering whether, as' he moved, his light-coloured garments had been descried from the fort. He heard the sound of many voices from the other side, the whinny of a horse, the clink of metal; but there was nothing to indicate any unusual circumstance, and drawing himself a little forward, still keeping as much as possible in the shadow of the bush, he peeped over.

The ravine was deep, deeper even than he had expected. Even in the gloom he could see its opposite side and the walls of the fort, but he could not see the bottom of the ravine; he only heard the swirl of the water over the rocks far below, and fancied he could just discern an occasional dash of white foam. Opposite rose the grim wall of the fort. Bob scanned it anxiously for the sign of a sentry; there was none. He realized that none was needed. Below the fort the ground shelved rapidly for several yards to the edge of the ravine, then bent inwards before it became a perpendicular wall to the invisible bottom. Bob looked all along the space from left to right, and marked one spot where the inward curve was broken by what appeared to be a horizontal rocky platform, like those large flat slabs sometimes encountered exceptionally among jagged rocks on the sea-shore. Beyond this platform, up the shelving bank, he espied a narrow winding path which was visible for a few yards, then disappeared into the face of the cliff to the left of the fort. In the cliff-wall itself, just above the platform, he caught sight of what appeared to be an iron staple, though this seemed so unlikely that he thought his eyes might have deceived him.

"A sentry's post, I suppose," said Bob to himself, "though it is evidently never required. Only a bird could cross the ravine. I wonder what its width is."

It was difficult in the growing darkness to make a guess; still, it could hardly be less than eighty feet across. The width varied a little to right and left of his position, but only by a few feet at the most. Bob saw only too well that the fort was indeed, as his informants had said, on this side inaccessible. The question suggested itself: Could it be reached from the bottom of the ravine at some remote point to left or right? At the spot where he lay the descent on both sides was too precipitous to be scaled even by an expert mountaineer; but it was possible that at some distance the cliffs would be lower as well as less steep. In that case he could descend on one side and ascend on the other. But he might need assistance in his climbing. He remembered that Alpine climbers roped themselves together for safety's sake; it would be a reasonable precaution to return for Ah-Sam and the chief, so that with their joined straps they might help him in case of need.

It was now so nearly dark that the risk of being discovered was much lessened. Rising on hands and knees, he prepared to make his way back up the hillside; but he suddenly remembered the cleft he had noticed on this side of the ravine, at right angles to it, and it occurred to him that he ought to take a cursory look at this also. Crawling within the belt of trees, he rose to his feet and walked rapidly as long as it was safe, then wriggled along from bush to bush till he came to the edge of the opening, and looking over found that it was in the shape of a long wedge, like a slice cut out of a large cake. The sides of this also were precipitous, and the bottom was out of sight.

He looked along the cleft from the narrow inner end to the wider outer end, and there noticed a long dark object lying transversely across it. He thought at first that it was possibly a sapling which had been uprooted and fallen, but this idea was negatived on his approaching the spot. The object lay, not on top of the cliff on either side, but a foot or two below. Walking, still with caution, close up to the place, he was surprised to find that the two sides of the cleft were connected by a stout bar of iron, the nearer end of which he felt was firmly embedded in the rock, reminding him of similar poles used at home to support unsteady arches or prop up tottering houses. Obviously no such purpose could have been intended for this bar, and he vaguely wondered why and when it had been placed in position. It had clearly been there a long time; it was much rusted, flakes of rust coming off as he touched it.

Leaving the cleft, he returned as quickly as possible to the spot where he had left Ah-Sam and the chief. The former rose to meet him.

"Well," said Bob, "has all been quiet?"

"Yes, massa; no piecee man come this-side, no bobbely, not'ing."

"I want you to come along with me. Hide your baskets under the shrubs, but bring the straps; we may require them."

In a few moments he was leading the way in a direction at an angle to the path he had taken, past the narrow end of the cleft, and then on a line parallel with the edge of the ravine. He walked for nearly a mile, finding as he proceeded that the ground, while undulating, was in general on almost the same level as his starting-place. Suddenly, however, it made a sharp dip, and going to the edge of the ravine he saw that the cliffs on both sides were less precipitous and less lofty. The sky had for some time been growing lighter, indicating the rising of the moon; and peering over the edge he saw the water of the torrent sweeping along in foamy current below. The sides of the ravine were covered with stunted trees, by means of which he saw that descent or ascent might be facilitated. Telling Ah-Sam to join the three straps together, he took one end and climbed down the rocky slope, carefully placing his feet, and stopping at intervals to allow the men to make sure their footing behind him. Having reached the brink of the stream, he bade his followers remain hidden among the trees; then he waded into the water, and began to ascend the opposite side, carrying the strap with him to assist in his descent by and by.

The moon, emerging now and then from among the flying clouds, threw a fitful radiance over the scene as Bob scrambled up the steep acclivity. Stepping with great care, pulling himself up by overhanging branches after he had tested them, endeavouring not to displace loose stones, he at last with one final heave gained the top, where he sat down to recover breath and look around him. The white moonlight clothed the neighbourhood with a ghostly glamour, throwing up in bold relief the grim outlines of the fort far up the ravine. No tree or other obstacle interposed between it and him; the ground for some distance from the edge had probably been kept bare purposely. But some hundred and fifty yards to his left there stood a dark patch of firs, he could not tell of what extent; to gain that would at any rate bring him a little nearer to the fort. Throwing himself on his face, he crawled towards it, pausing every few moments to listen. It seemed a long time before he reached the firs: it was really only a few minutes; but at last he gained their shelter, and stood erect, stretching himself in relief.

A light wind sighed in notes of gentle melancholy among the branches, though above his head he saw between the tree-tops the heavy clouds drifting rapidly across the sky. He moved carefully among the firs, pausing now and then to listen and to take his bearings, for he was anxious to avoid the risk of losing his way as he returned. The trees at the edge of the clump were set far apart, and between their trunks he saw three firs forming a group on the other side of the ravine. These he took as his landmark. Then he walked into the heart of the patch, where the trees grew thicker, treading lightly on the deep compost of fir cones, wondering whither his steps were leading him.

Suddenly he halted. A faint sound had touched his ears from a point ahead—a sound like the clink of steel. He listened, his body bent forward resting on his right foot, his left foot raised upon its toes. The sound had ceased; he now heard nothing but the rustle of the wind. He went on again, but after a few steps he was again arrested by the same sound, the same slight clink. Again he waited, for a longer time. Hearing nothing, he took a few more steps, and emerged almost unawares upon a small clear space. Instantly he darted on tiptoe behind the nearest trunk. In the centre of the clearing a figure had caught his eye, a motionless form whose outlines in the suddenness of its discovery he had had no time to distinguish. He waited, scarcely daring to breathe; his heart thumped against his ribs, he heard its thuds. But there was no sound from before him—yes, he caught again the clink-clink, louder, more prolonged.

He waited, then ventured to peep out from behind the trunk. The figure was still there, in the same spot, in the same attitude, motionless. Strain his eyes as he might, Bob could detect, in the darkness of an overshadowing cloud, no sign of movement. A gust of wind came sighing through the copse; yes, the figure does move, and as it moves there comes again the clink-clink. Then all is still again. A nameless uneasiness seized upon Bob;

a cold, clammy perspiration broke from every pore; he watched the figure as if fascinated. Again a gust of wind; again the slight swaying movement; again the soft clink-clink; again the perfect stillness.

Bob could bear the suspense no longer. Between himself and the figure stood one slender sapling, an accident of growth. With heart wildly beating, he stole out and tiptoed towards this fragile cover. He reached it just as a stronger gust swept through the plantation, and at the same moment a sudden beam shot from beneath a cloud and filtered wanly through the tree-tops. The figure swayed more violently; the clink-clink became the rattle of chains; and in the moonlight Bob saw with horror, but at the same time with unspeakable relief, that the form was a human skeleton, chained upright to a post.

He remembered what Ah-Sam had learnt in the inn. This no doubt was some hapless wretch who had been caught wandering on the spot and chained there, with who could tell what accompaniment of cruelty, to die of starvation or exhaustion. Grim reminder to Bob of what his own fate would be if he fell into the hands of this Wild Man of the Hills; of what perhaps Kobo's fate had already been! For a moment he paused, surveying the grisly object. "Poor wretch!" he murmured. Then with lips resolutely set he pursued his way.

Keeping as nearly as he could judge a course parallel with the edge of the ravine, he crossed the clearing and plunged into the firs on the other side. In a few minutes the copse thinned, then came to an end; there was nothing but open country, rough, but clear of trees, between him and the fort. The ravine, he thought, must be about five hundred yards on his right. In that direction, where the ground sloped down to the edge, he saw a low hut; a similar building lay at almost equal distance on his left. Were they the huts of sentries? he wondered. He waited at the edge of the copse. From the hut on the right came no sign, but on the left he saw in the moonlight a figure emerge from behind the building and walk slowly towards him. Bob stood motionless. Surely he had not been seen? No, the man approached but a few steps, then returned and disappeared.

Bob's pulse had resumed its natural beat; he felt cold and strangely tired, but the suspense, the uncertainty, the eeriness of waiting for he knew not what, had gone. All his senses, all his intelligence, were bent towards the fulfilment of his purpose. He must go on, whatever the risk. Waiting for the moon once more to ride behind a cloud, he stole forward between the huts. For a quarter of a mile all was dark, then a gleam shot forth; he dropped to the ground and lay still. He waited long, turning on his side to watch the black clouds scudding overhead. At last the moon was again obscured; again he stole forward, and he had come within an arrow's flight of the fort, and was hidden from the huts by a dip in the ground, before the moon reappeared.

He could now take a leisurely view of this face of the stronghold, bathed and blanched as it was by the moonbeams. Two figures were moving up and down upon the wall, two others on the top of the flanking tower to his left. He saw the opening, black and ominous, of the fort's only gateway. Here and there around him the grass was blackened as if by a temporary encampment. If he moved, his light clothes would show against these dark patches. He wondered whether it would not almost be safer if, avoiding them, he should continue his progress only when the moon shone.

He still lay watching, vainly trying to imagine some means of entering the fort, when he heard the clang of arms, then a great creaking and groaning. Hardly daring to peer over the brim of the hollow in which he lay, he saw the huge gate swung open outwards. Even as the thought struck him that this was surely an unusual incident at such a time of night, a man on horseback came out, set his horse to a fast trot, and clattered by within a hundred yards of Bob's position. He flattened himself against the ground and held his breath; he felt the tremor of the earth under the horses' hoofs; he heard his heart beating. But the horseman did not slacken his pace; the clatter became fainter. Again there was a groaning and creaking, and the great gate clanged to. All was silent.

For a full hour Bob lay there, while the light of the moon came and went, vainly endeavouring to think out a means of accomplishing his ends. It seemed to him that he had come in truth on a wild-goose chase. The walls of the fort rose sheer from the ground to a height of at least twenty feet, smooth, regular, with not a foothold from base to crown. He could not hope to scale them. Even if he could do so, what chance had he of finding Kobo? He must himself be instantly discovered. The walls were out of the question. What of the gateway? As he had just seen, the massive gate was shut at night; no doubt it was closely guarded by day. Supposing an opportunity offered of slipping in in disguise, how could he make use of it? He knew nothing of the language. He would gain admittance only to be detected, arrested, and despatched.

Thus all his puzzling was in vain. At length, with a feeling of despair, he rose during a temporary darkening of the moon, and made his stealthy way back towards the patch of firs. He groped his way through, shuddering as he heard the clinking of the chained figure, emerged on the opposite side, and finding the three trees he had chosen as his landmark, safely reached the edge of the ravine. There he waited. The moon had sunk behind the distant hills; in the darkness he would run the risk of alarming his enemies if he attempted to descend, for this side of the ravine was steep, as he knew, and he could not get down without making some noise. So, crouched under the edge out of sight from above, he waited, cold, tired, and heavy of heart, through the night till the chill dawn. Then with infinite care he let himself down from tree to tree, passing the strap round a trunk and holding firmly to it until his feet were secure below. He reached the stream, waded through, and found his two companions waiting with oriental patience where he had left them.

"My say no can do not'ing," said Ah-Sam, glancing at his master's drawn, pale features.

Bob was too tired to reply. Under cover of the trees the three threaded their way back to the spot where they had left their provisions concealed, and there, making sure that no alarm had been raised in the fort, they sat down to their breakfast. Bob had no appetite. He forced himself to eat, for he knew not what further trial of endurance might be before him; then, feeling the need of sleep, he lay down behind a spreading bush, and bade the other two keep watch in turn.

The day passed alternately in sleeping and in discussing the situation. Neither Ah-Sam nor Sing-Cheng had any suggestion to offer. The former stolidly adhered to his opinion that nothing was possible. The latter said in effect, "Don't ask me to plan. Tell me what to do, and I will do it."

Bob got neither help nor comfort from them. The stock of food was rapidly diminishing. The two Chinamen ate without sparing; and if only for this reason, either something must be done at once or they must all return on their tracks. The sense of his powerlessness stung Bob like a goad. At one moment he was on the point of giving up; then with the thought of Kobo in the power of Chang-Wo came a fresh spurt of determination. All through the day fits of despair alternated with renewed efforts to solve the difficulty, until his mood of nervous irritability was almost past enduring. Ah-Sam and the chief talked constantly in low whispers, and with such solemn looks of concern that Bob felt they would help him if they could. It occurred to him once to ask them what point they were discussing so gravely, and he could have knocked their heads together in sheer vexation when Ah-Sam replied:

"My tellum Sing-Cheng littee pussy boilum stew, makee numpa one topside chow-chow. Hai yah!"

At last, thoroughly worn out with the strain, as darkness sank over the hills Bob fell into an uneasy sleep. It was crowded with dreams—of recent happenings, of his school-days, of his childhood among the Cumbrian dales. He turned restlessly from side to side, sometimes muttering, sometimes calling to his friends, giving his two companions, as they in turn took watch, matter for wonder and concern. At last he found himself on his back, with eyes wide open, staring up into the starlit void, his pulse beating furiously, his nerves aquiver. He had awoke at a moment when in his dream a terrible accident was on the point of happening. The scene was the school gymnasium. He was swinging on one of the ropes of the giant-stride, and seemed to have worked up a velocity only to be obtained in dreamland. On the next rope before him swung his chum, and he felt that some demon of speed was whirling him down upon the boy, with such force that he must inevitably do him serious hurt. Only by his own agility and muscular strength was the injury averted; and he woke trembling from the nightmare — to a scene of absolute peace beneath the clear cold stars.

Suddenly he sat bolt upright, uttering a low exclamation that caught the ear of Ah-Sam, taking his turn of duty.

"I have it! I have it!" he cried. "Ah-Sam, wake the chief. There is a long journey before you."

Sing-Cheng was soon roused from his snoring slumbers. Then Bob, his nerves still quivering with excitement, told Ah-Sam what he must do. With the chief he was to set off at once for the large village of which they had heard. It lay probably about sixteen miles away over the hills. They were to enter the village and explain that their master's mule-cart had broken down several miles away through the snapping of the traces. They required ten yards of new rope. When they had bought this they were to say, as by an after-thought, that, rope being very dear in their village far to the north, they would like to purchase a larger quantity to have a stock always in reserve, and to sell again to neighbouring farmers. They were to ask for at least one hundred yards. Further, they must procure more food, and return with their loads as soon as possible.

The chief looked discontented when this errand was explained to him. He had evidently expected some scheme for the instant conquest of the fort. But Ah-Sam reminded him of his promise to do anything he was bidden, and he assented with a shrug.

The moon was up.

"If you start at once," said Bob, "you will cover several miles before the moon sets. When it is too dark to see your way, rest. On your return, don't come within five miles of the fort by daylight. Wait until dusk, then hurry back to me with all speed. Ah-Sam, I trust to you; be careful, be quick."

The men took the money he gave them, and with the customary low obeisance marched away. At the same time Bob stole down to the wedge-shaped cleft in the side of the ravine, and, keeping under cover, spent some time in looking up and down it, and across to the fort. The moon was disappearing when he returned and threw himself down again to rest and think.

Chapter XXIV
In the Enemy's Gates

A Long Rope—A Trial Trip—A Miss—As a Thief in the Night—Chang-Wo Takes His Ease—Tantalus

The next day passed so slowly that it seemed as though it would never end. Bob was full of all kinds of apprehension as to what had befallen Ah-Sam and the chief. He wished he had accompanied them; then saw how unwise it would have been so to do; his presence would only have been a source of danger, and, except in an actual fight, he could be of no use. He ate sparingly of the remaining food; till the men returned he could not be sure of their being able to procure a fresh supply. If they proved unsuccessful, all three would be on short commons indeed.

Dusk fell. There had been time for them to go and return. Bob waited anxiously. Hour after hour passed; the moon rose, and climbed higher and higher into the sky. Where were the men? He was anxious about their fate; but he fretted also because, even if they returned in safety, it was growing too late to do anything that night. He walked up and down like a sentry, stopping at the end of his beat to listen, how often he did not count. At last, when he judged it must be nearing midnight, he heard a soft footfall, and in a moment saw a man's form approaching. Holding his pistol ready, he waited until the man came within a few yards of him, then called softly, "Who are you?"

"My Ah-Sam, allo lightee," came the answer in a whisper.

Bob lowered the pistol, and the Chinaman stepped forward panting, and dropped a heavy bundle at his feet.

"Where is Sing-Cheng?"

"He one piecee li wailo, he hidee. Chang-Wo look-see. 'Ch'hoy! two piecee man', he say; 'my catchum, killum'; one piecee man no makee muchee bobbely; he come this-side allo lightee; Chang-Wo no can look-see he."

"I see, you come one at a time; Sing-Cheng will give you time to get here, then come himself. A good idea of yours, Ah-Sam. Now tell me how you got on."

They had reached the village at early morning, said Ah-Sam, and made their purchases with no difficulty. On leaving the place they had thought it advisable to make a slight circuit, and had unluckily, after an hour's march, come plump upon two of Chang-Wo's men on horseback. One of the men had instantly recognized Sing-Cheng, and attempted to lay hands on him, while the other made at Ah-Sam with his spear.

"And how did you get away?" asked Bob.

"Killum, one, two," replied Ah-Sam simply.

"The horses?"

"He lun wailo chop-chop; my no can catchee."

"Towards the fort?"

"No, massa; lun far far wailo that-side."

He pointed in the opposite direction. Bob gave a sigh of relief.

"Did you see any more of the brigands as you came?" he asked.

"Look-see one, two, t'lee; he makee my hidee; my come this-side velly slow, galaw!"

In a few minutes the chief arrived, bearing his share of the burden. Both he and Ah-Sam were exhausted; in any case it was too late to attempt anything that night; and Bob told the men to eat and rest, for there would be work for them on the morrow.

When, next day, dusk was deepening into night, a sentry on the wall of the fort abutting on the ravine might possibly have seen, if it had occurred to him to look, a figure moving by almost imperceptible degrees along the face of the cleft opposite. The course followed was along a narrow ledge some feet below the top, leading from the inner end of the cleft to a spot immediately below the stout iron girder whose presence and purpose had given Bob so much food for conjecture. Arriving at the girder, the figure reached up, cautiously passed the looped end of a long rope over it, and, threading the other end through the loop, drew it tight over the girder and pushed it gently with the stripped branch of a sapling towards the centre. Then he retraced his steps along the ledge, carrying the loose end of the rope. The slack, dangling in the cleft, displaced a stone, which fell with a rattle to the bottom. The stealthy form hurried his pace to reduce the length of the slack, fearing for a moment lest the fall of the stone might have been heard in the fort. But there was little risk; stones must frequently drop down the sides of the ravine; and in any case the rope, in the almost total obscurity of the narrow cleft, was invisible from the farther side.

At the nearer end of the ledge Bob rejoined Ah-Sam and the chief, who were crouching by a couple of stout saplings that overhung the deep gorge beneath. Making fast to one of the saplings the rope he carried, he sat down and spoke in low tones to the Chinaman, explaining the scheme which he had devised after hours of meditation.

The situation was a simple one, yet one that called for nerve and unbounded courage. Immediately opposite the cleft, on the other side of the ravine, was the small rocky platform, with a staple in the wall above. The width of the ravine, as Bob estimated, was some eighty feet, but it was impossible to make any more accurate calculation; it might be more than eighty, it might be less; and a few feet one way or the other would make all the difference in the plan he had conceived. He had come to the conclusion that the iron girder which had so much piqued his curiosity had an intimate connection with the platform and staple. It had been there in the old chief's time; nobody knew when or why it had been placed in position, but Bob felt convinced that girder and platform had been intended to serve as a means of ingress to or egress from the fort if it should chance to be invested. A besieging force, relying on the apparent impossibility of scaling the side of the ravine, would be unlikely to maintain a guard there. But Bob's idea was that, suspended from a rope fastened to the girder, an active man could swing across the chasm, and, if the length of the rope were properly adjusted, could land gently on the platform, make good his footing by grasping the staple, and thereby prevent himself from falling backward with the return swing of the rope. If the rope were too long, he would of course run the risk of being dashed against the wall of the ravine beneath the platform. If it were too short, he would fail to reach the staple and swing back into the cleft; and as the return swing would obviously not carry him to his starting-point, he would again swing across the ravine, and so the pendulous movement would continue until he came to rest perpendicularly beneath the girder. He would then either have to climb the eighty feet of rope until he reached the iron bar, or drop the sheer two hundred feet to the bottom of the cleft. There was a further danger. On the return swing the man might, owing to oscillation in the rope, fail to enter the cleft, and be carried against its jagged edge, probably with sufficient force to stun, disable, or even kill him. Clearly the attempt would be full of danger; but it was this hazardous feat that Bob had resolved to attempt.

One necessary precaution could be taken in advance. It was to discover by experiment the length of rope needed. Bob guessed that the ledge on which he stood, at the narrow end of the cleft farthest from the ravine, must always have formed the springing-ground; its position therefore governed the length. Having explained to his two companions what he had in mind, he cut their expostulations short by borrowing some of their upper garments, which he made into a soft bundle. He weighted this with some heavy stones, tied it to the rope, and then, as the moon threw a dim light on the opposite side of the ravine, he placed the bundle in Ah-Sam's hands and made his way to the neighbourhood of the girder. Arriving there, he lifted his hand as a signal to the Chinaman to loose his hold on the bundle, and anxiously watched its course. It swept through the cleft, across the ravine, came to rest apparently within a yard of the platform, then swung back, making a giddy oscillation and narrowly escaping the wall of the cleft, until as it approached the ledge Ah-Sam caught it by means of a noose in a shorter rope. Its unsteady return journey gave Bob some alarm, but he surmised that with the greater weight of a man the rope would probably have risen higher and taken a more direct backward swing.

The experiment was sufficiently satisfactory, and then Bob explained to his amazed listeners what he proposed to do. He would himself risk the attempt. If he got safely across he would fix the rope to the staple and make a preliminary investigation of the pathway leading upwards from the platform. Should he require assistance he would return and loosen the rope, which would then swing back to a position perpendicularly under the girder. Ah-Sam meanwhile was to crawl to the extreme end of the ledge just below the bar; he was to obtain a hold of the rope as it swung loose, return to the innermost end of the cleft, and swing across the ravine as Bob had done. On the other hand, if Bob found that nothing could be done from the platform, or if he were detected, Ah-Sam was to cover his retreat with the revolver.

"What Sing-Cheng do allo tim'?" asked Ah-Sam when he had grasped his own instructions.

"He will remain behind. Tell him so."

When the chief understood this he was greatly indignant, and began to protest in loud tones. Bob checked him peremptorily. He felt that if he gained admittance to the fort precious time would be wasted if he had to give orders to Sing-Cheng through Ah-Sam, while if two men were unable to effect their purpose it was unlikely that three would succeed. He did not consider it necessary to argue with the chief, but pacified him by saying that, if Ah-Sam crossed over, he was to take the Chinaman's place at the end of the cleft and watch carefully lest it proved necessary to cover the retreat of the two from the other side.

All was now ready. But Bob waited for nearly an hour until the moonlight fell full upon the platform and the staple above it. Then he rose, placed his right foot in the loop of rope from which he had removed the experimental bundle, and stood on the ledge, grasping the rope firmly with his right hand. It was an anxious moment. He felt a sudden shudder run through his body as he hesitated on the brink, looking at the black gulf before him, and realizing that he was in very truth taking his life into his hands. But his hesitation was but momentary. With a determination and a hope that were themselves prayer he set his lips, pulled the rope taut, and dropped, his companions holding their breath as they watched him. There was little jerk as he fell, but it seemed an eternity before the swift motion through the air began to slacken on the upward swing. Suddenly, just as he felt that he was coming to a stop, he saw the staple above him slightly to his right. He jerked himself up and sideways in the effort to catch it with his unoccupied left hand; he touched it with the tips of his fingers; then the sagging rope became taut again; he fell swiftly downwards, felt a slight jerk at the lowest point of the rope's course, twirled round and round, and grazing the wall, it seemed by an inch, shot upwards towards the ledge. He had only time to wonder whether Ah-Sam would catch him with the loop when he again came to rest and began to fall downwards. There was a sudden constriction about his waist; he felt a sharp pain; then, to his relief, though to his discomfort also, he was steadily hauled in, and landed breathless, exhausted, and dazed on the ledge beside Ah-Sam.

When he was again able to take stock of his surroundings, he observed that Ah-Sam had fastened to one of the saplings one end of the rope by which he had been landed. But for this precaution the two men on the ledge could scarcely have arrested his fall, but would probably have been dragged themselves headlong into the cleft.

"That was well thought of," said Bob to Ah-Sam. "Now, I must have another try."

"No, no," returned Ah-Sam. "Massa too muchee tired; Ah-Sam tly one tim'; massa no can do evelyting."

"Your turn by and by. When I have rested a little I'll drop again. It can be done. It will not be so strange and breathless the second time."

He waited until he felt completely recovered from the experience, which, though lasting only a few seconds, had been a very trying one; then he rose for the second attempt. This time he placed his left foot in the loop and grasped the rope with his left hand, leaving his right free. He sprang off with his right foot, down into the gulf. He went through the same series of sensations as before, except that he was more conscious of the motion and more alert at the end of the swing. There was the staple again; again on his right side; he flung out his arm as rapidly as he could, touched the iron, caught it, obtained a good grip. As he did so, the whole weight of his body was thrown on his right hand; but the strain was only momentary, for instinctively advancing the right leg he reached the edge of the platform, and with a forward jerk he stood safe but breathless on firm rock.

Waiting for a few moments to steady himself, he released his left foot from the rope. Then hitching the end to the staple, he made his way cautiously up the path. It was broader than it had seemed from the opposite side of the ravine. At the point where the path had appeared to vanish into the cliff he now saw that it entered a low tunnel. Going into this, treading warily, he found that he had come to a flight of narrow steps. It was pitch dark. With his hands lightly touching the wall on either side he crept up, waiting after each step, anxious, suspicious, his ears strained to catch every sound, his eyes peering for any light above him. Suddenly the steps ceased; he was on level ground again; he stole forward on tiptoe for what he thought must be between twenty and thirty yards. From the direction of the tunnel he guessed that he must now be near one of the flanking towers: the left-hand one overhanging the ravine. There was still no light, still no sound; this was not surprising, for the whole garrison save the sentries were probably asleep. Yet, if he found no light, his enterprise almost certainly must fail. He went on, groping, conscious of the musty atmosphere of the passage. He could see nothing: his hands were outstretched, and he moved them now to the right, now to the left, touching the walls on both sides.

All at once his right hand came upon an obstacle immediately in front of him. It was either the blind end of the tunnel or a door. His heart sank as the thought crossed his mind that the tunnel, so long in disuse, might have been bricked up. But moving his hand over the obstructing surface he felt that it was of wood, and in a moment he touched something cold that projected an inch or two towards him. He pressed it gently, pushed it, tried to lift it, then bore down upon it; it yielded suddenly, and from the other side came the unmistakable click of a latch. He held his breath, waiting motionless for more than a minute, fearful lest the sound should have been heard by someone on the other side. All was still as death. Keeping the latch depressed, he pushed the door gently, then more firmly. There was no yielding. Again his heart sank; was the door bolted on the inside? Had he come thus far only to be baulked at last? But doors might open outwards as well as inwards. He pulled gently at the catch, and stopped with a start, for he heard the dreaded creak of a hinge. The door had begun to open towards him; through the inch-wide opening a draught of cold air played upon his face.

Had the creak been heard? He waited, listening. The silence was still unbroken. Then he began to pull the door towards him by almost infinitesimal degrees, and with every least movement there was a faint creak that sent a thrill through him. Yet it was better to risk many slight and interrupted sounds than one loud and prolonged; and he continued, lessening the strain on the hinges by giving an upward pressure upon the catch.

It seemed an age before the door was sufficiently open to allow him to wriggle through. He waited again; then moved slowly and warily forward, to find within a few paces that his foot was arrested by another step. He had come to a staircase. This time the flight wound round and round, and as he rose higher a glint of moonlight fell through a narrow slit in the right-hand wall; he must be on a winding stair within the tower. He left the dim light behind and came again into inky blackness; then, at another turn, another slit gave entrance to the pale beam. At last, after mounting until it seemed that his winding course would never end, he came into open air and full moonlight; he was on the roof of the tower. Before stepping out from the shelter of the stairway he glanced eagerly to right and left. The roof was vacant. It was hexagonal in shape. He wondered whether it was overlooked by other towers. Dropping on his knees, he crawled under cover of the wall that intercepted the moonlight, and made his way thus to the parapet. With relief he saw that the other towers were no higher, but apparently indeed a few feet lower. Completing the circuit of the roof, he came to another stairway immediately opposite the one he had just left. He entered cautiously, and found that this also was a winding stair, differing from the other only in the fact that there were no patches of light from slits in the wall. He went down step by step, quietly, until at a turn he was brought to a sudden pause by the sight of a small lamp burning in a niche opposite a heavily-barred door. For a minute he stood still; then stepped silently down until he came to the door. He listened; he ventured to place his ear against the wood: there was no sound. Waiting for a brief space, he hovered between advancing and retiring; then, with quickening breath, he moved on past the door until he came to the foot of the staircase.

He there perceived that he was in a narrow passage, with matting underfoot. It was dark, except at the farther end, which was slightly illuminated by a dull glow, evidently the reflection of a light from some point round the corner. Proceeding with cautious movements towards it, he came to a spot where the passage made a sharp turn to the right. He dropped to the floor, and, after listening to make sure that no one was approaching, ventured to peep round. At the end of the passage he saw a half-open door, through which the light was streaming; and now he heard the low hum of voices, and in the distance a faint clatter as of cooking utensils. On his left was a massive door clamped with plates of iron. It was shut. Bob guessed that he had been following a passage that led round the inner wall of the tower, and that the iron door was the principal entrance to the tower from the central courtyard of the fort. On the right hand, opposite this door, he saw a broad corridor or entrance-hall, illuminated by a large oil-lamp. He rose and peeped round the corner; the corridor ended with another door richly hung with silk.

He waited for a moment. If either door should be suddenly thrown open he was lost. He almost feared lest someone should hear the beating of his heart, so madly was it thumping. It was touch and go. The risk was great, but he had a great purpose. He stepped into the corridor, and crept along towards the silk-hung door.

Lifting the curtain, he found that the door stood slightly ajar. He held his breath as he peeped round, and spied, in the midst of a magnificently-furnished apartment, crowded with the rich spoils of many a raid, the one-eared Manchu Chang-Wo, reclining on a divan, and smoking. He wore a loose jacket of blue silk above his pantaloons, and a skullcap. His features had the same impassivity that always characterized him; from his face one could never have guessed whether he was happy or the reverse. As Bob looked, Chang-Wo raised his hand, and with the knuckles struck a small gong that stood by his side. Bob wondered with no little alarm from what quarter the summons would be answered, and gripped his revolver. From a door on the left of the apartment a burly Manchu entered. To him Chang-Wo addressed a few curt words; whereupon the man kow-towed and disappeared through the doorway. There was a sound of voices, then light footsteps in the passage at the end of the corridor—a continuation of the passage up which Bob himself had come. He flattened himself against the wall just as three figures crossed the end of the corridor in front of the iron door, and went along the passage towards the staircase by which he had descended. They were no doubt carrying out the order Chang-Wo had just given. What if, on their return, they should take the nearest way to their chief's room and come down the corridor instead of along the passage and through the door leading, as Bob conjectured, to the kitchen? In that case they would certainly discover him. He could not risk discovery, so tiptoeing along the corridor he followed the men, calculating his pace by the sound of their shuffling footsteps ahead.

He came in a few moments to the foot of the staircase, and knew by the hollow sounds coming down that the three men had ascended. Their mission apparently was either to the roof or to the heavily-barred door he had passed on his descent. The passage led on past the opening of the staircase, and as it was quite dark in that direction Bob resolved to go on for a few steps and await the men's return, trusting to the darkness to conceal him. Listening near the foot of the stairs he heard the clatter of the bolts as they were withdrawn at the door above, then the creak of rusty hinges. There was an interval; then he heard the men returning, and as they came down, with the sound of their voices was mingled the clank of chains.

They descended slowly, and as with care. They reached the bottom; they entered the passage; and then in the dim glow Bob saw that there were not three men now, but four. The fourth, a smaller man than the rest, was being half pushed, half dragged along, and all the time his every movement was accompanied by the clank-clank of metal. Bob felt a rush of blood to his face; his fingers tingled as though with galvanism. He pressed on after the group. They came, as he had done, to the great iron door. As he had done, they turned into the corridor opposite; and they passed into Chang-Wo's hall by the draped door where Bob himself had but a few minutes before been peeping. Almost reckless of consequences he followed them. They left the door half open, and from the folds of a silken hanging he beheld a piteous scene.

Between two of the Manchu guards Kobo was held up before his enemy. He was but the shadow of his former self. Bob could not see his face, but he saw his thin manacled wrists, he saw the hollows in his neck, and these, with the drooping helplessness of his attitude, were evidence of something too terrible for words.

Chang-Wo was speaking. He took the pipe from his mouth and jerked a word at the third Manchu, who went into the kitchen and returned with a metal can. Then Chang-Wo spoke to Kobo, snapping out the syllables in a harsh staccato that matched well the cold cruelty of his stony face. It mattered little to Bob that he could not understand what the Manchu said, or what Kobo replied in a thin husky whisper, scarcely audible. He heard a mocking note in Chang-Wo's voice; he saw the cup held before Kobo's face, but just beyond his reach; he saw Kobo's head move slowly from side to side as if making the gesture of refusal; and he guessed that this was the extremity of torture to which his friend had been put: that he had been kept without water, and that a brimming cup was now being offered to him in the hope of tempting him to betray his country.

For some minutes the scene continued—Chang-Wo's cold metallic voice addressing the fainting Japanese; Kobo murmuring his steadfast refusal; the Manchu offering the cup. Then suddenly it ceased; Chang-Wo, his expression never changing, flung up his hand; the water was taken away; the two guards wheeled Kobo round, and in the moment before Bob turned to retreat he caught one glimpse of his friend's face.

"God in heaven!" he muttered, and, white to the lips, went silently over the matting to the foot of the staircase.

Chapter XXV
Nemesis

Gagged and Bound—Flight—Into the Depths—Too Late—Last Wishes—Taru—At Rest

Bob went up the winding stair, past the door now unbarred, until he came to a spot where, unseen, he could see. After him, at a slower pace, ascended the Manchus with their haggard, tottering captive. They hauled him into the room, shut and barred the door upon him, and descended to their quarters. Bob waited till their footsteps had died away, then he too descended again; if he was to accomplish his purpose he must fix the positions of the rooms so firmly in his mind that he could move without error or stumble. He stole once more along the passage around the wall, down the corridor leading from it to Chang-Wo's room, back to the passage and along it farther until he came to a door opening to the kitchen, from within which he heard the voices of the servants. Then he returned to the stairway, mounted to the roof, went down the outer stair, and so through the tunnel to the platform above the ravine. He looked across to see whether the moonlight would reveal the form of Ah-Sam at his appointed post; but the Chinaman had kept out of sight. Bob himself could be seen; he loosened the rope from the staple and sent it flying downwards. It was caught as it swung under the iron girder. A few minutes passed, then he saw the form of a man swinging across towards him. Holding on to the staple, Bob caught Ah-Sam at the end of the swing, once more secured the rope, then retreating to the shelter of the tunnel he explained in a whisper to the amazed and breathless Chinaman what he had discovered and what he meant to do.

For some hours the two waited there in silence, until Bob thought the occupants of the tower must be asleep. Then he led Ah-Sam by the way he himself had traversed until they reached the passage at the foot of the inner stairs. Bidding Ah-Sam remain there, he stole forward to reconnoitre. As he came down the stairs he had seen that the lamp opposite Kobo's dungeon was still burning, though dimly; he now saw that the lamp in the corridor also was still alight. Did Chang-Wo keep these lamps constantly burning? Was he, like all tyrants, fearful of assassination? The constant lights, the massive iron-barred door in the passage, suggested that he did not trust his followers; he himself was a usurper and an assassin; might not the measure he had meted to others be measured to him again? He ruled by fear; when men ceased to fear him his authority would vanish like a pricked bubble.

Bob went along until he came to the door into the kitchen. It was half open, and peeping in, he was concerned to see that the three men were immersed in a game of "go"; two playing, the third looking on. He wished they were asleep. Scarcely daring to breathe, he stood in the passage for what seemed hours, ready to flee or to fight as the moment might require. The players were absorbed in the game, exchanging only rare monosyllables. They were no doubt gambling, and to them the stakes were important.

At last the looker-on, the man who had answered Chang-Wo's summons, turned away, retreated to a corner of the room near the door of his master's apartment, and curled himself up for the night. Bob gave an inaudible gasp of relief. The other two played on; when would this long game be ended? The minutes lengthened themselves into at least an hour before one of the men rose with a sudden exclamation of anger, and, seizing his opponent, knocked his head smartly against the floor. Having taken this revenge for his losses, he went to his corner, spread his couch, and prepared for sleep. The victor, a much smaller man, bore the assault with a patient shrug, and, rubbing his head, tied his paltry winnings in a bag which he took from somewhere among his clothes. Then he too retired to rest, leaving the lamp burning.

As soon as heavy breathing and snores in three different tones told that all were asleep, Bob returned for Ah-Sam. He whispered a few words to him, then both tiptoed along the passage until they came to the kitchen door. Ah-Sam entered alone. A few minutes elapsed; he returned to the passage, and handed Bob a soft pad of cloth a few inches long and a strip of cord, himself retaining a shorter piece. Bob looked his approval of his follower's quiet and successful search, and both went into the room.

The big fellow lying nearest Chang-Wo's door was clearly the toughest customer of the three, and Bob had decided to tackle him first. He was lying on his back, and his mouth was wide open. Bob crept to his head, Ah-Sam stood at his feet. With a sudden pounce Bob slipped the pad of cloth between his jaws; at the same moment Ah-Sam seized his feet and began to tie them together, and Bob endeavoured to pinion his arms. The Manchu's position rendered this difficult; he wriggled over, and his arm striking against the floor, roused one of his companions, who half rose upon his elbow. Seeing that Ah-Sam had firmly bound the feet, Bob left him to complete the trussing of the first man and rushed over to deal with the second. The half-dazed fellow had just sat up and begun to look about him when Bob dropped upon him, dealing him a blow that rendered him for the moment harmless. But before Bob could recover his balance, he was himself pulled to the ground by the third man, who had awakened in full possession of his senses. Giving a shout, he got his left hand upon his assailant's throat; Bob was upon the floor, helpless to resist the horrid clutch. He writhed, he was choking; he felt already that all was over, when the pressure suddenly relaxed; the Manchu fell, a huddled heap, to the ground. Ah-Sam had disobeyed orders. He saw what was happening to his master, and, finding the first man still wriggling, had given him his quietus with the knife, and then darted across the room, to deal in the same way with Bob's opponent.

Bob sprang to his feet. Chang-Wo must by this time have been awakened by the commotion, and might escape by the farther door. There was no time to lose. Pulling the dead Manchu from before the door, Bob flung himself against it. The catch on the inside gave way; he burst into the room; there was a blinding flash, and a bullet crashed through the woodwork within a few inches of his head. In the middle of the room stood the Manchu chief, with a pistol in his hand. Bob made a dash for him, but keeping his eyes on Chang-Wo he failed to notice a pile of quilts on the floor. He tripped. The figure of Ah-Sam coming in support was seen by Chang-Wo, who waited no longer, but rushed to the door leading into the corridor, and slamming it behind him, disappeared.

Bob was after him in a moment. The door, he already knew, had no fastening on the outside. He pulled it open, and, followed by Ah-Sam, dashed into the corridor after the fugitive. He heard the pad of rapid footsteps ascending the stairway. Springing up as fast as the narrow winding steps allowed, he gained the roof just in time to see, in the thin light of dawn, the gigantic Manchu disappearing through the opening opposite. Bob leapt across the roof to follow. Down the stairs he plunged, staggering, recovering himself, gaining on the heavier man in front of him. So eagerly did he pursue that he forgot the existence of the door at the foot of this staircase, until, coming suddenly full tilt against it, he was brought up with a painful shock that rendered him almost breathless. He remembered that the door fastened on the other side; had there been time for Chang-Wo to slip the bolt against him? He pressed it; it did not yield; he went back a few steps and flung himself against it. There was a creak, a slight yielding; pray heaven the bolt is old! Ah-Sam is by his side. Together they hurl themselves against the door with all the force the confined space admits. The bolt is torn from the woodwork, the door flies open, and the two dash through.

But with this interruption Bob bethought him of the man he had felled in the kitchen. He might, he would, recover consciousness, and alarm the garrison.

"Back!" he cried to Ah-Sam, halting for an instant. "Back, and secure that man. Do not kill him."

The Chinaman, after a moment's hesitation, ran to do his master's bidding. Bob ran on, stumbling through the tunnel, down the path, towards the platform. Then he saw that a rope-ladder hung from the staple. Chang-Wo must have kept it in readiness in the passage or on the stairs, and snatched it up as he ran. As Bob emerged on to the narrow platform the bandit was facing about to take the first step downwards. But with the quickness that had always served him, he saw in a flash that, once upon the ladder, he would be at the mercy of his pursuers, who could cut the rope and hurl him infallibly to destruction. One bound, and he caught at the rope by which Bob had crossed, slipped the noose over the staple, and, with a desperate courage that extorted Bob's admiration, flung himself off the platform into the abyss, just as Bob came within arm's length of him. At the brink Bob stopped, watching as if spellbound the hazardous course of the swinging figure. It grazed the angle of the cleft by a hair's breadth, spinning round and round at the end of the rope; then as its speed decreased on the upward flight, and it finally stopped, to begin the backward swing, Bob caught sight of another figure, a crouching form on the ledge below the girder—it was Sing-Cheng, who, obedient to instructions, had spent the livelong night watching in silent patience on the spot where Ah-Sam formerly had been. The sun was just rising across the opposite hills, and Bob saw the face of the Chunchuse chief, and noticed its expression of rage and hatred as he peered over the precipice at the swinging figure. In his right hand he grasped his revolver. Bob had an impulse to call to him, and bid him spare the wretch beneath; but even with the thought he recognized its hopelessness. Nothing could now intervene between the hunter and his prey. The drama must play itself out.

A Question of Seconds

A Question of Seconds

Meanwhile beneath the girder the rope swung heavily backwards and forwards for some time before it came almost to rest. Then, all unconscious of the fierce eyes watching him from above, the Manchu began to climb up the rope, slowly, painfully, carefully, for he knew the cleft and its ragged bottom two hundred feet below. Foot by foot he ascends; he is more than half-way up; thirty more feet and he is safe—when he suddenly catches sigh of the stooping enemy on the ledge above. He stops his upward progress, twisting his legs round the rope to ease his straining arms. For a few seconds he remains thus; Bob, watching with fascinated eyes, sees not a shade of emotion on his face. Above, the ruthless enemy; below, the jagged rocks; both alternatives are fearful. To drop is certain death; to ascend is to meet an armed foe. But a man may miss his aim; it is here a chance in a million. It is the only chance, and Chang-Wo takes it.

He climbs up a few more feet; his eyes are now fixed unswervingly upon the waiting enemy. Reading their expression of vengeful hate, he stops again. At that instant a shot rings out, and from behind Bob a flight of birds spring with clattering wings into the air, almost smothering a scream of pain from the dangling figure. He has loosed his hold with the right hand; the right arm falls helpless to his side. He swings round, still clinging to the rope with the left hand, though he knows full well that with one hand he can never raise himself. For half a minute he hangs thus, swaying; the strain is unendurable; he lets go his hold, and without a cry falls into the gulf.

A moment afterwards there was a sharp report from the wall of the fort above Bob, followed by a babel of shouts. Bob, who had watched the scene before him in silent horror, saw a puff of dust struck from the side of the cleft just above the spot where Sing-Cheng lay peering gloatingly down upon his lifeless enemy. The chief instantly rose to his feet, glared for an instant towards the fort, then raised his hand and shouted a few words to the men who, as Bob surmised, though he could not see them, were now lining the wall. Whatever the words signified, they had an instantaneous effect. The clamour ceased. Then the chief raised himself to his full height, and began to harangue the crowd, turning this way and that, pointing with his finger, using many strange gestures to emphasize the words that fell in a rapid staccato from his lips. He spoke long, and the crowd heard him in complete silence. When his speech came to an end, he put the tips of his fingers together, and made three dignified movements with his head. Then he stood waiting.

Immediately afterwards Bob heard a great bustle and chatter from the unseen crowd. All seemed to be talking at once; the noise was like that of a hundred parrots holding a parliament. Again silence fell, and from the wall a loud voice shouted what was apparently a brief question to the stolid, immobile figure on the other side of the ravine. The answer came instantly, with a proud gesture, and was received with a storm of approving shouts from the crowd.

At this moment Ah-Sam came from the tunnel and stood beside Bob, who turned to him and asked:

"Is all safe in the tower?"

"Yes, massa; one piecee man makee no bobbely; he tied velly muchee tight, galaw!"

"Ask Sing-Cheng yonder what is happening."

Ah-Sam stepped forward and called across the ravine. The chief replied in a few words.

"What does he say?" asked Bob.

"He say come this-side velly soon; he hab catchee allo piecee man, now allo belongey he."

"Made friends with the enemy, has he? How is he coming here?"

"He go long down that side; come lound chop-chop. He velly muchee topside man this-tim', galaw!"

"Tell him he will find me in the tower."

Bob did not understand what means of persuasion Sing-Cheng had found, but he had complete faith in the man's discretion. As soon as the chief had disappeared up the cleft, Bob went in haste with Ah-Sam back into the tower; he felt with a deep sense of relief that there was now nothing to prevent the release of Kobo.

They returned to the kitchen. Bob suspected that the keys of the dungeon would be found on the person of the big Manchu who had slept by Chang-Wo's door, and told Ah-Sam to search him. In half a minute the keys were in his possession, and with eager steps he hastened along the corridor, up the staircase, until he came to the doorway. The lamp had burnt itself out; the passage was so dark that he had to feel for the keyhole. Then he threw open the door and entered the room. It was in darkness, save for the thin light filtering through a narrow slit high up in the wall. In the middle of the room lay, amid his chains, the huddled figure of the Samurai. Bob went up to him, stooped, and touched him on the shoulder. In a low, husky whisper came an exclamation that he did not understand.

"Speak to him," murmured Bob to Ah-Sam; he feared lest the sound of an English voice might prove disastrous to the overwrought prisoner. At Ah-Sam's first words the prostrate man stirred and opened his eyes. He tried to lift his hand, but it fell back, and the chain clinked against the stone floor.

"Mr. Fawcett!" he murmured. "Water, water!"

Reproaching himself for forgetting, in the excitement of the moment, the scene he had witnessed in Chang-Wo's room, Bob sent Ah-Sam back to the kitchen, whence he returned with a full cup. Handing this to his master, he knelt down and raised the prisoner's head. Bob held the cup to Kobo's lips, allowing him to take only one sip at a time. The Japanese gave a sigh of ineffable content; for several minutes not a word was spoken by any of the three; Bob's heart was too full for speech. Presently Kobo signified that he had drunk enough, and Bob placed the cup beside him on the floor.

"Thank God I came in time to save you!" he said, laying his hand on Kobo's. He had a terrible sinking of the heart as he felt the thin hand—it was mere skin and bone, the hand of a skeleton; it was clammy to his touch.

"I thank you, Mr. Fawcett," said Kobo feebly. "I thank you, but it is too late. I am dying."

"Don't say that," replied Bob. "We'll take you out of this horrible place. In the fresh air and sunshine, with good food, you will be yourself again."

"Tell me," went on the prisoner, in the same low, difficult tones, "did you give my message to the general?"

"Yes; I remained with him, and was able to do something to guide the Twelfth Division. We are across the Yalu, sir."

"Banzai! Banzai!" exclaimed Kobo with sudden vigour. "The Russians are beaten?"

"Thoroughly—driven from all their positions; we captured forty of their guns."

"Banzai! My country! She will win. I know it. We have crossed the Yalu: then we shall drive the enemy before us—from Kiu-lien-cheng to Liao-yang, from Liao-yang to Mukden, from Mukden to Harbin, from Harbin— Ah! why should we drive them farther? Dai Nippon shall come to her own."

"But yourself, sir; we must take you out of this. You will be more comfortable in Chang-Wo's room, and then, when you have rested and eaten, we will take you slowly into the Japanese lines, and you will live to see the triumph you have done so much to secure."

Kobo shook his head.

"I cannot stand," he said. "I shall die. But what is death?—Rest, peace, eternal quiet."

Bob felt a lump in his throat.

"Help me lift Kobo San," he said, turning to the Chinaman.

Tenderly they carried the slight figure between them down the stairs into Chang-Wo's room, where they laid him on the soft quilts that still bore the impress of his enemy's form. And then Bob saw that there was indeed no hope. Kobo was almost unrecognizable. He was haggard, emaciated to a shadow; but for his open eyes he would have seemed a corpse. At Bob's orders Ah-Sam hurriedly prepared some food, but after one or two mouthfuls Kobo refused to take any more.

"Rest," he said; "I want rest, that is all. I thank you."

His eyes roved round the room as though in search of something or someone.

"Your enemy will not trouble you again," said Bob. "Chang-Wo is dead."

"He died first! He has starved me, beaten me; he kept me without water—how many days? I do not know. He tempted me, held a cup before me; I might drink if I would do as he wished: betray my country. We Japanese do not fear death.—My servant! Have you any news of him?"

"No, I have not seen him since I left you."

"No matter. Taru will know how to die. If he should survive, and you meet him, tell him to return to Nikko; my wife will have need of him. And my son, my boy Takeo in England. You will see him? You will tell him?"

"Yes; I will go to him as soon as I can."

"I thank you. Will you give me a little water?"

Kobo lay back on the padded quilts, and his eyes spoke his thanks. Bob was troubled, and watched him in silence. Ah-Sam, with stolid countenance, was busy preparing a meal for his master. Suddenly through the walls of the tower penetrated the sound of a multitudinous discharge of firearms. Bob rose to his feet, and leaving Kobo in Ah-Sam's charge hurried to the top of the tower, his mind filled with apprehension. Was Kobo's end to be disturbed? From the roof he saw a strange sight. The inner wall of the fortress was thronged with the garrison, who were shouting and gesticulating with excitement. The huge gate stood wide open, and beyond, half a mile across the green plain, a tall figure had just mounted a beautiful horse, which had evidently been taken out to meet him by three men from the garrison. The horseman rode up slowly, and as he approached, Bob saw that it was his late companion, Sing-Cheng.

At the gate of the fortress the chief halted and made a speech to the men, who responded with loud cries and another discharge of their rifles. Then he rode through the gate into the courtyard. Looking up, he caught sight of the solitary figure on the roof of the tower. Instantly springing from his horse, he bowed himself low to the ground, and ordered the surprised Manchus to do the same. The kow-towing over, he sent a man to knock at the outer door of the tower. Bob hurried down, and bade Ah-Sam open the door. Sing-Cheng entered, bowed humbly to the Englishman, and followed him into Chang-Wo's room. He gave one glance to the figure prostrate on the floor, looked a mute question at Ah-Sam, and then explained what had happened.

As he stood at the edge of the cleft, looking towards the wall, he had recognized among the crowd one who had been his comrade when he himself had served the old chief. Addressing him by name, he had reminded him of his own former importance in the band before the chieftainship had been usurped by Chang-Wo. He explained that Chang-Wo had met a terrible fate through his ill-considered adhesion to the Russian side in the great struggle now desolating the country. Chang-Wo was dead; if he had lived, the extermination of the whole band could only have been a matter of time. But now he, Sing-Cheng, the chief of a rival band, had disposed of his old enemy and proved himself a better man. Let them accept him, therefore, as their new chief. He would lead them with more success; under him let them relinquish the losing side and do yeoman service for the conquering Japanese. The alternative? If they did not accept his leadership he would deliver them into the hands of an army of Japanese whom he had guided into the neighbourhood, and they would be slain to a man. The strong tower of the fortress was already in the hands of two powerful friends of his, who had crossed the ravine by an unheard-of means, had faced the Mountain Tiger in his lair, and driven him headlong to destruction.

The bold offer had been accepted. Sing-Cheng had demanded that an escort of three men, with a horse suited to his dignity, should meet him at the distance of a li from the fortress, and, as Bob had seen, he had ridden in to receive the submission of the garrison.

The chief's story was hardly finished when one of the garrison came running in with a message. Sing-Cheng instantly went out into the courtyard.

"He say Manchu hab catchee one piecee Japanee," explained Ah-Sam.

"Follow the chief, and bring me word what is happening," said Bob.

A few minutes passed. Kobo was restless, his eyes wide open with a look of strained eagerness, his breath coming and going in quick feeble pants. Bob sat by his side, moistening his lips at intervals. Presently the door opened, and Ah-Sam first appeared, restraining a small gray-headed man, who seemed to be in haste to enter.

"One piecee boy Kobo San," said Ah-Sam to his master.

The man came forward eagerly, and Bob saw that it was Taru, his friend's servant. The little Japanese flung himself down at his master's feet, and muttered a few words brokenly. Kobo smiled. Beckoning to Ah-Sam, Bob went out of the room, leaving the two lifelong friends, master and man, together. Outside he learnt what had happened. The rider whom he had seen leave the fortress on the memorable night when he had reconnoitred the position had returned, bringing with him the disguised Japanese servant, who had been making his way by devious routes to the haunt of his old enemy. Taru had explained to Ah-Sam that while in Yongampo he had heard that his master had been captured by Chang-Wo, and had instantly set out to track him; if possible to rescue him; if not, to die with him. He had come safely to within two miles of the fortress, and then fallen into the hands of a small party led by the Manchu courier.

For half an hour Bob remained in conversation with the chief, discussing through Ah-Sam the measures that were to be taken to consolidate his new authority, and to do service to his new allies, the Japanese. Then Taru came hurriedly from the tower, and asked Bob to return with him. They found Kobo now raised to a sitting posture. His eyes were closed, but he opened them as Bob entered. He was pale with the pallor of death.

"I am going—to my fathers," he whispered.

Bob sat down by his side, and looked at him with dim eyes. He breathed painfully; Taru, on the other side, gave him at intervals a spoonful of water.

"I rejoice to have—two faithful friends," said Kobo. "Mr. Fawcett, Taru will—return to Nikko; you will remember—Takeo, my son in England. I shall rest."

He closed his eyes and remained silent. Taru took one hand and held it fast, Bob held the other. He waited, sad at heart, grieved that Japan was to lose one who had served her so well. He thought of the long hours of agony this hero must have suffered; the tortures of hunger and thirst, the fierce temptation that must have assailed him. Kobo had been reticent of details, but Bob understood that he might have purchased his life by disclosing the methods of the Japanese secret service. How small a thing, thought Bob, to meet death bravely in the heat of battle! in a moment a man passes from full life to quietude. But to endure such horrors as Kobo had faced without flinching needed another kind of courage, a higher mind, a greater soul. Bob thrilled with sympathy and admiration, and all the time felt an aching disappointment that he had not been able to avert this tragic martyrdom.

Kobo's eyes slowly opened. In tones almost inaudible he said a few words in Japanese to his servant. Taru bent to the floor, and placed his master's hand upon his head. Kobo looked at Bob, and attempted feebly to press his hand.

"It is good-bye," he said. "I am going into the dark—which is rest. Good-bye."

Bob could not speak. There was a moment of silence. The dying man gasped painfully.

"Taru," he murmured. "Taru—sayonara!"

His head sank. Taru waited a few moments; then, lifting Kobo's hand, he rose saying:

"Be at peace, dear master."

Chapter XXVI
Old Friends and New Prospects

Compulsory Leave—Andrew B. Charteris—Looking Ahead—The Busy Bee—Smuggling Ah-Sam—Schwab Proposes—A Blessing

Kobo was buried in a glade among the trees near the fort. Bob placed over the grave a stone from the ravine—a flat slab washed smooth and white by the torrent; and upon this Taru scratched a simple inscription in Japanese characters. The chief meanwhile had sent men to find the body of Chang-Wo. What indignities the already mangled corpse might have suffered but for Bob's presence need not be told; Bob insisted on a decent burial, and made the chief promise that the grave should not be desecrated. The dead man's effects were thoroughly examined, and a discovery was made which threw light on a matter always puzzling to Bob—the presence of Chang-Wo in Tokio. Among his belongings were many papers, charts, and maps of Japan and the surrounding seas, plans of the Japanese ports, memoranda of military details—all probably intended for Russian use in an invasion of the islands, and kept by the Manchu until he could depend on getting a good price for them. These Bob made into a bundle; then he prepared to return with Taru and Ah-Sam to the Japanese head-quarters.

A few days later the services of one of the army doctors with General Kuroki's force were required for a young Englishman who had just been brought into camp by four coolies, led by a Japanese and a Chinaman. Sunstroke had laid Bob low on the day after leaving the fort. The unusual exertions which he had undergone since his adventure with the Cossacks had tried his constitution more than he was aware, and the final excitement and strain of Kobo's rescue had left him too weak to withstand the effect of the sudden heat. He was unconscious when he reached General Kuroki's quarters, and the doctor who examined him looked grave.

It was some days before he came fully to himself, and then the doctor, though he foretold a complete recovery, declared that it would be a matter of time and rest, and emphatically forbade Bob to think of active service for months to come.

"But I must get back to the fleet," protested Bob. "I'm a kind of deserter, and though I couldn't help being captured, and everything else has followed from that, I sha'n't be able to help feeling guilty when I report myself to Admiral Togo."

"You'll do nothing of the kind. We're a long way from the coast; in any case we can't spare a cruiser to carry you to Port Arthur; and if we could, I shouldn't allow you to go."

"What's to become of me, then? I can't follow the army; and I'm sure I don't want to be left behind in a Manchurian village."

The doctor's reply was interrupted by the entrance of General Kuroki himself. After greeting Bob, the general took the doctor aside, and for some minutes the two were engaged in conversation. They spoke in Japanese, and Bob, with the impatience of an invalid, felt annoyed at being the subject of a discussion which he could not follow. At length General Kuroki turned to him and said:

"I hear you want to rejoin the fleet, Mr. Fawcett. That is an entirely creditable wish; but the doctor is quite right, you must not think of it. You need not be disturbed about your quarters, however; we shall not leave you to the tender mercies of the Manchus. I'm going to send you to Yokohama. Stay," he added, as Bob began to protest, "it is quite fixed; you will be escorted to Chemulpo as soon as the doctor gives permission. For my part, I shall be glad to be rid of you." The general smiled. "Don't take that personally; I have had the pleasure of sending a report to the illustrious Emperor detailing the services you have rendered us since you left the fleet, and your adventurous expedition for the rescue of Kobo San. You have good friends, sir. Ever since you started on your quest I have been pestered by telegrams from a lady, first from Seoul, then from Yokohama—a Mrs. Pottle, who has been most energetic in enquiring after your welfare. Mrs. Pottle has given me more trouble than all the press correspondents together, and that is saying a good deal. I wired to the lady when you were brought in, telling her of your illness, and hoped that I should hear no more from her. But her telegram has now become a daily event, and only this morning she wired: 'Send him right along, I will nurse him like a mother'. So you see, Mr. Fawcett, that in getting rid of you I get rid, as I hope, of Mrs. Pottle."

For all his disappointment, Bob could not help smiling.

"She is a most determined woman," he said; "quite capable of leading your army, sir, with her umbrella. Well, I'm in your hands, general; it's very kind of you to be bothered with me at all. I only wish I had a chance of doing something; but I suppose that when I am quite well again the war will be over."

"I hope so," said the general gravely. "We have hard work before us; many good lives will be lost; but we shall persevere, and who knows—?"

Bob was welcomed by Mrs. Pottle at Yokohama literally with open arms. He had never been so much fussed over in his life as he was during the next few days. His health had improved with the voyage; but he was still only the shadow of his former self, and Mrs. Pottle showed that she had undertaken in all earnestness the duties of nurse. Bob found her energy rather trying, but he endured her ministrations with patience, for they were alleviated by the presence of Ethel Charteris, whose enthusiasm was displayed in a quieter and more winning manner. Mrs. Pottle was by no means short-sighted, and after a time she began to leave Bob more and more in her niece's hands, much to his contentment.

One day she returned from her usual morning expedition through the town accompanied by a stranger—a tall grizzled gentleman, sparse, keen, yet bearing an undefinable resemblance to the lady. Ethel was seated at Bob's side on the veranda of the hotel when she saw the two figures approaching.

"Good gracious! It's poppa!" she exclaimed, and fled to meet him.

Mrs. Pottle came up first, rustling in Japanese silk under a chrysanthemum parasol.

"See what you're responsible for!" she exclaimed. "Here's my brother, Andrew B. Charteris, come right out to fetch us. Says he couldn't make head or tale of our letters, and couldn't size up the attractions of Yokohama, and so he's left his business in a critical situation to see what his sister and daughter are doing. I hope you and Andrew will get along, Mr. Fawcett. He's a silent man, but a real good hand at taking stock of things. Here he is."

Mr. Andrew B. Charteris came up with Ethel clinging to his arm. The introductions were made.

"Heard a lot about you, sir," said Mr. Charteris. "Real glad to meet you in the flesh."

"There, Andrew, you don't mean anything; but if you had known Mr. Fawcett before, you wouldn't have said just that. Poor boy! he's little enough flesh on his bones now."

"H'm! Nature has wonderful recuperative powers," said Mr. Charteris, who after this profound remark walked on into the hotel with his daughter.

A week passed—a time of quiet enjoyment to Bob, who had still more of Ethel's company now that Mrs. Pottle had her brother to pilot round, as she put it. There was only one drawback to his happiness. One day he was surprised by a visit from a high court functionary, who had come to command his attendance at the palace in Tokio at a certain hour next day. Bob made a wry face when the functionary was gone. He guessed that this unexpected honour was due to General Kuroki's report to the Mikado, and was sufficiently boyish yet to hate all fuss, as he told Ethel.

"I think you are quite wrong," she replied. "You have done splendidly, and it is only right that the Mikado should thank you himself. Why, I know young men in San Francisco who'd give their eyes to be invited to see a real live emperor."

He went to Tokio, and certainly did not look unhappy when he returned. Mrs. Pottle bombarded him with questions about what had happened.

"Oh, it was all right," said Bob. "He's a very good sort; so's the Empress. It wasn't the formal affair I expected. They had me in their private apartments and gave me some tea, and the Emperor said uncommonly nice things, and presented me with—this."

He held up a ribbon with a gold ornament attached.

"My!" exclaimed Mrs. Pottle, "what's that?"

"It's the insignia of the order of the Sacred Treasure."

"Mysakes! Only think of that! Well, I'll say this; it's no more than you deserve. There!"

"I'm so glad," said Ethel.

"What's it worth in cash?" drawled Mr. Charteris.

"Oh, poppa, you unromantic, practical, shocking old man! The idea! It's perfectly priceless. Mr. Fawcett wouldn't part with it for anything, I'm sure."

"I sha'n't tempt him. I don't cotton to fal-lals of that sort. A thumping cheque would have been more to the point. Say, Mr. Fawcett, you ain't a rich man?"

Bob flushed at the blunt question, and Ethel blushed in sympathy.

"No offence!" added the old man, his eyes twinkling. "It's just this way. I've been thinking for a week, Mr. Fawcett. It ain't right for that tramp of yours across the Manchurian hills to be thrown slick away. How long do you suppose this war will last out?"

"That's more than I can even imagine," replied Bob. "I don't see how Port Arthur can hold out much longer; they are closing in on it; and as to the land campaign, the Japanese generals are driving the Russians from pillar to post. If the Russians are wise, the war will end with the fall of Port Arthur."

"Ah! and then?"

"What do you mean, sir?"

"Well, I suppose the Japs—"

"Poppa!" interrupted Ethel. "Don't use that horrid word—call them Japanese."

"Anything to please you, my love. I was going to say that I suppose the Japs—Japanese, I mean—are not running this war for nothing. They'll want to develop the country—what?"

"No doubt."

"And they'll keep an 'open door', eh? Well, what I've been thinking is this. When the war ends, it'll be time for me to slip in with a syndicate to work out some of the minerals—what! And it seems to me, from what I've heard and seen of you—especially what I've seen—that you're the right sort to be of use. You know the country; say, you've had a practical training—not wasted too much time on defunct languages, eh? and what's most to the point, you've got a pretty level head, and I'll go bail you ain't afraid of work. So, if you're agreeable, we'll strike a bargain. What?"

"I accept your offer with pleasure, sir," said Bob, his face flushed, his eyes shining. "I've always wanted to live an active life, and—"

"Shake!" said the American, relapsing into his usual laconic mode of utterance. Mrs. Pottle gleamed benevolence through her eye-glasses, and Bob's eyes sought Ethel's.

A few days later, one of the liners of the *Pacific Mail* was steaming across the ocean from Yokohama towards San Francisco. On the deck sat a group of three—the same three who had foregathered on the voyage out to Nagasaki seven months before. Morton and Desjardins, finding that their chances of seeing anything of the actual fighting were not improving, had asked to be recalled, and were returning by way of New York. Bob, with sick-leave from the Japanese government, had accepted an invitation to spend a few weeks with Mr. Charteris in San Francisco. The three were lolling on their deck-chairs, when a fourth figure was seen slowly rising from the companion-way.

"Well, Schwab, feel better?" shouted Morton.

"Zanks, Mr. Morton, I am vat you call fairly gumfortable. Ze sea-illness attack me not zis time so bad. Indeed," he added expansively, "I gommence to enjoy myself."

"Ah! de beautiful sea, de beautiful sun!" exclaimed Desjardins. "I look up into de blue sky lovly above, and it make me feel all de vorld is poetry."

"Bosh!" snorted Morton in his downright way. "Excuse me; no poetry in the world but what you put there. I ain't built that way; no Englishman who can eat a beefsteak is. No!"

"But, monsieur, you do yourself, you do your nation, im-mense injustice. Par exemple! vat vas it I hear last night ven I promenade myself beneas de so silent stars? Assuredly it vas de sweet voice of Mademoiselle Charteris who give a lesson to de boy Ah-Sam. I listen; I am charmed; it vas a little poem, so short, so simple, I learn it by 'art at once:

"'Ow doss de leetle beesy bee-e
Impr-rove each shinin' hour-r,
And gader 'oney all de day-e
From every openin' flower-r-r!

So it begin, and—"

"I see Madame Bottle!" suddenly exclaimed Schwab, rising clumsily from the deck-chair into which he had subsided. The others rose also and hastened along the deck towards a group of two ladies and a gentleman coming in their direction. Schwab at once took possession of Mrs. Pottle; the others manoeuvred for the place at Ethel's left hand, the right being occupied by her father. Desjardins lost his chance by waiting to make an elaborate bow; Morton, for all his bluntness, was a bashful man; so that Bob had no great difficulty in securing the position. Morton consoled himself by arranging deck-chairs for the ladies, and the company grouped themselves, Schwab still next to Mrs. Pottle, and Bob retaining his place at Ethel's left hand.

"We've been hearing of your English lessons to Ah-Sam," said Morton to Ethel.

"Have you? Oh yes! I don't like his pidgin English at all. It would be so much nicer if he could speak properly, and the poor man is really so eager to learn."

"How does he get on?" asked Bob.

"I think he is improving, but it is very slow. I read in a magazine the other day that learning to recite poetry is a great help, so I have been teaching him a very easy little poem, explaining it as I go along in just the same simple language I use to my Sunday-school class. He is so intelligent."

"There he is," said Bob. "Let us see what he makes of it" (with a glance at Desjardins). "You don't mind, Miss Charteris?"

"Not at all," replied Ethel, with a faint blush, "—if you are not too severe an examiner."

"Here, Ah-Sam!" called Bob.

The Chinaman came up and bowed humbly.

"Miss Charteris has been teaching you about the little busy bee. We should like to hear you say it."

"My no can talkee missy so-fashion," said Ah-Sam, looking troubled.

"Never mind that. Say it your own way."

Ah-Sam looked at Ethel.

"Come, Ah-Sam," she said; "remember how I explained it to you."

The Chinaman put his hands behind his back, hesitated, then fixed his eyes on the nearest ventilator, and in his odd sing-song chanted:

"What-for one piecee littee pidgy bee
Wantchee go workee allo bloomin' day-lo?
He go 'long smellum evely littee tlee;
Ch'hoy! catchee jam-jam; bimeby chop-chop wailo!"

The colour of Ethel's cheeks had deepened from pink to scarlet during this recitation. Morton gave a titter at the second line, then cougned and looked solemn. At the end they all glanced at one another and burst into an uncontrollable fit of laughter. Ah-Sam looked deprecatingly at his young mistress, and began to make humble obeisance with his hands.

"Thank you, Ah-Sam," she said. "You said it very nicely. You may go now.—What a shame!" she added, turning to the others when he had gone, "to hurt the poor man's feelings so. He did his best."

"And clearly showed that he had studied your commentary more than the text, as is the way with students of English," said Bob. "Never mind, Miss Charteris; Ah-Sam's a good fellow. I am hardly yet reconciled to his transference of allegiance from me to you."

"Nor I," said Mr. Charteris drily, with a grim look at his sister.

"Now, Andrew, don't go into that again," said Mrs. Pottle. "There's no rule without an exception. Our legislators are mostly right, I allow; but when they make a law that excludes all Chinamen from our shores—well, they have to reckon with me. I confess I smuggled Ah-Sam on board; he's the exception, a most exceptional China boy. Ethel took a fancy to have him for a servant, and I'll land him right down at San Francisco, laws or no laws."

Mr. Charteris shrugged.

"Fawcett," he said, "come and take a turn with me. We must talk over that prospectus—eh, what?"

"Yes, and I must write up my diary for the *Argonaut*," said Mrs. Pottle, rising, and sailing away towards a table specially reserved for her beneath the awning. Herr Schwab looked glum on her departure; he took no part in the conversation of the others, and when Ethel by and by left the group and strolled away by herself, he too got up, refilled his big pipe, and walked to a spot where, leaning on the rail, he had Mrs. Pottle in full view. Puffing solemnly, he watched her for a long time as she wrote on and on in complete unconsciousness of his lingering gaze. At last, putting his pipe into his pocket without knocking out the ashes, he went below. Soon he returned, laden with several bulky tomes, and staggered up to Mrs. Pottle's sheltered corner, where he placed the volumes in a pile beside her table, and heaved a sonorous sigh. Mrs. Pottle looked up, glanced from Schwab's face to the books, then resumed her writing, just as the German was bringing his right hand down on the crown of his wideawake. He wiped his gold-rimmed spectacles, replaced them on his nose, and sighed again.

"Don't you feel well, Mr. Schwab?" said the lady, preparing to pack up her papers.

"Quite vell, madame, I zank you—egzept in vun sbot," he said. He had his hat off now, and as Mrs. Pottle looked curiously at him he made her a profound obeisance, and in a hurried, slightly anxious tone, said:

"I beg leaf, dear madame, to bresent you zese few volumes *Brockhaus Encyglobaedia*—last edition, viz colour blates."

"Really, Mr. Schwab, it is very good of you, but—no, I couldn't think of it—I—"

"Ach, it is nozink; it is nozink. Ze Gairman heart, madame, ven it is touched, do not zink of egsbense; it vibrate only viz sentiment. Besides, I buy zem halfprice."

Mrs. Pottle had both hands on the table, and was gazing through her eye-glasses at Schwab in speechless amazement.

"Allow me, dear Madame Bottle, to egsblain. You, no doubt, haf forgotten ze moment—vy should you regollect?—ven you ar-rive on zis ship: ze moment ven—vat shall I say?—ven you stickfast in ze too-narrow gangvay. Oh! madame, zat vas ze obbortunity of my life; I vas ready. You, Madame Bottle, vas Andromeda; I, Hildebrand Schwab, vas Berseus. Madame, I bush you zrough.... And at zat moment—I—fall—in—lov!"

"Oh!" gasped Mrs. Pottle, half rising to escape. But she could not leave the corner she had so carefully chosen without passing Schwab; his bulky form concealed her from view; and feeling a prisoner she fell limply back into her chair.

"Lov!" continued Schwab, as one declaiming an oration; "lov! vat is it? Madame, I seek it in *Brockhaus Encyglobaedia,* vol. eleven:—'Lov is a highly gomblex emotion azzoziated viz ze value vun put upon a berson or a objeck.' Vat, I ask myself, is ze value I put upon zat beautiful objeck—I should say berson? Madame, I—I cannot gif estimate—I, Hildebrand Schwab, vat gif estimate by ze zousand. Ergo, I am in lov: *quod erat demonstrandum.*"

Mrs. Pottle said something, and again essayed to flee, but Schwab spread himself and solemnly waved her down.

"Stay, madame. It is not merely zat I am in lov; I am also in business. I haf ze honour to offer you double bartnership. My hand, madame, my heart—my Gairman heart—I blace zem at your feet. And viz zem go ze rebresentation of ze solid house of Schlagintwert, ze gorresbondence of ze *Düsseldörfer Tageblatt* vat circulate in Werden, Kettwig, Mülheim, Odenkolin, and ozer blaces; besides fery bromising agencies in Ruskin edition de luxe, batent mangle, hair restorer, zentrifugal bomp, bianola—"

Schwab was so intent on his formula that he was not prepared for a sudden convulsive movement on the part of Mrs. Pottle, who seized her sunshade, and, sweeping the bulky wooer from her path, fled below. He stood for a moment in solemn stillness; then he took out his pipe, emptied it of ash, refilled and lit it, and, blowing great guns, gathered the volumes into his arms and walked away.

Meanwhile Mrs. Pottle had almost fallen into the arms of her brother, who was bringing from his cabin a paper to show Bob on deck.

"Now, Jane, Jane," expostulated Mr. Charteris mildly "you are too old to take flying leaps like that."

"Oh, Andrew, Andrew!" said Mrs. Pottle, with a burst of laughter, "I am not too old to have an offer."

"What do you mean?"

"My! I can hardly tell you for laughing. I have had a proposal of marriage—at my age! Guess who from?"

"Not Bob Fawcett?" said Mr Charteris with a sudden grim suspicion.

"Bob Fawcett!" Mrs. Pottle almost shouted with laughter. "You are just an old goose, Andrew. No; from Mr. Schwab, Hildebrand Schwab, who tried to woo me with a German encyclopaedia. It just beats anything!" ,

Mr. Charteris grunted.

"Knows that Isidore left you a pile, I suppose."

"You're not complimentary, Andrew. Mr. Schwab called me a 'beautiful objeck', fell in love with me because he had to help me up the gangway, 'bush me zrough!' Oh!——"

The recollection was too much for Mrs. Pottle; her portly double chin shook, and she was breathless with laughter.

"I advise a visit to the stewardess, Jane," said Mr. Charteris. "Excitement is dangerous—at your age."

"Wait a moment, Andrew," said his sister as he made to ascend the ladder. "You thought Bob might have fallen a victim to Isidore's pile? You're as blind as a bat to everything but business. Let me tell you a secret, sir. Bob is head over ears in love with Ethel."

"Eh?"

"And Ethel, though of course she won't admit it, is, his, well——"

"What?"

"Yes!" said Mrs. Pottle inconsequently. "Don't look so fierce," she added, patting his arm. "Bob's a good fellow; you won't be disappointed in him."

"Well, Jane," said Mr. Charteris slowly, "I allow that you surprise me. I guess I'm pretty well pleased. To be sure, I never reckoned on Ethel marrying a Britisher; she don't take no stock of 'em as a rule. But I'll say this: I don't care who the man is—Yankee, Britisher, or Australian; but if he's a worker, a fellow who'll get on, a good sort, and real fond of my gal—hang me, he shall have her—if she's willing. What!"

Glossary

C=Chinese, J=Japanese, P=Pidgin-English. The Chinese substitute *l* for *r*, and add the terminations *-ee*, *-um*, and —*lo* to many words.

allo (P), all, every.

banzai (J), lit. "ten thousand years!", an exclamation in salutation of the emperor, equivalent to *Vive le roi!*

belongey (P), often equivalent simply to the verb *to be*.

bimeby (P), by and by, afterwards.

bobbely (P), noise, uproar.

bottom-side (P), down, below.

catchee (P), to get, have.

ch'hoy (P), an exclamation.

cham-tow (C), to cut off the head, execute.

chop-chop (P), quickly.

chow-chow (P), food.

daimio (J), a feudal and military chief whose income exceeded 10,000 *koku* of rice(*koku*=5.13 bushels).

-ee, a pidgin-English termination.

first-chop (P), best, excellently.

galaw (P), a common exclamation.

geisha (J), a dancing and singing girl.

hai (J), an exclamation used in answering.

ha-loy (P), come down.

hara-kiri (J), suicide by cutting open the abdomen.

hayo (J), early: *o hayo*, good-morning.

he (P), he, she, it, they, him, her.

iniside (P), within, in.

joss (P), god.

joss-house (P), temple.

joss-pidgin-man (P), priest.

kimono (J), long outer garment.

komban (J), good-evening.

koto (J), a kind of lyre.

kow-tow (P), to bow humbly.

li (C), a Chinese mile: 250 *li* make 1 degree.

littee (P), little.

look-see (P), look, examine.

makura (J), a rest for the head.

meshi (J), boiled rice.

muchee (P), very.

musumé (J), girl, young lady.

my (P), I, me, my, mine.

no can do (P), cannot.

numpa (P), number: *numpa one*, first-rate.

o (J), an honorific prefix used in addressing or speaking respectfully of a person: *o hayo*, good-morning.

obe (J), a long sash worn round the waist.

one-tim' (P), once.

pan (J), bread: *pan taberu daro*, I want something to eat.

pidgin (P), business: *pidgin-English*, English as spoken by Chinese at the ports.

pidgy (P), busy.

piecee (P), used with numerals: *one piecee man*=a or one man.

plopa (P), proper: *allo plopa*, all right.

saké (J), a fermented rice-beer.

sampan (C), a Chinese punt.

samurai (J), lit. one who serves the emperor; a member of the military class formerly privileged to wear two swords.

san (J), a title used with names.

sassy (P), saucy, proud.

savvy (P), know, understand.

sayonara (J), good-bye.

shogun (J), commander-in-chief; the title of the ruler who for several centuries supplanted the Mikado.

side (P), place, direction: *this-side*, here; *that-side*, there; *what-side*, where.

so-fashion (P), in that way.

tabemono (J), a gift of food.

taberu (J), I shall eat.

tadaima (J), presently, at once.

that-side (P), there.

that-tim' (P), then.

this-side (P), here, hither.

tim' (P), time.

topside (P), above, superior.

topside-pidgin-man (P), missionary.

uma (J), horse.

wa (J), a particle.

wailo (P), away, to go away, run away.

wantchee (P), to want.

what-for (P), why.

what-side (P), where.

what-tim' (P), when.

yen (J), dollar.

yinkelis (P), English.